A

COMPLICATED

LOVE SONG

2015 First Place Gold Medalist for Urban Fiction
Independent Publisher Book Awards

Dedication

Willaton Burns, you are a wonderful, self-sacrificing husband, lover, and friend. Because of you, this book is realized. I thank and appreciate you more than words can express what my heart feels.

Tarik, Malik, and Jakim, my Burns boys to the third power, you are fine young gentlemen that make me proud. I thank you for your support, patience, and *anyhow* love.

Ethel Vance, my thick-n-thin friend, your love, prayers, receptive ear, and encouragement are God sent and Lynda appreciated.

I thank, salute, and honor the true entertainment Divas whose remarkable stories gave Bettina Charles her breath of life. You paid for the applause with your talent, heart, soul, and privacy.

Acknowledgements

Dorothy Jones, you gave me life and are the strongest person that I've ever known. I finally understand that you challenge me the most because you recognize my gifts more than anyone else.

God-mom, Dr. J.C. Hayward, your daily phone calls are special and always end with "I love you."

I honor my oldest sister, Nina-Jonetta Jones. Thanks for your example and for setting the bar so high that, even in my near failures, I end up floating among the stars.

I lift up my middle-big sister, Jee-Jennifer Joyner and my sisters/first cousins: Hattie Ruth Williams, Deborah Moore, Maxine Andrews, Judy Faye Savage, Bobbi Moore, Linda Moore, and Denise Ransome.

Supportive friends are rare finds—Janis Pace, Dorene McKnight, Kimberly Turner, and Cynthia Brower.

I give many thanks to my reading village. I'm grateful for your watchful eyes—Dr. Wilbur Bower and Dr. Dorothy Burns.

For all the Pastors that helped to shape my spiritual life, I thank you for preaching, teaching, and touching me directly—Reverend Doctors John T. Jennings, Sr.; A. Michael Charles Durant; Glen A. Staples; Grainger Browning, Jr; Jo Ann Browning, and Ostein Truitt.

Then, there's the hardest-happiest serving Pastor I've been privileged to know, the Rev. Dr. Robert A. F. Turner. I thank you for your prayers, support, your unique and contagious laugh, and listening ear.

A COMPLICATED LOVE SONG

LYNDA JONES-BURNS

Heart 2 Hand Publishing

PUBLISHED BY HEART 2 HAND PUBLISHING
a division of Heart 2 Hand Inc.
Printed in the United States

ISBN: 0990423301
ISBN 9780990423300
Copyright © 2015 Lynda Jones-Burns
All Rights Reserved

Book Layout, Sketches, and Graphic Images:
Lynda Jones-Burns
Additional Illustrations:
Christopher Moore (Image of singer on cover),
Gene Gregorio (Joseph-Lee Manor & a part of the tombstone),
and Tarik Burns (Heart 2 Hand Logo & other part of the tombstone)

www.heart2handpublishing.com
www.acomplicatedlovesong.com

ATTENTION CORPORATIONS, ORGANIZATIONS,
AND BOOK CLUBS
Quantity discounts are available for bulk purchases that will be used for educational, business, or sales promotional purposes. Lecture and book club engagements are also possible.
For more information, please contact: 301-653-6978 or email: acomplicatedlovesong@msn.com.

Foreword

Buckle Up! You are about to go on a roller coaster ride—from the valley of pain to the summit of ecstasy. A Complicated Love Song exposes you to the passion of a young woman's dream of stardom—the deep family secrets that lie just below the surface and the incredible love stories that keep a heart beating in a cocoon that embraces you throughout. Difficult to put down, and when you do, the words will linger in your soul. Beautifully written, eloquently told, and captivating. A must read!

Dr. JC Hayward
Journalist

A
COMPLICATED
LOVE SONG

Table of Contents

1

CLUB TREVI'S

BETTINA Bethany Charles stood behind the podium with her leather Nike sneakers comfortably crossed so that her toes on one foot were on top of the toes on the other and began her salutatorian address. The extra-long shiny gown covered her feet completely and closely matched the even shinier tasseled cap. She had chosen her public school-issued graduation uniform from the selection bin that accommodated taller students for that very reason. Her goal to feel cozy, casual, and cleverly camouflaged had been achieved.

To reduce her uneasiness, Tina's mind began to wander as words continued their vocalized flow. *When this speaking torture is over, I'll change into my pumps for the reception. With the complicated love song I have as a family, I know it's going to be hilarious. Because of its capacity, my backpack always wins out over a purse. There's plenty of room for everything including my shoes and this hideous cap and gown.* The young scholar reprimanded herself. *Focus Tina on the task at hand because you're starting to veer off course.* "After spending my first 10 years indoctrinated by patriotic traditions of parents in the military, I was transplanted to the southeastern United States. Absent the expected southern drawl, my vernacular was designated by you guys as proper. That often made me the subject of unsolicited conversation." The young lady primarily known as Tina paused until the majority of the laughter had subsided. "That is why I put great effort in steering clear of situations like this one—speaking in length to an audience of my peers mixed with well-dressed strangers."

In her high school yearbook, Tina was listed "Most Talented, Most Studious, and Most Likely to Be Chosen as a Runway Model." It was her classmates' best attempt to acknowledge their 1982 salutatorian's many gifts that were set apart by her amazing voice, intellect, and beauty. The oval face of the 17-year-old presenter complemented her body. She was 5 feet 8 inches tall and 107 pounds, with long limbs that supported her statuesque silhouette. From vastly different perspectives, Tina was called bony-thin by her Great-Aunty Trudy and considered curvaceous by the other two great-aunties in her close relational tribe.

Aunty Gina spoke softly as she bragged to intentionally rile up the meaner of her two sisters—the one seated next to her. "Our baby girl is all grown up and down right beautiful. Every ounce of fat in her body is stored in the right places—boobs, hips, rump, thighs, and calves. I can't wait until this dignified ceremony is over. Then, Tina can show off the new dress I bought her to wear for the graduation reception."

Aunty Zooni shook her head to convey concern while whispering her response. "With those long lashes, hazel-colored eyes, and no common sense, all I see is trouble with men folk in the very near future."

"What you call trouble, I see as fun and bonus opportunities for advancement."

"You would see it that way." Aunty Zooni slammed the program booklet down forcefully on her lap, poked her sister hard in the side, and grunted. "Dammit! So, it begins. Tina's saying whatever the hell is rolling around in her head. The words aren't even close to the prepared speech we helped her write. How dare she intentionally embarrass me in front of my colleagues? That group of teachers is part of my social circle."

"Must you take it so personally? That's Nadine's child and sophisticated standoffishness came with the package." Aunty Gina chuckled. "I hated high school too and am enjoying the look on her principal and teachers' faces. Besides, she's speaking the truth." Simultaneous shushing came from Aunty Trudy and Pappy John, seated to the left and right outer sides of Aunty Zooni and Aunty Gina.

With the goal to reduce the length of her oration, Tina intentionally scored 70 on a final exam in order to drop her grade and position down from valedictorian. As she headed toward her speech's finish, she exuded exceptional, natural stage presence. Her eye contact and gestures were excellent as she maintained an eloquent timbre. "It was much easier for me to manage pronunciation in the controlled environment of a song's measured cadence. That is where I succeeded at converting my speech into a less pronounced accent that was peer approved."

Pappy John began massaging his clean shaven, dimpled chin as his smile extended to the corners of his eyes. *I am so proud of our daughter. — Nadine, I know you're listening and smiling from heaven.* John Chapman's attendance at his adopted daughter's graduation was his first visit to the south in seven years. Her guardianship had been an inherited and shared responsibility. Aunty Gina was on "Tina Patrol" for about eight months of the year, and Pappy John took the reins during the summer and a few of the major holidays.

Tina shifted her feet. "Singing in the glee club here at Brawley High is where I gained acceptance. Just as I found a way to fit in, I welcome you here today. As requested by my classmates, I will deliver my conclusion in the form of a melody — And, I thank you."

Tina proceeded to belt out a jazzed-up, eyebrow-raising rendition of the school song. In addition to receiving a standing ovation after a lengthy hold of her final note, she was well-pleased with the end result. She did what came natural in her own unique way.

Friday, June 25, 1982

As patrons entered the front door of Club Trevi's, the booming bottom-beat assaulted their senses on impact. The energy was high and the party palace was nearing the end of its *TGIF* Happy Hour, having offered free drinks to ladies arriving before 9:00 p. m. The incentive added an extra boost to the already outrageously electrifying atmosphere. Trevi's was a large venue, by North Carolina standards, occupying four storefronts in a nine-building strip mall. It was located on the outskirts of Greenville close to a major highway—easily accessible to East Carolina and a slew of other colleges and universities. There was also a series of secondary routes nearby, drawing people from several two-stop-sign towns. One of them was Scotland Neck, an unsophisticated, country community that had been Tina's home for the past seven years.

Club Trevi's was the place where people came to escape the mundane and dabble in some of the Bible Belt's forbidden pleasures. It comfortably and legally accommodated four hundred party-goers at a time, including women with bodies for sale, ladies looking for love, and dirty old men auditioning for full-time jobs as *sugar daddies*. Because this particular Friday ended the first summer session for a number of nearby colleges, the club overflowed with students ready to party and be entertained. In addition to preparing to perform a second set at Trevi's, Tina was one of those relieved souls, having just finished her finals earlier that afternoon. The truncated schedule had been exhausting. Each day in the summer session equaled a week in a regular semester and was crammed with research papers, lab experiments, and exams. Trying to fulfill her family's expectation of getting her college degree, she graduated high school while taking courses at ECU.

The time was drawing near for Tina's second set. After twenty minutes of checking the door and the watch she pulled in and out of her backpack, she exited the broom closet/dressing room, sidestepping her way across the club's tattered carpet. She passed an area with five rows of tables, seating four people each, and all of them were full. Hors d'oeuvres and beverages were being served at the tables, which were draped in bright red cloth with a votive candle resting on a glass coaster as the centerpiece. This added an eyedropper full of ambiance to the otherwise noisy and somewhat seedy surroundings. It was obvious to Tina that, with the college invasion plus the locals, the popular hotspot was bordering on exceeding its capacity. *Clearly Manuel is not overly concerned about a possible infraction of the county's building occupancy code,* she surmised. The club owner's track record for bending and breaking the law was well known to those in need of an exemption.

The stage was the large open area's focal point—a simple, raised platform positioned against a back wall. The club's bar was next to that, stretching 30 feet from there to the front door. Because Trevi's was known for pouring liberal shots of alcohol, Manuel strictly enforced his rule against bar loitering. There was a three-drink minimum and an open-tab requirement for those seated at one of the twenty much-sought-after barstools.

Tina approached a woman she had befriended over the past two months. Appreciating her directness from their initial introduction, she referred to herself as a Freelance Specialist of Sexual Favors. "Hello Miss Jackie, have you seen my cousin?"

"No baby, but I really enjoyed your singing earlier tonight. Your sweet voice and smile will be missed around here."

"Thank you, Ma'am." Tina put a folded five dollar bill in the woman's palm and kept moving. *Who am I to judge since I too am on the list of the unlawful? I'm getting ready to sing a final set in a club in which I'm a bit too young to be performing.* Since the age of three, Tina's natural abilities in music and dance were enhanced with lessons in piano and ballet. God-given sexiness in addition to training came in handy when aspiring to sing and "strut her stuff" for a living. With that as her plan, her gig at Club Trevi's had been a chess move in the right direction. The stage was hers on Friday nights, and this was the last show of a two-month arrangement. It was a giant step up from the church choir, local pageants, and the glee club, which summed up the majority of her past experience. She was deemed a solo artist by her cousin and wannabe manager whose current whereabouts were unknown.

Tina mumbled a bunch of "excuse me's" as she squeezed her way between the tables. Most of those seated had seen the young singer's first set and were anxiously awaiting the next. Tina felt awkward and was angry that she had to move through the club and interact with audience members prior to performing. *When I find him, he's getting two earfuls. Before going on stage, I should be in a dark corner maintaining.* Done with her eyes closed, her preparation was a process of taking a series of deep breaths as she slowly counted down from ten to one. She learned the exercise from her beloved adopted mother as a way to calm herself and regain control.

"Bettina Bethany Charles, you're as red as a ripe tomato," Momma Nin often said. "Sit over there and *maintain* until I see a difference in your countenance." In the recent high school graduate's past experiences, she had tapped into the special brand of meditation prior to school exams, medical injections, encounters with her Aunty Zooni, and musical performances. On this night at Trevi's, however, instead of engaging in the prescribed *maintaining*, she was in the middle of a trek across the club. Along the way, she deflected remarks from people who had no inhibitions about expressing their love for her as she passed by their tables.

"You were great!" one man hollered.

"Pretty lady, you rocked the house!" yelled another.

That was followed by an old-school comment. "If fries come with that shake, I want a double order!"

One request was shouted from a table full of music majors. "Can you sing 'Rainbow High' again? You hit every note, in both octaves, with your full voice and that was amazing!"

Tina nodded, smiled, and continued moving forward. This conveyed that she was on a mission, unable to pause and chitchat. Yes, she was aloof, but thoughtfully so, able to dismiss people without them knowing. She was innately sassy, way too literal, and slow to distinguish good intention from deception. As a result of unfortunate circumstances, Tina had been displaced several times, causing her to be reserved, feel nomadic, and remain unsure of where to truly call home. She also suffered from recurring nightmares that left her emotionally confused, frightened, and often fatigued.

Without acknowledging a single one, Tina spotted several members of her church. *I know the Pastor's wife will receive a full, inflated report about my activity here at Trevi's, but I could care less.* Marylou Jennings was the First Lady of Mount Pleasant Hill Baptist Church—the home worship center for Tina and most of her extended family. The senior minister's wife was known as a vocal distributor—a person highly skilled at spreading private information about the people in the town. "When Bettina Bethany Charles was a baby, her parents died in a car accident," said the First Lady whenever discussing Tina's situation. "That's when her aunt and the white man took over raising the child. Don't let that news travel any further, however. If it does, you never heard it from me." Eavesdropping on that and similar conversations had caused Tina to downgrade Mrs. Jennings' character.

To the world at large, the middle-aged adopters were Colonel Nadine Bethany Charles-Chapman and General John Archibald Chapman. In 1951, the military-lifers committed a reprehensible offense—a white man and a Black woman got married. By crossing the bold line of segregation, they entered the ranks of a very small minority of interracial couples. As army officers, they were able to choose the path of least resistance and escape full-fledged persecution. They opted for duty stations outside the United States.

To Tina, they were the parents she adored—Momma Nin, the lullaby letter writer—Pappy John, the devoted husband and father. Together, the trio had 10 years of close-knit bonding, making cheerful memories in two cities located in neighboring countries. While working, their home base was a military township in Landstuhl, Germany. Leisure time, such as three-day weekends, annual leave, and most holidays when they remained in Europe, was spent 290 miles away in their elegant second home in a suburb of Paris, France, called Les Vésinet. Regrettably, the happy-go-lucky Tina diminished when losing Momma Nin to a heart condition and a worn-out battery. That is the reason Bettina Bethany Charles was living in Halifax County, North Carolina, being guided by three spunky, sixty-something great-aunties.

In 1961, Colonel Nadine had been the recipient of one of the first implantable pacemakers. After fourteen years, the device had run its course and Momma Nin was too weak to endure the replacement surgery. Having accepted the diagnosis of a death sentence with approximately one year to live, she devoted most of that time to her adopted daughter, not only through direct interaction while she was alive, but also in reflection through the letters she had written.

Because of the words Momma Nin left behind, she remained the greatest influence in Tina's life—despite passing away when her precious child was 11 years old. In addition to providing motivation, the letters were also a history of heritage—the who, what, when, where, and how of the colorful Charles-Watkins-Smith clan. In all, there were three binders full of writings entitled Lullaby Letters held in a safe deposit box at Fitzgerald National Bank. Per stipulations of Momma Nin's Last Will and Testament, Tina would receive a volume of the letters and hope chest items at different intervals in her life. Volume one's 50 letters had been presented to her at age twelve. Upon turning sweet sixteen, she had received the second batch of writings.

Tina safeguarded the two volumes that were in her possession in a worn, orangish-brown, hardback leather briefcase that she called Brief de Vaughan. When she was away from home for extended periods, her briefcase was a close companion. She may have forgotten clothing and other personal items, but she never forgot her letters. Tina rarely missed a day without thinking about Momma Nin by reading or reflecting on excerpts from her bequeathed Lullaby Letters.

Upon reaching the front edge of the parquet dance floor, Tina came to an abrupt stop. Track lighting and disco ball effects lit the sixty-by-sixty-foot square with alternating flashes of color. The dozens of bodies swinging and swaying as they danced to the upbeat tempo were close together, back-to-back, and elbow to elbow. Depending on the movement of the lights, the faces came in and out of focus. Some danced as couples, but most bounced and jiggled in clusters of males and females. With the 1980's edginess and free-to-be-me sounds of R&B, Pop, and Rap, it really didn't matter who danced with whom.

The exception was an occasional slow song where grinding bodies appeared to be having sex in a standing position. Whether fast or slow, all the tunes were amped up to near-deafening decibels. The music was being piped through huge, state-of-the-art speakers strategically placed throughout the trendy club. Except for the words of DJ Darnell that were broadcasted through his fancy microphone, all other communications were delivered using a combination of screaming and exaggerated hand gestures.

Tina stood on her tiptoes and strained her neck while moving it back and forth in an attempt to locate Carlton on the dance floor. Pray tell, "Who in the hell is Carlton?" That was a question often posed the first time anyone saw him accompanying Tina. The accurate response was, "All that could be imagined." By relationship, Carlton Andrew Charles was Tina's older cousin, best friend, protector, confidant, and acting manager. By all reported sightings, he was attractive—with light-brown eyes sparkling against dark, silky skin. The Charles-Watkins-Smith clan's recessive, funny-colored eye gene had been passed down to both him and Tina. Carlton had a naturally chiseled torso and long, smooth legs to balance out his 6 foot stature. He wore tight-fitting pants to accentuate what he believed to be his most attractive asset— the rear side of his body.

Carlton described himself best. "I am a flamboyant mover and shaker all day and in every way. In addition to my birth name, you can address me as The Lovely or Mister Montgomery. Atmospheric conditions impacting my mood determine the name I choose to respond to. Mostly, it depends on the time and situation, Honeychile."

Although refusing to discuss his past, he was severely damaged because of it. At age eight, Carlton's life changed drastically and spiraled downward after his father, Andrew Montgomery Charles, Jr., was killed in Vietnam. Seeing dollar signs while in search of a new revenue stream, his mother, Vanessa, remarried too quickly to figure out that her new husband's money came by way of ill-gotten means. With the help of her abusive loser-of-a-husband, she ended up addicted to narcotics. This placed Carlton in a precarious position of being hardened by his environment—growing up in a Washington, DC neighborhood riddled with crime and deviant behavior. In 1972 at the age of thirteen, Carlton left his abusive home, completing a part of his maturation process on his own in the streets of DC. His playground was a domestic warzone of drug dealing, theft, prostitution, and murder—only eight blocks from the White House, the residence of the leader of the free world.

Facing criminal charges at age fifteen, Carlton stood before the judge, interrupted his court appointed attorney, and answered on his own behalf. "Your Honor, sir, I choose curtain number two."

The judge reared back in his executive chair. "Excuse me young man, what did you say?"

Young Master Charles tapped on the microphone that was attached to the podium where he stood in family court. "I said I choose the second option. Obviously, I'll take the five-year sentence in the boring, hillbilly south with my Great-Aunty Gina over the same amount of time in a jail cell at juvenile hall in the nation's capital. You could've saved the city's money on this attorney fellow here. That was a low brain wave decision."

With the sentence so ordered, in August of 1974, Tina and Carlton's worlds collided by virtue of being placed in the care of the same great-aunty to finish out their rearing. During those years, the two cousins developed their special bond of solidarity. Upon turning twenty-one and with the assistance of Pappy John, Carlton's juvenile file was sealed. In that time, he had changed a great deal, opting to remain in Scotland Neck in spite of being in possession of his freedmen's papers. Having made a pact with Tina, he kept busy running his Aunty Trudy's beauty salon until his little cousin was ready to fly out of the nest alongside him.

In preparation for that joint departure, Tina and Carlton set out on their serious road to fame six months earlier, in January of 1982. No coaxing was necessary to get their Aunty Gina on board because she was Tina's biggest fan—equally supportive and protective of both her great-niece and great-nephew. Her major concerns were for their safety, for her to be kept informed, and for them to respect her house rules. With parental guidance in place, Carlton put together a band of mediocre talent and convenience—a four-cousin ensemble of men in their fifties moonlighting as musicians. Rufus, the keyboardist, worked as a sorter in the local tobacco factory. Duberry and Clevon, the lead and bass guitarists worked in the textile mill making socks and underwear. Cornelius, the drummer, was a cook at The Pit, the Charles family carryout. It was owned by Cousin Alonia who was known for his award-winning vinegar-based North Carolina, minced barbeque. As a close-knit team, the band of four cousins' combined musical ambition had nothing to do with the limelight. Rather, the attraction to Club Trevi's stage was the free booze arranged by Carlton as part of their compensation package. The cash component of forty dollars each was incentive as well—at least eight dollars more than a full-day's pay in their barely-above-minimum-wage jobs.

As a next step, Carlton set up rehearsals around everyone's schedule and helped Tina add sexually suggestive sassiness to her choreography. Then, he booked several small-time performances at a county fair, a family reunion, and a nearby college's spring fling. Following that, his efforts were rewarded with a taste of the big time in their tiny universe. Carlton negotiated an eight-week singing engagement at Club Trevi's. In spite of being preoccupied part of the time with partying and other forms of self-gratification, the end result of his hard work was quite impressive for a rookie acting-manager.

Tina was open to performing for almost any occasion with the exception of funerals. She refused them regardless of her ties to the dearly departed. When a request would come up, Carlton turned it down quickly, knowing there was no convincing his little cousin to make an exception. From time to time, he would make a blanket statement to her about funerals. "There will be one funeral that you will sing at and that's mine. If you don't do it, I'll jump out of the casket and beat you down. Then, I'll haunt you for the rest of your life."

Tina's response was consistent. "Whatever, Carlton. By the time you die, I'll be bent over, gray haired, toothless, and too old to sing."

2

MISSION: FINDING CARLTON

UNABLE to find Carlton on the dance floor, Tina resigned herself to the fact that there would be no pep talk or last minute adjustments to her performance. With that understanding, she backtracked across the club, ending up at the edge of the bar next to the entrance to the stage. Manuel, the owner of Club Trevi's, seized the opportunity to sneak up on Tina from behind. He pressed his body firmly against hers, making sure she felt the end result of him having a hard-on. He lowered his head, causing his goatee to touch her skin.

His lips and tongue wet her ear as he whispered. "Damn! You're wearing the hell out of that tight little dress." He was referring to the short garment that her Aunty Trudy called a "harlot's negligee" and warned her not to wear. "You sing good, but you look even better," said Manuel while pressing his stiff joystick against her body even harder. "I've been enjoying your view for two months now. How about you lose your bodyguard and hang out with me after closing? Tapping your plump, young ass would be a nice way to end—no, I mean to take a break from—our professional relationship. I want you back here singing real soon. Don't worry; to better your mood during our little send-off, I'll give you a little toot to powder your nose before we get started."

Tina cringed internally as the kinky hair on Manuel's goatee brushed against her baby-smooth, soft shoulder. It smelled like cigarettes soaked in moth balls, felt scratchy, and was in desperate need of grooming. Most bothersome were Manuel's heavy breaths hitting her cherished necklace. In addition to lullaby letters, Momma Nin left her daughter a hope chest filled with sentimental items and heirlooms. There was a patch work quilt, an apron, a table runner, and some monogrammed towels that had been made by her grandmother, *Big Momma*. Tina's *Smarty Pants* doll, a carefully wrapped dish set, linens, baby clothing, and a family Bible were also enclosed. Collected from around the world, Momma Nin included a variety of antique lattice lace fabrics in hopes of them being incorporated into Tina's wedding gown one day in the distant future.

Momma Nin Lullaby Letter Excerpt

Just like lattice that is crisscrossed in countless ways, may these varying patterns of lace accent your wedding gown like roses growing feverishly and fruitful.

Inside of the larger dowry chest was a 12-inch-wide, cedar container referred to in the sixth letter as a *Glory Box*. It was filled with a valuable collection of jewelry—some purchased by Momma Nin— most passed down through several generations. Dearest to Tina was an ultra-thin wedding band held on a slim, gold herringbone chain that she named *Love Golden*. Since receiving it, July 1976, seldom was it removed from around her neck, just as indicated in Momma Nin's instructions on how to handle the piece of fine jewelry once belonging to her mother with care. As a coping mechanism or when in deep contemplation, Tina would slide the golden wedding band up and down its chain.

While tilting her head away from his lips, Tina turned to face the man she privately called "Mister Nasty." *Damn it!* She shouted in her mind. *Where in the world is Carlton? He should be here preventing stuff like this.*

In mid-motion of turning around, head bartender Barney handed Tina her standard drink—about 10 sips of hot tea, lemon, honey, and a shot of brandy. Minus half a shot, Momma Nin called it a hot toddy and had given it to her as a child at the first inkling of the sniffles. Repurposed, the potion was a part of her pre-performance ritual to prepare her throat for singing and to send a silent salute to Momma Nin. In this instance, Tina took a few sips of the drink, lowered it to her chest, and used the cup to place distance between her and Manuel. While thinking of a suitable response and subtle retreat, she was saved by an abrupt pause in the music, followed by DJ Darnell's booming voice.

"Gals and guys, Club Trevi's always brings you the best in live entertainment. Since you asked for more, she's back to sing another set. As most of you know, this is her last night performing here for a while, so let's send her off right. Ladies and gentlemen, I need y'all to make some noise for Miss Bettina Chaaaaaaarles!"

The dance floor cleared and most of the crowd directed their attention to the stage. Tina finished her drink in one gulp, handed the empty glass to Manuel, and climbed the three wooden steps. In about five seconds, she was standing behind the microphone in the dark at center stage. Claps and yells of approval injected Tina with a burst of adrenalin that was intoxicating. As the makeshift spotlight hit her body, she was instantly transformed into her alter ego she had named Tosha Ray. Tucked away deep inside that persona, all her inhibitions disappeared and were replaced with Carlton inspired sensual sassiness.

As part of her carefully designed introduction, the only sound coming from the band was a continuous tap on the cymbals. With a wide-open hand covering her face, Tina took her audience on a seductive tour of her body. She moved the outstretched palm downward from her chin to her neck, gliding across each breasts in turn. Descending further to her left side, she slid her hand inward across her tummy, using fingertip play to trace the area surrounding her belly button in a circular motion twice. It was easily accessible through the cut-out in her ultra-short, stretchy red polyester dress. Delicately, she gestured toward her crotch and closed her hand to a fist. Appearing to scoop up her own vajayjay, she lifted it up to her mouth, opened her hand, and blew the imaginary coochie into the audience. Choreographed by Carlton and censored by Tina, the visual was well received. It was sexy, but not vulgar. Absent any music, the yells of the crowd made a shrieking beat of their own. Tina tapped her right foot three times to signal the band to start playing.

As Tina covered three, up-tempo top 10 hits, the crowd remained lively. They yelled, rocked, danced, and sang along to the familiar lyrics. Tina ended the set with one of her original songs. The motivation to write them was ever-present—memorialized in one of Momma Nin's lullaby letters.

Volume II: Lullaby Letter 84

Dearest Tina, since you were an itty-bitty girl, you scribbled out your thoughts. Actually, before learning to write, you mocked the church sermons you heard by reciting funny parables. They made me and others in shouting distance of your voice laugh hysterically. As if a divine assignment, you turned any situation into an opportunity to entertain.

Sometimes, I sit back and read one of your little stories and am always amazed at the way you animate sentences. Your words dance off the pages. Just like your father Donnie, you were born with stories in your heart and a God-given gift to put them on paper.

Tina, I want you to always be mindful of the fact that God grows impatient with slothful recipients of His blessings. To not lose your gifts, I want you to use them as much as you can. Your poetic words will serve as therapy, enabling you to write through your most difficult times as well as highlight your joyous experiences. — A world wrapped in wonder through wisdom written in words, Momma Nin ∎

With inspiration from Letter 84, Tina put many of her heartfelt words to music. Some were grief relief emotions never to be publicized. Most were lullaby lyrics to share. All were part of a continual composition she called A Complicated Love Song. *I'm sure Momma Nin would be supportive; even though, this type of animated performance was not her preference.* For the wound up crowd, Tina chose one of her most provocative tunes to close out this final set at Club Trevi's. Her sexually suggestive movements flowed to the rhythm of the beat.

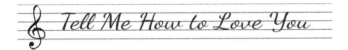

Tina sang:

> *If you need me, tell me*
> *If you want me, tell me*
> *Show me how to use my mouth*
> *And move my head from north to south*
> *Tell me how to be for real*
> *Show me how to make you feel*
> *Help me better understand*
> *Tell me how to do you, man*
> *Please—tell me—tell me how to love you*

Six fraternity brothers wearing the same tee-shirt pushed their way to the front of the stage slightly off center. They gave no thought to blocking the view of the people seated behind them. They urged Tina on with howls and pumping fists. To play up to the six-pack of barking dogs, she turned her body in their direction. She moved her hips and midsection slowly in the fashion of a belly dancer as she continued to sing.

> *If you need me, tell me*
> *If you want me, tell me*

Show me how to open wide
And move my hips from side to side
Show me how to use my hands
To move my body at your command
Help me better understand
Tell me how to do you, man
Please—tell me—tell me how to love you

The people surrounding the stage weren't the only generators of electricity and noise in the club. They were absolutely not the only one's grooving and moving to the beat of Tina's song. Down a corridor near the back of Trevi's, there were moans, groans, and heavy breathing coming from the men's bathroom. The last and largest of the three stalls at the end of the L-shaped restroom was a well-known, semi-secluded rendezvous point. With a deep knee and back bend, two pairs of feet covered in pants dropped to the floor could be seen from the gap at the bottom of the stall. The heated exchange took place over the sink, facing away from the porcelain throne. "This feels so good!" slurred Carlton as he directed the movement from behind his obliging sweetheart. Tony Alexander was a 5-foot-9 inch tall curly-headed cutie, with a copper skin tone. At 21 years old, he showed no traces of hair on his face or on his silky smooth body. With his manicured nails and hands pressed against the cold, tiled wall, Tony vowed. "I'm yours forever—together, no matter what."

In this pleasure-seeking moment, Carlton had no thoughts of enduring adoration. He said to himself, *I'm not feeling this yours-forever business. One of us, not me, needs to slow it way down.*

Clouded by marijuana and the impact of hard liquor, the tackiness of the bathroom backdrop—transient bystanders, sticky floor, flickering lights, flushing toilets, and overall filthiness—heightened Carlton's senses and satisfaction. It also demonstrated deliberate, detached disrespect towards Tony. He was treating his steady lover like a quick pick up. While absorbed in a haze of sexual euphoria, he left the management of his client/cousin/best friend hanging on a hook in that bathroom stall. Carlton hadn't totally forgotten about Tina, but had every intention of resuming his responsibilities at the completion of his climax.

In the front of the club, Tina was on the last verse of her song.

> *If you need me, tell me*
> *If you want me, tell me*
> *Show me how to move it fast*
> *To slow it down, to make it last*
> *Show me how to bump and grind*
> *To stroke you right and blow your mind*
> *Help me better understand*
> *Tell me how to do you, man*
> *Please—tell me—tell me how to love you*
> *Please—tell me—tell me how to love you*

Tina ended the set with liquefied digit play. From bottom to top, she licked the back of her pointer finger, directed it at a random man in the crowd, and motioned him to come to her. The music stopped and the song ended with that provocative directive. Along with unanimous claps from all, some women yelled "Yay" and most of the men barked and whistled. Tina showed her appreciation with a curtsy to stage left, one to stage right, and a bow and kiss blown from center stage. *I'm an exceptional performer and I live for the smiles on people's faces and their applause.*

By the time she exited the stage, her alter ego Tosha Ray, her smile, and her naughtiness were gone. All that remained was a pissed-off Tina on a mission to find Carlton. It dawned on her to ask the lead bartender who was the keeper of all the club's dirty little secrets. "Have you seen Carlton?" Tina's hunch did not disappoint. Barney pointed in the direction of her missing-in-action cousin. Upon learning of his whereabouts, she chastised herself for not thinking of the location on her own. Motivated by anger, she hurried down the dimly lit hallway and headed to the restrooms. Ignoring the sign that designated gender, she pushed the door open, whizzed by men at urinals, made a sharp left turn, and bent over to look under the stall. Instantly, she identified her target by his pants. Tina knocked on the door forcefully, folded her arms, and tapped her foot impatiently.

"Come out of there!" she yelled. "I'm ready to go home!"

After way too much time, the sought after older cousin unlocked the door and stuck his head out. "Hey, Tee-Tee." Appearing only somewhat presentable as his clothing had been pulled hastily into place, Carlton and then Tony exited the stall clumsily. The disgusted diva turned her back to them both and marched toward the exit. The two bad boys followed Tina out of the bathroom in single file, touching the wall periodically in order to maintain balance.

In response to shocked expressions of the onlookers, Carlton shouted. "Don't be mad. Be glad when royalty crosses your path."

3

SNEAKING IN

WHILE easing out of the car at three-thirty in the morning, Tina exhaled a deep sigh of relief, having arrived home safely from Club Trevi's. She propped her backside against Carlton's candy apple red Mustang, his sixteenth-birthday present from Momma Nin. He and his appease-to-please boyfriend, Tony, kept the attention-grabbing, seven-year-old Ford in *mint* condition. While leaning on the preciously pampered vehicle, Tina pulled her stilettos off—the right heel and then the left. She put her index finger midway her lips and shushed Carlton, followed by a verbal warning to be quiet. He had slammed the passenger door way too hard after fumbling his way out and up to a posture that was partially vertical. Yes, he should have been the driver, but he was too drunk to do so. In addition to everything he ingested throughout the evening and on into the wee hours at Trevi's, he took swigs of *Tennessee Jack* during the entire ride home. This was one of those nights where every attempt to achieve numbness was nullified by the brain's ability to preset its mode to anguish.

Tucking her pumps under her left armpit, Tina rushed around the car to Carlton's side and got there just in time to catch him before he toppled over. Unable to support his dead weight with one arm, she let her shoes fall to the ground and kicked them under the car's front tire. Steadying her cousin required concentration and the use of all the strength that her petite frame could muster.

This irregular movement caused Tina's harlot's negligée of a dress to rise while displacing her undergarment. The result produced two plump, fully exposed butt cheeks. Although feeling an uncomfortable rub and a slight breeze, she had no free hand to rescue her leotard-styled panties from the deep crevice of her behind. Luckily, darkness was the only witness to this front yard, ass-bearing, struggle-with-Carlton fiasco.

After repositioning her body underneath his, Tina staggered with Carlton toward Joseph-Lee Manor, the Charles family homestead since it was built in 1846.

Momma Nin Lullaby Letter Excerpt

My precious child, not only does your home have a name; it became a colloquialism, woven into the fabric of the language in our town and vicinity. After your grandfather, Joseph Leonard Charles, Jr. died, my mother known to all as Big Momma, began referring to the house by my daddy's nickname, Joseph-Lee. In a short time, it seemed that the name stuck to the very foundation of the two-story, colonial estate. It was one of a few former slave plantations still standing. As such, the house was of historic value to the state of North Carolina and was ground zero for Charles family business affairs and gatherings.

It took me years to accept Joseph-Lee Manor as my responsibility. Yes, I was the eldest of Joseph Leonard, Jr. and Big Momma's two children, but I had plans. Since Donald Leonard Charles, their youngest child was a boy and twelve years younger than me; I wanted the task to be dumped on him, eventually. Regrettably Tina, as a carefree young adult, my baby brother and your biological father were not on my top ten list of major concerns.

Once maturing to understand Joseph-Lee Manor's family importance, I gave it quite a few makeovers through the
years. Adding the first-floor bedroom suite was the most
outstanding. After deciding to move back in, I needed quarters to match the high-brow living to which I had become
accustomed which also provided built-in privacy. ∎

The bedroom suite's most impressive feature was its private side
entrance, which made it quite easy to slip into the house undetected.
Sneaking in was the very thing that Tina and Carlton were in the process of doing. They had staggered their way to the porch and this secondary, inconspicuous entryway. While not asking for much, entering
and exiting by her prescribed curfew was their Aunty Gina's prime
directive. Later, once the sun came up, Tina would be leaving for her
annual summertime visit with Pappy John and she wanted a smooth
departure. In light of her current predicament, avoiding a verbal lashing could only be achieved through deception.

Filled with guilt and frustration for having disobeyed the matri-
arch, Tina reprimanded her wayward cousin while admonishing
herself. "Carlton, when you sober up, I'm going to kill you!" she threatened, speaking softly, but with heated emotion. "Everything about this
is wrong. You're pissy drunk, my shoes are under your car, and I just
drove all the way from Greenville without a license." Tina looked stern-
ly at Carlton and shook her head with authority. "I need to be well
rested to face Pappy John tomorrow. Instead of worrying about waking
Aunty Gina, my only focus should be on figuring out how to deliver my
bad news to Pappy John. It's the script you and I wrote together prior
to your drunken stupor."

Appropriately used pronouns such as "you and I" and the word
"stupor" were deemed by Carlton as part of his cousin's highfalutin vo-
cabulary. "Your mind and mouth can't shake the years of being an up-
per-crust American living on European soil," he said often to tease her.
As strategically plotted and followed through by her adopted parents,

Tina's advanced education and cultural enrichment had been on a level befitting the daughter of high-ranking officers in the US military.

Refuting parts of her soliloquy, Carlton slurred. "Don't be so testy. I'll go back and get the damn shoes."

Tina shushed him again. "Forget about the shoes! You can barely stand up. Right now, all I need you to do is be quiet!"

"Okay, okay, The Lovely's lips are set on silence."

Tina released her grip on Carlton long enough to unlock and open the door. Finally, the two emotionally lost lambs reached the inside of the inherited private quarters. Mimicking a small apartment, the space opened up to an inviting sitting room. It was adorned with a cobblestone fireplace, sofa, side chair, two end stands, and a coffee table. About three months after Momma Nin's passing and at the urging of Pappy John, Tina relented and gave Carlton rein to redecorate her outer parlor. Because of the sensitive circumstances, he had used restraint back when Tina was younger and appropriately fashioned the room in a manner befitting an adolescent female's style preferences—rather than his own—layered with brazen and flashy overtones. Each piece of furniture was unique, yet tied together by pastel shades of peach, green, and bone. Overall, a soft tone of girly-girl chic was conveyed. There was also a doll collection of lovely ladies from all over the world. It was displayed in a glass curio and hugged a corner of the room.

In addition to femininely fabulous furnishings, Carlton had more recently retrofitted the sitting room with the latest in freestanding cabinets. This modern eye-grabber was a made for the 1980s entertainment center. It was equipped with adjustable shelves to hold the most up-to-date electronic technology as well as general trinkets. For Tina, this meant that the entire left side of the unit was reserved for music appreciation. There was a component set bundled with a radio receiver, a cassette tape deck, an automatic arm turntable, two large speakers, about twenty 45-rpm records, and two shelves dedicated to alphabetized albums. The cubby holes on the right side of the wall unit held her favorite books, whatnots, and framed photographs of happy times with Tina and family—mostly of Tina and Momma Nin.

A new color television rested on the wall unit's center shelf. It was a graduation present that came along with a check from Tina's faceless maternal grandparents. They were another loose screw in her life, vowing to never engage in direct contact with her. Thus far, in the first 17 years of Tina's life, they had been true to their word. Periodic gifts and money served as their method of communications as opposed to openly acknowledging a biracial grandchild. Like his older sister, the baby brother followed coincidentally. Just as Momma Nin had married a white man in John Chapman, Donald Leonard Charles married Christina Chambers—Tina's Caucasian, biological mother. In either case, through bloodline or by adoption, Bettina Charles was biracial. As a practice, she gave away many of her missing-in-action grandparent's offerings or took them under the umbrella of complete detachment. In terms of the television, she accepted it because of Carlton's insistence. Putting it lightly, he found it rude and insulting to return such a lavish gesture of goodwill.

Specifically, Mister Montgomery's actual feelings about the television were expressed demonstratively with one hand on his hip and the other waving in Tina's face. He said, "Ain't no damn way a brand, spanking new colored TV is gonna enter the doors of Joseph-Lee Manor, and we ain't gonna enjoy it. Oh hell no! You can be pissed off at the Chamberses, madder than mad, and curse them with a voodoo spell for all I care. Whatever you do to deal with your Chambers-anger is gonna happen while sitting down in front of your crazy ass grandparents' color TV set. Thank you very much."

With Carlton resolving the television issue, Tina knew exactly what to do with the Chamberses' check. Unlike all the other contributions from her grandparents that had been sent to the lawyers managing her trust fund, this $25,000 windfall profit was mailed directly to her. Tina made a decision to tell no one in the family about its existence, except her collaborating cousin. "Carlton, since the funds miraculously ended up with me, I'm keeping the Chamberses guilt money. It will be the primary source to finance our relocation."

Tina's well-situated financial portfolio was the product of a combination of planning and windfall. The planned component was Bettina's portion of Momma Nin's assets which included life insurance, savings, retirement dividends, and property. The windfall was a creative collection of contributions from the Chamberses. Over the years, the unexpected gifts kept coming—$50,000 at five months old, $25,000 at age twelve, and $25,000 at age sixteen. If the Chamberses maintained their consistency, the teenager's trust fund would be receiving another $25,000 contribution in five days—upon her turning eighteen-years-old.

Momma Nin Lullaby Letter Excerpt

To cut down on jealousy, Aunty Gina and I made a pact to keep the cloaked grandparents' financial gestures a secret from Aunties Zooni and Trudy. I need you to be mindful that monetary blessings or a lack thereof do strange things to kinfolk. This is especially true when the dividends are dispersed inequitably to a singled-out benefactor. —That would be you Tina, in this case. ■

Because of the soon-to-come birthday bonus, Tina thought it was fine to discreetly retain her absentee grandparents' graduation guilt gift. *Mailing it directly to me must have been intentional and I've never been required to report the contents of my private mail to my guardians in the past. No point in starting now. Besides, I'm almost grown.*

Double doors separated Tina's outer parlor from her shrine of a bedroom. It was spacious, with a walk-in closet, and a private bath. After giving Carlton authority to decorate the sitting area, she had snatched the control right back, assuming a contrary position as it related to her bedroom. She adamantly stressed that it remain as close as possible to the way her precious benefactor left it. Year-to-year and instance-to-instance, Tina dismissed countless urges from assorted family members to loosen her stronghold grip on what they perceived as painful memories of sickness and death. Her main guardian Aunty Gina's plea was soft, sweet, and sympathetic. "Tina, changing the bedroom will not make you forget about Momma Nin. You'll always carry Nadine in your heart."

Her heaven-bound Aunty Trudy pushed her point with a prayer and preaching. "Tina, the Bible tells us to let the dead bury the dead. It's sinful to be so stubborn, allowing a den of Satan's thieves to steal your joy."

Tina's bitter and brazen Aunty Zooni bellowed like a belligerent bully. "Who's the child and who's the adults around here? We need to grab some brushes, paint, and new linens. Then, march on in there and change the damn room to something more suitable."

Of course, Cousin Carlton defended Tina with tenacious testimony. "Girl, don't let those old biddies drive you to drink. In this case, the definition of mine is yours. It's your room and your world, so do what the hell you wanna do!"

Tina's response always aligned the closest to Carlton's sentiments with only a few differences. Her words were brief and accompanied by tears and a tantrum-like temperament. "Momma Nin's—I mean my bedroom is perfectly fine the way it is, so leave me alone and stop talking about it!" A slammed door and retreat to the back corner of her walk-in closet would follow. Curled into a ball, she would sit with thighs touching her breasts, arms wrapped around her legs, head perched on her knees. After an adequate amount of pity-party time, Carlton or Aunty Gina would coax her out of the closet.

With that, Tina's half-modern, half-dated bedroom suite was, by far, the largest sleeping quarters in the house. To no family member's surprise, Momma Nin left most of the kit and caboodle to her precious Bettina. The bedroom suite, the house, and the land were all a part of her inheritance. Similar to the youthful Momma Nin, Tina possessed live-in-the-moment, teenager tendencies and was ill-equipped to understand the totality of her bequeathed estate and those who relied on her benevolence.

Tina did a quick recap of the night's journey while dragging Carlton the last few feet into the center of her outer parlor. In what seemed like forever, she had exited the car, staggered up the driveway with her co-conspirator, negotiated the four side-porch steps, and crossed the threshold of Joseph-Lee Manor—touching down in the sitting room portion of her suite. She was breathing heavily and was in agony from bearing much of the weight of her taller and heavier accomplice. Tina bent over as low as possible, letting Carlton land face down on the carpet. Exhausted, burdened with the weight of culpability, and sparsely clothed, she walked into her inner parlor and collapsed on the bed, quickly falling asleep.

3:28 a.m.—Tina was so cold that goosebumps covered her skin and her teeth chattered. *Surely Aunty Gina's flashing, as she calls it, caused her to leave my window open, making this early morning in June feel like a blustery winter night. I am very frustrated because my blanket is floating above my head just out of the reach of my outstretched arms. I'm feeling so embarrassed because my nightgown is raised up showing these two little knob thingies that recently started growing on my chest. The stranger watching me from a distance is getting a long look at them and all the rest of me. I don't know how to make him go away.*

Tina was startled awake by imaginary excruciating pain. It was accompanied by actual accelerated breathing and an increased heart rate. She sat up in bed and searched the hazily illuminated darkness. She always left her nightlight on the dim setting.

For the second time this month, a similar, horrifying nightmare has startled me awake. A quick room scan gave her comfort. *It's a few days short of my eighteenth birthday and I'm okay. Why am I dreaming about an eleven-year-old grief-stricken me? As I creep at the door of adulthood, I'm beginning to make less sense.* Safety reassured and respiration normalized, Tina drifted back off to sleep.

4

MORNING TIME

"GREENVILLE,** Tarboro, Scotland Neck, and the like—it's Morning Time, Saturday, June 26, 1982! WGTS is the best of the rest," yelled the DJ's voice from the clock radio. Showered and dressed, Tina entered the kitchen and prepared the remedy that had become a frequent requirement following Friday night performances. Too young to be pouring alcohol, she made sure that all in the house remained silent before proceeding. She dropped ice into a glass, sprinkled in salt and pepper, and added a vodka shot, tomato juice, Worcestershire sauce, lemon, and celery. She took a sip and placed the strong drink on a tray next to a small bowl of water and a cup of French roasted, black coffee. At some point earlier that morning, Carlton had crawled from the floor to the sofa. Tina walked over to him, placed the tray on the coffee table, and pressed her butt towards his stomach to carve out a seat for herself. She used a Momma Nin method to awaken Carlton. After shaking his shoulder, she splashed cool water from the bowl onto his face. The combination of the actions brought him around to a vague awareness.

Tina forced the Bloody Mary into his hand and demanded. "Drink it fast because it's time to get up." The cousins' plan had been to always rise early despite receiving minimal hours of sleep. This made them appear well-rested to the one whose opinion mattered the most. Because Tina had a plane to catch, waking early on this particular Saturday had a dual purpose.

After taking three sips of her coffee, she began to scold her ne'er-do-well cousin. "I can't believe you abandoned me on our last night at Trevi's. When DJ Darnell asked me to do a second set, I was happy and surprised because we never had to do that before. I wanted to change things up a bit, but needed the advice of my, absentee, acting manager!"

Carlton responded from a place of half-hearted remorse. "Tina girl, don't be mad. I did my job for most of the night."

"Exactly, most—not all—not the parts when I needed you the most. In the first set when the microphone was screeching, you didn't notice. Rufus had to stop playing the keyboards, slip off the stage, and walk over to get your attention."

"Yes, but didn't I fix the problem?" defended Carlton. "Let's not forget who got the gig at Club Trevi's in the first place—dead smack in the center of the action. Last night was our biggest crowd so far. Yours truly, The Lovely, outdid herself as usual. Bam!"

"That's not the point. You should have stayed focused the entire time. By the end of the night, all my adult chaperones, you, the band, and Tony were tore up drunk, high, or both. It was ridiculous and risky—me dropping him off and driving the two of us home without a license. Remember, I'm the almost eighteen-year-old younger cousin, not you."

Carlton consumed what was left of his drink and allowed Tina adequate time to vent. "Although we shouldn't focus on the negative, go ahead and get all the hostility out of your system. Please note that anger creates frown lines that interfere with a flawless complexion."

"As I was saying, I looked up and saw that you had disappeared. Of all the meeting places—Manuel's office, the broom closet/dressing room, the band's Impala—you chose the bathroom. You can't behave like that in public and you should be more respectful toward Tony.

Doing what you were doing—where you were doing it—wasn't cute at all. Quite frankly, it was common and embarrassing."

Tina's harsh and judgmental comments about Carlton's professionalism awakened him fully and caused him to fire back adamantly. Not wanting to disturb everyone else in the house, he used exaggerated head movements and flailing hand gestures to express his outrage. "How in the hell am I gonna embarrass you from a locked stall in the bathroom? Child, please!" Carlton said dismissively. "I decided to do what I was doing with somebody I wanted to do it with—nobody decided for me. Anyway, Little Miss Thing, let's not get all grand. You weren't exactly acting like *Snow White*, you know. What's the difference in what you were doing on stage and what I was doing in the bathroom? Both of us were fulfilling fantasies and getting off by making people feel good. Carlton was being The Lovely and you were rocking it hard as Tosha Ray."

With different paths leading them to very similar circumstances, it was as if the two, through a twist of fate, were joined at the hip. The Vietnam War had stolen the life of Carlton's birth father and his mother and stepdad were dead to him emotionally. Both of Tina's birth parents and adopted mother had passed away while her adopted father lived too far away to make a continuous impact. As a result of their deep-seated pain, the two misfits' mantra was "us against the world." They nursed their emotional hardships with perilous behavior that included excessive drinking, promiscuity, toying with older men, and driving without a license. As always, the disagreement ended in a stalemate. Neither was capable of remaining upset with the other for very long. Frankness and honesty were the sealing agents of their unbreakable bond.

Since Tina was incapable of remaining angry with Carlton and agreeing with his analogy about their behavior being similar, she made light of a serious situation. "When you disappeared, I had to deal with yucky Manuel the Nasty, on my own. His eyes and hands were all over me and that nappy goatee was scratching my shoulder. It was so gross!"

Carlton chuckled. "I thought you were all hot and bothered for older, hairy-faced men. Are you sure you weren't feeling a happy tingle from the touch of that nappy-ass goatee?"

"First of all, I'm not out of my mind crazy about anybody. Secondly, I like slightly older guys—handsome, tall, with silky smooth mustaches—not BB gun pellets. There is a huge, huge difference between what I think is hot and Mister Nasty."

Carlton entered Tina's walk-in closet and retrieved clothing from his stash. Knowing their magnetic attraction to trouble, this sleepover arrangement was one of their carefully crafted countermoves. His actual bedroom was one floor above and to the left. Aunty Gina's room was the home's original master suite. It was positioned around the bend at the other end of the hallway and Aunty Trudy's was next to his. The close proximity to both was too risky for a drunken Carlton to sneak up the stairs to his own room. There was another bedroom on the first floor, but it was reserved for guests.

As the conversation continued, Tina rechecked her luggage against a hand-written list. It was time for her summer getaway with Pappy John. Although shortened significantly from two months to ten days, Tina wanted to ensure that nothing essential was left behind. She was told to come prepared with clothing for both hot and cold weather. Most importantly, she triple-checked Brief de Vaughan to make certain that each of Momma Nin's lullaby letters was accounted for and filed in the correct order.

A few days earlier, after a long military career and years living abroad, Tina's adopted father had finally retired and relocated to the States—but was far from being settled-in. Upon returning from his vacation with Tina, he would be staying with a friend because his Washington, DC apartment would not be available until the end of July. Pappy John felt that a trip to Colorado was a great time-killing distraction from the blues of this major transition in his life. It gave him an opportunity to visit family, friends, and to uniquely celebrate his daughter's eighteenth birthday.

While using Tina's private bath, Carlton talked to her through the cracked door. "And you, Little Miss Bettina Charles, had that crowd in a trance like a charmer with his snake. They had you do a second set because they loved you so much."

With a sheepish grin, Tina nodded in agreement. "I was hotter than hot on stage and my mind was caught up in the music. The entire performance felt so-o-o good—like I was floating on a cloud!"

In that moment, Tina and Carlton had become self-absorbed, rendering them ineffective sounding boards for each other. Tina elevated her ego while her older cousin listed his smart maneuvers in an attempt to counter the lapse in judgment of the bathroom escapade.

"Now, do you understand the method to my madness?" asked Carlton. "I told you that changing some of the lyrics would hype up the crowd. Those guys went crazy for your sex talk, especially when you said, 'use my mouth and move my head from north to south.' And let's not forget my talent as a stylist," Carlton bragged with a sense of total victory. "By me bumping up your hair and working your makeup, we pulled off you being fabulously flirty—real good."

In addition to acting manager, Carlton was hair dresser and clothing stylist extraordinaire. As his canvas, Tina had progressed from pubescent cute to star-quality beautiful. Her almond-shaped eyes sparkled and were defined by her thick, naturally arched eyebrows. Her heavy-cream-n-coffee complexion complemented her sandy-brown, wavy hair, which cascaded more than six inches past her shoulders. Her luscious lips had already started to invite trouble. Aware of their power, she often used a pouty mouth to draw men in while she was singing. When engaged, her smile was wide and brightened by pearly white teeth. While staring in the mirror and dragging her fingers through her hair's lengthy strands, Tina's demeanor shifted to contemplation.

"I'm going to miss Club Trevi's—especially those weekly doses of that flying-high feeling I get when singing," she said with a longing in her voice. "After celebrating my birthday with Pappy John, I'll be back here to sing at the wedding. That will be my last time performing for who knows how long."

Tina was not just a pretty face who could sing and dance; she also was keenly intelligent. Her educational foundation was an advanced curriculum received in grade school in Landstuhl, Germany courtesy of the US Army's impeccable academic program. By the end of her 10th grade year back in the States, she had breezed through America's high school requirements ahead of schedule. In fulfilling her obligation to become a college graduate, she had devised an ambitious two-year plan.

Step one of the plan was Tina being accepted into a higher learning early admissions program. This enabled her to attend college full-time while remaining on Brawley High School's attendance roster—able to participate in extra-curricular activities suitable for a sixteen-year-old at the time. To keep her grounded, Aunty Gina and Pappy John insisted that Tina participate in the high school glee club. Attending the senior prom was also required, but she was allowed to take Carlton as her date. His explosive personality and antics contributed to the yearbook recording the event as the best prom in school history.

Step two was for Tina to test out of everything allowable. At the end of placement exams, she was awarded twenty-one credit hours—three credits each—English 101 and 102, US History, College Algebra, Biology, and French 203 and 204.

Step three was to complete the next two arduous years of higher learning—tuition paid in full by Tina's trust fund. Carlton did the honors of getting his cousin to ECU daily, giving them further time to bond and perfect their exit strategy. On average, she remained there for seven hours either in class or in the library with her head buried in a book. Because piano and voice were especially tailored and last on her schedule, Professor Michael Milton, Sr. would drive her home. He lived in Rich Square, a tiny community next to the small town of Scotland Neck where his prize pupil lived. In addition to his new role as her college dean and academic advisor, he had also been her private piano instructor since she was 10 years old. Their bond was close and he was instrumental in Tina's acceptance to the early admissions program.

It was common knowledge that Professor Milton was a single father, who had raised his, now, grown son with the assistance of a live-in uncle. When the university or Joseph-Lee Manor wasn't convenient for piano lessons, they took place at the Professor's home. That is where Tina uncovered the huge secret that the uncle was actually her teacher's abusive long term boyfriend.

Friday, September 7, 1979—*A few days earlier, Hurricane David's wind gusts and 15 inches of heavy rainfall had caused damage to ECU's campus and closed it for a week. Joseph-Lee Manor was still in the dark, so the instruction was moved to Professor Milton's home. Tina sat in the living room at the piano attempting to drown out verbal insults that were coming from her teacher's bedroom. "I found this phone number on the back of a photo in your pants pocket," yelled the man she had known as her professor's uncle and roommate. "I know you're screwing this fair-faced freshman who sits front and center in your piano basics class. I've snuck a peek here and there and noticed how he looks at you."*

Tina's entire body jumped as she heard two hard slaps, someone crashing into something, and items being knocked over. Ten minutes later, Professor Milton returned to his seat at the piano next to his student. Pretending all was well, her eyes registered a cut in the middle of her instructor's bottom lip. Periodically, he used his handkerchief to wipe the trickling blood. Tina recalled with clarity, "This explains the black eyes and bruises I've seen on the Professor from time to time. They were put there by his jealous and irate live-in lover."

With the two-year plan set in motion, Tina approached college as if it were high school, taking classes back-to-back all day, every day. Her most unforgettable course was Geomorphology—the study of rocks, sand dunes, and continental drift. Oddly enough, it was a required course despite her major in Fine Arts. The torturous experience involved a two-day camping trip on the Outer Banks of North Carolina. Urinating in bushes, building a shelter, and waking up wet from dew on the ground were equally horrible, but mandatory in order to pass the class. Tina's life consisted of studying most of the time, singing, and playing the piano. Her most uplifting and recurring activities were her summer trips to Europe with Pappy John by way of Washington, DC.

Upon reaching the end of the two-year master plan, Tina had earned a total of eighty-seven credit hours—twenty-one by way of placement exams—fifteen each for Fall 1980 and Spring 1981—eighteen each for Fall 1981 and Spring 1982. Due to the results of her best efforts, Tina walked across Brawley's stage with a high school diploma and an *East Carolina* transcript that was thirty-five credit hours short of the 122 hours needed to graduate. To get closer to the goal, she enrolled in the college's first summer session in May 1982. In the span of five weeks, Tina completed an additional six hours—bringing her total credits up to 93. On the verge of an emotional collapse, she was still short 29 hours. For Tina, she had failed to earn that college degree—breaking her promise to Momma Nin, Pappy John, Aunty Gina, and Professor Milton. Tina was the epitome of an academically overdosed teenager.

She nervously asked Carlton, "What do you think will happen when I tell Aunty Gina and Pappy John that I'm taking a break from college and moving with you to New York City?"

"It might interrupt their regularly scheduled programming, but they can't block your decision. In four days, you'll be eighteen years old and that's the day that our plan goes into effect."

Tina had become obsessive about calculating and recalculating the numbers. "This professional venture of ours is scary and expensive. Based on New York's high cost of living, our money will barely last a year if we're really careful."

Tina and Carlton's plan lacked the benefit of wisdom. It was akin to skydiving out of Joseph-Lee Manor's nest with no safety instructions while sharing a single parachute.

A dashing and fully clothed Carlton exited the bathroom, walked over to his best friend that he had long ago lovingly dubbed Tee-Tee, and placed a reassuring hand on her shoulder. The fingers of his free hand glided from the crown of her head down the back length of her hair. "Honeychile, twelve months is a long time without extra baggage—no college, no nappy hair to tame at Aunty Trudy's beauty salon, and no nagging relatives." The Lovely heard movement coming from another part of the house. "Speaking of nagging relatives, it sounds like the ones living here are up and on the way to the kitchen."

5

KITCHEN CAUCUS

SOUNDS of thumping feet walking down stairs signaled the awakening of the house's remaining occupants. Aunty Gina, the reigning commander, reached the kitchen with her sidekick older sister, Aunty Trudy, trailing closely behind. She discarded what was left of Tina's brew, making her own special blend of Borger House Coffee sprinkled with cinnamon. The large kitchen's décor spelled out down-home country—a wooden table for eight, necessary appliances, and flowery wall paper—yellow background and burnt orange, faded daisies. Two plug-in devices eliminated the need for pots, pans, or turning on eyes on the stove. After Momma Nin's death, elaborate, southern-style breakfasts had been down-sized to coffee and toast with a choice of strawberry or peach preserves on most mornings. Instead of gorging on food, a kitchen caucus convened to address violations of house rules.

Passed down for generations, Aunty Gina bellowed the Charles-Watkins-Smith family command for summoning young folk accused of disobedient behavior. "Bettina Bethany and Carlton Andrew Charles," she yelled, "get your narrow behinds in this kitchen right now!"

In response, Tina shouted. "Yes, Ma'am, Aunty Gina, we're coming." Then, she spoke directly to her cousin. "Let's get this over with.

We've angered the good fairies." Tina used a designation of goodness to distinguish her Great-Aunties Gina and Trudy from the fire-breathing dragon personality of her Great-Aunty Zooni.

To convey alertness, Tina and Carlton entered the kitchen with wide-eyed exaggerated expressions. Tickled internally by their theatrics, Aunty Gina continued the poker game. Portraying her best impression of a lioness, she began to roar. "Trudy told me that she heard y'all stumbling in the house after three in the morning. My rules haven't changed. Carlton, you need to have your butt in this house by two a. m. or twelve thirty when you're chaperoning Tina. If you're going to be later than that, you have to call, each and every time."

Tina whined. "Why are you yelling at us? We made our curfew. Aunty Trudy must've been hearing things."

Filled with sentimental emotion about Tina's departure and approaching a milestone birthday, Aunty Gina conceded and reduced her lioness roar to a house cat's purr. "Since you just graduated high school plus doing that early college thing, I'm giving you a pass on missing curfew, but don't make it a habit. And you, Carlton, I truly hope you weren't out there driving drunk?"

Carlton answered with assurance. "Oh, Aunty Gina, I swear on a stack of Aunty Trudy's Bibles that I wasn't driving drunk last night."

Carlton's response made Tina clear her throat and let out a little giggle, well aware that she had done the illegal driving.

Dressed in overalls and ready to work the fields, Uncle Ed entered the kitchen. He was a soft-spoken hard worker with a consistent goal of staying out of the three sisters' volatile discussions. "Morning all," he said.

In unison, Gina, Trudy, Carlton, and Tina answered. "Good morning."

As the chatter continued, Ed accepted the coffee mug from his wife Trudy and hurried out the back door. It was located on the right side of the morning room, which exited onto the rear screened-in porch.

Preceded by additional, disorderly thumps and bumps down the stairs, a booming male voice rang out from the hallway. "Hey, Ed, wait up! I'm coming!"

It wasn't surprising that Aunty Gina had a man sleep over, but quite shocking that it had become a recurring activity with a single suitor. Although not expressed, Tina felt uneasy around Aunty Gina's many men friends. *Why does my anxiety level spike with each introduction to one of Aunty's friends as she refers to them? Although Larry seems harmless like a child, I can't shake my uneasiness. I'm most certainly well acquainted with her revolving door process after seven years of observing it.*

In Larry's case, Tina was cordial, but kept her distance, continuing her practice to lock her bedroom door at night. The thought of being intruded upon worried her to the point of nausea and panic attacks that disrupted her sleep. When adding the special lock years earlier, Aunty Gina insisted that she and Carlton have access to a spare key in case of an emergency. Tina obliged and it was hidden in her sitting room on the entertainment unit inside of her soundtrack album of *The Wiz*.

With his shirt half-buttoned and his fly unzipped, Larry tripped his way into the kitchen and gave a one-word greeting. "Hey."

In unison, Carlton and Tina said, "Hey."

Trudy said, "Gina, you're turning this house into the Devil's workshop, allowing Larry to use his Satan scepter to have his way with you."

Carlton's laughter blurted out unexpectedly. "Now, Aunty Trudy, that was funny!"

Ignoring her sister and with a sheepish grin, Gina extended her beau an admiring head to toe greeting. "Good morning, Larry." As he zipped-up his fly, she finished buttoning his shirt.

Carlton sighed. "Ahhhh! Isn't that nice? Momma Bear is helping her baby cub finish dressing." Tina poked Carlton in his side.

At 43, Larry was 16 years younger than Gina. He was big and burly, standing at 6 foot 2. He had a scruffy beard and consistently looked disheveled. Outlasting the average suitor, he had the distinction of holding Gina's attention for 3 straight months. After kissing her on the lips and administering a firm squeeze to her rump, he headed out the back door.

Gina said, "It's so nice of Larry to help Ed with the crops."

Carlton spoke softly to Tina. "The busier the hands, the longer the stay."

Zooni the Evil One brushed shoulders with Larry as he exited and she entered the kitchen. Although not living at Joseph-Lee Manor, she would engage in daily drive-bys—spraying bullets from her mouth with messages originating from the back gates of hell. Her goal was to beat the spoiled brat out of Tina and to return Carlton to the gutters of Washington, DC, from which he was spewed. As was her usual practice, she proceeded to dominate the conversation. "I don't know where Larry's rushing off to, but I know it ain't the library with his non-reading self. And Carlton, I told you about leaving that gosh darn car halfway up the driveway."

"Damn! My peaceful spirit just ran away," mumbled Carlton.

Trudy continued seeking the truth. "With the Lord as my witness, I know I heard those youngins sneaking in late last night. It's just so sinful to lie when you know God is looking and listening."

Zooni used Trudy's testimony as ammunition. "Gina, you letting that youngin break the rules again? Even though she'll be with John Chapman in a matter of hours, you're in charge around here at Joseph-Lee Manor for reasons I don't understand. Do something to discipline that gal! If you don't, she'll return from her visit rolling over you like a tractor."

Carlton clamored. "Ring-a-ling-a-ling! I hear a bell letting me know it's time to go. Tina, say your good-byes. I gotta get you to the airport and me back to Trudy's Place. I don't take my first appointment until three this afternoon, so I'll be working half the night." Trudy's Cut-n-Curl was known to the locals as Trudy's Place. Carlton was the supervisor, lead beautician, and makeup artist. With Aunty Trudy appearing only a few hours per month, he managed the shop with the assistance of her daughter, Hattie Mae, and his sweetheart Tony. Clients from neighboring towns traveled to Scotland Neck because of Carlton's artistry—mimicked well by Tony and not so well by Hattie Mae.

"I'm out of here. Later!" Carlton quickly jumped up and rushed toward Tina's room. Instead of leaving the house through her private entrance, he went back into the kitchen to give his little cousin a hint to follow him and get out of there. He had Tina's garment bag on his shoulder and carried her heavy suitcase with the opposite hand. He looked straight at her, motioned toward the backdoor, and headed outside. When frustration would reach its boiling point in Joseph-Lee Manor, Tina would sometimes reflect on a reality check mental pacifier—her mother's words of advice.

Momma Nin Lullaby Letter Excerpt

There will be times when your high-class upbringing and your Great-Aunties' plain-folk living will clash—as should anything that is in exact opposition. Proper etiquette and deportment that John and I instilled prepares you for audiences with Presidents and Queens while your kinfolk training helps you retain respect for the common touch. Being armed with both sides of the coin will give you a well-earned advantage in people skills regardless of a person's station in life.■

While moving close to her great-niece, Gina demanded. "Zooni, stop butting in." Reaching out to Tina, she smiled and stroked her hair. "You gotta lot of traveling ahead of you, so pay attention to everything and everybody."

"Yes, Ma'am."

"My, My, My! When you get back, you'll be eighteen years old. I'll have your birthday cake ready and we'll do something special like go shopping in Raleigh—anything you want. I'm a phone call away. Be good and remember that I love you."

"I love you more and you and Larry behave yourselves while I'm gone." *Because Aunty Gina gets rid of her men friends so quickly, who knows if he'll be here when I return? I hope so because he seems to like her very much and doesn't make me feel as sick and nervous as most of the others.* Tina kissed Aunty Gina on the cheek, clutched the handle of her brown leather Brief de Vaughan tightly, and headed out the back door behind Carlton.

Aunty Zooni shook her head in disgust. "Gina, you treat that child like she's your girlfriend or a princess. In my math book, eighteen don't add up to Tina being grown. When she gets back from visiting that white, anti-social father of hers, you need to beat her non-listening ass until she hears again—able to recite the house rules forward and backwards. That's what you need to do." Aunty Zooni took every available opportunity to pull rank over Aunty Gina, her younger half-sister.

Seduced and impregnated at 14-years-old, Gina's mother bled to death shortly after giving birth to her. With limited resources, Gina's maternal grandparents placed her in the care of the family of the middle-aged man who committed the disgraceful act. Prior to doing so, they named the newborn Eugenia as a constant reminder of the offense. Gina was the fifth child of Eugene Watkins. In order of birth, her older siblings were Big Momma (*Naomi*), Zooni (*Arizona*), Trudy (*Gertrude*), and Vance. Older sister by twenty-three years, Big Momma raised Gina alongside her 2-year-old Nadine (*Tina's Momma Nin*). Growing up together, Momma Nin and Aunty Gina were best friends and closer than most sisters. With the rest of the small community, they were aware of the circumstances of Gina's birth—that they were actually niece and aunty respectively. Tina's father Donnie (*Donald Leonard*) was born thirteen years later—well after the gossip had died down. The family lineage was a tangled web of Charleses, Watkinses, and Smiths.

After shedding a few droplets of tears, Tina wiped them away quickly and jumped into Carlton's car. This time, she was lawfully positioned in the passenger seat. "Momma Nin's letter was so right. Aunty Zooni is as mean as a black snake."

"Yeah, she's that, on loan from Hell, and an evil bitch too," Carlton added. The cousin/best friends looked at each other and laughed uncontrollably.

Just as he put the car in reverse, Tina screamed. "Stop!"

He pressed down hard on the breaks and returned the lever to park. "What in another world is wrong with you?"

She jumped out, grabbed her pumps from behind the Mustang's front tire, and hopped back into the car. "All right now, we can go."

Charles-Watkins-Smith Family Tree
Double-Cousin Roots

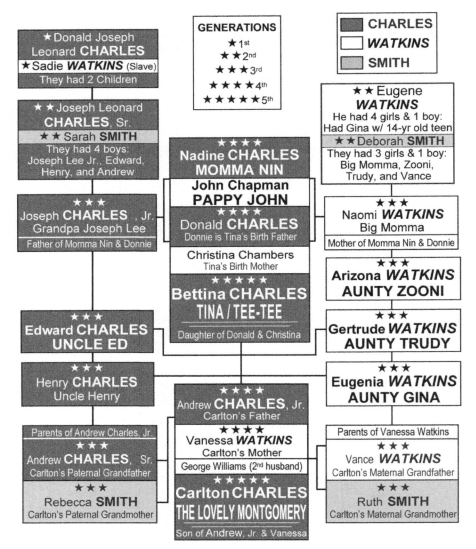

- Donnie & Christina died in car accident. Momma Nin & Pappy John adopted their niece Tina.
- Momma Nin passed away in 1975. Pappy John & Eugenia (Gina) have joint custody of Tina.
- Carlton's father Andrew Charles died in Vietnam in 1967. Mother remarried George Williams.
- Naomi (Big Momma), Arizona (Zooni), Gertrude (Trudy), Eugenia (Gina) are sisters.
- Joseph Lee. Jr.. Ed. & Henry are the three Charles brothers that married three Watkins sisters.

6

ROCKY MOUNTAIN HIGH

CARLTON reached Raleigh-Durham Airport in plenty of time to check in at the service counter, hand over luggage, and order burgers and fries. Once screened by an airport security's metal detector, he and Tina sat down and ate at the departure gate. Hunger was his excuse to camouflage the duty of baby-sitting until it was time for her to board the plane. Upon arriving at her destination, Tina would join her father for a tinge over a weeklong, western-style birthday adventure. Most of her birthday celebrations had taken place in DC, centering on the theme *Independence Day in Washington.* Unlike the past, Tina had no idea of what to expect, but she was excited about exploring unchartered territory.

Pappy John was a native Coloradan, bred in Boulder County less than one hour north of Denver. He arrived two days ahead of Tina to visit his family, particularly his three siblings—James, Thomas, and Ava, and their spouses, eight grown children, and seven grandchildren. Cousins and close friends were also included on his visitation list. As the oldest, he felt it his duty to maintain a relationship in spite of them displaying various degrees of intolerance through the years. Now that his parents had passed on, his resolve was even stronger. In Tina's absence at these spontaneous family reunions, Pappy John always came armed with photos and stories marking her achievements. This kept his daughter in the mix, without ruffling relational feathers or subjecting Tina to an unpredictable undercurrent of racism. Out of all of his relatives, his baby sister Ava showed the most genuine interest in her niece's well-being. She was quick to recognize that her brother's comments were different than usual, light on listing accomplishments and heavy on reflection.

Pappy John shared that the fifth month of her life and eleven, twelve, and sixteen years of age stood out as the most unforgettable of all his years with Tina. At five months old, she entered his life. At eleven, with the passing of his wife, he became a single father. At twelve, America's bicentennial year, Tina received her first volume of Momma Nin's lullaby letters. At age sixteen, he presented her as a debutante in Europe. Now, as his Tina stood at the entrance of adulthood, he would be there to escort her over the threshold. To his surprise, family members other than his sister were actively participating in the conversation. He went on to tell them about his intentions to make Tina's milestone Bornday special, having chosen five-star accommodations at the historic Royal Canyon Hotel. It was located in the heart of downtown Denver. Ava laughed when her brother explained that Bornday was a Tina term coming straight from her naming game list. Other family members thought the list was cute as well and were impressed with Pappy John's attention to details in caring for his daughter.

Upon awareness of the airline agent hovering, Carlton stood, gave Tina a big hug, and backed away from the departure gate. While blowing kisses in her direction, he moved quickly, knowing that she would be perturbed by what was coming next. "Bye-bye Tee-Tee, I'll call you on your Bornday and will see you in ten."

"Bye Carlton and I love you." Although knocking on the door of adulthood, it would not be opened for another four days. An announcement rang out that children traveling alone would board the aircraft first and the one being paged was Tina. The embarrassed, five-foot-eight, almost young adult lowered her head and moved as directed. She followed the attendant onto the airplane like an obedient unaccompanied juvenile and endured being monitored throughout the flight. Waiting on the other end, her response was sheer relief as she disembarked with escort and was signed over to Pappy John. "That is officially the last time the airline staff gets to treat me like I'm two years old," Tina said with assurance.

Having ridden in this rodeo many times, daddy dear was prepared with two forms of identification and Tina's revised birth certificate, showing him as her father. Examining them as they were returned, the daughter poked and twisted her lips to the side to convey her displeasure. "Pappy John, these IDs are lifeless and so businesslike. Promise me that you will take new photos that show your softer side." Tina and her father engaged in a tender embrace.

"I'll add new ID pictures to my lengthy to-do list."

In a lineup of men between forty and sixty-five, Pappy John would be identified as a handsome and virile fifty-two-year-old. At his actual age of sixty-two, women tossed many smiles, double takes, and subtle pickup lines his way. His olive, naturally suntanned complexion was a trait from his mother's Mediterranean lineage. The smoothness of his skin's texture was an added kiss from God. Pappy John was medium build and stood erect, appearing taller than his six-feet-one-inch height. With healthy eating and plenty of exercise, he was in excellent physical condition. He had an attractive, balanced face with deep brown eyes, a straight nose, a well-defined jaw, and a dimpled chin. His black hair was moderately streaked with gray, and he was cleanly shaven. He had a charming personality with a clever discriminately used sense of humor. When engaged, he would pull harmless pranks on those in his inner circle, particularly on Tina.

Traveling west from the East Coast, Tina left Raleigh at twelve noon and arrived in Denver at 3:00 p. m. Pappy John cashed in those two extra hours of sunlight immediately. He hit the highway and drove Tina all around, introducing her to the magnificence of his home state. His first stop was a ridge on a foothill of the Rocky Mountains, overlooking a breathtaking view of downtown Boulder. While pointing toward the state's largest university and his alma mater, he yelled. "Behold the black, silver, and gold. Let's Go, Buffs!" Tina chuckled, having never seen Pappy John display such gleeful emotions.

Other than being of European descent, Pappy John had shared very little of his heritage. Now, he was completely transparent, using his voice like a volume of Momma Nin's lullaby letters. As he shared information about his ancestry, Tina held tight to his every word, thinking surely that her father's about-face openness was the result of the thin air at this mile-high elevation of 5,280 feet above sea level. "My heritage labels me as a Welsh American. I'm proud to share that distinction with eight US Presidents, including Jefferson and Lincoln. My paternal grandparents migrated from Wales. It is a country with a fair amount of mountainous terrain and is part of the United Kingdom."

"I knew there was something kingly about you," Tina quipped.

"With many options as a skilled miner, my grandfather settled the family in Colorado because he was drawn to the majestic Rocky Mountains and the choice of mining for gold, silver, copper, or coal. As a young child, I enjoyed listening to my grandfather's stories about the folklore and customs of the Old Country."

From another hillside, Tina looked into the distance. "I'm fascinated by the sheer beauty of this place. The sloping landscapes are unique and the Flatiron rock formations take my breath away." In focusing downward, she was curious and cautious, gazing on a desolate area in the valley about the size of a baseball field. Its soil was a sandy-clay constitution and was covered with burrows—dozens of holes and tunnels dug in the ground by a small animal she could not identify. Some were jumping in and out of their dens and others were sitting erect on their hind legs for minutes at a time—heads moving from side-to-side.

Tina asked tentatively. "What are those squirrel-looking things making those noises?"

Pappy John was ready with answers, elated to be in this dream moment, standing on a hillside in Colorado with his daughter. "They are called black-tailed prairie dogs," he explained. "They have a sophisticated system of communicating vocally. They call out warnings to the colony, alerting them about the size and distance of a lurking predator. I did a study on them when I was in college."

Noticing Tina's jumpiness, he said, "Pumpkin, don't be nervous; they are harmless little creatures to us." His words did not ease her tension, so he seized the opportunity to tease and scare her. "Look over there and over there. The furry creatures are closing in on us!"

As he laughed, Tina held onto his arm, pulled the back of his shirt, and screamed. "Stop scaring me! Let's go. I've seen enough of these prairie thingies."

Upon reaching the suite, Tina and Pappy John engaged in a usual hotel practice, ordering room service and watching a made-for-television movie. Being with Pappy John was Tina's safe haven; just as performing was her ultimate place of comfort. She was having an incredible time, and the fun was just beginning.

Over the next three days, Tina and Pappy John were constantly on the go. In close proximity to the hotel in an area called Larimer Square, they shopped, sampled the delicacies of a few specialty restaurants, and walked the one mile to the state capital building. Tina was captivated at the sight of a group of miming artists that were providing street entertainment. Dressed in whiteface and using no speech and syncopated movement, they used the motions of their bodies to act out stories.

Seeking thrills, Tina and Pappy John went white water rafting in the Clear Creek River. The starting point of the adventure was thirty-five minutes away from the hotel in a town called Idaho Springs. They were dressed in wet suits, helmets, splash jackets, and certified life preservers. Slightly cautious, Tina and Pappy John listened carefully to the professional guide's safety instructions. "The front center of the raft is the least likely place to fall overboard."

Armed with that information, Tina and Pappy John sat in that most centralized position and abandoned their oars to anchor themselves by holding onto a thick rope. "Don't worry baby girl, we won't be falling overboard," assured the overprotective father. With hands busy gripping the twine, the paddling duties were left to the remaining six passengers. Fortunately, the rowing requirement was minimal because the river's gradient and steepness kept the raft moving at a steady pace. The motion of the water's current was like taking a ride on Mother Nature's roller coaster. True to its name, the white water was extremely clear.

During the eighteen-mile ride, the scenic view was spectacular under the cover of brilliant blue skies. There were unique rock formations, mineral deposits, and jagged cliffs. Animals were spotted along the riverbanks, including muskrats, beavers, and an occasional mountain goat on the high hillsides. Tina screamed when a huge bird flew overhead a bit too close to their position. "Oh my word, what is that humungous thing with a fish clutched in its bill?"

"It's a great blue heron," answered Pappy John. "That massive wingspan explains why it's ranked as one of the largest birds in Colorado."

"That's for sure."

Although Tina was enjoying her western vacation, her body was tested as she not only had to adjust to the elevation, but also adapt to extreme fluctuation in temperature. "Pappy John, these weather conditions are so drastic. From wearing shorts and sandals earlier today, I'm bundled up like a snow man, wearing a winter coat tonight. It went from ninety to forty degrees in a matter of hours."

"Isn't it wonderful? We get to snuggle up in front of a fireplace and roast marshmallows in June."

"All I know is that I'm suffering with sunburn and a mild case of frostbite in a single day."

Pappy John offered Tina solace. "Unlike the east coast, at least the ninety-degree days are humidity free."

"I guess that's a bright side."

The two daredevils chose gliding in a motorless sailplane as their next adventure. Tina was brave until arriving at the location—and witnessing the activity up-close. "Wait a minute! I didn't know this encounter is a one-person-at-a-time affair." Tina barely blinked while watching Pappy John go first. She carefully analyzed each step of the process. Her father, the gutsy human cargo, was strapped into the front seat of the glider plane. The experienced pilot steered the red-baron-looking aircraft while seated directly behind his eager passenger. Pappy John was surrounded by an all-glass awning, enabling him to have a clear and open 360-degree view of the scenery.

Once her father was back on the ground safely, it was Tina's turn to engage in the experience of flight without a motor—just her, the pilot, and the glider. Upon being buckled into her seat, Pappy John double-checked to make certain that Tina was hunkered down securely. Once the glass hatch was locked, she was on her way, being towed to the preplanned altitude. *Ready or not, I'm on my way up into the clouds.* Because of the peacefulness of the quiet glide, Tina's anxiety dissipated, enabling her to focus on the sights. Per Pappy John's selection, the traditional plane with an engine hauled the sailplane up to the height of 3,500 feet. There, the towrope was released and the sailplane soared freely with steering support from the pilot. At the chosen elevation, Tina could not only see the foothills, canyons, and Flatirons, but also glided across the full length of The Buffs' university campus.

Throughout the journey, the panoramic perspective of the mountains was incredible. "I'm marking this feeling of explosive exhilaration as the purest form of flying that I will ever be brave enough to experience. It's close, but still not as intense as the elation I feel when performing." Upon the pilot's offer to let her handle the controls, she promptly declined. "I prefer to focus on the carefree floating sensation and concentrate on what I hope will be a slow descent to the ground."

All was well until the first jolt of the glider's attempt to land. The sailplane's wheels touched down violently. Tina's body was subjected to rough, wobbly jerking on an uneven, gravel-laden runway. Upon planting her feet on solid ground, she ran to Pappy John and made an emphatic declaration. "I feel like I have whiplash because that landing was brutal. My thrill-seeking cup is not only full, but it is overflowing with a lifetime's worth of good memories."

7

ORLEANS STREET VACATION

SINCE there was no parking anytime on the street where Kelly King grew up, she pulled into a space up the hill and around the corner. She draped her purse over her shoulder like a sash, needing both hands to carry two gift boxes. *In spite of my crazy schedule, I found time to shop for my parents and come bearing gifts—a dress and shoes for mom and a fedora hat for dad. Since I missed all the special celebrations this year, I had to do something to pacify my guilt.* She locked the rental car and began walking down the hill. Her dark sunglasses hid her brown eyes, but not her fair skin, red full lips, and pudgy nose. Her head was elevated and her gait was stiff and pompous, pushing the point of severed ties with a Baltimore, Maryland community that hadn't been her home in eleven years. Her sexy and expensive business attire was straight off the runway—a gray suit with a long, hip-length jacket and a short, thigh-high skirt. The emphasis on her curvy hips and thick, shapely legs was like flypaper, though it attracted eyes and hissing catcalls instead of flies.

While striding along, Kelly was dowsed with the flavor and energy of the neighborhood, passing children playing street-suitable games and teenagers being teenagers. Some were loitering in an alley, some talking competitively, and others shooting baskets into a netless hoop attached to the side of a brick wall. She also encountered small groups of women and men congregating along the sidewalk.

You still have it girl—mad skills at deflecting barrages of whistles, pickup lines, and gawking. The neighborhood hasn't changed much. I'm so relieved that no one recognized me as Kelly King, music industry power-broker—an entertainment, business magnate. The magazines kill me with their classifications. Anyway, not being called-out saves me from making empty promises to listen to tape recordings that, at best, will be passed on to the interns for review and most likely a quick disposal. Crushing dreams was a part of Kelly's job description at Walden Records. Also called The Label, it was one of the music industry's overachieving babies—a mega-successful independent record company.

As executive vice president, Kelly had risen to the top like dry cream in coffee. She wore many hats at the company. Her high-level responsibility was to set the course and implement the vision of Arnie Peters, The Label's owner and president. She held biweekly meetings with department heads to be briefed on divisional activities and to deliver operational mandates. Although her job was multifaceted and involved operating puppets from behind a curtain, her name and face often appeared in magazines and on television, especially award shows. Many of the artists she managed achieved celebrity status, as well as financial and award-winning success. Her role in those accomplishments was duly noted.

Upon reaching the corner, Kelly paused to readjust her packages. She was standing under a lamppost that served as a light source as well as a directional sign. It identified the intersection as Collington and Orleans Street. *I see nothing new about Baltimore's Orleans Street. I'm in the inner city and most of the houses are small, attached, and congruent—shaped like narrow, square boxes.* Kelly theorized using sarcastic intent. *How well-conceived were these row house jewels—jammed together so tightly. Maybe people were smaller back when they were built.*

There were so many units compressed on a block that it took Kelly a measly six strides to walk from the end of one row house to the beginning of the next. The feature distinguishing one from another was a change in the color of brick. The options were style one: sandy-brown; style two: deep red; and style three: light-gray accented with blue and beige bricks.

At the extreme top edge of most of the dwellings, there were intricate carvings trimmed with white crown molding. Because of their flatness, the rooftops could be walked on—from one end of the block to the other. Each structure had black railing only on the right side of four white marble steps. They led to a flat area at the front door called the stoop. As well as row upon row of little houses with stoops, the white marble steps had been an iconic feature in Baltimore since the late 1700s. They were made from the same magnificent marble found in Cockeysville, Maryland, and used in the construction of the Washington Monument.

These marble steps are a notable symbol of neighborhood pride, but I still cringe when thinking about their place in my past. I spent years on my knees scrubbing the grime off of them. It was dreadful. Her tools were a metal-bristled brush and a tin pail of warm water with a powdered cleanser called *Bon Ami.* The steps were a central meeting place where neighbors gathered to socialize. As part of the interaction, women competed for bragging rights. *Thanks to my hard work, momma was praised often for having the cleanest marble steps on the block.*

In a phone call from the airport, Kelly had given a list of marching orders to Benjamin Franklin King. "Daddy, don't forget that your job is to keep mom from making too big a fuss half the time and criticizing me to death during the other part of my visit. My purpose for being home is to escape my high-pressured job, hide from my boss, and to rest my mind and body."

"I'll do my best, but your mother is Queen of the castle. Oh yeah, that important document came, so I stuck it in the usual place."

I'm finally here, but my arms are aching from carrying these packages. Kelly stood in front of the row house that belonged to her parents. It was style three: light-gray bricks accented with blue and beige. Near the middle of the block, it was pressed together like a sandwich, sharing walls with neighbors on both sides. There was room for just a few details on the exterior of the house—a main floor with a single paned window and a slender slate-blue front door. There was one short window in the basement and three narrow sixteen-inch-wide windows on the second story.

Although the exterior looked like all of the others, the interior of the hundred-plus-year-old house was ultramodern. Upon returning to Orleans Street, Kelly often reflected on a heated argument she had with her mother. "Listen mom, I'm fixing this place up before it implodes. All I need is for the press to report that Kelly King is allowing her parents to live in a death trap."

Through the victory of that impassioned battle with Kay-Dee Davis King, the stubborn mother agreed to her daughter's demands and total interior renovations commenced. They involved combining rooms and updating the plumbing, electrical systems, and all of the appliances. An interior decorator chose and arranged furniture, artwork, and exercise equipment. For three months during the transformation process, Kelly's parents were forced from Orleans Street into a luxurious two-bedroom condominium. It was a few miles away, across from the spectacular Inner Harbor, the cornerstone in a massive plan of urban renewal. *I intend to buy this new property and lure my parents from Orleans Street for good.* When the renovations were completed, well-intent was overridden by reality. The mother handed the keys to the condo back to her daughter, opting to return to the now decked out row house and the familiarity of the community that surrounded it.

Kay-Dee listed reasons. "My friends are there, my house is there, and I know the bus routes like the back of my hand. This hotel condominium has been a nice change of pace, but me and Ben King are heading home." Over the years, the executive vice president had grown exhausted by the combat it took to share the wealth of her success with her parents, especially her mother.

Kelly climbed the four steps and stood on the stoop, trying to unlock the door while balancing the packages on the lap she made with her bended knee. Hearing the phone ring, she tried to hurry her actions, causing the door to spring open. As if on a sheet of ice, she slid on several letters that had been pushed through the slot by the mail-man. Using her arms to break her fall, her parents' gifts flew forward. The music executive chastised herself. *I forgot that the mail would be scattered on the floor by this time in the late afternoon.*

Kelly was not surprised by her parents' absence. It was time for her father to pick up her mother, a nondriver, from her job at a fresh seafood carryout in the world-famous Lexington Market—open since 1782. With her husband's pension and her only child's contributions, Kay-Dee's need to work was not about money. The, now, part-time hours kept her busy as well as enabled her to stay connected to her long-standing customers. She had served them faithfully for more than twenty-two years.

The phone had stopped ringing by the time Kelly stabilized her body. While kicking off her heels, picking up the gifts, and carrying them into the living room, the phone rang again. Grabbing the receiver in time, she answered it. "King residence, may I help you?"

The voice said, "Please hold for Mr. Peters. Thank you."

"Kelly, where in the hell have you been and where are you now?" asked her ornery boss. He was Arnie Peters who was considered to be a tyrant by most of his staff. The executive directress, however, saw past his personality flaws and found him to be fascinating and attractive. "I've been trying to reach you since last night!"

"We both know I'm on vacation. And, since you're calling me on my parents' phone, you know where the hell I am." Because he considered her brilliant as well as a mouth-watering seductress, she was the only person who could get away with speaking to the great and powerful Mister Peters with such an attitude of overt insubordination.

"I want an update on the request I made that falls under your jurisdiction. Where is the pop artist your team was supposed to deliver?"

Informally for a time period that continued to stretch, Kelly single-handedly ran Walden Records' main headquarters in New York City. Arnie trusted her immensely although he never got close to verbalizing that sentiment. Kelly was annoyed. "Arnie, this doesn't sound like an emergency. I just walked in the door so at least let me empty my bladder. I will have to call you back." She hung up the phone and rushed to the bathroom.

For more than six months, Arnie Peters had been busy establishing a West Coast presence. As a self-proclaimed lobbyist, he attended meeting after meeting trying to get Black music videos reasonable airtime. For him, that meant more than a single Black artist being featured as part of regular programming. Arnie coined the music-video products *Triple-Ems*, which stood for "mini-musical-movies." Songs were becoming hits based on a video telling a poorly plotted story that relied heavily on sex and violence.

Arnie mentioned his intention whenever a microphone was stuck in his face. "Although I have no problem with sex and violence in videos, I want to offer the viewers a bit of refinement." Those enhancing elements included large-scale productions, quality cinematography, and sensible plotlines. In addition, he felt that the time was right to feature a versatile, Black female artist with an amazing voice, great dancing ability, and a gorgeous face—all wrapped in a sexy sellable package. The process would require the involvement of a top feature-film director and crew to assist his company's internal team. Before moving forward and making the substantial financial investment, Arnie wanted to guarantee run-time. His number one target was *National Video Television*—which was taking the world by storm—known simply as *NVT*. Sold on the concept, the network awaited Arnie Peters's delivery of a Pop-Diva goddess—one that was marketable to their sponsors—and they would guarantee multiple plays.

From the bathroom, Kelly heard the phone ring four times and disconnect. By the time she wiped, flushed, and washed her hands, the phone rang again. *I need to stop giving Arnie the phone number of every place I go. It's my own fault that he's driving me crazy on my downtime.* "Hello!" she answered.

Again, the voice said, "Please hold for Mister Peters. Thank you."

"Good, you're back—personal business finished, I assume."

Kelly used a much calmer voice. "Yes, Arnie, I'm done."

"Good, and like I was saying, I need my new superstar—like yester-day! No more demos of thug-girl rappers. In that gangster genre, I'm waiting for the dust to settle, the hustlers to leave the game, and the kingpin producers to stop killing each other. After that, we'll kick ass promoting it."

"That's duly noted."

Arnie boasted. "As I predicted over a year ago, there's a tiny ripple that will eventually turn into a gigantic wave. A few Black music enter-tainers are being viewed as artists without a designation of race."

Although it was 1982, systems were still in place that kept music sung by Black artists in separate categories from their white counter-parts. Even the Detroit sound, with its broad appeal and proven cross-over track record, was clumped together in the Black-only categories when it was time to present honors. National television coverage am-plified the disparity during the annual music award season—recogni-tion based on race and then style and sound. Black music designations included blues, jazz, soul, R&B, and recently rap. In turn, there were misfit white artists no longer qualifying as rock musicians. A remedy was created called "Pop"—first labeled as music with jazz and blues rhythms sung by white artists. Trends in record sales were slowly rede-fining Pop as a unified sound equally sung and enjoyed by all races. Arnie was a fervent believer in the new philosophy and was determined to force the industry to change. His plan was to place a mega-Pop artist who happened to be a Black woman into the game.

Arnie continued. "You see, Kelly, this crossover to the Pop vibe is a movement for Black and white artists who fit. For those who don't, the current genres will always be there. But when it does fit, it means broader worldwide audiences, leading to untapped revenue streams. My problem is that my break-out artist is somewhere out there in limbo land—unsigned to my Label."

"Yes, Arnie, I understand."

"Apparently you don't. I can smell the shit as it's churning, but Walden Records is still at the damn starting gate." Arnie was a brute who expressed himself loudly using offensive phrasing—often flavored with foul language.

Kelly offered a praise report instead of a direct response. "Did you read the latest article in *Black Ventures Magazine?* They said that we're on target to be 'Music Corporation of the Year,' based on the gold records awarded so far by ARC." The Association of Recording Certification was the organization that qualified albums and singles sold based on an intricate auditing process. It awarded gold and platinum records to both the artist and their record company. Gold awards were for five hundred thousand units up to platinum, which was for sales of one million units or more.

Kelly's attempt to appease Arnie with a list of accomplishments was waning. "We've got twelve R&B top twenty-fives—six of them are top tens. Three of those have been flip-flopping as number one now for the sixth week in a row. I know we'll get at least three, probably four more gold singles in the next two fiscal quarters."

Absent enthusiasm, Arnie responded. "R&B is Walden Records' bread and butter. I expect those results in what we do best. What does ARC say about our ratings on the Pop charts? Not a damn thing! We don't have a dog in that fight and that's not acceptable. I always deliver on promises—especially the ones I make to myself."

Kelly sighed. "It would be helpful if you weren't so picky. Besides the rappers, the Artist & Repertoire Department has been out there doing their job—hitting the pavement, reviewing recordings, and identifying hopefuls. My A&R leads sent you some pretty good demos of decent young talent and you turned them all down." Knowing what was coming, Kelly moved the phone about eight inches from her ear.

"Dammit! Pretty good ain't good enough," Arnie shouted. "The season has passed for financing mediocrity. The demos you sent reeked of one-hit wonders—not elegant or sexy enough for video. Our next new artist will have staying power and versatility and will be classified as a Pop artist who maintains R&B top chart status."

Arnie's silence was Kelly's permission to proceed. "In other words, you want me to pull a rabbit out of my ass."

"Exactly! I don't just want A&R on this. I want the whole damn company out there searching, including the music production managers—everybody."

"I promise you that, in some way, the entire East Coast office is involved in this search. Matter-of-fact, the director of the Artist Operations Division is leading a demo-sampling session that begins tomorrow and continues every day thereafter. If anything shakes, they'll let you know."

"They? Won't you be running the sessions?"

"I-I-I told you—I'm taking a week or two off."

"Or two—are you kidding me? This is a bad time!"

Now Kelly lost control. "Arnie, any time I take off is a bad time. It's been a year with me grabbing a day off here and there and I'm exhausted."

"That's irrelevant because I wake up exhausted."

Kelly gave no response to Arnie's last statement in order to avoid his trap to make her argue with him. "Oh, yes, I almost forgot. If you want me to be able to leave the country, I have to renew my passport. I plan to take care of that personal matter during my time off."

Unsuccessful at provoking his female equivalent to change her plans, Arnie yielded. "All right, Kelly, do what you need to do, but I wish you'd take one week instead of two. I gotta go." He slammed down the phone.

8

PASSPORT TO TRUTH

Tuesday, June 29, 1982

BENDING the truth to her advantage, Kelly slowed down Arnie's assault. She had already performed the steps necessary to get a replacement passport with the help of Angela, her administrative assistant. With a certified letter from Kelly, a copy of her birth certificate had been sent from the City of New York's Department of Health and Vital Records. Although she grew up in Baltimore, Kelly was born in New York City. It was her mother's first stop after fleeing North Carolina. She was grateful that her Uncle Frank needed help with his newsstand in Harlem—138th and Seventh Avenue—just when her mother showed up at his doorstep in search of a safe haven and a job. Kelly couldn't imagine the storyline of her childhood penciled in with scenes of her picking cotton and shucking corn. Having never visited a country community, her disdain and phobia for the Southeastern region was based on her mother, aunt, and favorite cousin's accounts of their rural American backdrop.

Kelly's mother, Karen Davis King was known to all as Kay-Dee. Her gloom and doom story had painted a drab picture for her daughter. "As a little girl sprouting up down South, I remember the unhappy faces of grown folks that had gotten used to surviving. Even your grand-parents were uneducated. They were stuck sharecropping to pay down on debt that kept rising," Kay-Dee recounted. "We were one of four families living on Mister Billie's farm, doing back-breaking work in the tobacco and cotton fields from sun up to sun down."

Kathy, the registered nurse and social worker, was Kay-Dee's older sister by three years. As the second downtrodden testimony, she added her take on the story. "I was glad when my baby sister escaped Tarboro, North Carolina and made it safely to Uncle Frank's place in New York City. She was free-spirited and a pathetic field hand. That's what farm workers were called back then. Down the road a piece, once liberated by my college education, I chose to stay in Edgecombe County and help others improve their living conditions."

Kelly's two-year younger cousin Katrina added. "The sad thing is that not much has changed for many of the people—the ones still trapped by ignorance. They were raised to be obliging servants—slaves to the landlord and shackled just the same." With such wholesome de-pictions of small-town USA, who could fault Kelly for possessing a nega-tive stereotype?

Once Assistant Angela gathered all the necessary information, the passport request was mailed. It included Kelly's replacement birth cer-tificate, a completed passport application, a two-inch by two-inch color photo, and a check for a hundred and fifty dollars. It paid for the application fee and an additional fifty dollars for expedited service. Knowing she'd be in Baltimore, Kelly had the document sent to her parents' address. Based on her father's confirmation, the envelope holding the replacement passport had already arrived. He had placed it on top of the refrigerator in a basket set aside for mail still coming to the house for his daughter.

Kelly reached up, pulled the basket off the refrigerator, and re-trieved the sought-after letter. The envelope was sent from the US

Department of State, Washington Passport Agency. Such awareness gave the music executive a sense of patriotic inclusion, receiving a document that represented a personal affiliation with America. As she carefully opened the letter, the phone rang again. Wondering what Arnie wanted this time, her attitude was unpleasant.

"Hello, what does Mister Peters want now?" Kelly asked.

The voice on the other end said, "Aunt Kay-Dee, is that you?"

"No, this is Kelly—Katrina, is that you?"

"Oh my God, Kelly, it's you! I've been trying to get in touch with you for a whole week. Your staff refused to patch me through. Even your assistant Angela, wouldn't take on the task. I called you here at Aunt Kay-Dee's because she told me that you were taking a vacation and coming to visit."

"I'm so, so sorry, but I was more than swamped and forced my entire team's hands. The walls of my crazy world were crushing me. Even though I was missing in action, I gave strict instructions for them to handle anything that you needed. Please tell me it's been happening?"

"Oh yes—absolutely. They've been great!"

"That's a relief because your wedding is important to me. Having Angela take over in my absence was my way of helping with the plans as the big day is drawing near."

From a small child, Katrina spent each summer in Baltimore with Kelly. Both mothers, Kay-Dee and Kathy, vowed to maintain a tight sisterly bond and to raise the girls as close companions. Through the years, the relationship strengthened as designed, making them more like bosom buddies than first cousins.

Katrina complained. "Because you know them by name and not association, you're the only one I can turn to when one of them acts crazy."

"Who is it this time?"

"It's none other than the ring leader, Grandmommy."

In Kelly's thirty years of life, she had never seen her grandmother, but for photographs. In fact, Katrina and Kathy were the only link to the Carolina connection of her mother's immediate family. A stamped-out explanation for the lack of relationship with the Davis bloodline had been fed to Kelly and Katrina through the years.

The sanctioned story was quite elaborate. It had been used often by Kay-Dee and her husband Ben King, Kathy and her husband Stephen, and Uncle Frank and his wife Aunt Kelly-Louise. The girls were told that their grandparents, Kathleen and Malachi Davis, ruled the extended family with ironclad gloves of rigidity, bitterness, and blackballing. Within their nuclear family, the household was managed with strictness, verbal lashings, and corporal punishment. As it related to Kathleen and Malachi's feelings about their two children, their oldest daughter could do no wrong. Kathy's intelligence was scarcely surpassed by her obedience and loyalty. Their younger daughter was given no room to error. Kay-Dee failed at each attempt to cross T's and dot I's to a spit-polished shine. While growing up, the girl's coping mechanisms were quite different. Kathy responded to her nurturers' penal parenting with devoted deference while Kay-Dee reacted with defensive defiance. In 1951, a breaking point in the chastisement had been reached, resulting in a family rift. At sixteen years old, Kay-Dee fled her parents' strict and physically abusive household. Her protective sister, Kathy, was so implicit in the escape that she used her part-time job's money received for washing clothes to pay for the bus ticket to the recently opened New York Port Authority Bus Terminal.

Because Uncle Frank and Aunt Kelly-Louise allowed their niece to move in, a permanent wedge was driven between the brothers, Frank and Malachi. In addition, Kay-Dee was ostracized by her parents, meaning separation from most North Carolina-based relatives. As the years passed, the bitterness became frozen in time and an acceptable family fact of life. However, Uncle Frank and Nanna-Weezy, Kelly's pet name for her great-aunt, were doting grandparent figures to Kelly—showering her with love measuring the magnitude of an entire Davis's village. In turn, Katrina was the center of her grandparents' joy—able to do no wrong in their eyes.

Pumped with such a thorough understanding of family dynamics, the cousins concluded that they could do nothing to change zebra stripes and mule stubborn tendencies. Focusing on something in their control, Kelly and Katrina forged an alliance of solidarity and care expressed toward each other down through the years.

"What's happening now?" asked Kelly.

"Grandma has lost her ever-loving mind," whined Katrina. "Last week, she decided to look at the invitation that I had given her over two months ago. She's refusing to come to my wedding unless the location is changed. I'm scared that other relatives will follow her lead."

"That sounds ridiculous! Why should she care where the wedding's going to be held? Since she's acting ugly toward you, her favorite grandchild, I don't know what to say about this new level of crazy. Remember, I've never met the woman—Thank God!"

"The church hosting the wedding made sense on so many levels. My fiancée's father is the minister of music and I recently became a member even though we'll be moving away. The church is completely renovated and the sanctuary has a wide center aisle—just perfect."

"With that being the case, I suggest that you go ahead with your plans and deal with the fact that some relatives may not attend. Who knows? Their absence might be a good thing."

"You always make me feel better," praised Katrina. "Since you'll be on vacation, it would have worked out perfectly for you to be at my wedding? After all, you should be my real maid of honor. I hate that our immature older family members can't get along. It's funny that you've been around the world many times, but never down here to North Carolina."

"I know. In addition to me never meeting any of the family down there, can you believe that my mother has not seen Grandma Kathleen in over thirty years? Now, that's craziness on steroids."

"Yeah, it's heartbreaking. Aunt Kay-Dee is an especially sweet person and her mother is missing out on so much. It makes me very sad whenever I think about it."

Kelly focused on lifting her little cousin's spirits. "Oh happy-glad Trina, come back to me. You're the belle of the ball who isn't allowed to be sad. All your energy should be focused on having the most amazing wedding day ever. I practically bought every item on your gift registry."

"I told you not to do that," scolded Katrina. "You already paid for the reception and the honeymoon."

Kelly changed the subject. "I can't believe that you landed a husband before me."

"We both know that you haven't been looking for one. You'd have to divorce your job in order to have time for a marriage."

"Oh, don't you know me so well? On a serious note, even though I won't be there in person, I'll be thinking about you the entire day. Well, I'm sure Arnie is trying to call me again, so I better hang up now."

"Speaking of Mister Peters, I hope he's fine, by the way. Tell your secret-lover-man boss that Katrina said hello."

Kelly spoke using a raspy tone to denote a whisper. "Hey, don't say that so loudly. Anyway, I know your wedding day is going to be really special. Love you with a whole bunch of hugs—good-bye."

"I love you back and my hugs are bigger—bye-bye."

Finally having an uninterrupted moment, Kelly opened the envelope and examined her passport. The stiff navy-blue backing made the embossed gold lettering and emblem of the American eagle even more pronounced. She opened the cover and stared at her image. It was a good likeness—showing reddish-brown hair, an oval face, high cheekbones, and just enough freckles to be considered cute—about six per cheek and five on her nose. After tucking the passport into her purse, she went back to the envelope, realizing it contained another document. It was the replacement birth certificate used by the government for verification and then always returned with the passport.

It dawned on Kelly that this moment represented the first time she had ever looked at her certificate of birth. All prior instances that required the document, including the procurement of her original passport, had been handled by her mother. Since the document was folded in threes, that was how Kelly opened it. The first fold unveiled the top portion of the document, citing New York as the city of origin and a statement of authentication.

It read:

This is a certification of name and birth facts on file in the Bureau of Vital Records, Department of Health, City of New York.

The next fold revealed the certificate number, the date filed, and the date issued in the Borough of Manhattan. Other specifications read:

Date of Birth: SEPTEMBER 29, 1952
Name: KELLY DONNITA CHARLES
Sex: FEMALE

Immediately noticing that her last name was different, Kelly was dazed, as if she had been sucker-punched in the face. She opened the third fold, exposing the complete document. The last two lines of specification read:

Mother's Maiden Name: Karen Denise Davis
Father's Name: Donald Leonard Charles

Believing that exhaustion had caused her to hallucinate, she closed her eyes, shook her head, reopened her eyes, and read the detail again. Her second examination did not convert the information to what had been her truth for thirty years. She reached in her purse, grabbed her wallet, and retrieved her social security card, feeling the need to verify her own name.

The social security card read:
KELLY DONNITA KING

The name flip-flopping made her even more confused. Kelly re-folded the birth certificate, adding a few extra creases in order for it to be small enough to fit inside the tiny pocket on the lower right side of her suit jacket. She hated the fact that most business apparel designed for women did not have real pockets. Anxious for the truth, Kelly rushed upstairs to her parents' bedroom closet. From the far left corner, she pulled out a small, hard green suitcase with a weak lock that wasn't latched. This old piece of luggage was the sole repository for the King family's full arsenal of vital records—insurance policies, marriage license, car title, deed to house, and three certificates of birth—her mother's, her father's, and hers. She opened her original birth certificate and it cited the same shocking information as the replacement copy, still resting inside her suit jacket's miniature pocket.

Her continued search of the suitcase uncovered two letters sent from the Social Security Administration. The first envelope was addressed to the person she just met: KELLY DONNITA CHARLES and contained a Social Security card still intact—perforation in place. The second envelope was addressed to the person she had known all her life: KELLY DONNITA KING. The Social Security card was missing. That made sense because it had been in her possession since she used it to procure her first summer job as a teenager. The second envelope contained an additional item—a letter printed on government stationary with a one-sentence statement.

It read:

This is a reissue of Form SSA-3000 due to a name change.

That brief notation spoke volumes. It supported the fact that Kelly Donnita Charles and Kelly Donnita King were one and the same. Apparently, her parents had changed her last name to match Ben King's early on—prior to her entering grade school. The reissued social security card was the tangible proof that her last name had been officially changed from Charles to King. This awareness caused Kelly's mind to do somersaults. She felt distrust toward her parents and her Aunt Kathy. As it related to Uncle Frank and Nanna-Weezy, they were memorialized in her heart and could do no wrong. In terms of relatives, Katrina was the only one she still trusted completely—positive that she too had been left in the dark. Because of the pending wedding, Kelly refused to burden her best friend with this shocking news. Unlike her, she knew Katrina would drop everything and run to her side. Although experiencing indescribable loneliness, she refused to be that selfish—not this time.

9

A QUEEN AT EIGHTEEN

GETTING Tina out of bed at 5:15 a. m., the hotel's wakeup call had done its job. In what felt initially like a lifetime, the forty-eight days since graduating high school had disintegrated into particles of nothingness. After brushing her teeth and rinsing with mouthwash, Tina looked into the mirror and grinned at the brand new person. It was Wednesday, June 30, 1982, and Bettina Bethany Charles had officially turned into a *Queen at Eighteen*. With exactness, Tina followed the directions Momma Nin had placed in the prologue of her second volume. As instructed, she woke up early, opened Brief de Vaughan, and retrieved Lullaby Letter 86. It was in the binder with the rest of the letters, but sealed and tucked inside of a translucent pouch. Upon tearing open the envelope, her face lit up with joy as she read her special birthday greeting.

Volume II: Lullaby Letter 86

Dearest Tina, in believing that this lullaby letter was not opened until the date and time I specified, I hope you woke up early to read it and that I'm the first person to say HAPPY, HAPPY BIRTHDAY! In hoping that you're still playing your naming game, I also wish you a HAPPY, HAPPY BORNDAY! Your imagination's interpretation of the world has always been precious. It's difficult for me to envision you, my fresh-faced little Bettina, as an eighteen-year-old young woman. I want you to rest in knowing that I'm smiling with the angels and thanking God for your safe arrival at adulthood.

As you should've been told, this milestone birthday comes with a gift of five thousand dollars. Use a portion of it to activate your vision and have fun under the guise of common sense. Prepare to stumble and fall over some of your decisions, but I hope you get up quickly and move on. In embracing adulthood, I ask that you never hand over your innocence, openness, and optimism to the constraints of mainstream maturity. —*Trusting that your birthday blessings become bountiful benefits, Momma Nin* ■

Tina interpreted Momma Nin's words as a sign of motivation, encouraging her to press forward with her plans. Her internal liberty bell began to sound off ramblings of independence. *I am eighteen years old, am free from all the permission slips of childhood, and can legally sign my way into hell and back if I like.* The hour had come for the bank to release holdings of thirty-one thousand dollars to Tina's care and for her New York City apartment's lease to be legally binding. Tina's financial dividend was a combination of a five-thousand-dollar birthday gift plus her first monthly stipend of one thousand dollars, both coming from her trust fund. Having been in Tina's possession for over a month, the Chamberses' twenty-five-thousand-dollar graduation gift represented the bulk of her discretionary funds.

Although having a reason for overexcitement, Tina talked herself down from the treetop of jubilation. She was hell-bent on moving forward with her plan to toss a grenade of disappointing news at Pappy John. *My sneak attack will be launched at the dinner celebration this evening. People tend to be extra nice and forgiving on a person's birthday.* After wounding my dear father, I'll return to Scotland Neck, face the music of Aunty Gina and the Aunty-ettes, and sing at the wedding. When that is over, my old business will be finished and I'll be free to focus solely on conquering New York City.

Just as Tina returned Letter 86 to the binder, the phone rang. She hurried to answer it while trying not to awaken Pappy John from a well-earned, extended slumber in the hotel suite's second bedroom.

"Hello, Tina speaking."

"Happy Bornday, Miss Grown and on Your Own Hussy!" Carlton teased. "You made it to Canada, girl—the last stop on the Underground Railroad—to the land of fantastic freedom. Feels good, huh?"

Tina giggled. "Not sure. I haven't done anything adult yet. For breakfast, I'm going to order a couple of mimosas—a little orange juice and lots of champagne."

Carlton agreed. "You ain't said nothing but a word! Tony's here and we're talking on the telephone loudspeaker—no hands, Honeychile? Can you hear us okay?"

"I can hear you fine and probably better if you stop screaming."

From the background, Tony yelled. "Happy Birthday, Miss Queen at Eighteen!"

Tina looked at the clock. "Thanks, but if it's six here, it's eight there—much too early for Carlton to be awake."

"So true, but today is special. Guess where we are?"

"I thought that in a couple of hours you and Tony would be on your way to New York City."

"Tina Boo, we're not on the way—we've arrived to the land of plenty of everything under the sun! I'm standing in the living room of our apartment waiting for the furniture to get here. I don't know what happened, but this place is nothing like the one we picked out of the newspaper. I called Mister Brown and he told me that I was at the right address. So who am I to argue when it's beneficial to us? The cab driver who brought us from the train station said that we're on the Upper East Side. It's just like *The Jefferson's*: 'a deluxe apartment in the sky.' The building's a high-rise on 86th Street with a bunch of elevators, and we're on the twenty-fourth floor. Our front door is stamped

2407 in shiny gold letters. Down in the lobby, there's a doorman on duty around-the-clock and a conci-something service that helps with anything. I ain't ever seen a building like this and I already had two requests—to walk a dog and mail some letters."

"So, what did you do?" asked Tina.

"On my way back from walking the dog, I put the letters in the mailbox. The Lovely ain't doing nothing to be kicked out of paradise. By the time you see the apartment, it's gonna be hooked up to the max, fabulous, and fierce."

"I can't wait to see it," Tina replied in a tone that lacked enthusiasm.

"What's wrong with you, Birthday Girl? You sound like somebody just ran away with your smile and your happy heart."

"My mind is focused on later—on telling Pappy John that I'm taking a break from college and moving to New York City."

"You've been in Colorado four days and haven't told him yet? If you want, I'll do it. It's a mess to be stressed on your birthday," Carlton said with authority and assurance.

"Thanks, but no. I have to do this myself. I'm the grown and on my own queen at eighteen—remember? I'm telling him tonight at dinner, for sure."

"Do what you must. Anyway, when the beds get here, Tony and me are gonna take them for a test drive."

"Carlton, feel free to do what you want on yours, but stay away from my bed and I mean it!"

"Girl, you know I'm just playing. See, I got your mind off your troubles."

"Yes, you find a way to do it, each and every time. And by the way, don't forget about our budget—no purchases besides what's on the list."

Tony responded. "No worries. I'll make sure he behaves."

Carlton jumped in. "All right, Tina, we got work to do and you got a birthday to enjoy. Love you. Happy Bornday! Bye."

❧

Even though most screamed girly-girl, Pappy John participated in the majority of the *Tina-Time* activities. On this eighteenth birthday, that meant facials at 9:30 a. m., manicures and pedicures at 10:30 a. m., and enduring a *Tina's Choice* movie at 2:00 p. m. She selected the blockbuster film: *E. T.*—definitely not on Pappy John's must-see movie list. He reasoned, *At least the film is presented in Dolby Stereo, enhancing the cinematic experience with four-channel surround sound.*

Per Tina's insistence, they arrived early enough to have the twentieth position in line to enter the theatre. Although an afternoon show, the hottest movie in America created a line that wrapped around the corner. When the doors opened, Tina grabbed Pappy John's hand and pulled him along. "Let's stop for popcorn," he yelled.

"Not yet. First, we have to claim our seats."

Tina's aggression merited a dead-center position. With that secured, she placed her order and Pappy John spent the previews standing in yet another long line. Eventually, he returned with popcorn, hotdogs, sodas, and milk chocolate balls in two varieties. One was concealing mint and the other was wrapped around peanuts.

At the movie's end, Pappy John offered commentary. "It took two hours to tell a story about a homesick extraterrestrial, befriending a few kids, phoning home, and riding bikes with them in the sky."

There were opposing critiques from the father and daughter. Tina gave the science fiction film a thumbs-up for being magically fantastic. Dozing minutes at a time during the viewing, Pappy John rated the movie a thumbs-down for flying right over his ability to comprehend the reason for the hoopla.

With a short walk back to the hotel, there was plenty of time to dress for the birthday dinner. The reservation was for 6:30 p. m. with a grace period of arriving early, on time, or not at all.

10

FIGURED OUT ALL WRONG

CUSTOMERS made cooing sounds to register their subtle satisfaction regarding Pappy John and Tina's entrance into the Royal Canyon Hotel's five-star restaurant. They stood there on display, waiting for the maître d' to seat them. She wore a black, pleated chiffon gown—sleeveless with a sweeping full-length skirt. He was dressed in a classic white, one-button, tuxedo dinner jacket with a satin shawl collar. His satin bow tie and trousers were black and his pleated front shirt was white. Tina was such an old movie buff that she compared this real-life situation to her thoughts of cinematic romanticism. *This is like Casablanca with a twist. Instead of 1942 in Morocco at Rick's Café, it's 1982 in Denver, Colorado, at Novelli's. Rick Blaine's heart was broken by Ilsa, his old flame, and Pappy John's heart will be crushed by me—Bettina, the daughter he adores.*

After eating the amuse-bouche, Chef Pierre Novelli came out to greet the birthday girl. In his best French interpretation of English, he said, "Mademoiselle tonight is une spéciale occasion pour vous turning dix-huit. A fabuleux cinq course meal will be presented pour votre pleasure."

Each course was a culinary masterpiece, plated to perfection like a work of art. The protein performed exceptionally well as the star of every dish—escargot, sea scallops wrapped in apple wood bacon, and grilled Colorado Lamb tenderloin. The vegetables, starches, and garnishes added color and artistic design—baby carrots, asparagus, summer squash, Yukon gold potato purée, and fresh chives. Because the meticulous preparation of French cuisine unveiled slowly, it gave Tina adequate time to present her case to her father. Once the first course was served, she dove right into the discussion, explaining how she first caught the performance bug.

Saturday, November 30, 1974—Ten-year-old Tina sat on a booster seat in the Imperial Theater's front row center bedazzled by the Broadway smash hit musical 'Pippin.' From a dark stage canvas, a wonderful melody played as dozens of wide open hands in a multitude of hues and sizes swayed to the beat. Appearing to be suspended in midair, they moved forward. Brightly spotlighted, Ben Vereen's face appeared between his open palms. With the remaining audience forgotten, his brilliant smile greeted Tina. His fulfilled mission had convinced her to 'leave her fields to flower and her cheese to sour to waist an hour or two because they had magic to do.'

Tina became teary-eyed as she spoke. "Pappy John, it was Momma Nin's last earthly Thanksgiving and the three of us spent the holiday in New York City. I was ten years old and we went everywhere. The place I remember the most was Broadway, the play *Pippin*, and Ben Vereen. You remember, don't you?"

"Oh, baby girl, of course I do. That's one of the memories that pulls me through my toughest days—the ones when I miss Nadine the most."

"Ever since then, words from the musical's opening song have been my theme. I say them to myself all the time, 'Bettina Charles, you've got magic to do.' Sometimes, I feel like I'm getting ready to explode or fly away. Momma Nin's lullaby letters are my guide, explaining how dreams come true through action. Now that I'm old enough, I'm ready to do the hard work—to put my passion to practice on a grand scale. I want to sing and dance my way into the hearts of people the way I did at my high school graduation. The pleasure I gained was amazing and I want—I need to feel like that again and again."

Tina slid a document across the table to Pappy John. It detailed her exceptional, but incomplete academic record. "For two years, other than singing and spending time with you, my life has been filled with studying and nothing else." As her voice started to quiver, she paused, took a few sips of water, and then continued. "That transcript you're holding shows eighty-seven credits—mostly As and a few Bs. I ignored your advice to take a break until the fall semester and instead, spent the last five weeks in ECU's first summer session—not smart. The two courses required that I be in each class four hours every day with exams every week. I guess I was trying to prove that I did my best to finish. With the six hours yet to be posted, the total is ninety-three credits—twenty-nine short of completing my degree."

"Pumpkin, your hard work will pay off in a big way one day. Haven't I told you how proud I am of you?"

"Yes, but what I'm getting ready to tell you is going to make you the opposite of proud—disappointed." Tina took a deep breath, called upon her stored-up courage, and poured out her soul. "Those ninety-three hours are it for a while." After a moment of silence to gauge Pappy John's reaction, she continued. "My Bornday present to myself is to take a break from college and go after my dreams—with Carlton by my side, of course."

"I knew Carlton would appear somewhere in the background of this picture that you're painting. And where exactly are you two going?" Although knowing her plan and having already interceded on her behalf, Pappy John wanted to hear the details directly from his daughter. He was troubled by her delay in bringing this irrational news to his attention.

Tina dropped the whininess from her voice and spoke with assuredness. "I'm taking a year off from college, moving to New York City with Carlton, and auditioning like crazy until I get a job in a Broadway musical or a dramatic play or singing in a famous club." Tina paused to inhale the oxygen necessary to finish her well-rehearsed recitation. Sill, failing to gauge Pappy John's anger meter due to his relaxed facial expression, she continued. "If that doesn't happen right away, I'll try out to be the first Black Rockette dancer or some other job involving live performance—something—anything to put on my resume. I know I have the talent. You and everybody around have told me that I do, but what I don't have is experience."

In addition to academics, Tina had done the work to fine-tune her talent—fifteen years of piano and twelve years of voice and dance. Relative to on-the-job training, her curriculum vitae lacked the necessary credentials. She had not performed for massive audiences or participated in large-scale productions. In fact, Tina was certain that Club Trevi's was the only relevant experience worthy of her acknowledging on paper.

The energetic young adult hesitated, hoping that Pappy John would interject feedback. When none was forthcoming, her rambling continued. "Professor Milton has a good friend who works closely with a Broadway music director and he also knows a few producers in the music industry. He's going to try and get me an audition. If that works out, Professor said that his friend's friend would introduce me to some of the right people—casting directors, agents, and managers. Once Carlton and I find somebody to help us make a professional demo recording, his friend might be able to get it to a large record company—maybe."

An exasperated Tina decided to rest her case. After several seconds of stillness, Pappy John broke his silence with cross-examination to expose the loopholes in his daughter's proposal. "Professor Milton's friend and his friend's friend have way too many 'ifs,' 'mights,' and 'maybes' attached to their assistance. Although well-intended, I must conclude that the Professor's associates are shaky at best and will likely lead to dead ends."

"L-l-like him, h-h-his friends are eccentric and y-y-your hunches are probably right. Other than that, however, I've got it all figured out."

"Wait, Tina, I'm not finished poking holes in your plan that you re-inforced with plastic wrap. Your biggest problem is money. The stipu-lations of your trust fund have been explained to you many times—no four-year degree, no twenty-five thousand dollar payout. That leaves you with one thousand dollars a month plus your five-thousand-dollar birthday present—nowhere near enough money to live in New York City—with no job—just you and Carlton running around from audi-tion to audition."

Tina's monthly stipend was based on a forty-hour work week at a rate of six dollars and twenty-five cents per hour, remaining constant regardless of inflationary factors. Momma Nin wanted Tina to be com-fortable, but not lazy. If she needed additional money, she would have to earn it. With compounded interest minus the initial payout of six thousand dollars, Tina's very tightly controlled trust fund was approxi-mately $435,000. Other than her monthly stipend, she would receive a ten thousand dollar birthday payout at the age of twenty-one and the twenty-five-thousand-dollar payout if ever obtaining the coveted col-lege degree. Besides those dividends, Tina could not even sneeze at the majority of her money until reaching the age of twenty-five. At that point, with or without a degree, she would receive the full benefit in addition to the right to keep or sell the Les Vésinet property. Joseph-Lee Manor had to remain in the family, under her control, but never sold.

With now or never courage, Tina dropped the bomb. "I know you're going to be upset, but I really do have things figured out. For graduation, the Chamberses sent a check directly to me for twenty-five thousand dollars. They had never done that before, so I took it as a sign to move forward. I didn't tell you because I thought you and Aunty Gina would make me put the money in that stupid trust fund until I turned twenty-five. What's the point of having money if you aren't allowed to spend it until you get really old and stop dreaming?"

"Tina, the fact that you think twenty-five is really old is a big reason why the stipulations of the trust fund are in place."

"Well, I gave the graduation money to Mister Vaughan, who helped me fill out paperwork for checking and savings accounts. They officially opened this morning."

Preston Vaughan was senior vice president of Fitzgerald National Bank, which was headquartered in Washington, DC. He'd been a friend of Momma Nin's since college and an acquaintance of her husband John Chapman since 1953. Preston Vaughan helped to open Tina's trust fund back in 1964 with the Chamberses' first fifty-thousand-dollar offering.

Pappy John said rhetorically. "Twenty-five thousand dollars is a huge secret to keep from your guardians for more than six weeks, don't you think? But it's done now. So, as of today, you have a total of thirty-one thousand dollars. That's enough money to pay for a lot of recklessness, but wisdom is not for sale. It's something that is earned through experience over many years."

Tina had never seen Pappy John so disappointed in her and she tried to demonstrate her foresightedness. "Carlton and I gave a lot of thought to choosing an apartment. We spent lots of time at ECU's library looking through the *Times* and *Post* newspapers. W-we made a list of two-bedroom apartments, renting for less than two-thousand-dollars a month. Uncle Doug helped us choose the best one, somewhere in Manhattan."

Douglas Brown was a CPA and investment banker. He had been Pappy John's best friend since army officer's training school and the buddy he would be bunking with in DC. The Brown family's venture capital corporation had extensive high-end real estate holdings in Manhattan—luxury condominiums for sale and apartments for rent. Unfortunately, all he could offer Tina was advice because the apartments on her list were owned by slumlords, definitely not under Brown Properties' jurisdiction.

With intent to patronize, Pappy John interjected. "Oh really! You went to Douglas without telling me? Interesting!"

"Yes, sir. The apartment we chose rented for twenty-five hundred dollars—higher than our price range, but Uncle Doug said that it was the best one on our list, by far. After adding up a year's rent plus the four thousand dollars we spent on furniture and household things, we still have eight thousand dollars left. That's pretty good budgeting, isn't it?"

Pappy John interrupted. "From the eight thousand dollars, you need to subtract utilities, groceries, and incidentals like toiletries clothes, and entertainment. I assume you two will be club hopping like most young people your age. Most importantly, to get around town to auditions, you need bus, subway, and cab fare."

Tina used the palm of her hand to tap her forehead. "Utilities, groceries, and the rest are important. I can't believe we forgot to put them in our budget."

"Yet, you have it all figured out. Baby girl, God placed a Pappy John and Aunty Gina in your life for a reason. We're supposed to be there to remind you of the small, but really important details. With everything we've been through as a family, I thought we had earned each other's trust."

Realizing the level of pain caused by her deceit, Tina's heart sunk extremely low. "I do trust you a hundred percent, but what I did had nothing to do with trust. I was trying to get my way by being sneaky. Pappy John, I'm really, really sorry and I hope you will forgive me."

"Maybe in a few years' time." Pappy John nodded and smiled. "Admitting guilt is a very grownup thing to do, and, of course, I accept your apology. There's always room in my heart to forgive the most important person in my life. Now, have you told me enough of this lengthy story to lighten your awful burden of guilt?"

"Yes, yes, and yes. I feel so much better!"

"Good! Now, it's my turn to make a confession. I've known about the money and your apartment search for about five weeks, one less than you. Shortly thereafter, I told Gina and we made some decisions together."

Tina's eyes widened to their full capacity. In disbelief, she asked, "If you knew, why didn't you tell me? Why did you make me go through all this stress?"

"You chose to keep me in the dark and I chose to let you think I remained there. Tina darling, in addition to my friends, Preston and Douglas are professionals. They are bound to full disclosure as it relates to you and certain financial activity. Other than them as your legal advisors, Aunty Gina and I are the co-executors of Nadine's estate and have a certain amount of responsibility until you turn twenty-five years old. And in this case, you should be grateful that we were involved.

Douglas came to me troubled by your choice of living quarters. The apartments that made your short-list were a cause for alarm—high-crime neighborhoods, roach and rat infestation, no laundry facilities, no elevator, and no amenities that would help to protect your safety. Oh, yes, and the twenty-five hundred dollar cesspool apartment you chose was five flights above a twenty-four-hour convenience store and located in a red-light district."

"But, Pappy John, I'm confused. Carlton is in New York right now and has already moved our furniture into a really nice place. He said that we're on the twenty-fourth floor, with a huge lobby, several elevators, and a doorman. That's nothing like the apartment you're describing—thank God."

Pappy John said pompously, "That's why it pays to have a father and friends in high places. Brown Properties leased you a luxury, two-bedroom apartment, on the Upper East Side for an amazing price—four thousand dollars a month. And that's the cost after the two thousand dollar discount. You are responsible for twelve thousand dollars. That will be the first check written with that new account of yours. Be sure to include a detailed, handwritten thank you note to Douglas. Minus your part of the rent and the furniture you've already purchased, there should be a balance of roughly fifteen thousand dollars. I expect you to manage it well, taking care of food, utilities, tips for the doorman, et cetera. By the way, without an establishment of credit and steady employment, a cosigner was required to enter into an above-board leasing agreement and that was me."

Tina sat and looked at her father in total amazement and adoration. *Although he's not overjoyed about my decision, he's helping me figure everything out. And, that's my Pappy John.*

11

BORNDAY SURPRISES

Q UEEN at eighteen or not, Tina was grateful, relieved, and confused. She didn't understand how a celebration she had ruined
royally was still working out in her favor. Pappy John was seated across
from her extending love and support in spite of her deceit and disappointing news about taking a hiatus from college. A silent praise pause
commenced to commemorate her blessings. *My bare feet just walked
across sand heated at 110 degrees without me getting a single blister.*

Tina spoke, almost inaudibly. "After writing my twelve-thousand-
dollar check, plus the two-thousand-dollar discount from Uncle
Doug's family's business, there's still a ridiculous amount left to pay—
thirty-six-thousand-dollars. Without money from my trust fund, I can't
afford to rent that kind of apartment for an entire year." Tina needed
answers to trace the trail of a mysterious revenue stream.

"I'm very appreciative about Uncle Doug's kindness. The generosity, however, didn't stop with him, nor should my gratitude."

Pappy John daughter's persistence coaxed the anonymous donor
out of anonymity. "In order to capitalize on the unprecedented discount, an entire year's rent comes due on July fifteenth. Once your
twelve thousand dollars are received, a year's rent will be paid in full."

Tina pressed for more information. "That's an amazing miracle, but it still doesn't name my secret Santa."

Pappy John conceded. "For the sake of moving forward, the private contribution just turned into a Bornday surprise. Since you were insistent on going to New York, I paid the balance of the year's lease. I needed to know you were in the safest environment possible." Pappy John subsidizing Tina's dream was done with much trepidation—knowing that he had unlocked the cage and released his daughter into one of the largest concrete jungles in the world.

Tina gasped in astonishment, placing her hand over her mouth. "Pappy John, thank you so-so-o-o much. This means everything to me, mainly that you believe in me enough to support my dreams in such a huge way."

"Whether fully understanding or not, I'll be your biggest fan in whatever career you choose—always applauding from somewhere in the wings."

With a deep sense of gratitude, Tina made a vow. "I promise to work extra hard, every minute, and hopefully land my first job right away. With the support of you and Aunty Gina, there's no limit to what I can accomplish."

"Hold on a minute, I have a few conditions. There are two promises that must be made."

Pappy John's face got extremely serious and Tina leaned forward to pay close attention. "What are my two conditions?"

"You must finish college by your twenty-first birthday. I'm doing my best to drill the Charleses' academic accomplishments into your head and heart, but feel like I'm failing miserably at taking over where your mother left off. "

"I think you're doing a fantastic job. Your preaching of the college subject is much more intense than Momma Nin's gentler approach that she covered in her Lullaby Letters."

"Your news to leave school for New York City says differently, so I'll repeat the academic charge again. Nadine's father graduated from Howard University in 1910—among a very few Blacks able to attend college at all back then. Your Momma Nin followed him in 1943 and Donnie followed them, finishing in 1956. Your completion date must be added to this unbroken chain of achievement. It would be dishonorable for you not to receive your degree. Also, it would make me break a promise to my wife that I'd make sure you graduated college."

With such a serious first promise, Tina had no idea about the subject matter of the next. "What's the second promise?" she asked.

"This one is lighthearted, but just as serious. You must make sure that the 'some other job having to do with performing live' does not involve a pole, G-string, or money being thrown in your direction."

Knowing that she had 100 percent of Pappy John's support with his special blend of humor thrown in, Tina glided around to his side of the table, sat on his lap, and gave him a long kiss on the cheek and a big hug. With no knowledge of the unlikely pair's relationship, interest in them heightened. Most restaurant patrons reacted in some way that included pointing, hissing, and squirming.

After returning to her seat, Tina squealed with excitement. "Pappy John, I promise that I will finish school and place the degree in your hand before I turn twenty-one." In her spoiled, whiny voice, she rolled her eyes and giggled. "I also promise that I will absolutely not become a stripper." As always, they sealed the deal by pinky swearing.

Gradually, the people seated around them had cleared out. On the other side of the restaurant behind a half wall and columns, the dining room was buzzing with activity and filled completely with patrons.

Pappy John made an observation. "It's eight thirty and we're the only ones left on this side of the restaurant. I hope it isn't a hint that we've overstayed our welcome."

Tina asked, "Is everything okay? I'm accustomed to subtle reactions to our public father and daughter routine, but never have we cleared an entire side of a restaurant. Do you think the lap sitting, big hug, and kiss were too much?"

Concern was quickly put to rest with Chef Novelli's return to the front of the restaurant, delivering the dessert course. Two sous-chefs accompanied him, pushing carts filled with decadent desserts—crème brûlée, chocolate mousse, soufflés, crepes, cream puffs, and apple tarts. Novelli said, "And now as the finale. Pour vous, Mademoiselle, I have prepared a magnificent assortment of desserts pour vous and your entire famille."

Mixing English and French, Tina and Pappy John assumed that Chef Novelli misspoke when stating: *entire family.* As the overhead lighting brightened the restaurant, the pastry chef entered the room holding a three-tiered cake—pink buttercream icing, accented with chocolate musical symbols, and eighteen burning candles. This awesome display was accompanied by a concert of voices yelling surprise and happy birthday, coming from all directions. Initially, Tina was startled by the presence of about thirty-five strangers—white people of all ages who knew her name and were wearing party hats and blowing party horns. As introductions were made with her father's siblings taking the lead—James, Thomas, and Ava.

Tina stood up and began hugging her family. "It's so nice to meet you Aunty—I-I-I mean Aunt Ava." While trying to explain to the Westerners, the young niece was interrupted in midsentence.

"You don't have to explain. We've already been briefed on your naming game and are eager to learn more of your unique terminology." Her Aunty Ava's warm words of understanding were like a hatchet that demolished Tina's walls of apprehension and caused light-hearted giggles to flow indiscriminately. When observing his family's demonstration of love, the heavy burden caused by the hate of racism had been lifted. Overcome by power of prudence and blind justice, Pappy John sobbed loudly like a broken man. Shortly thereafter, tears flowed freely throughout the room.

The next four days were a nonstop party in and around the cities of Denver and Boulder. Starting early the following morning and after denouncing daredevil activities, Tina's newfound family took her on another frightening adventure. At 4:15 a. m., a fifteen-passenger van pulled up to the Royal Canyon Hotel, filled with relatives and two extra seats for Pappy John and Tina. They headed west of Denver and drove an hour and a half to reach the Central Rockies. At sunrise, eight of them shared a hot air balloon and floated nine thousand feet above a Colorado valley. The magnificent eight were Tina, Pappy John, his three siblings, and their spouses.

On the ascent, Tina expressed her uneasiness. "I'm quite nervous for us all. We're rising so high in a basket that's being held in the air by a balloon."

Laughter was her collective response.

Ava assured, "I promise that everything is fine."

Pappy John stood in the right back corner of the giant basket—breathing in big gulps of the clean air and feeling a gentle breeze while watching the answer to an often-requested prayer. *For the first time in a moment of apprehension, Tina is not holding onto my arm or tugging at my clothing. She's found solace in my side of her family.*

Ava held Tina's right hand, Thomas held her left, and James had his hands on her shoulders. They eased her tension by engulfing her with love—pointing in various directions across the panoramic view. They drew her attention to the plains, rolling hills, and free-ranging animals. Some were big horn sheep, deer, and elk. Although seeing the Flatirons from a hillside and a sailplane, Tina thought the views from this nine-thousand-foot elevation were unmatched, stunning, and spectacular.

After the hot air balloon excursion, while surrounded by the protection of relatives, Tina became fearless, enjoying every minute of kayaking, cave exploring, and hiking up steep and rocky hillsides. While moving about, Ava and her brothers were disturbed by the double takes and stares that Tina was receiving. In those actions, they saw a representation of their former selves, producing a very sorrowful shame in them.

While in a gift shop, a curious sixty-year-old white woman, eased up to Ava, whispered, and asked, "Is that young lady a Black person or is she just very, very tan—like extremely sunburned tan?"

Ava wrapped her arm around Tina's shoulder before answering the awkwardly stated question. "Oh my! I never noticed, but my niece is a beautiful young woman that happens to also be Black. Would you like to be introduced?"

With a goal to chastise and not make acquaintances, the now, not so curious woman backed her way out of the general store and eased into the front passenger seat of a station wagon. Shortly thereafter, her husband screeched the tires as he drove away swiftly. There were a few, similar encounters and many surprised looks that occurred throughout the day. When the looks were accompanied by racial slurs, her aunty and uncles tried to intervene, apologizing continuously until Tina stopped them. She followed Momma Nin's advice to, "whenever possible, turn unawareness into a teaching moment."

Tina explained. "I looked it up and found out that Black people make up less than 1 percent of the population living in this area. Other than a few ugly comments, most people were just curious and that doesn't bother me at all. Pappy John taught me to be proud of who I am."

Tina politely engaged in conversations, answering very unusual questions. She even obliged an extremely bizarre request from a strange woman. "May I touch your hair?" Once finished her tentative two-finger glide, the woman said, "Besides being coarser, it's hair just like mine." Tina smiled and remained silent.

Ava whispered. "We'll just let that comment float away to the far-off land of stupidity." In a private moment, she confessed to her niece. "I want to apologize on behalf of the family, especially me and my brothers. Much more than the woman who touched your hair, we have spent a lot of years being silent bigots, acting narrow-minded, and ignorant. Sorry is not enough. There are no words to express our level of regret."

After hugging her Aunty Ava, Tina offered reassurance. "What happened before is not important to me. I have you guys now, and, together, we have a lot of tomorrows."

Piled onto the adventures already enjoyed, the family took Tina fly-fishing and horseback riding, and they toured several gold mines. On the Fourth of July, they attended a festival that included a huge community picnic of various towns in Boulder County and ended with an amazing fireworks display. The pyrotechnics appeared as if they were spewing out of the mouth of the mountains.

On the following morning, July fifth, it was time for Tina and Pappy John to leave Colorado. At the airport, another crowd of around thirty-five people showed up. This time, they gathered to say good-bye. Unlike at the restaurant, there were no strange white people—just relatives and friends, each of whom Tina could call by name.

During the flight home, there was no talk of newfound family, dreams, or moving to New York City. Tina and Pappy John slept like babies all the way to Dulles Airport. They rested peacefully, having succumbed to the elated exhaustion of being showered with an immeasurable amount of love.

12

IDENTITY CRISIS

UNIMAGINABLE, mind-boggling revelation convinced Kelly that the goals to rest and rejuvenate her body and soul may not be possible on this trip to Orleans Street. She slowly walked down the stairs from her parents' bedroom stunned, confused, and angry. The woman arriving in Maryland as a mover and shaker had been reduced to a vacillating vessel with an identity crisis. Her mother and father would be home soon and she wondered how she would face them— what would she say and do? How much of this sordid tale did Ben King know? Kelly often bragged about her father's career as an army sergeant. *After stealing the heart of a woman twelve years younger, daddy converted his final assignment into a civilian position at Aberdeen Proving Grounds in Maryland. That transfer was the reason I grew up in Baltimore instead of New York City.*

All her life, Kelly witnessed her father's overt expression of love for his wife, treating her like royalty. *If I wait until a man like Ben King comes along, I'll be single forever.* Knowing her father's propensity to please her mother, she was certain his role in hiding her identity was minute—aiding and abetting by remaining silent. Kelly did not want to hurt her father, but she knew he would be bruised by the daggers she planned to throw at her mother. Although she had unconditional love for Ben King, she was filled with curiosity about Donald Leonard Charles—who was he, where was he, under what circumstances had he connected with her ultraconservative mother. Having long determined that she looked a little like Kay-Dee and nothing like Ben King, she wondered if many of her un-explained features were the result of genes inherited from Donald Leonard Charles.

Kelly sat down at the front window inside her parents' row house, resting on a wooden chair with a double-padded cushion. It was her father's favorite place to sit. She tried to divert her thoughts to external things, attempting to slow down the reeling of her mind. As was her outward manifestation of managing stress, she tapped her nails on the ledge of the windowsill. To take her mind off of her identity crisis, she leaned forward and pressed her nose close to the window screen to begin a process of engaging in random reflection. *Do cars blatantly zoom past the house, ignoring the twenty-five-mile-per-hour speed limit? Is there a flagrant disregard for the law or the result of semantics—Orleans Street's abrupt convergence with Pulaski Highway?*

Kelly turned her focus to people—some walking back and forth and others sitting on stoops. *I know that a small fraction of them are up to no good, but most are simply killing time. For those with limited education and resources, the probability is low of them doing anything other than stoop-gazing—sitting on a street like Orleans—watching people and cars go by. I wonder who possesses the greatest contentment between me and a single one of them. Clearly, I'm experiencing an all-time low in my sense of self and well-being. I'm in need of parental affirmation to combat my identity crisis.*

While deciding on the next detached distraction, two familiar voices hit her ears. Upon turning her head in the direction of the sound, her parents seemed to magically appear on the outside of the house. The window screen's wire mesh made it easy to see and to talk back and forth. From the sidewalk, her mother yelled. "Hey, Kelly, thank God you finally made it home! It's been so long since your last visit; I wasn't sure you remembered how to get here from the airport."

Although filled with contempt, the music executive remained silent. *The last thing I want to hear is my mother's sarcasm.*

Her father gave his greeting from the stoop. "Hey, Baby Girl, it's good to see you."

Kelly thought, *No matter how old I get, my father will never stop calling me 'Baby Girl.'* She answered him. "Hey, Daddy."

Ben King's heart smiled. *No matter how old she gets, my 'Baby Girl still calls me daddy.*

With a turn of the key and several more movements, her parents reached the living room and were standing above her head. Their presence caused Kelly's voice box to freeze, so her body chose its own course. She stood up and hugged her parents—mother short and loose—father long and tight. Then, she retrieved the birth certificate from her small suit jacket pocket, opened it fully, and handed it to her mother. As a silent signal of disdain and separation, she folded her arms, kept her eyes glued on her parents and back-peddled to the other side of the room. She was careful to negotiate her way around the coffee table. Upon reaching the loveseat, Kelly sat down, crossed her legs, and waited for them to finish examining the certificate of truth. *I wonder who will speak first and to whom. Maybe they'll talk to each other and then to me—or leave the room for a private conversation.*

The pitch of silence in the room was high enough to shatter glass. It stilled the air, making seconds feel like minutes. Then, her father made the first move. He released the hold of his side of the document and kissed his wife on the forehead. As an ordinance specialist, testing ammunition, large guns, and warheads, Ben King was well-versed in detonation. If it were to occur, he welcomed the ensuing explosion, believing it to be long overdue to destroy the thirty-year-old secret. He decided to excuse himself, taking leave from his wife and his daughter. "You two need some time alone to talk and to listen to each other. I'll be out for a while—gonna meet up with the guys at Charley's." He placed his hat on his head, grabbed his keys, and made a final statement before leaving. "The love I feel for both of you will never change." After closing the front door, he paused on the stoop to light his pipe and then navigated the four steps slowly. He turned left at street level, walked a few blocks up, and crossed a busy intersection. *Lord, those two lovely ladies are the most precious treasures you've given me. Please let us grow stronger as a family as you guide us to the other side of this uncovered secret.* Shortly thereafter, Ben King reached his destination—the neighborhood bar and billiards—a place where many mature former soldiers congregated.

Once the two women were alone, Kay-Dee meticulously followed the order of the creases to slowly fold the birth certificate back down to a small square. She walked across the living room, sat down on the loveseat beside her daughter, and placed the identity document in the palm of her wounded child's hand. Although a nominal seventeen-year difference in age, their attitudes were North Pole to South Pole distances apart. One was a jet-setter while the other had never flown on a plane. One dined in the finest gourmet restaurants while the other preferred a southern cooked meal at home. One had a bachelor's degree in communications and a master's in business administration. The other had earned a GED in night school. One attended movie premieres and fundraising galas, and the other opted for church revivals and bazaars. Even with their differences, Kay-Dee and her only child spoke by phone several times a month at a minimum, no matter where Kelly was in the world.

Kay-Dee tried to lessen her nervous embarrassment by placing a humorous spin on her compound questions. "Will you move a muscle or blink to let me know that you're in there—that you're not in shock—and that you're okay?"

Brazenly bitter, Kelly asked, "Is it true? Is this Donald Leonard Charles man my father?"

Through the years, Kay-Dee had been heavy laden by the weight of her secret and decided that the straightforward truth was the overdue antidote to lighten her load. "Yes, Kelly, your birth father is Donnie-Lee—Donald Leonard Charles."

"As much as we speak on the phone, I thought we talked and fussed about everything. I found Donald Leonard Charles by accident. Were you ever going to let me know that he was my father?"

"I've wanted to tell you for years, but the timing was never right. At first, you were too young to understand and then, too content as you grew up."

"How could you be dishonest for thirty years? Every time you looked at me it was a direct lie to my face. You ingrained the concept of deceitfulness in me early, teaching me to write my last name as King instead of Charles. What kind of mother would do that?"

"When looking through my eyes, all I saw was you and Ben's closeness. The two of you always had a beautiful father and daughter relationship. I didn't know how to break in with my awful and surprising news."

Kelly started to ramble. "But how? Not how—I know how people get pregnant—When—How? There are pictures of daddy—my Benjamin King daddy—holding me as a baby." Kelly stood to her feet. "You know what, mom? Explaining won't change a thing. My luggage is still in the rental car and that makes it so much easier. I'm sorry, but I have to get out of here. My purpose for coming was to have a nice visit with my parents and to relax. It's obvious that won't be happening now. This Donald-Leonard-Charles-being-my-father thing is way too much for me to handle."

The executive vice president walked to the front door and slammed it. Kay-Dee followed closely behind, opened the door, and pleaded with her daughter. "Kelly, please don't go. Don't leave angry like this. Talking it through is the road to recovery."

"And where did you hear that, on one of those ridiculous talk shows?" The mother's words fell on obstinate ears, damaged by betrayal, unable to entertain a long-overdue confession. There had been horrendous horror in Kelly's past and years of therapy had strengthened her constitution. She could feel herself slipping and began to console her spirit. *I refuse to allow this lie to expose my heart to a deadly dose of excruciating pain. The symbolic door housing my severe emotional devastation has been appropriately sealed for a very long time.*

Similar to her father's exit, the bruised daughter stood on the stoop, lit a cigarette, sashayed down the stairs, and headed up the street. The touch of the handle on the rental car's door caused her entire body to freeze. This was a life-altering crossroad. *If I get in this car and drive away, I know I'll end up on a highway of no return. I would be duplicating the thirty-year-long ostracism that exists between my grandparents and my mother.*

Instead of fleeing the scene, Kelly walked to Charley's pool hall to speak with the man who offered reassurance her entire life—the father she loved so dearly. Upon seeing his daughter walk through the front door, Ben King returned his cue stick to the rack and sat down with her in a corner booth. It was near the bar on the quieter side of the billiard hall. He did the ordering: Buffalo wings with extra blue cheese and alcoholic *Palmers*—iced-tea, lemonade, and vodka.

Kelly made a general observation, being unable to jump headfirst into the discussion. "It's been years since we've sat down in here together. Other than the change to colored televisions, the place looks the same."

"That's right, but, we're here to work through your feelings—just like with the Frank and Kelly-Louise tragedy. If we worked our way through that, we can do the same with this surprising discovery. So, instead of beating around the bush, we've got serious things to talk about. I'm sorry that you had to find out about your birth father in such a shocking way. I must say, however, that I'm relieved that you finally know the truth."

"Daddy, why didn't you tell me?"

"It wasn't my truth to tell."

Kelly scolded him. "Instead, you chose to spend your life with a liar."

"Let me be clear. I'm not here to listen to potshots aimed at my wife and your mother. I'm here to wash windows so you can make your judgments from a clearer view."

"I'm sorry, daddy, but, I feel so angry—like my whole life is one big lie. Since momma is the source of the lie, I want to make her suffer. I feel like she's controlled everything in my life, including who I am or who I think I am. I'm just so confused."

"You have a right to your feelings and it's your decision how to react to them. But, if you're saying your mother controlled your life, then, from what I can see, she did a pretty damn good job. At seventeen years old, she chose to stay in New York and raise her baby girl. She sacrificed a lot and lost even more, the love of most of her family. She doesn't deserve to lose you too, but that's your burden to bear. If you like, I can tell you what happened from when I stepped into the picture and how I saw things."

"Daddy, I would like that very much."

"I remember so well the first time I laid eyes on your mother because that's when the clock of my life started over. Although it was a month after you were born, there were no signs that she had just had a baby. Other than her beauty, I noticed right off that she seemed to be on a serious mission. She was working at your Uncle Frank's newsstand. I was in the last four months of my duty tour at Fort Hamilton in Brooklyn. I stopped at the newsstand while waiting for a good buddy to pick up his girlfriend from work at a coffee shop on Seventh Avenue. I bought a pack of extra-mint gum and squeezed your mother's fingers after placing the nickel in the palm of her hand. At that moment, I had a deep desire to rescue her and have been trying to do that ever since."

"Daddy, that's so sweet."

"Your mother is very sweet and at the time was very young, but had been forced into an adult world that was way over her head. Two days later, I got permission from your Uncle Frank to ask her out. He gave me a yes nod, but wished me luck in catching her. I figured out her work schedule and would be there every day at her quitting time. Before I could make a move, she'd take off running down the street. Later, I found out that she was rushing home to you.

After two weeks, I decided to run after her—down Seventh Avenue—all the way to 125th and Morningside. I blocked the entrance to the building where she lived and made a breathy plea. 'My name is Benjamin King and I think you're as beautiful as a flower, but with lightning speed like a shooting star. I already got your uncle's permission and would love to take you out.'"

"I'm assuming she said yes, so what did you do."

"The first thing I did was jump hurdles over all the low fences in the neighborhood while planning our first date."

"Where did you take her?"

"Because at seventeen, she was too young to get into any of the fancy clubs, I took her to dinner and a movie. Although I was twelve years older than Kay-Dee, your Uncle Frank and Aunt Kelly-Louise thought me having a stable job and being settled was a good thing under the circumstances."

Kelly asked, "So, when did you find out about me?"

"On our first date, all the customers in the restaurant and I heard it together."

Your mother screamed out, "I have a brand-new baby girl and am not with the father." Then, she stood up. "If you have a problem with it, I can leave right now. I have my own cab fare to get home."

"Once convincing Kay-Dee to sit back down, the rest of our story was magical."

"Daddy, that's so sweet. The sad thing for me is that you're an endangered species—the last of your kind."

"And you're my daughter and are truly loved by both me and your mother. There's no need for you to have an identity crisis."

13

LOVESEAT CONFESSIONAL

TAKING the longer route home, Kelly and Ben King talked about any and everything, except Donald Leonard Charles. The stockpile of questions and curiosity remaining had to be addressed by Kay-Dee. She was the apprehended perpetrator, ready to confess on behalf of herself and the co-defendant—whereabouts unknown. Heading west on Fairmount, father and daughter walked about six blocks before turning onto Collington. After maneuvering high traffic on Fayette Street, they stopped at the rental car and retrieved Kelly's luggage from the trunk. Bearing a heavy physical and emotional load, momentum carried them down the hill. After a turn onto Orleans, they crossed an alley and entered the family's row house. Kelly followed her father into the living room. He kissed his wife and continued to the kitchen, leaving mother and daughter face-to-face. Kay-Dee's prayer to see her child again had been answered quickly. Tucking away her shame and guilt, the mother was prepared to confess—armed with details to respond to her daughter's quest for answers.

The forty-seven-year-old mother took her thirty-year-old daughter by the hand, guiding her back to what had not been a loveseat during their earlier heated exchange. Now, it would serve as a confessional. Having promised her father that she'd give Kay-Dee a chance to explain, Kelly tempered her attitude and willingly sat down with her mother. In many ways, Kay-Dee was forty-seven going on seventeen, trapped where her childhood ended abruptly. She went from being validated to a villain, from dances to diapers, from fun to feedings, from classes to cleaning, and from worry-free to working full-time.

Kay-Dee took a deep breath before releasing a part of her soul that had been deeply buried and was badly scarred. It had held the details of a thirty-year-old secret. "I was sixteen and Donnie-Lee was seventeen when we first started dating. We had to be super sneaky because your grandparents were so strict. Since we could only see each other at church, we were very active in Sunday school, the youth choir, and the junior usher board—making sure no one ever saw us alone." Although Kelly tried to appear non-receptive, Kay-Dee noticed subtle movements in her only child's forehead, eyes, and mouth. She prayed that in revealing the truth, nothing would be said that would cause her daughter to flee for a second time.

Kay-Dee explained. "I felt so lucky that Donnie-Lee chose me out of all the girls he could've dated. He came from money—going off to college, not needing to pray for scholarships. He was very nice and thoughtful—bringing me candy—writing me unsigned poems I could claim I had written. I remember our first romantic encounter so clearly. It was the last Communion Sunday in the year, December 30, 1951. After the church service was over, Momma and Kathy were in the kitchen cleaning the little glasses and trays used for Communion. Daddy was with the rest of the deacons and trustees counting money and having a meeting. Kathy was three years older and was home on winter break from A&T State University. She maintained a 4.0 grade point average and was praised for being smart and I was tortured for disgracing the family by receiving an occasional B+. It didn't matter to your grandparents that, at sixteen, I had already been offered scholarships from Bennett and Spelman Colleges. After church, my parents let me go home with Mrs. Scott, my English teacher, to borrow books for a report I was writing. I told my mother that my teacher would bring me home and told Mrs. Scott that a cousin was picking me up. Of course, Donnie-Lee was posing as the cousin."

Although not ready to speak, Kelly hung onto Kay-Dee's every syllable. It was the first time she had heard anything about her mother's teenage years. Kay-Dee continued. "Donnie-Lee picked me up in his Buick. It was black and shiny—handed down from his sickly mother who was no longer able to drive. Although it was wintertime, I don't remember being cold. I do remember the magic made in the backseat of that Buick. In that first intimate expression of love, I became pregnant with you."

From the loveseat confessional, Kelly forced out her first words since sitting there. "Although it's awkward listening to you talk about being with somebody other than daddy, I'm glad I came out of such a loving experience."

Kay-Dee was grateful to hear Kelly break her silence and elated that her words were not harsh. "For around two months, Donnie-Lee and me saw each other when we could. Then, minus two cycles, I figured out that I was pregnant. Like the special big sister she was and still is—your Aunt Kathy made a special trip home from college and tried her best to save me. I stood behind her as she told mom and dad the news about me being pregnant."

Dad started yelling. "You're a Trampy Jezebel, the worst of all sinners!"

Kay-Dee's face displayed the pain as if it were reoccurring. "Momma's hands did all her talking. She knocked me down and split my lip with one hard smack across my face. Then, dad used his leather belt and your grandma used a switch from an old oak in the back of the house. She called it her favorite tree because of the rubber-like limbs, making an extra strong switch for whipping youngins. I really thought they were going to beat you out of my womb, but your Aunt Kathy jumped in the way and took half of the lashes for me."

Kelly reached back, grabbed the tissue box from the end table, and pulled out about ten pieces—one tissue at a time. She kept half of them and gave those that remained to her mother. Each woman desperately needed this tear-wiping and nose-blowing break in the incident report.

After clearing her nostrils and her throat, Kay-Dee pressed forward. "The very next day, your grandparents put me on a bus and sent me to Uncle Frank in New York City. Just like that, the only life I knew ended. I was gone away from Donnie-Lee and everything that was important to me, except your Aunt Kathy. She wrote me in secret for a whole year. I only wrote her back at her college's address until she broke out of our mean parents' prison and got married."

Kelly's anger had transformed into sympathy for her mother, and now Kay-Dee could see an overt change in her daughter's countenance. "In the version of this story you fed me and Katrina all these years, Aunt Kathy paid for your bus ticket and you just showed up on Uncle Frank's doorstep."

"Well, ninety percent of what we told you two girls was true. Me and your Aunt Kathy just left out quite a few details. By the way, she did give me her clothes washing money. I used most of it to buy sweets during my pregnancy. I had awful cravings for hard candy and chocolate bars. Your Uncle Frank was big on self-sufficiency and made me pay for each and every piece I got from the newsstand."

Breathing a sigh of relief that Kelly had calmed down, Kay-Dee proceeded. "I remember each second of that Monday night—September 29, 1952. Because I was so young and terrified, they let Aunt Kelly-Louise be with me in the delivery room. She held my hand and then held you before I did. You two bonded right away. She couldn't have kids, so you gave her the chance to take care of a newborn. I named you Kelly in her honor and she came up with the middle name Donnita. She said that Donnie-Lee should be honored in some way, especially having no idea that he had just become the father of a beautiful baby girl."

"Are you saying that you went through the whole pregnancy without him knowing?"

"As hard as it was, yes. I couldn't tell Donnie-Lee at that point. He had mentioned our running away together several times. Had he known about my pregnancy, I know he would have delayed college to be with me. Besides, I couldn't bear being hated by my family as well as his. Including me, to this day, only four people know the name of your real father—Uncle Frank and Aunt Kelly-Louise, God rest their souls, Ben King, and now you."

"Why didn't you tell Aunt Kathy? She's your sister and best friend."

"I figured that if she didn't know who he was, Mom and Dad could never punish her for not telling them. That's the reason they beat me so hard when they found out I was pregnant. They wanted a name and I wouldn't give them one. I was not going to get Donnie-Lee in trouble. I was sure daddy would try and kill him. All they knew was that it was a boy from Mount Pleasant Hill Baptist Church."

"Did everybody call him Donnie-Lee? Oh no, the Charleses were quite refined and called him Donald Leonard. I called him Donnie-Lee because we were sweet on each other."

"That's really special. You gave my birth father a pet name. Well, when did grandma and grandpa find out I was born?"

"The same night that you came into the world, Uncle Frank dialed the number and I talked to them. They didn't ask if you were a girl or a boy, but they did tell me I could come back home."

A confused Kelly asked, "So why did you stay in New York when you wanted to go back home so badly?"

Fresh tears were released from Kay-Dee's eyes. "Mom and dad said that I could come home, but I had to leave you in New York with Uncle Frank and Aunt Kelly-Louise. There was no way I was gonna trade you in for a ticket back home. They expected me to give birth, deposit you like a church offering, and come back home like nothing happened. That was the last time I spoke to them."

"Now I feel guilty. When you chose to keep me, you gave up going back home, going back to school, and even back to your Donnie-Lee. I'm pretty sure I would have chosen to go back to my old life if it were me."

"Kelly, you need to hear me good! With my many mistakes through the years, I did three things right—I had you, I kept you, and I married Benjamin King."

"I'm glad you were able to find some happiness in such a sad situation. So, what happened next, after I was born?"

"Well, to take care of the two of us, I worked at Uncle Frank's newsstand full-time. After work, I'd rush home to our apartment. I couldn't take the chance of getting stuck in the elevator—it was broke half of the time. I would run full speed up the stairs to apartment 5H. I scooped you up and cared for you the rest of the night. You were and still are everything to me. I guess my way of showing it needs work, but you're never too old to learn. I'm willing to try and do better if you give me the chance."

Ben King returned to the living room and placed a tray on the table. It held an uncorked bottle of red wine, two glasses, slices of sharp cheddar cheese, thin crackers, and honeydew melon squares. After arranging everything nicely on the coffee table, he disappeared upstairs to the bedroom, letting the TV watch him as he fell asleep.

"Daddy told me that he had to chase you down to get a date."

"That's right! This tall, handsome man in a green military uniform showed up at the newsstand day after day. I had no idea that he liked me until he ran me down at the door of the apartment building. After realizing he wasn't an ax murderer, I thought it was a very romantic thing to do."

"Daddy told me how you flipped out on the first date with him."

Kay-Dee giggled. "Oh yeah, I did make a pretty big scene. I needed to let him know about my baby, so I just blurted it out. Right after that, I showed him your picture. He was happy and excited, the total opposite of what I thought would happen. The next Saturday, the three of us went on our first date together. We rolled you around Central Park in your stroller. You took to Ben right away."

"I can't imagine anyone who wouldn't like daddy. He's such a kind and loving person."

"That's why I said yes right away when he asked me to marry him. On Valentine's Day, the Saturday after I turned eighteen, February 14, 1953, your daddy, Uncle Frank, Aunt Kelly-Louise, you, and me went to Abyssinian Baptist Church and got married. You were five months old. The next week, we moved to Baltimore with your dad, and he never left our side. Uncle Frank and Aunt Kelly-Louise would come down on weekends to be with you. That gave me and Ben time to get to know each other better. From our first date, I loved him as a man, but I grew to love him as my husband."

"I don't want to do anything to hurt daddy, but I really want to know more about Donald Leonard Charles. I have resources and I intend to find him. I'm not sure if I'll tell him who I am, but I really want to see what he looks like."

"Kelly Baby, I'm sorry, b-but Donnie-Lee passed away years ago. He died in a car accident when you were twelve years old. I didn't find out until four years after it happened." Kelly and her mother paused to sip their wine. After about a minute, Kay-Dee cut through the silence with additional details. "When I found out, you were a junior in high school and had already received two college scholarships. I didn't see anything good coming out of telling you at that point. The life that you dreamed about was just beginning to take form and you were so happy in it. Then, you were off to college and straight to graduate school from there. With what you dealt with in finding Uncle Frank and Aunt Kelly-Louise brutally murdered, I refused to burden you with anything else."

"After therapy, we agreed not to discuss that anymore."

"Yes, but watching you fight through that pain was awful. I know that you're the strongest woman I know. I, however, am not. Maybe coward is the right word to describe myself. As time passed, I used life as the excuse for not telling you and I am sorry and hope you will forgive me."

Kelly had learned more about her mother in that loveseat confessional than she had learned in her entire life. She realized that her mother had suffered enough in the past in addition to the anger she had piled on earlier that afternoon. "Mom, you're much stronger than you think. You're not a coward, and I absolutely forgive you."

As they hugged, tears flowed freely, requiring more tissue. "Thank you Kelly so much for not hating me."

"Even though Donald Leonard Charles is dead, he must have living relatives and I intend to find them. Maybe I can get a photo and possibly learn some details about his life."

Kay-Dee wanted to help. "Well, I do know that Donnie-Lee came from a well-to-do Black family with many college graduates. They lived in a big house at the end of this little town called Scotland Neck. My home, Tarboro, is about twenty miles away in the next county over called Edgecombe. I remember Donnie-Lee talking about a much older sister who had a big time job in the military. Also, he was very close to an aunt called G-Geba—Gee-Gee, G-Something like that. If his family still lives in that house or in the area, some of them probably go to Mount Pleasant Hill Baptist Church. I'm sorry, Kelly, but that's all I can remember right now."

"Although it feels strange, I'm glad I know the truth and daddy is definitely relieved. I love him more than anything, and no Donald Leonard Charles will ever change that."

"I'll help you find answers any way I can, except going to North Carolina. I'm not that strong. Because of my hurt and fear, I'm not going to my only niece's wedding and I feel awful about that."

Then, Kelly remembered her earlier conversation. "In all the craziness, I forgot to tell you that Katrina called before you and daddy got home. She said something about Grandma not going to her wedding because of where it's being held."

"Oh my God, Kelly, I think I figured something out!" Kay-Dee rushed over to the book case, searching in and around volumes and magazines until she found Katrina's invitation. Kelly was looking over her mother's shoulder in wonderment.

"Mom, what is it?"

"I glanced at it and stuck it away, without thinking twice about it. Kelly, look where Trina's getting married."

The invitation read:

Mount Pleasant Hill Baptist Church
Scotland Neck, North Carolina
Saturday, July 10, 1982

Both mother and daughter had the same expression of astonishment on their faces. Kelly said, "Now, I get it!"

On the same page with her daughter, Kay-Dee hissed. "That old woman is holding tight to her bitterness. I'm the reason that she wants Katrina to change churches? She can't get around the fact that her wayward child's fornicating took place there. "

"That's right. She knows the boy that got you pregnant attended that same church."

"And your Aunty Kathy told me that our parents stepped foot in Mount Pleasant Hill one more time after finding out I was pregnant. Once dropping me at the Enfield bus station, they headed straight to the church and cussed out the Pastor, the choir director, and the head of the junior usher board. Of course, they were quickly escorted out of the church all the way to daddy's car."

The loveseat confessional ended with the uncovering of the wedding church mystery. The mother and daughter agreed not to burden Kathy and Katrina with their discovery.

In her old bedroom, surrounded by dolls from her childhood, Kelly was unable to fall asleep. Thoughts of Donald Leonard Charles were unyielding. After much deliberation, she made a decision, sat up, and called her assistant in New York City. Kelly's needs were always the priority. She had no problem awakening Assistant Angela at two in the morning, having done it many times before.

Trying to pull herself out of a punch-drunk sleep, Angela answered the telephone in an incomplete state of lucidity. "Hello, Angela Carson speaking."

"Hey, it's me."

Upon recognizing her boss's voice, clarity came quickly. "Yes, Ma'am," replied the administrative assistant.

"I've decided to go to Katrina's wedding after all. Don't tell her because I want it to be a surprise. Schedule the flight, departing very early on next Saturday, the morning of the wedding. Until then, I'll be here in Baltimore with my parents."

Knowing her boss's pet peeves, Assistant Angela grabbed a pad to write down the particulars yet to be spoken. "Is there anything else?" she asked.

"Yes, find me a low-key driver who also does security. I don't want to raise eyebrows by coming to a small town with an entourage. Make sure he's prepared to sit, wait, and shadow me until I'm back on a plane heading the hell out of North Carolina. And most important-ly, no matter what he says, don't tell Arnie anything about my plans. Thanks and let's talk later in the week. Good-bye."

14

THE WEDDING SINGER

Saturday, July 10, 1982

DRIVING the eighty-five miles from Raleigh-Durham Airport to Scotland Neck took about an hour and a half. That was more than enough time for Kelly to change her mind about attending the wedding—to tell her driver to reverse direction and take her back to the terminal. Instead of being *First in Flight,* as the state motto of North Carolina suggested, she decided to stay the course, enter unfamiliar territory, and deal with the unknown. Remaining steadfast required Kelly to intermingle with a church full of dapperly dressed outsiders— more than half of them blood relatives. Katrina and her parents would be the only familiar faces.

On the way to the church, Kelly occupied herself by focusing on the sights—field after field of corn, cotton, and tobacco. She was awe-struck and antsy like a child, seeing free-roaming cows and pen-fenced hogs for the first time. The sights and smells held her attention until interrupted by the driver's announcement. "Ma'am, you have reached your destination."

As the town car pulled onto the consecrated grounds, Kelly's heart rate increased and her stomach began to quiver. From the backseat, she looked through the smoky glass at bronze, embossed lettering that read *Mount Pleasant Hill Baptist Church*. Kelly's visual verification of the church's name, coupled with a glance at her watch, confirmed that she was in the right location at the correct time. Once the back passenger door opened, the music industry mogul literally needed the strength of her driver to pull her up from the car and onto her feet. "Thank you Chadrick. I needed your help more than you know."

"Not a problem Ma'am. I'm here at your service." As she was escorted up the stairs onto the vestibule, her eyes did a quick scan of the church perimeter. She wondered which locations had served as secret rendezvous places for her mother and Donald Leonard Charles.

After signing the guest book, Chauffeur Chadrick left Kelly in the hands of an usher who escorted her down the center aisle to a reserved section on the bride's side of the church. Observing her apparent style and grace, many eyes followed the mystery woman to her seat—apparel adhering to the wedding's colors branding that Kelly had chosen herself. She was wearing a modestly designed white chiffon dress with a sweetheart neckline, knee-length hem, and a three-quarter sleeve jacket. Following the prominent wedding color, all her accessories were fuchsia—the waist jacket, her purse, shoes, and her pillbox-shaped hat with a veil. Arriving at the premium pew, she took her place of prominence—third-row, end-seat, and on the center aisle—next to Pastor Jennings's wife, Marylou. After introducing herself as the bride's first cousin and close friend, she flipped through the pages of the wedding program, unable to concentrate on a single word. She was nervous for Katrina and panicky on her own behalf—wondering if anyone in the room had a connection to her birth father. How would she go about engaging in such nosey interrogation while making it seem off the cuff? Feeling a hemisphere away from her comfort zone, the act of undercover investigator was going to be much more difficult than handling music executives in a boardroom.

Kelly decided to cozy up to the church's First Lady, thinking she must surely be a good source of information. She lifted her veil, handed over a business card, and answered a few questions about having broken through the glass ceiling in the music industry. "Being a woman challenged continuously by hungry male sharks is a task I tactfully take on. It's easy to counter-punch when you've overly trained for the contest. As a favor for me, please let my career conquests remain a secret between the two of us for now—like girlfriends."

"Your world renowned success is safe with me and my husband of course because we are one flesh as the good book says."

"I won't be opposing the Bible, so I guess telling him is fine."

The First Lady was elated internally. *My dear pastor-husband won't beat me this time. Meeting a famous producer is the biggest news ever.*

Kelly looked around and absorbed the church's exquisiteness. "This sanctuary has character as well as celestial beauty." The music executive wrote out a three thousand dollar check and placed it in Sister Jennings hand. "Please accept this love offering to be used for the building's up-keep. I'm sure fundraising can be challenging. My mother is the head of the building fund committee at her church in Baltimore and obviously, I'm her number one supporter when allowed. Donating per event is the only way she accepts my financial assistance."

After a close examination, First Lady Marylou tucked the check inside her purse and was overcome with the desire to serve as hostess and schmooze up to the special guest. "Oh thank you very much. Your donation is quite generous and will go a long way to help pay for our recent renovations. They included brighter and additional lighting, great acoustics thanks to a new audio system, central controlled air, triple-twined carpet, and red plush cushions added to each wooden bench throughout the house of prayer."

Kelly thought that, even with the renovations, her mother's memory was on target. *Mom gave a very accurate description of a church she hadn't visited in thirty years.*

The daughter's internal praise of her mother was interrupted by a smiley-faced usher holding a neat stack of hand fans. Each was shaped like a slice of bread, had a tongue-depressor-looking handle, and was made of a heavy paper stock. Kelly was instructed to take one and pass the others down the row. The three design choices included an image of a bronzed, stringy-haired Jesus; a photo of Martin Luther King, Jr. dressed in a brown suit, and a sketch of Willow-Matt's Funeral Home. Pews packed with people strained the new central air system, causing heat to linger. This made the hand fans a welcomed manual tool for cooling the body.

The music executive selected the bronze Jesus fan and the First Lady chose MLK in brown. Per instructions, the rest were passed down the pew. As the choir casually entered the loft, Kelly wondered if their robes had come from the courting-closet her mother and Donald Leonard Charles had used as a meeting place. She blushed from the inside out, envisioning two teenagers tossing goo-goo eyes back and forth from their respective singing sections in the youth choir.

As a sign that the auspicious occasion was about to begin, the mother of the bride and grandmother of the groom were ushered to the sanctuary's right and left front pews. The groom's mother had passed away when Michael was a child. Katrina's grandmother refused to take part in any way.

Having pulled the veil of the pillbox hat back down over her face, Kelly remained under the radar—not recognized when her Aunt Kathy passed by. Both husbands were wedding participants. Katrina's father, Stephen Brown, was waiting in the wings to escort his beautiful daughter to the altar. The groom's father, Professor Milton, was at his post as minister of music.

His first act as maestro was striking a deep and thunderous chord from his wind-driven pipe organ. He was accompanied by two students—one playing the traditional piano—the other producing harmonic percussion sounds using the Hammond organ.

That attention-grabbing chord was effective in alerting the entire building to the start of the wedding. Upon raising his hand to end the chord, the music shifted to that of basic accompaniment—supporting background to undergird the vocal soloist. Because this was the wedding of his son, the goal of a near-perfect musical performance was paramount in his mind. The choir led off, softly humming the harmony and the soloist joined in at the verse.

Tina sang:

> *When I look at you*
> *I see the best part of me*
> *Not fearing who I am—the one I can see*
> *But where I am, is where you want me to be*
> *When I look at you—I'm so happy and free*

From an unidentified location, clear and clean tones were being sung by a faceless performer. Kelly's first observation was that the mystery singer's voice was captivating and had a professional quality. Telltale signs were apparent—controlled breathing, richness of tone, inflection, and projection. As the bridesmaids, groomsmen, ring bearer, and flower girls made their way down the center aisle, their march was to the beat of soft music and rich, melodic vocals that reverberated throughout the sanctuary.

Tina sang:

> *When I look at you*
> *I see the face of my friend*
> *A listening ear—to share my secrets, and then*
> *The special one—on whom, I can depend*
> *When I look at you—I look once and again*

The choir joined in, singing with Tina at the chorus.

It's not a surprise and no way to disguise—
Lost in Love—is the place we will be
Lost in Love—made for just you and me
Lost in Love—a bond so happy and free
Lost in Love—the name of our destiny

A beautiful, complicated love song set to music was being delivered with exceptional style and composition. The vocal choreography was presented as a serenade to each individual listener, with an ultimate goal of providing the wedding attendees with collective satisfaction. As a producer in need of a wow factor, the invisible soloist reminded Kelly that a single day was all that remained of her vacation. *Come Monday morning, I'll revert back to an Alpha Lioness on the prowl to fulfill my boss's latest request.* During her almost two-week absence from The Label, she was kept up to date by Angela whose reports were similar. Although Mister Arnie Peters was in Los Angeles, the head honcho's conference calls were intense and felt strongly in New York City. They shook the earth and set off atomic blasts on a daily basis.

Kelly moved her thoughts away from Arnie and refocused on the wedding. She gave the mystery vocalist high scores for technique. *I'm certain that the visual presentation won't measure up. Will the lyrical vessel show her face at all?* Kelly's internal scrutiny ran a gamut of valid reasons for a cleverly concealed soloist. *Her features are probably revolting. Maybe she has a critical case of bulimia or morbid obesity that has irreversibly injected her with low self-esteem. On the other hand, humility could also be the culprit because there's no mention of a soloist in the wedding program.* Kelly compared what she uncovered to an anomaly in her profession—one she had yet to witness. *No artist at Walden Records would ever agree to sing without receiving, at a minimum, the subtle accolade of a byline—especially one with such great pipes.* The voice she heard was a naturally rich alto, with a range reaching as high as first soprano.

Kelly was not in her plastic world and the wedding singer's missing visual supported her modesty theory. *For once, the focus is in the right place—on the wedding party, not the wedding singer.* Even so with an unsatisfied curiosity, she scanned each member of the choir slowly, unable to identify the soloist. No one was holding a microphone and the vocal contribution of the entire group was a harmonizing series of oohs and aahs. Then, at the start of the third verse, the owner of the golden voice entered the sanctuary from a hallway behind the choir loft. She walked down a narrow, short aisle onto the dais platform to the right side of the pulpit next to the piano. She was not draped in a robe like the rest of the vocal ensemble. Instead, she was wrapped in a chiffon dress with a short mini hemline—fuchsia-colored to match the bridesmaids' gowns. Her dress was strapless, revealing gorgeous shoulders and formfitting, accentuating a sleek and sexy silhouette.

Tina sang:

> *When I look at you*
> *I see a heart that understands*
> *Courage to—face hard times, once again*
> *Prepared to act—the way that life just demands*
> *When I look at you, against all odds we will stand*

This beautiful young woman had electrifying stage presence and was capable of emotionally charging an abbey of nuns. She stood there belting out the song's bridge, which was an octave higher with a key change. This was Kelly's first experience of being awestruck by a performance rendered from an amateur talent.

Tina sang:

> *In good times and bad—whether happy or sad*
> *In sickness and strife—for the rest of our life*
> *With God on our side—we'll forever abide*
> *Hand in hand—among the stars in the sky*

Again, the choir joined in, singing with Tina at the chorus.

It's always the same so we have to proclaim
Lost in Love—is the place we will be
Lost in Love—made for just you and me
Lost in Love—a bond so happy and free
Lost in Love—the name of our destiny

Kelly turned to First Lady Marylou for answers. "Do you know anything about the beautiful young lady who is singing?"

The First Lady answered with pride. "Her name is Bettina—from one of Halifax County's finest families—the Charleses. Her great-grandfather, Master Donnie, built this church. It's all been documented by Carolina historians."

A sour note touched down on Kelly's taste buds. *Does she mean master as in slave owner? Even if that's the case, I'm going to sidebar the unexpected fact and focus on her mention of the last name Charles.*

"So, the soloist's last name is Charles?" *I desperately need confirmation.*

"Absolutely. She's the one and only Bettina Bethany Charles."

A chill rushed through Kelly's body upon hearing the last name Charles repeated. *I didn't have to go very far or dig too deep for answers after all. I'm sitting in a North Carolina church hearing the name Charles spoken aloud several times.*

The First Lady continued. "We call her Tina and she's dealt with more pain and problems than most old people I know."

Things are always too good to be true. Of course, the little songbird has a closet full of skeletons. Kelly made a quick mental list of the golden voice's potential problems. *She's probably a high school dropout, a thief, a drug abuser, a cutter with suicidal thoughts.*

With the large bridal party slowly sashaying down the center aisle, there was plenty of time for chatter. Now, on a first-name basis, Kelly asked, "Marylou, what exactly do you mean? What kind of problems does the child have?"

"Our precious little Tina lives with her Aunty Gina."

Kelly's mind went straight back to the previous week—to Kay-Dee's memory block when she said, *Donnie-Lee has a favorite aunt, whose name started with a G—Geba—Gee-Gee, G-Something like that. I'm pretty certain that this Aunty Gina and my mother's mystery G-Something surely have to be the same person.*

Before Kelly could ask another question, she was stopped by a piercing stare. An old woman, sitting in the row ahead and a few seats down, turned around and rolled her eyes at them with a churned-up expression—translating to *lower your damn voices.* The message was received and Kelly and First Lady Marylou decreased their volume to a barely audible whisper.

The First Lady murmured. "Oh my goodness and no offense, your mean ole grandmother showed up after all! She swore to Katrina that she wasn't coming to the wedding and low and behold there she is." Kelly fought to keep the surprised shock that she was feeling hidden on the inside—externally looking at her grandmother, in person, for the first time.

The First Lady pressed on. "Me and Katrina turned it over to the Lord and there sits the answered prayer. Now, I'm hoping that we prayed for the right thing and Sistah Kathleen won't do nothing crazy."

Kelly's inner thoughts converted into mental yelling. *In addition to the high probability that Tina's Gina is my mother Kay-Dee's G–Something, the old woman shushing us is definitely my Grandmother Kathleen—the one who tried to trade me in for Kay-Dee's ticket back home.*

Tina sang:

> *When I look at you*
> *I see the one who I adore*
> *A smile that lights a brighter world than before*
> *A bond to last—now and for–e–e–ver more*
> *When I look at you—great things we will explore*

First Lady Marylou chimed back in. "Well, I'm sure you're quite familiar with your grandmother's nonsense, so instead of boring you with more of that, let me finish telling you about Tina."

Kelly grinned as if she was well acquainted with her grandmother's saga. She shook her head, "Yes, that would be nice," she encouraged. "I'd like all the juicy details." *My hunger about the Charleses has lasted for thirty years, so I need to be fed all that you're serving up.*

"God sent Tina's singing gift straight through her father," replied the First Lady. "He used to stand close to where his daughter's standing right now—singing the most sinful of souls to salvation."

Kelly's mind screamed to her consciousness. *Daughter, daughter, did she say daughter?* Kelly made sure she was externally calm and then asked, "What is her father's name?"

"Donald Leonard Charles, but I called him Donnie. When he and his wife died in a car accident, his only sister raised Tina. By the time she was a preteen, Donnie's sister died too and that's how Tina ended up being raised by her Aunty Gina."

As the last members of the bridal party positioned themselves at the altar, Tina belted out the chorus for the final time. Then, she ended the song slowly in a sweet, soft tone. She stretched the length of her last note, letting it softly fade away.

For the final time, the choir joined in, singing with Tina at the chorus.

> *Lost in Love—is the place we will be*
> *Lost in Love—made for just you and me*
> *Lost in Love—a bond so happy and free*
> *Lost in Love—the name of our destiny*
>
> *In joining our life as husband and wife*
> *In what we've become in uniting as one*
> *A team forever—just Lo-ost in Lo-ove*

The First Lady's revelation about Donald Leonard Charles being Tina's father was one shock too many. Kelly's inner thoughts turned into a mind-to-mind discussion with herself about the talented young woman being her little sister. The one named by her cousin-best friend as the genuine maid of honor was questioning the timing of this discovery. *After so many years of darkness, why is the enlightenment coming all at once? I'm having difficulty breathing and need to get out of this church immediately.* She searched for the nearest exit. Had she eyed a convenient one, Katrina's wedding would have been interrupted in possibly a very unforgiving way.

Kelly imagined Katrina's rage as she said, "First, you refused to come to my wedding and then you showed up, but ran out before I made it down the aisle!" Kelly waged war with her internal system of fright and flight, trying to prevent her own adrenaline from running wild.

Just at that critical moment, the instrumental serenade of "The Wedding March" commenced under the direction of Professor Milton. The bride appeared in the back of the church, looking flawless in her professionally applied hair and makeup—courtesy of Carlton Charles Montgomery. As Katrina and her father took the first few steps to begin the slow saunter down the center aisle, Kelly abruptly stood to her feet. Her breathing difficulty had advanced to the stage of hyperventilation. Fortunately, her need to rise coincided with the entire church of wedding attendees jointly standing in honor of the bride. God had shown pity, sparing both Katrina and Kelly traumatic outcomes—catastrophic disaster averted. As the audience clapped, cameras flashed and the music played loudly, Kelly took a series of deep breaths and focused on keeping her feet firmly planted on the church's new triple-twined carpet. Steadily, her respiratory problem reduced to a coughing spell.

By the time Katrina and her father were halfway down the aisle, Kelly's body turned in the bride's direction like the rest of the wedding onlookers. Internally, however, she was trapped in a haze of an alternate reality—a victim of contextual reassignment. This amounted to a fundamental change of what she thought was her past. Instead of originating from a seed implanted by her nurturing dad, Benjamin King, Kelly's existence sprang forth from a sperm deposit injected during a puppy love session between her mother, Kay-Dee, and a faceless birth father named Donald Leonard Charles. The truth of that encounter altered Kelly's present, placing her in a church at a wedding receiving revelation from a First Lady named Marylou. The result of the altered past and present transformed her future. Now, it would include, at a minimum, an Aunty Gina and from what she could determine visually, a much younger sister named Bettina Charles.

No matter how difficult, Kelly fought to portray a reasonable level of composure, knowing that a full view of the bride was forthcoming. When Katrina reached Kelly's pew, their eyes met, rendering the veil's concealing power ineffective. Katrina broke tradition and motioned her father to pause. Her excitement at laying eyes on her cousin/big sister/best friend was uncontainable. "Oh my God, you made it to my wedding after all." With a huge smile on her face, she reached around her father and hugged Kelly. The secret maid of honor's center aisle seat made it a convenient maneuver.

"Yes, I found a way to make it happen." From Kelly's perspective, her little cousin's joyful gesture foiled her plan to maintain a low profile. From every pew, there was lots of murmuring—people trying to figure out the identity of the mystery hugger—the one wearing a fuchsia pillbox hat with a pulled-down veil.

15

PHOTO OP-TRODUCTIONS

AT the end of the wedding, the overjoyed mother of the bride exited the church, revealing her connection to the famous woman people had already started to recognize. "Yes, she's Kelly King, the popular music producer and Katrina's first cousin and best friend." This caused many of the wedding guests to behave like buzzards and swarm Kelly with introductions, programs to autograph, and flickers from their cameras.

First Lady Marylou scattered the vultures. "Y'all need to head on out of God's Holy place and do your socializing on the church yard." Once alone, Kelly gave herself permission to succumb to a moment of vulnerability. With it, the weakened woman, in the fuchsia pillbox-shaped hat with a veil, sat down in a corner of the sanctuary feeling woozy. She had overdosed on the potency of too much information. She used her pause to acclimate to the double-sided family drama—the discovery of a talented baby sister on her birth father's side—the sucking up of unknown kinfolk on her mother's side. Other than Katrina, of course, she decided to prioritize one person instead of dispersing her attention among the many channels. She intended to enter the treacherous waters, negotiate her way around the leeches, and retrieve the oyster's pearl. *My little sister, Bettina Charles, is the jewel that I seek—well worth the sacrifice of whatever level of inconvenience I have to endure. I'm not sure how to proceed, but barging up and saying "Hey, Sis" is not the answer.*

Internally, Kelly began to feast on a nice slice of karma. *How quickly I received a big piece of poetic justice. I'm situated in a quandary similar to my mother's. I'm in the possession of a poignant secret and have learned quickly that certain life-altering truths aren't so easy to tell.* After deep contemplation, she concluded that there was no quick-fix solution. *Because I know nothing about Tina's emotional state, it's imperative for me to tread lightly, gradually increasing the water's temperature. I will engage Bettina Charles from a professional capacity as a music mogul. It's the least traumatizing way to enter my baby sister's life. After all, I was immensely impressed with Tina's talent, regardless of the apparent bloodline connection.*

Twenty minutes into her cooling-down period, Aunt Kathy came rushing back into the sanctuary with a summons from her daughter. "The First Lady told me you were in here. The photographer has finished shooting the bridal party and Katrina refuses to take a single family photo until you Kelly are in the mix."

"Those sound like my best friend's marching orders to me." Kelly refreshed her makeup, stood, and pressed the wrinkles from her dress. "Aunt Kathy, please lead the way."

Outside, Kelly joined her formerly estranged relatives and smiled on cue as the photographer directed. The wonderful dynamic was that Katrina and Kelly stood side by side, holding hands through each and every click of the camera. During the entire photography process, Tina was a distance away, watching Carlton and Tony, who were busy touching up the makeup and hair of the ladies in the bridal party.

With Carlton's larger-than-life personality, he and Kelly were quickly on a first-name basis. She became a bigger fan upon receiving the First Lady's most recent revelation. "Besides being Tina's first cousin, he's her best friend and sidekick. The two of them are pressed together like a peanut butter and jelly sandwich."

Carlton was shrewd, waiting for the right moment to play his introduction-to-Bettina-Charles card. Kelly had chauffeur Chadrick watching and ready to run interference. This would give the executive a chance to engage Tina, should she make a move to leave prior to them meeting. The last snapshots taken on the church grounds were the result of Carlton's observation. "Surely a mistake must be the reason, but all participants of the ceremony have been photographed with the bridal party with the exception of the wedding singer."

Kelly jumped on the subject like a pig in slop. "Carlton, you are quite perceptive. Would you please bring her over so that the oversight can be corrected? Besides, I was looking for an opportunity to personally congratulate the young woman on a singing job well done."

Carlton put all hair care products and makeup in his assistant Tony's care, dashed away, and promptly ran over to Tina. On the short walk back, his words were hastily delivered and instructional. "Miss Big Time Music Executive wants to take photos and have a little chat with you. Tee-Tee, I need you to flash all thirty-two of your bright whites. Let her know that you're interested in singing professionally and are looking for a helping hand."

"That's a lot to say all at once, but I'll do my best."

"You better. We've gotta make the most of a once in a lifetime opportunity to speak with someone like Kelly King." In quick fashion, the photographer took about ten photos—no time for a verbal exchange. After that, the bride and groom and most of the remaining guests jumped into cars to take the country road drive to the reception. This included Tony, who traveled with the bride. Of the few stragglers still lingering, the important ones were Kelly King, Carlton, and Tina.

In his role as acting manager, Carlton kicked off the conversation. "Well, as you've already seen, Mister Montgomery and his team have been busy keeping our bride looking fabulous. Although difficult, let's not focus on The Lovely. With that said, Carlton will just move on to making introductions."

Kelly picked up on the fact that in a short time her high-spirited cousin had referred to himself in the third person by three different names. *Interesting,* she thought, *but I can't worry about that right now.*

Like a model presenting the big-deal curtain on a game show, Carlton waved his arms and hands up and down Tina's body. "Kelly King, meet Bettina Charles—Bettina Charles, meet Kelly King."

Showing respect, Tina bent her head slightly and smiled. "It's very nice to meet you." The sisters shook hands.

Taking mental notes of everything, Kelly gave Tina points for good manners and noticed an unidentifiable accent that was opposite the expected southern drawl. "The pleasure is mine. You are stunning, absolutely gorgeous. I couldn't see the whole visual from where you were standing in the church. More than that, I was quite impressed with your vocals."

"Thank you, Miss King. Hearing that from you means a lot."

"I'd love to hear more. Are you singing at the reception?"

Two different answers were spoken simultaneously.

Carlton said, "Yes."

Tina said, "No."

Kelly was puzzled and searched both their faces for the truth. Baffled as well, Tina stared at Carlton, anxious to hear the details about this nonexistent performance.

Carlton chimed in with confidence. "As Miss Charles's acting manager, allow me to explain. She won't be singing at the reception but will be performing at the same location later on tonight. Sometimes, Trevi's takes on extra business like this highfalutin wedding reception, but mainly it's the hottest dance spot anywhere near here. At seven tonight, the Pumpkin Reception Hall turns back into Club Trevi's and Miss Charles kicks things off at nine o'clock."

Kelly looked to Tina for corroboration of what her gut told her was a fabrication of the truth. The Wedding Singer did her best to establish an out clause for Carlton's blatant lie. In the time it took to cough and clear her throat, Tina had successfully manufactured a plausible response. "I'll be singing at the club tonight as kind of an opening act, if the reception ends on time. But I'm sure you weren't planning on staying around that long."

Kelly was overjoyed that an opportunity had presented itself to spend more time with Tina without forcing an exchange. "Certain things are worth waiting for, so I'm looking forward to seeing you later tonight." Kelly waved while getting in the backseat of the town car.

Once it was completely out of site, Tina punched Carlton in the arm. "You know darn well I'm not singing at Trevi's tonight! I'm supposed to be spending the evening with Aunty Gina, making sure everything is accounted for and packed. Remember the plan, Carlton? We'll be on our way to New York City tomorrow evening! You and Tony are going to the wedding reception to do hair and makeup—it has nothing to do with me. I can't believe you lied to Miss King and I lied to her as well! That was a once-in-a-lifetime chance and we blew it—actually, you blew it!"

The very offended Carlton rebutted. "That's a lie from the pit of hell. I didn't blow shit!—at least, not today. Anyway, you should be shouting all over the front of this church. Tonight, Kelly King will be hanging out in a club in North Carolina just to hear you sing!"

Tina yelled. "But I'm not singing! Fridays were the nights when I sang at Trevi's. Manuel's biggest dance night is Saturday. He's not going to let me sing." Determined not to cry, she calmed her body and lowered the volume of her voice. "Carlton, I need you to go to that reception, make up a good excuse about why I'm not singing, and get me some type of contact information for Miss King. Do that for me and I'll take it from there. Now, please drive me home. I'm done talking about this."

Tina often became deadly silent when reaching this level of being severely upset. She sat in the passenger seat of the red mustang pale with her lower lip protruding in a sulky pout. She remained silent the eight minutes it took to get her home to Joseph-Lee Manor. Once there, she got out of the car and started walking quickly toward the house. Carlton blocked her way by running at full speed to jump in front of her.

He pleaded. "Bettina Charles—Tina—Tee-Tee—talk to me!"

Tina chose the quickest path to being left alone and answered him. "What Carlton?"

"Tina, I know this seems crazy, but you will be singing at Trevi's tonight. I promise. I got this." Carlton looked at his watch, noting that it was one thirty in the afternoon. "I'll call you in an hour *or so* with details." His choice of words reminded Tina of a miserable childhood experience.

> **July 5, 1974**—*Momma Nin was hospitalized for the purpose of taking a battery of tests in addition to having a procedure. Since adopting Tina at five months old, the separation represented the first time that the mother and daughter had spent a night apart. The fact that her favorite great-aunty was dividing her time between her and a man she called Bernard made the needy niece extra miserable.*
>
> *"Aunty Gina, where is your husband Uncle Henry?" Tina asked loud enough for the stranger to hear.*
>
> *"He's somewhere doing what I'm doing—minding?"*
>
> *"Mining what—coal or minerals? I didn't know you or he did that."*
>
> *"What I'm trying to tell you Tina is that it really doesn't matter."*
>
> *Tina shifted to a more important subject. "When will Momma Nin return?"*
>
> *"She'll be back in a week or so and you need to be more polite to my special friend," Aunty Gina responded.*
>
> *After asking over and over, Tina was never given a definition of the time span represented by the words "or so." In the life of a ten-year-old, "or so" ended up being a very long time. Ten days later, Momma Nin returned and the mystery, whisky smelling man was gone.*

Refocused on standing in the front yard of Joseph-Lee Manor, Tina was furious. "*Or so!*" she yelled. "You know how I hate *or so!* It means nothing to me!"

Carlton quickly apologized. "Forgive me already. I had a slip of the tongue. It's hard to keep up with all the words and little things that are touchy issues for you. Anyway, let me rephrase. I will call you in less than two hours. Now, go in the house and do your special meditation. I'll take care of the rest. Can you please do that for me?"

Tina knew when her cousin was serious and was certain that he would do his best to make something happen. "All right, Carlton, all right! Go and do whatever. I need to relax my mind before my brain explodes. You better call me in less than two hours and tell me something—good or bad."

Carlton jumped in his car and zoomed down the small town's major highway at his usual pace, averaging fifteen miles above the speed limit. He was on a mission to get to the club/reception hall at lightning speed. Club Trevi's was one of a very few venues in the area large enough to host an event the size of Katrina's wedding reception. Located thirty miles away from Scotland Neck, it was the same upbeat dance hall where Tina headlined for a two-month period that had ended just fifteen days earlier. Manuel, the club's owner, was about making money as goals one through a million. Renting the venue for important affairs was a clever method of advertisement, exposing his club to a broader audience. A large number of the special event attendees always remained for the *after party*—the ones interested in extending their good time. Manuel was masterful at managing these activities—ending them no later than 7:00 p. m. and having the entire venue cleaned, transformed back to its original purpose, and fully opened to the general public by 8:00 p. m. that same evening.

Tina entered the house with a red, puffy face that expressed gloom and doom. Aunty Gina knew better than to inquire about Tina's obvious woes. To do so would place her on the receiving end of bratty, dismissive remarks. Even Aunty Trudy received the message to back off, find a corner, and intercede through silent prayer. Fortunately, Aunty Zooni was absent, doing something rare—tending to matters at her own home. Instead of words, Aunty Gina presented her great-niece with her favorite food of comfort—a turkey sandwich with Swiss cheese, fresh baby spinach, and a good coating of mayonnaise on both sides of the bread. After eating and washing it down with a glass of sweet tea, Tina went to the office to call her healing agent. Pouting to Pappy John generally made her feel better, but this time it did not. She was upset with herself for lying to Kelly King. She had made the decision to support Carlton in his usual game of exaggeration.

To prevent herself from sinking into a very dark place, she used the strongest weapon that she had—*maintaining.* She sat on the side porch breathing slowly while swaying back and forth in Momma Nin's favorite rocker—the one on the left side of the door closest to the private entryway. With eyes closed, Tina absorbed the sounds in the air as if they were soothing music, allowing her mind to float away in the distinctiveness of each audible vibration. The most pronounced rhythms included the periodic rumbling on the highway of anything passing—from a car to a tractor trailer, farm equipment pounding in a distant field, chickens scattering about, and the steady chirping of a variety of birds.

16

SETTING THE STAGE

BY the time Carlton arrived at Club Trevi's, the wedding guests were being served hors d'oeuvres under a tent outside the club. The wedding party was on the inside being organized for the receiving line. With all facets of the reception being handled by outside sources, Manuel was free to posture, mainly on the end of his bar. It was mid-afternoon and he was on his second shot of Hennessy.

With heart attack symptoms of chest discomfort, anxiety, and nausea internalized, Carlton's carefree exterior coolly camouflaged the pounding of his heart and head. Nonchalantly, he walked over to Trevi's owner and made his request. "Can we talk privately like now? Something to fear around here might change your glad to sad and most certainly make you pissed-off mad."

After a moment of suspiciously studying Carlton's serious expression, Manual decided that gaining more information was the prudent thing to do. He extended a short invitation and began to calmly walk toward his office. "Follow me." Mister Montgomery was trailing a distance behind, consuming the contents of half-finished champagne flutes from waiters' trays while heading to the back of the club.

Once the door was closed, Carlton said, "I've been working hair and makeup for this fabulous wedding. I'm talking First-Lady-Nancy-Reagan fabulous, but you already know that 'cuz you're hosting the reception and all. Anyway, Tina was the wedding singer, and one of the guests was this big deal famous lady who was so impressed with my little cousin's singing that she wanted to hear more." Sensing that he had piqued Manuel's curiosity, his colorful account of the day's events continued. "Since Miss Big Time Lady is leaving tomorrow, I sort of exaggerated slash lied and told her that Tina was performing here tonight after the reception. I wanted to fill you in just in case someone asks if she is singing. Obviously, there's no way Bettina Charles is gonna sing here tonight—not now."

Instead of listening closely, Manuel was thinking about his answer. He responded quickly. "You're damn right! Nobody schedules something in my club without asking me first. But thinking about Tina's cute little ass puts me in a charitable mood." Manuel sat on the edge of his desk and lit up a Newport. "Mister-Miss Montgomery or whatever the hell you call yourself, you need to listen closely. Right now is the time you need to start begging and offering something up to make me say yes—yes to Tina and that pretty, young, plump ass singing here tonight."

Carlton pulled out bubble-gum-flavored lip gloss and began applying it to his lips. When they were nice, glossy, and moist, he placed his hand—just one hand—on Manuel's crotch. With that hand, he stroked the joystick and its two nodules simultaneously. Upon getting a fluid rhythm that reaped pleasurable protrusion from Manuel, he withdrew his hand.

In a very sensual voice, Carlton teased. "And I was ready to make you a very delicious offer, but like I said, something's going down that changed my mind. Once I tell Tina, there's no way I could get her to sing here tonight or any night—even if I begged. Well, I delivered my message, so toodle-loo. My work is done. I need to get out front and help Tony with the styling duties for the wedding party."

Carlton turned and walked toward the exit. The taller Manuel rushed over, reached above Carlton's head, and held the door closed. Manuel demanded. "Wait a minute, Mister Lovely. It ain't that damn simple. You don't pull me away from my drink, at my bar, into my office, and give me some half-ass story. Ain't gonna be no bullshit ass toodle-loo until you tell me more. I know you and so far, I'm not following."

Carlton smiled, knowing that the bait was on the hook. He put on a frightened expression before turning around to face the fish. Moving close to Manuel, he whispered. "Since you're threatening to place me into captivity, I'll confess. A reliable source told me that undercover law enforcers are lurking around and their eyes might possibly be looking in your direction. They said something about a *Sting.* You know, like the movie." Carlton walked back to Manuel's desk while doing a pat-down of his own body. He reached in his back pocket, pulled out a small plastic bag that held marijuana and tossed it on top of Manuel's clutter. Carlton back peddled a few steps. "Oh! Holy damn! I forgot I had this illegal substance in my possession."

Manuel picked up the package and tried to return it. "Don't give your stuff to me! I got my own sweeping to do."

Carlton said nervously, "Well, I bought it from you, so I suggest that you put it in the dust pan with the rest of your stash—I mean your trash."

Manuel lifted his right pants leg and pulled six little bags of weed out of his sock. He lifted his other pants leg, reached in his left sock, and pulled out four little bags filled with a white powdery substance. Then, he bundled them together with Carlton's bag of product and placed them in his filing cabinet—top drawer inside of a folder marked *Taxes.* He asked, "Does your source know if I have time to really clean up?"

At that point, Carlton was certain that the fish bit down hard on the bait. He was definitely holding the club owner by the balls. "Manuel, for right now, I recommend that you stay cool and just do some light housekeeping. A suggestion would be for you to place any loose controlled substances in that file cabinet and keep it locked. For tonight, all distribution and consumption of illegal substances here at Trevi's needs to stop. Since they'll be watching you like a hawk watching a chicken, me and my crew will make sure that all of your feening-ass clients chill out." Carlton paused just to see the beads of Manuel's sweat, and then he continued. "You know some of my peeps—the ones connected to Tina—Rufus, Duberry, Clevon, Cornelius, and Tony?"

Manuel, who was hanging onto Carlton's every word, shook his head. "Hell, yeah, I know your posse. Most of them have been down with me since forever—for real!"

Carlton lowered his head sorrowfully and said, "Oh! Damn! That's right, we won't be here. I take back my offer to help you. Miss Big Shot is pressed for time and wants to hear Tina sing tonight. Since she's staying down the road at the Renaissance, I figured Tina can sing there in one of those conference rooms. The vibe won't be like Trevi's—a real joint—but it will have to do. And Manuel, you know that even The Lovely can't possibly be in two places at one time. That means it's just too bad and so sad for you, huh? Me and Tony will clear out of here quickly right after this wedding reception is over."

Manuel lit a second cigarette and started to pace back and forth. A light bulb went off in his head and shocked his brain. "What if we do something that benefits the both of us? You and your crew do the lookout thing for me and Tina can sing here tonight. If you don't tell her what's really going down, she'll sing, right?"

Carlton answered tentatively. "As long as she doesn't know what's up, I'm 99 percent sure I can get her to do it. Oh, wait a damn minute, I forgot. That 99 percent for sure number has to drop down to 45 percent because of another small problem."

Manuel hunched his shoulders. "Small problems can easily be fixed—so, what is it?"

Carlton cautioned. "You and your hotdog stand deenie-weenie! For me to get Tina to sing, you gotta do something that I'm sure is quite unfamiliar—and that is to act like you got some sense—like be a gentlemen. She was freaked out about you rubbing all over her the last time she was here. Get what I'm saying? Keep your hands and your other body parts to yourself."

Manuel's hand gestures resembled those of a football referee waving off an incomplete pass. "No problem, no problem. It's all good.

The only thing Tina gets from me tonight and from now on is respect," he said to his highest capacity of conveying sincerity.

"Well, if you can hold up your end, I got mine. Now, may I please leave? I need to go and handle the Tina-singing-here-tonight part of this situation. Before I skedaddle, I gotta tell Tony that he'll have to keep performing the styling duties without me. That's not going to bring sunshine to his afternoon." For maximum theatrical value, Carlton turned to leave and reversed his action. "Oh yeah, the band of four cousins needs to hook up with me for a quick rehearsal with Tina. Once I get her to agree to sing—that is. Instead of them, I'll leave a few unfamiliar faces of my crew to do the first lookout *thingy*. If that's alright with you, they'll hang around here with Tony—posing as reception guests." There was no faceless crew, but Carlton improvised to spice up his farce.

Manuel said, "Yeah, man, that's fine. They can do their lookout thang and you go take care of the Tina thang. When this is over, trust that I'm gonna hook you up real good—right?"

With his back turned away from Manuel, Carlton gestured a thumbs-up, walked out the door, and yelled. "No problem!" Then, he mumbled to himself, "You small, burned fry in a happy meal asshole!"

Once Carlton was out of sight and before Manuel made it across the doorsill, a large male presence with an unfamiliar face forced him backwards into his office. It was Kelly King's tall, muscular chauffeur Chadrick delivering directives on behalf of his nameless employer. The club owner was given five hundred dollars. At an inflationary rate, three hundred was for an hour and a half worth of half-priced drinks plus a two-hundred-dollar tip. After placing the money in his hand, the big bad chauffeur put a bug in his ear. "Miss Bettina Charles's performance this evening is a 'go,' come hell or high waters—even if caused by a heavenly inflicted flood."

Upon his return from Manuel's office, Kelly caught chauffeur Chadrick's subtle nod—conveying that the club owner had been appropriately schooled and was in the process of carrying out her wishes. That confirmation prompted her next move. Kelly placed a phone call to her assistant, Angela—initiating an action designed to increase the after party's external noise. With overture activities completed, Kelly rejoined the wedding party. Standing in the receiving line next to her Aunt Kathy, she smiled, shook hands, and hugged *some* of the wedding reception's guests—certain relatives with inviting personalities.

Seventy-five minutes after making the promise to his little Tee-Tee, Carlton placed a call. The phone rang inside of Joseph-Lee Manor. Tina was nonresponsive—mentally locked away inside her unconventional method of contemplation. She was brought back to the present by Aunty Gina, but it required yells and a shoulder shake. After informing her great-niece that Carlton was on the phone, Tina practically knocked her Aunty down—pushing her way from the porch into the house. She whisked through her sitting room, traveling swiftly past her Aunty Trudy, who was trying to give her the phone's receiver. Instead of grabbing it, she continued into the office to take the call in private.

Tina yelled. "Got it! You can hang up now!" After hearing the click, which indicated that Aunty Trudy was disconnected, she said anxiously, "Hello."

"Hey, Miss Spoiled-Ass Brat Cousin. I need you to put some cucumber slices over those puffy eyes. Oh, I know you've been crying—even though I told you no worries. Why, you ask? Because tonight at nine o'clock, to be exact, you'll be singing at Trevi's just like Mister Montgomery promised.—BAM!!!"

A skeptical Tina asked, "Oh my God, Carlton, are you serious?"

"Like the heart attack I almost had earlier. Has The Lovely ever let you down?"

Tina started screaming and jumping. "Carlton, how did you pull this off? Then again, I don't wanna know, but thank you. Now that I have another chance, I know I'm going to blow Miss King away. Oh wait, what about the band?"

"Already done—I told you I got this. Everybody'll be at Joseph-Lee Manor at five thirty for a quick run through. It's only three songs and they know them already—easy as pie."

"Oh Carlton, I thank you. I thank you so, so much! I gotta get off the phone to start getting ready. I'm so excited! I can't wait to get on that stage. Hurry up and get home. Love you, bye!"

17

THE GRAND RECEPTION

HEARING Tina scream, Aunty Gina rushed to her great-niece's side and was quickly brought up to speed on the reason for the excitement. "Miss Kelly King is a close relative of the bride, was at the wedding, and will be at Trevi's tonight to hear me sing again. Carlton arranged everything with Miss King, Manuel, and the band. My best friend-cousin is a genius miracle worker, you see."

"Who is this Kelly King person?" asked Aunty Gina suspiciously.

"She's just one of the biggest producers in the music industry."

With no immediate recollection of the powerful woman, Aunty Gina was doubtful about her ability to help Tina and cautious about her motives even if she could. To prove credentials, Tina shared several articles about the music executive that had appeared in three national magazines. They had been saved as part of her women in entertainment collection resting on a shelf in her sitting room. After reading each article carefully, Aunty Gina's level of skepticism increased and no line of conjecture was out of bounds. "Why hang around a small town to go to a club to see a young lady perform for the second time in one day? As one of a few female music executives in Corporate America, this King woman has to be on the ball and tough as nails. At thirty years old, she's never been married and there's no mention of a significant other in any of these articles."

"Aunty Gina, what does that have to do with anything?"

"Tina, you just watch yourself because I hope Miss Executive doesn't have an appetite for something sweet, ripe, and unsuspecting that's beyond your talent."

"Now, you sound like Aunty Zooni."

"When it comes to you, I'm just overly concerned," said Aunty Gina while trying to appear more supportive. "If this second performance doesn't change her mind, I don't want your feelings hurt and your dreams crushed."

"That will definitely not happen. Momma Nin and Pappy John taught me to never give up and to believe in myself no matter what."

Aunty Trudy broke in with scripture. "Faith moves mountains and prayer changes things."

"That's right and besides, Carlton and I are moving to New York City where hundreds of opportunities are waiting. I know that my talent will make room for me with or without Miss Kelly King."

Tears began to drizzle down Aunty Gina's face. "I'm overly emotional because my babies will be leaving me tomorrow after seven years under my charge." At the end of a tight hug, she added encouraging words. "Tina, I believe in you too and know that you will amaze Kelly King like you do everyone else."

Providing comfort, Aunty Trudy rubbed her sister's back as they left their great-niece alone to prepare for her performance. Tina went straight to the living room and sat down at Willie Chambers. She gazed at his eighty-eight keys for several minutes before touching them. During this pause, a nostalgic mental flash carried her back to the feel-good memory of receiving her most precious gift.

Friday Night, December 20, 1974—*A ten-year-old Tina stole the show by playing the piano, singing, and dancing her way into the hearts of the audience that packed the pews at the Mount Pleasant*

Hill Baptist Church's Christmas Showcase. Expecting a special gift when she arrived at home, Tina blew through Joseph-Lee Manor's front doors into the living room. There, she was stunned by the bulkiness of her mammoth-sized Christmas surprise. It was a top-notch piano—a black, hand-polished Steinway baby grand. After a barrage of ear-piercing yells to convey thankfulness, Tina sat down and tentatively examined her new colossal pearly keyed instrument. Like all other meaningful things in her life, she put her naming game to practice and christened the piano Willie Chambers in homage to the person listed on the delivery receipt. When questioning the dispatcher's name, Tina was told that William Chambers had been instrumental in arranging the figurative and literal details—getting the oversized baby grand piano placed inside of the living room of Joseph-Lee Manor.

Regardless of the naming convention, Tina's reasonable assumption was that the Steinway was a gift from Momma Nin and Pappy John and she proceeded to put it to good use. From that point forward, at least five evenings a week, Tina spent time at Willie Chambers. Other than Carlton and Brief de Vaughan's contents, he was her closest companion.

Tina's recollection of her most special Christmas moment ended as usual—with a bag of mixed emotions. On the one hand, she returned from her trip to the past with feelings of cheerful joy. They included mental pictures of her little self, giving hugs and kisses of gratitude. It also made her smile, remembering her own small fingers moving up and down the keys of Willie Chambers. On the flip side, her mental homecoming came with luggage filled with tears and piercing heart pain. That moment was a jarring reminder of her greatest loss. It was the beginning of Momma Nin's decline, lasting eight months until she passed away.

As for the authentic donors of the baby grand, Tina learned the truth almost six years after its receipt.

Momma Nin Lullaby Letter Excerpt

Dearest Tina, your Willie Chambers piano was a gift from your missing in action grandparents Willie and Victoria Chambers. I wanted to hunt them down and strangle them for dropping such a huge memento in your life without interjecting their physical presence. How could such generosity come from two selfish people? With me dying, I so badly wanted them to be in your life. I knew you'd need them so much when the time came. Tina, I have concluded that some strains of racism are incurable. I reasoned that it had to be the case if your beautiful face, talent, and personality didn't heal their hearts. I sent photos and videos of you and their only response was to periodically send more gifts and money. The fact that I failed to unite you and your grandparents was one of my biggest regrets. Right away, a deep connection was formed between you and Willie Chambers. As you practiced technique, you played your way through grief and sadness as well as moments of joy. Your abilities were amazing and you played to me daily—escorting me to the gates of heaven. Promise that you will never stop using your musical talent.—Hearing you happily from heaven, MOMMA NIN. ∎

After reflecting on her most memorable Christmas, Tina mimicked Professor Milton and played a resounding chord by pressing all ten fingers down on Willie Chambers's keys at the same time. She spent five minutes playing Momma Nin's favorite symphony, Chopin's "Nocturne Opus Nine." After that, Tina began her vocal exercises, singing scales up and down her voice's register. Repetitively, she chanted. "Me-May-My-Mo-Moo—Me-May-My-Mo-Moo—Me-May-My-Mo-Moo."

While Tina was preparing for the amateur hour of her life, Kelly's command performance was well on its way—filled with multitasking to the umpteenth degree. Now that the after party venue was secured and the running of interference was set into motion, Kelly focused on doting duties of devotion for the remainder of the wedding reception. Putting first things first, she downgraded Katrina's sorority sister's role from maid-of-honor at the marriage ceremony to a full, grown flower girl after that. Kelly sat focal-point central next to Katrina and placed the college friend at the end of the bridal party's table beside the children. Katrina did her best to smooth things over with her stand-in college roommate. "As I've shared with you many times, my first cousin is just being herself. She's pushing the point that she is my authentic maid of honor. I appreciate you being so understanding because Kelly King can't help but act large and in charge."

In applicable fashion, the business executive proceeded to direct the action of the wedding planner, caterer, waiters, and Tony. To personally assist the bride, her actions included lifting Katrina's train when necessary, holding her flower bouquet when both hands were required for things like the first dance, organizing the single ladies for the bouquet toss, and leading the toast to the happy couple. She even wiped Katrina's face after the cake-cutting/cake-smashing ritual.

Throughout the wedding reception, Kelly was introduced to quite a few aunts, uncles, and cousins on her mother's side of the family. She enjoyed some of the verbal exchanges, particularly with relatives her age and younger. She found it interesting that the majority of the sucking up was done by her much older relatives. During the three-decade-long cold war, they were the ones with some level of culpability in ostracizing her mother. Kelly's Aunt Kathy used two elbow pokes in her side to identify the major culprits as they approached. Other than a smug look here and there, Kelly received them lukewarmly. As it pertained to the ring leader, her Grandmother Kathleen, she maintained restraint and simply extended well-wishes on behalf of Kay-Dee, the banished daughter. Kelly realized that her presence at the wedding celebration, her professional success, and her over-the-top catering to Katrina delivered bruises and scars of envy more effective than words of an outward assault.

Kelly's final mission was assisting Katrina with changing her clothes for departure to the first-class Hawaiian honeymoon she paid for and helped plan. There was no question that Kelly adored Katrina, but her love for anyone was contingent upon personal benefit at best and not being an inconvenience to her in most cases. This North Carolina invasion was no different. Kelly's top-shelf hijacking of the wedding reception was a success—a brilliantly executed done-deal—finished an hour earlier than Trevi's maximum ending time for special events.

Although appearing modestly altruistic while accomplishing pin-pointed objectives, a feeling of separation overtook the executive vice president. Katrina's face conveyed a similar expression of a strong sense of loss. This honeymoon send-off felt different from any previous good-bye moments between the cousins. It had a feeling of finality. Separately and from the inside out, both women had acknowledged a shift in priorities. Katrina's marriage and Kelly's increased career-focus had produced a natural redefining of their relationship.

Disengaging her tight hug, Kelly said, "This is it. My running buddy is no longer free to roam. Just like with the evolution of my career, life gets busy, complicated, and time is scarce. Your marriage has to be the priority—over me, our grandparents, and over everybody. Promise me that you'll remember that."

"I won't forget—I promise." Katrina stuttered. "M-Michael's promotion and us moving to Oklahoma City makes it easier. While he's focusing on Federal government business, I'll be keeping house and hopefully rocking a baby or two real soon."

"Hawaii is a wonderful setting to work on that project." Kelly moved close to Katrina's ear. "Listen, even though our calls will be infrequent and our face-to-faces almost non-existent, you know I'll always have your back. Keep the number to my private line in the forefront of your mind at all times."

"I will. You're always there when I need you and that's a great insurance policy to have. It means the world to me. I love you."

"I love you more."

The cousins wiped each other's tears—followed by another tight embrace—followed by farewell.

Manuel was sitting in his office, feeling perturbed as his club was being prepped for the after party featuring *Bettina Charles Live*! He reared back in his executive chair, confused and terrified. He regretted accepting the bribe money but was comforted by the fact that he was too afraid to refuse it. "This crazy songbird shakedown thing is far above my pay grade. I'm just a small-town, small-time, drug-dealing club owner." Manuel lit a cigarette. "After the heads-up meeting with Carlton, a beast of a man, dressed in all black, stood toe-to-toe and threatened me in my own damn office. Was he an undercover cop, Tina's boyfriend or a relative crazier than Carlton? Regardless of who he is, I should be covered. I gave the okay for Bettina Charles to sing later tonight and told bartender Barney to charge half-price for drinks between 7:30 p. m. and 9:00 p. m."

With no other recourse, Manuel left his office and returned to the front of the house, leaning on the end of the bar facing the entrance. Although a few hours away, he kept checking the clock, knowing his uneasiness would remain until the sought-after singer walked through the front door of Trevi's.

Once the newlyweds' limousine could no longer be seen, Kelly hugged Katrina's parents, gave a universal wave to everyone else, and retreated to her suite at the Renaissance. After being driven the three short miles to get there, she was greeted in the hotel lobby by a front desk clerk who handed her three messages from the same person— her mother.

∽⟩

Knowing Kay-Dee's propensity to be melodramatic, Kelly took time to decompress from the spacewalk-of-a-day she had endured. Wrapped in a bathrobe after a long hot shower, she sat in a club chair with her feet resting on its matching ottoman. She stabilized her mood using some of her reliable calming agents—vodka, orange juice, and several cigarettes. Comfortably situated, Kelly returned her mother's phone calls. Right after saying hello, she informed Kay-Dee that she was pressed for time. The highlight reel she presented to her mother was succinct but detailed—a description of North Carolina's cash crops and the wedding ceremony particulars—smiling for photos, taking control of the reception, giving attentive support to Katrina, and encountering Grandmother Kathleen and assorted kinfolk. With the exception of Aunty Gina, other specific information about the Charles family was either spun or withheld. She decided not to burden her mother with her discovery of a little sister sired by Donald Leonard Charles until all dots were connected.

In a matter-of-fact tone Kelly said, "I think I found your Gee-Gee— G-Something mystery woman. Do you remember a lady named Gina?"

An excited Kay-Dee squealed before responding. "Oh my God, that's the name! For years, it's been hanging in my brain just out of reach. Yes, Gina—Donnie-Lee called her Aunty Gina and they were very close. Kelly, did you talk to her? Did she tell you anything about Donnie-Lee? Does she still live in that big house?"

"Mom, slow down with all the questions! Yes, Donald Leonard Charles's aunt—this Gina person—still lives in the big house. That's the beginning and the end of what I found out, and I'm not sure if I want to know any more than that right now. I go back to work on Monday and my assistant Angela warned me that things are crazy. In fact, I'm working tonight."

"You're working from North Carolina? I don't understand," her mother said with genuine concern.

Kelly proceeded to spin information about Tina, intentionally mincing words. "Well, Katrina had the most amazing wedding singer—a beautiful and talented young lady—just eighteen years old. She's singing at a local club tonight and I want to get a second look at her. That's why I'm rushing to get off the phone. I need to get ready so I can be there on time."

"Kelly, baby, I won't keep you much longer, but I need to tell you that I'm proud of how you're handling this whole thing about your birth father. Even though I don't deserve it, I'm thankful that you're talking to me at all and grateful that you're including me in what you're learning about Donnie-Lee and his family." There were a few seconds of silence between them.

With guilt about bending the truth, Kelly responded. "Mom, like I said, I'm taking it very slowly."

"I understand and think it's very smart to handle it like that—on your own terms and timeframe. I just want to tell you again that I'm sorry. I'm so very sorry for hiding the truth from you for all these years."

Now armed with personal knowledge about her vengeful Grandmother Kathleen, coupled with her own truth-hiding dilemma, Kelly had nothing but empathy for her mother. "Mom, I need you to promise me that you will never apologize about this Donald Leonard Charles thing again. I've forgiven you, but you have to forgive yourself."

"It's gonna take some time to forgive myself for hurting you, but I'll work on it." Tears accompanied Kay-Dee's words of remorse. "I almost lost your love and respect and that continues to terrify me. Well, as much as you want me to be, I'm here to help you through this thing with Donnie-Lee and your new and old families."

"Mom, I know you're there for me, just like always. I love you and will call you next week—good-bye."

18

BAND OF FOUR COUSINS

WITH a glance at the clock, Tina noted that her private performance preparation had gone on for almost two hours. During this process, she thoroughly rehearsed each of the three selections that would be showcased for Kelly King—repeating stanzas, verses, and bridges—rearranging chords using vocal inversion—perfecting octave changes while controlling her pitch. After that, she practiced choreography in front of the floor-length mirror hanging inside her bedroom door. Upon completing her showmanship practice, she took a bath as hot as she could stand—a Momma Nin prescription for unwinding. While in the tub, she had a piercing moment of reflection. In less than twenty-four hours, two opportunities to perform before a music industry executive were presented. They were occurring one month before the seventh anniversary of Momma Nin's passing. Somehow, through the solace, the acknowledgement served as a great source of strength. Tina imagined herself back there in the bed—nose-to-nose—sharing the pillow with Momma Nin when she whispered her last five earthly words. "Love—You—Bettina—Bethany—Charles."

The sentiment of that utterance inscribed an indelible stamp of affirmation on Tina's heart, reminding her of a spiritual connection to the power found in God's love. She climbed out of the tub and stared at the half-steamed mirror. Besides a naked, damp, unruly haired Tina, she saw a determined young woman, pursuing a path she hoped would lead to greatness. Succeeding in feeling relaxed and comforted, her emotional preparation required a final ingredient, a dose of self-assurance. She tapped into another Momma Nin tool to reinforce positive thinking. Using her inside voice, she said, "I have mustard seed faith that moves mountains and Kelly Kings." Louder, she proclaimed. "I have mustard seed faith that moves mountains and Kelly Kings." With firm conviction she declared. "I have mustard seed faith that moves mountains and Kelly Kings." As in past situations, that repetitive declaration caused Tina's embedded confidence to surface and wrap around her like a protective shield. The exercise invoked a self-belief of being a courageous conqueror geared up for the careful critique coming in a couple of hours.

Sufficiently toweled dry, Tina pampered her body, applying a thick coat of lotion and several head-to-toe sprays of perfume. She raised her hands high in the air and slipped into a curve-hugging, aqua, sleeveless mini dress. It was made of a stretched gabardine fabric, had a rounded, low neckline, and one-inch tank-top straps. As always, her undergarments were standard dance approved leotard bottoms. They were as essential to a singer-performer's dance costume as toe shoes were to a prima ballerina. The outfit was covered with one of Momma Nin's old housecoats—pink floral print, cotton, fastened with snaps from top to bottom.

Because it took some time to check on Tony as well as collect all the band members, Carlton arrived at Joseph-Lee Manor slightly before the motley crew—Rufus, Duberry, Clevon, and Cornelius. He busted through the front door yelling that Tina was on the radio. Clarifying, Carlton said, "I mean, Tina's not singing on the radio, but they are saying that she's going to be singing tonight." The hottest and only R&B–FM radio station in the area was advertising Tina's live performance. Like moths drawn to the light, everyone ran to the Great Room. Aunty Gina turned the radio on and up loud as family trickled in. Those present were Aunty Gina, Aunty Trudy, Uncle Ed, Larry, Rufus, Duberry, Clevon, Cornelius, Carlton, Tina, and Cousin Alonia, the owner of The Pit. He had heard the radio announcement and came rushing over to Joseph-Lee Manor. Aunty Gina gave an attendance report. "Aunty Zooni has teaching duties and will be here as soon as she finishes grading papers."

She lived ten minutes away in Hobgood where she was teaching summer school to students in jeopardy of failing. Tina's response was delivered facetiously only to Carlton's hearing. "Poor little children come to mind whenever Aunty Zooni and teaching show up in the same sentence."

"Speak the truth Tee-Tee and shame the devil as Aunty Trudy would say."

"What better incentive to study harder than to find out in advance that Arizona Watkins will be your teacher in summer school," said Tina accompanied with giggles. Aunty Zooni was overdue to retire but refused to do so.

While waiting for the commercial, the Great Room was buzzing with competing conversations—all about Tina—but from varying points of view. After a slew of advertisements, the awaited announcement started to broadcast, ringing loudly throughout the house. After a strong and commanding shush from Aunty Gina, all but the radio grew silent.

The DJ's voice sounded off with enthusiasm. "It's *Evening Time*, Saturday, July 10, 1982! *WGTS* is the best of the rest. Greenville, Tarboro, Scotland Neck, and the like—holla back. We got something to feel good about tonight. Our own little hometown cutie, Miss Bettina Charles, is singing her way into everybody's hearts. She's taking the stage tonight, nine o'clock sharp at Club Trevi's. Half-priced drinks will be served between seven thirty and nine o'clock, come rain or shine. When the club is full, it's full. So, you better get there early. Once again, Bettina Charles performs live at Club Trevi's tonight!"

Jumping accompanied the screaming of everyone present—everyone but Tina. Although elated, she expressed it differently. She converted her excitement to concentration, powering her determination to do her absolute best. She stood up and headed for the living room. While walking, she said, "Carlton, we need to get to Willie Chambers for our short rehearsal." With a little more excitement, she clapped her hands, added a little skip, and said, "Band of four Cousins, let's go." Those that she beckoned followed her. Everyone else remained in the Great Room, listening, waiting, and hoping that the advertisement would run again.

As planned, the band practice was short and sweet. It amounted to a run-through of questionable spots in each of the three songs— mostly their intros and endings. The rest of the session was more of a church meeting than a rehearsal. As church clerk, Carlton gave govern-yourself-accordingly announcements. "Attention! Attention! I need everyone to be focused and remain that way. Tonight's show is the most important one we've ever done. We've got to blow Kelly King away and make her forget she's in a club in the South. Is everyone clear?"

Rufus, the keyboardist, was already tipsy and spoke on behalf of the foursome. "Y'all didn't say nothing 'bout being on no radio. We can't fake what we ain't—big citified musicians and all. For the record, we ain't answering no—damn—questions."

Carlton responded. "And nobody's asking you to say a single word, Rufus. Matter of fact, the less said—the better. About this radio thing, none of us knew anything about it. Anyway, the only thing said was that Tina is singing at Trevi's tonight—nothing about anybody else. So, we all should be good to go?" Duberry, Clevon, and Cornelius shook their heads in the affirmative, understanding Carlton's words to be a non-negotiable command. Carlton continued. "Well, I say that everything is all good with an additional requirement. Y'all gotta hold off on getting sloppy drunk until after the performance—Cousin Rufus! With this radio commercial and all, I decided to pay double for your trouble and I know how y'all love extra money in your pockets. Am I right?"

Rufus perked right up and chuckled. "You got that right! Everything's all good."

Compensating them financially was inconsequential. When it came to her band, Tina's philosophy was the opposite of Carlton's approach. Hers was that of a beggar not being choosy. Other than second cousins, she understood that her musical crew was comprised of four older men—well settled in their ways—who did not share her lofty ambition about achieving stellar success. Her loose musical alliance with them was based on a right-now need. For tonight, that must-have requirement was that they play the correct chords while maintaining a steady beat.

To motivate her band of four cousins, she appealed to their fondness for their hazel-eyed little cousin. "Guys, I appreciate each of you so much. I can't do this performance without you and singing for Miss Kelly King is very important to me." Tina ended her plea with a prayer of benediction and disappeared into her bedroom. Carlton barked out strict orders while following the band of four cousins to the car that they shared—a 1974 Chevrolet Impala—olive green body, ivory hardtop, automatic transmission, and chrome accessories. Although the band members were close to the age of his great-aunties, Mister Montgomery spoke to the men as if they were children. "It don't make no sense. Standing all together, y'all look like four flat tires on a broken-down pickup truck. Remember what I said. Drive straight to Club Trevi's and no fooling around. I mean it!"

Carlton used the side entrance, walked through the sitting parlor, and used his customary vocalization to announce his entrance into Tina's bedroom. "Your brother from another mother is entering your boudoir my dear. Be straight because you know I don't like to wait."

"You may enter Monsieur Montgomery."

The stylist extraordinaire took one look at Tina and shook his head with multiple quick whips in the negative. "Girl, your hair is a *hot mess*, dipped in syrup to sweeten the aftertaste of your tawdriness. We have to quickly improve upon this gutter-in-a-back-alley situation."

Well-versed and technically sound, Carlton executed his styling interpretation of the 1980's trend of big hair crafted to be asymmetrical with a purposeful wildness. With the assistance of a blow-dryer, brush, curling iron, and hairspray, he tugged and pulled Tina's sandy strands into the desired level of submission. In comparison, her flawless, sugar-cookie-colored face was easy to accentuate—foundation lightly dusted with powder—eyeliner, blush, and bright-red lipstick sensibly applied. The final touch was a moderate coat of blue eye shadow, matching the color of her mini dress.

In record time, the transformation was complete and unanimously characterized by Carlton and Tina as exquisite, exotic, and sassy. It was definitely a night for Tina's alter ego, Tosha Ray, to shine. With very little time to spare, they rushed to the Great Room for the grand-guardians' critique. This time, there would be no sneaking out and in of Joseph-Lee Manor. The entire Charles-Watkins-Smith village was well-informed about Tina's audition for Kelly King.

The Great Room was true to its name, spacious and used mostly by the older members of the family. There, they lounged, listened to music, watched TV, and played games during the frequently held Friday night fish fries and Saturday night tomato-based beef stews. While Tina posed in the center of the room, Carlton reached around her body and pulled apart the snaps on her hand-me-down housecoat. This created a ripple effect—one snap disengaging after the other. Once opened, he slid the coverall completely off of his masterpiece, unveiling an aqua mini dress, no stockings, and spiked, three-inch heels—high, but not to the point of negatively impacting Tina's ability to dance.

Trudy said, "Lord have mercy on both of y'all souls! Tina, your private parts are barely covered up. You done turned your flower garden into Satan's doorbell—that's easy to be rung. Gina, don't let that gal leave this house like that!"

Zooni and her mouth had arrived. "You playing mommy is about over, so ain't no need in trying to tame her now. Gina done let the reins go completely. Come tomorrow the child's running wild and frisky free all the way to New York City. The last thing she needs is somebody talking her up on the radio. I know Nadine is tossing all around in her grave."

Though she rarely responded to her Aunty Zooni's chastisement, Tina was furious. "You don't know anything about what Momma Nin is doing," she snapped. Then, losing it completely, she snarled. "She's in heaven—somewhere you'll never be!"

Zooni responded. "Girl, who the hell you trying to sass? I will knock the taste out of your mouth!"

Carlton chimed in. "Say what? You ain't gonna knock nobody nowhere!"

Aunty Gina shouted. "Enough already! It's too much ugliness being thrown around. We—are—a—family that supports each other! Now, these babies need to get going on their way—out of here and this foolishness!"

Once again, Aunty Gina was serving as her great-niece and great-nephew's lifeguard, rescuing them from the shark bites of her sisters. Steadfast in her duty, she locked arms with Tina on one side and Carlton on the other and quickly escorted them to the front door. She gave Tina her usual kiss on the forehead and a smile. "You look just like the girls on that award show we watched the other night. All I want you to think about is doing your best." Then, she turned and hugged Carlton. "You done a fine job dolling Tina up. Now, y'all get going and make sure you—CARLTON—drive safely there and back! "

Tina and Carlton displayed sheepish grins, learning that Aunty Gina was aware of the illegal driving as well as some of their other transgressions.

Upon reentering the Great Room, Gina scolded her two older sisters. "Didn't I tell y'all to mind what you say around those youngins?

Times have changed! It's a different day and they gotta God-given right to follow their dreams. Nadine left me in charge—and the shot I'm calling right now is for the two of y'all—to let the two of them be."

After pouring wine and gathering snacks, the three sisters sat at the gaming table in the corner of the Great Room and worked on a 300-large-piece puzzle—a long-term Saturday night, sister-bonding activity. With vastly different methods of expression, all three aunties were hopeful and worried about Tina.

19

THE AFTER PARTY

LIKE a bat set free from Hell, it was 8:05 p. m. when Carlton and Tina arrived at Club Trevi's. They burst through the front door just before Manuel had a conniption. Knowing that the mystery man's eyes were on him, all of his actions were exaggerated. He ran around the bar and welcomed Tina with a slight bow, a handshake, and a loud greeting filled with repetition as a result of his nervousness. "What's happening, Miss Tina—what's hap-pe-ning? It's so good to see you—so, so good to see you! Things are set up for you—set up good for you, so follow me this way—follow me right down this hallway."

Tina was shocked and apprehensive about Manuel's tidings of great joy. Having recently performed there, she was well-acquainted with her changing station. During that stint, neither Manuel nor a member of his staff guided her there or anywhere else in the club. Tina whispered. "Carlton, don't leave me with Mister Nasty, not even for a second. He's acting crazier than usual. You better be where I can see you—before, during, and after this performance—or I'm out of here—Miss Kelly King or not."

When Manuel opened the broom closet/dressing room door, the space had been transformed. There were no brooms, mops, dust pans, cleaning supplies, or foul smells. The room was beyond uncluttered.

There were two folding chairs and a four-foot-long desk with a two-foot tall oval mirror—held in place by the angle of its tilt to the wall. A lamp resting on the left back edge of the walnut-colored desk served as an additional light source. It aided the naked light bulb hanging above in the center of the ceiling. A dangling white string was its on-and-off switch. "Everything's all good to go—your dressing room and your drink." Snapping his fingers, Manuel continued. "If you need anything else, holler and Barney will hook you up like that."

Once Manuel was out of sight, Carlton jested. "Tina-girl, if show-biz makes bastards human-like, then I can't wait until you get us there—to the land of fame and fortune."

Without Manuel noticing, the big, bad mystery man had slipped out of the club to carry out his number one job—that of a chauffeur—picking Kelly King up from the Renaissance and returning her to Trevi's. With no fanfare, she reentered the club dressed in her preferred business attire. She wore an expensive, breathable knit pants suit—black with a matching sleeveless camisole. Prearranged, Barney escorted Kelly to a reserved table. It was tucked away in front of a big post, catty-cornered in the back right edge of the staging area. While out of plain sight, there was an unobstructed view of the stage.

Courtesy of DJ Darnell, the atmosphere was cranked up with the latest and liveliest club music. Manuel and the chauffeur Chadrick had reclaimed their respective territory—leaning on opposite ends of the bar with about twenty feet of countertop between them. Each held a drink in one hand—rotating the hard liquor in a slow, but steady motion. While not acknowledging contact, their eyes met periodically as they cased the surroundings. From time to time, each man took a taste of his strong drink and then continued the glass's circular movement. This nonverbal posturing conveyed thoughts of "I'm bad" from the mystery man and "I'm pretending to be bad" from Manuel. In addition to the stalemate standing at each end of the bar, all its stools were occupied and all the tables were full—those surrounding the stage as well as the ones scattered around the room.

Tonight's fanfare and surge in attendance was remarkable to the local folk, but not coincidental. It had been seven hours since posing for photographs with her little sister Tina—a huge chunk of time for Kelly King to execute her multifaceted wizardry. In addition to taking control of the wedding reception, she had successfully persuaded and received aid from a dirty drug-dealing club owner. Then, she leaked her intention to return to the club to hear more from the wedding singer to a select group of her newly found cousins. The news quickly spread through the pool of younger relatives just as she intended. She told them and they told others. On top of that, Kelly had directed her assistant to broadcast the event using the most popular radio station in the area.

On this night, Kelly knew that she had outdone herself in upping the ante. The scene was set to see how Tina dealt with surprises, fans, foes, inebriated hecklers, and general pressure. She reasoned that her use of the customary Walden Records' scorecard would assist in her execution of an unbiased critique. It had a checklist of high-standard qualifications with close attention paid to the tiny details of a most excellent performance. Like all hopefuls tested before, the product—in this case, Tina—had to pass a clinical and cynical trial before being presented in any fashion—live or on tape—to Arnie Peters. Tina had to not only be talented and cute but also tough-skinned and adaptable to change with no advance notice.

Admiring her handiwork, Kelly sat there watching the chaos, stemming from an overcrowded, standing-room-only club. In addition to that, there were overwhelmed servers, overloaded bartenders, and people pushing and shoving to capitalize on half-priced drinks. Being catered to as a priority, bartender Barney delivered a double-dry martini to Kelly's table. It was heavy on the Tanqueray, had a splash of vermouth and two olives. She had switched her alcohol from vodka in her hotel room to gin in the club. Halfway through the drink, she realized that no change in beverage would mellow her mood. She was hyped to an unrecognizable degree in anticipation of Tina's performance.

Kelly, however, wasn't the only unusually antsy person in the building. Originating in the crude closet/changing room, there was hyper activity that included fussing, cussing, and rustling. As Tony powdered the oiliness away from Tina's face and Carlton teased her hair, she observed something so unlike her flamboyant cousin—noticeable nervousness and agitation. She decided to keep the information to herself, knowing how invested he was in her success.

Personally, Tina detested fear that manifested itself as a bad case of the jitters. Instead, she welcomed butterfly fluttering in the pit of her stomach. There was a difference. The elation was occurring inside of her at that very moment, propelling her forward. She pushed Carlton's arm down to stop his fiddling-around—an exaggerated message to alert him and Tony that it was time for her to perform. She rushed out of the makeshift dressing room with her stylist/cousin/best friend walking tentatively behind her with teasing comb in one hand and a can of hairspray in the other. Tony followed quickly behind them. At the edge of the stage, Carlton realized that he had forgotten to release his tools of the trade, so he handed them to Tony. With hands free, he clapped continuously like a head cheerleader or a proud mother. Placing the products out of sight on the floor, Tony joined Carlton's cheering squad. They were oblivious to the fact that the start of their praise preceded the performance.

Feeling lucky and blessed, Tina was grateful for the large and rowdy crowd. Like past performances, while being introduced by DJ Darnell and in the cover of darkness, she took sips of her hot toddy and took her place at center stage. When the modest club lighting hit her body, she snatched the crowd's attention with a vocal note originating in the lowest trenches of her voice's valley—resounding to the highest height of her register. She belted the sound out and held it with power for fifteen seconds. From there, she revved up the crowd, singing and dancing to her up-tempo lyrics. Her band of four cousin/misfit musicians eventually caught up to the speed of her pedometer. After the planned three songs were successfully delivered, the crowd begged for an encore, something she had never done. With a go-for-broke attitude, Tina obliged them with another up-tempo tune. She rendered a selection she wrote and had practiced with the band but had never sung in front of a live audience.

Tina sang:

Good As The Last Time

> *Hanging out in the club*
> *I was not looking for love*
> *Just taking sips of my wine*
> *Scoping for something real fine*
> *And then from out of nowhere*
> *Looked up and saw you were there*
> *And you were willing to share*
> *To make me feel—*
> *As good as you did the last time.*
>
> *No matter what you've done lately*
> *I just want you to take me*
> *Then I need you to make me feel—*
> *As good as you did the last time.*
> *Oh baby, no need to won–der*
> *All the stress I've been un–der*
> *Gonna tremble like thun–der—*
> *When you make me feel—*
> *As good as I did the last time.*
>
> *Waved my girls a good-bye*
> *Saw you and understood why*
> *Good thrills I know you supply*
> *New things I'm willing to try*

At me you started to stare
Told me you'd handle with care
Said you would take it from there—
To make me feel—
As good as you did the last time.

Kelly watched Tina and the audience. Then, she watched the audience and Tina. It was obvious that she was the attraction, drawing the crowd's attention like a magnetic force. The instrumental music accompaniment could be heard, but the musicians completely blended with the background's darkness. Unfamiliar with the provocative tune, Kelly wondered whether the song was self-authored. Regardless of the origin, she found herself involuntarily swaying to the beat of the verse as well as the catchy hook.

Tina sang:

After taking the town
A nice place to lie down
Soft music and French Champagne
Kisses while calling my name
Hard thrusts became the refrain
So good they drove me insane—

With me quite aware—
I let you come inside there—
To make me feel—
As good as I did the last time.

No matter what you've done lately
I just want you to take me
Then I need you to make me feel—
As good as you did the last time
Oh baby, no need to won–der
All the stress I've been un–der

Gonna tremble like thun–der—
When you make me feel—
As good as I did the last time

Tomorrow, come if you may
Forget about yesterday
All left that I have to say
Is thanks for giving today
Much more in e–ve–ry way—
To make me feel—
Even better than I did the last time.

The applause and yelling of the crowd conveyed to Kelly that Tina's performance had been received with the fervor measuring up to its delivery. With overhead lighting restored to its normal level, Tina allowed her eyes to zero in on Miss King's position for a few seconds. It was long enough to see that the round of applause coming from the music executive was polite and unenthusiastic. Unbeknown to Tina, and dictated by The Label's credo, Kelly was bound to exhibit a stoic, professional decorum externally. On the inside, however, she was outrageously impressed—rating the performance a "Triple-A" for Absolutely, Astonishing, and Amazing. Tina had proven her versatility—demonstrating a reserved ceremonial serenade at the wedding and a seductive, feisty, and energetic performance at Club Trevi's. The test scores to be used in Kelly's report to Walden Records were off the chart—high marks in singing, dancing, stage presence, sex appeal, spontaneity, ad-libbing, and crowd approval.

20

BACKSEAT BUSINESS

MAKE like a bird and fly away were the big bad chauffeur Chadrick's instructions to Carlton. He was supposed to bring Tina outside the club and deliver her to the backseat of Miss King's town car and then disappear. The business meeting was moved outdoors because the club was too noisy to conduct a civilized conversation—regardless of its brevity, which had been predetermined by Kelly King. Of course, Carlton paraphrased the instructions, ignoring the part about flying away. Unlike Manuel, he wasn't the least bit intimidated by the big and breaking bad chauffeur. He proceeded with helping Tina into the backseat of the town car, closed the door, pushed Chauffeur Chadrick out of the way, ran around to the other side, and slid in—sandwiching Kelly King between him and his little cousin. If Tina's look could administer execution by electrocution, Carlton would have received a fatal dose of electrical current—intended to be cruel and unusual punishment.

Responding to Tee-Tee's unspoken disapproval, Carlton vocalized his reply. "I'm not leaving your side all night, just as you ordered."

Kelly said, "Excuse me?"

Carlton responded. "Kelly that was not meant for you, but this is. Didn't our little Miss Bettina Charles steal the show by giving her all to the audience?" Carlton answered his own question. "Um huh, yes, she did. Tina, you did your thing, girl! You showed up and turned it out! What did you think, Kelly? I'm all ears because inquiring minds need to know."

Lighting a cigarette, Kelly was still wrapped tightly in her uppity business disposition. She responded matter-of-factly. "Miss Charles, your performance was impressive and I'd like to discuss it further tomorrow morning. Brunch at my hotel, The Renaissance—say around ten? It's my departure day, so I need to complete all business early."

As badly as Tina wanted a big break, she was emotionally and physically exhausted. Her psyche was wired to deploy a force field designed to lessen the pain of rejection, especially about her music. After Carlton lied to Miss King earlier that day, Tina had already run a mental scenario of losing the opportunity to connect with Walden Records. Therefore, a portion of her determined spirit had shifted to contingency mode and moved on to her next steps—hitting the pavement and knocking on doors upon reaching New York City. Tina's nothing-to-lose attitude surfaced as brassy arrogance and irritation. "You want me to come to your hotel to discuss *what*, Miss King?" she asked. "I know I'm talented—more than good enough to be a professional performer. If you don't think so, I'd rather end this tryout for an audition tonight. Like yours, my time is extremely valuable. I will be leaving town as well. I'm catching a plane tomorrow evening." Tina extended her right hand. "It was nice meeting you."

Not able to believe what he was hearing, Carlton interceded, reattaching the surname to display serious sincerity. "Miss King, Tina was dropped on her head earlier today right after the wedding and the effects are just starting to settle in. She will be at the Renaissance in the morning as you requested."

Tina spoke up. "I beg to differ. I'm quite sure that I won't be there. No offense, Miss King, but this is starting to feel like a game of stringing me along. As a standard, I try not to play games that I have no chance of winning."

Once again, Kelly's ears honed in on Tina's strange accent. She was caught off guard by the eighteen-year-old's bluntness, but not surprised by the obstinate demeanor. It felt to Kelly like a young and spunky self-portrait. She fought back an outward grin, thinking that Tina had stolen all of her lines. *She's trumping my urgency with her own valuable time and plane to catch. Miss Bettina is too much. Her born-to-be-a-starlet package even comes complete with the impatience and smugness of a Diva.* Kelly was curious about the nature of Tina's trip, but she knew an inquiry would be inappropriate and too casual. She reasoned that her little sister was correct. She had seen more than enough of Tina's talent and was definitely presenting her to Walden Records. The additional inquiry was to carry out the personal business of learning more about her birth father and his family.

Kelly directed her response to Tina, not Carlton. "Miss Charles, your candor is refreshing and you're absolutely right."

"She is?" Carlton added.

Kelly ignored him and continued with her comments. "You've been working your ass off all day and have earned the right to more information, so here it is. I want you in a booth in our New York City studio to cut a demo very early this Monday morning. My assistant Angela will contact you regarding the arrangements."

Carlton said, "There is no problem because we were flying out to New York City tomorrow anyway. It has to be a God-thing."

Kelly continued. "The morning meeting has a related but different purpose. I've heard and enjoyed your singing, but I've spoken to you very little. I'd like to learn more about you and some of the older members of your family—no offense intended, Carlton."

"None taken and instead of hearing about our family, you can meet them, if you're willing to come to Joseph-Lee Manor—I mean, our house in Scotland Neck. What about twelve thirty? The grand marshals of our guardian parade will be at church—not available to meet and greet until then."

Kelly thought that she had hit the jackpot, thanks to Carlton. *In one fell swoop, I get to chat with my little sister, meet relatives, and see the house where Donald Leonard Charles grew up.* "Yes, Carlton, that makes sense. The meeting will be at your house in Scotland Neck—the same town where the wedding was held, correct?"

Feeling back on track, Carlton dropped the formality. "That's right, Kelly. From your hotel, you pass right by the church and keep going for about a mile before reaching our house. You'll see a plaque that reads Joseph-Lee Manor."

"Miss Charles, I'd like the time to remain the same—ten o'clock. That will give me the opportunity to speak with you alone before meeting the rest of the family."

With an air of finality, Carlton said, "That sounds like a plan to me."

Kelly placed her hand on Tina's knee and asked, "Miss Charles was my explanation detailed enough for you?"

After a big toothy smile that lasted about five seconds, Tina's serious expression returned as she extended her hand. "Yes, Miss King that was an incredible amount of information. I appreciate you giving me this opportunity and I guarantee that Walden Records won't be sorry. It's been a pleasure, but I won't take up any more of your time. Thank you and I look forward to seeing you tomorrow—our house in Scotland Neck at ten o'clock."

Tina shook Miss King's hand and quickly exited the town car, leaving Carlton behind. "Kelly, it might not look that way, but Tina is super happy for this opportunity. It means everything to her. Well—toodle-loo—gotta be going. We'll see you tomorrow."

Before he exited the car, Kelly placed her business card into Carlton's hand. "Please give this to Miss Charles for me and I insist on seeing her alone in the morning. If that doesn't happen, my visit will be extremely short." As well as her professional information, Kelly's direct line to her office and her home numbers were handwritten on the back of the card.

Carlton exited the town car, ran back to the club, found Tony, and pulled him outside. As they smoked cigarettes, he shared details of the music executive encounter. "That heifer Kelly King ticked me off, insisting that she spend time with Tina alone. She may not know it yet, but me and Tina are a team. She threatened to make tomorrow's visit very short otherwise. I don't give a flying Frisbee about her little threat. I don't like when people command me around—hiding her warning by wrapping it in a calm, cool, and collected package."

Tony offered reason. "As a manager, sometimes you have to swallow your pride and do certain things for Tina's sake."

"You know what Tony? You always serve sensibility in your cups of sweetness."

"Baby, you deserve more than that. I wish I could leave with you and Tina, sneak into Joseph-Lee Manor, spend the night, and make you feel so-so much better."

"That would be yummy delicious, but somebody's got to get the four flat tires back to Scotland Neck. Unfortunately, Tony, tonight, it's your turn." As Carlton and Tony looked in the direction of the four cousins' parked car, their personal instruments were being loaded into the trunk by two multi-purpose members of Manuel's staff. In varying degrees of severe inebriation, Duberry, Clevon, and Cornelius were passed out in the back of the Impala. Rufus was dazed in the front passenger seat, and Tony was holding the keys to the old, but reliable, Chevy. Before parting company, a passionate kiss was exchanged between the two lovers. Then, Carlton sat behind the wheel of his red mustang and looked to his right at Tina. She slept soundly; the bell had rung and deemed her unable to continue.

Unlike many past experiences, this safe arrival home from Club Trevi's was absent any drama. There was no mischievous behavior, no illegal driving, and no stumbling up the walkway in the wee hours of the morning. Similar to the past, physical assistance was required to get one member of the duet into the house. This time it was Tina who needed to be aided and abetted. Effortlessly, Carlton carried her petite body through the private side entrance to Joseph-Lee Manor. He did so gently, without the least bit of disturbance to her peaceful flotation on a slumber's cloud. Tina's deep-sleeping stage had arrived quickly. It involved slow brain waves, no eye movement, or muscle activity.

As soon as Kelly entered the door of her hotel suite, she kicked her shoes off, reached for the phone, and called her boss. It was almost 9:30 p. m. on the West Coast, so she made an educated guess of Arnie Peters's whereabouts and called the number that corresponded. It was his personal line in the lounging area of his downtown Los Angeles office. He waited until after the third ring to pick up the phone's receiver. Only a handful of people had that particular number and he was a 100 percent certain that the caller was Kelly King. Thinking that she wanted additional time off, he spoke with intent to annoy. "Hello, Peters here, who is this?"

"Hey, Arnie, you know that it's me." Kelly braced herself for sarcasm and worse.

He chuckled. "Hello, Miss I'm On Vacation. How the hell is the world treating you out there, close to the unemployment line?"

"Ha, ha, Arnie. That's quite cute, but my vacation ended officially this morning. I've been busy busting my tail all day and I know you're going to be happy with my results."

"I'm almost afraid to ask, but what am I going to be so happy about?"

Celebrating her accomplishments in advance, Kelly poured herself a glass of champagne and undressed while she talked. "Arnie, I think—I take that back—I know I have what you've—what we've been looking for. I found Walden Records' next wow factor! She has the potential of being our biggest discovery ever."

Arnie demanded, "Whoa! Whoa! Slow down! Your words are muffled. What did you find?"

"Sorry, Arnie, I'm excited and I'm trying to get undressed at the same time."

"Now, I'm getting excited with you and wish I was there to witness your disrobing."

Kelly lifted the conversation back up to the level of business. "Yes, Arnie, I said that I found her. The search is over."

"And you're that sure? Please, proceed. Give me details. Can she sing—as in sing Pop—while top-charting R&B?"

"Yes she can, absolutely."

Annoyed, Arnie asked, "Absolutely what? I asked a series of questions."

"Yes, she's an incredible singer, one of—no, the best I've heard and without musical embellishments. Yes, she sings the hell out of Pop and with a European accent, if you like. And yes, she'll top the R&B charts—as sure as three-day-old bread will be stale."

"You kill me with those backward Baltimore expressions. Anyway, here's my next series of questions. Is she fat, unattractive, a ghetto queen, a country bumpkin, or a combination of my hell-no checklist rolled into one? We don't have time for a lot of grooming. Does she have stage presence? Answer my questions quickly and then tell me the bad stuff. I have a late meeting over cocktails to attend."

"I'm sorry for the hesitation, but I'm just over the top excited about this one. For the first time, mountains of prep work won't be necessary."

"And yet, I'm still waiting for my answers."

Before responding, Kelly inhaled a big gulp of air. "The answers to your specific questions are no, no, no, no, no, and yes. No, she's not overweight—not thuggish—not loud, not boisterous, or unsophisticated. Yes, her stage presence is amazing. She is quite shapely and cute as hell—gorgeous to the point that the camera will love her. She's extremely polished and dominates the stage in a way that keeps all eyes focused on her. She's perfect for The Label, but—"

"But what? I knew one was coming, so spit it out quickly, please."

"Well, she has a unique personality—sort of a pistol. She's self-directed, confident, sometimes cocky, and has a snappy tongue that will bite back hard if challenged."

"Are you sure you're not describing me or you?"

Kelly laughed, realizing that she had captured his full attention.

"Arnie, I find Tina to be—"

He interrupted. "Stop right there. Her name is Tina? I don't like it."

"That's her nickname. Her full name is Bettina Bethany Charles."

"Hell, no, on Bethany, but I'm jumping the gun. Stage name conversations are moot points anyway if she fails to impress me."

"I'm confident that your interest will be piqued."

"Well, you're not one to throw yourself in the ring to promote a lousy product, so I say go ahead with it. I want something to review no later than COB Friday."

"I can do better than that. I'll have a demo on your desk no later than Wednesday morning."

"Quite ambitious, but I'll hold you to it. Make sure the package is clean and complete—audio, video, and stills—no buts or excuses. I'm signing off now, good-bye."

After tending to Tina, Carlton escorted Aunty Gina upstairs to the sitting parlor of her large and comfortable quarters. The original occupant of the room was Master Donnie (*Donald Joseph Leonard Charles*) who built the home in 1846. After the untimely death of his barren wife Lucy, he moved his beloved slave Sadie and their two children (*Joseph Leonard and Josephine Lucille Charles*) into the plantation house. Within the interior of those walls, they lived as a close-knit family.

Seated comfortably in her sitting room, Carlton asked a question before giving his after party report. "Do you think this room is called the master suite because it was the quarters of the slave master?"

"I don't know, but it kinda makes sense. Do you see why Momma Nin and me sent you to beauty school and Tina to college?"

"Actually, it's Momma Nin and I. Tee-Tee corrects me all the time."

"That's what I'm talking about. Both you and Tina have good heads on your shoulders and I expect that you use them in New York City."

"Aunty Gina, we're going to be fine. By the way, we're supposed to be sharing that joint you sucked down to nothing."

"Forgive my selfishness, but age sucks before beauty, nephew darling. Besides, I haven't smoked this stuff in years. It does help with the pain I'm having about you guys leaving. Now don't forget to never introduce Tina to the bad choices we've made."

"Aunty Gina, I love her too much for that."

"Light another one up for the road or sky in this case. It's a salute to the two of yawl's flight to New York City."

Carlton and Aunty Gina looked in Larry's direction— still asleep in the adjoining bedroom. "By the way Aunty Gina, regarding tomorrow, Miss Kelly King asked to speak with Tina alone before meeting the entire family. That means your church plans can go on as usual. I'll just hang out with Tony at The Salon myself."

Aunty Gina was troubled. "How dare she order me out of my own home! Her high and mighty lifestyle stops before crossing the door sill of Joseph-Lee Manor."

"Aunty Gina, that's the same way I felt about her demands. Offended or not, we must behave ourselves for Tina's sake."

"For my baby girl, I'll have the house cleared out by ten in the morning, but that's where Eugenia Fae stops being ordered around."

After giving her the highlights of the after party, Carlton kissed his Aunty Gina on the cheek and headed down the hall to his bedroom.

2:30 a. m. — Carlton and Kelly's surrender to slumber was gradual, involving similar rituals. They both were sitting up in bed smoking a cigarette and consuming a nightcap—he next door to Aunty Trudy in Scotland Neck—she in a hotel room in Greenville. Both were in some level of contemplation regarding the events that had unfolded the way they had in the past twenty-four hours. With cravings fed, sleep followed a slight distance behind. The long emotionally charged day had melted away, bit by bit, like a candle left burning.

3:30 a.m. — Startled, Tina struggled to reach her blanket. *My private place is uncovered, it's hard to breathe, and something is in my mouth. I am extremely cold and frightened. I smell whisky and feel sharp pains down there like someone is stabbing me in the same place again and again.*

The shock of the imagery awakened Tina completely. Immediately, she was relieved that another nightmare had interrupted her sleep. The pain, however, was real. Her cycle had started and her cramps were severe. She went to her private bath, took two pain pills, showered, changed her nightgown, and put a pad in place. Returning to bed, she thought, *My body has a weird way of alerting me about pain. There has to be a better delivery option than these dreadful nightmares.* As Tina's spirit settled, her pain subsided. Then, deep sleep overtook her.

21

CITY LIMITS

ALTHOUGH she was not attending church this beautiful Sunday morning due to the meeting set by Miss King, Tina spent thirty minutes in prayer. She kneeled at the window in the corner of her bedroom by the side chair. Her petition to God was saturated with requests for intervention and deficient in her usual praise. Over and over, she repeated her appeal, beseeching the Lord to intercede in an enormous way. Because of the varied behavior of her cast of characters, Tina's prayer was very specific.

She prayed:

> *Dear God, please don't let my great-aunties embarrass me in front of Miss King. Make them behave and not talk about my makeup or my hair or my clothes. Change their nosiness into niceness. Bind up all butt squeezing and school-girl squealing in the presence of our guest. Dispatch a saint, other than Aunty Trudy, to testify and taunt the transgressions of others just until Miss King leaves Joseph-Lee Manor. Don't let anyone make Carlton mad enough to start cussing people out. And last, but real important, God, please keep Aunty Zooni busy grading papers at her own house. If she does finish grading those papers, make her Cadillac break down on the way from Hobgood to here. In Jesus's name, I pray, Amen.*

After repeating it for a third time, Tina was satisfied that her prayer was delivered successfully. To her surprise, Aunty Gina worked in concert with her to prepare breakfast, to speed up its consumption, and to rush everyone out of the house immediately after it had been eaten.

"I'm alone at last," she sighed and performed a final, unnecessary cleanliness check of the main floor's already immaculate surroundings. While placing refreshments in the Great Room, Tina was overcome with emotion about it being her last day living in Scotland Neck. Although excited about moving to New York City, she was sad about the reality of leaving the comfort of the familiar, especially Aunty Gina, Professor Milton, and Willie Chambers. Refusing to have a pity-party, she refocused on the situation at hand—the getting-to-know-you session with Miss Kelly King. While sitting on the third step near Joseph-Lee Manor's front door, she reviewed her mental script of the topics she planned to cover. At the same time, her ears were alert, awaiting the sound of a car pulling up the driveway.

Since Mount Pleasant Hill Baptist Church was on the outskirts of town, this was Kelly's first introduction to the municipality itself. From the car window, she saw fields and farmhouses and woods disappear as the country road slammed into the town. This caused the car's tires to screech as her driver's cruising speed reduced abruptly from sixty-five to thirty-five miles per hour. The unexpected decrease gave Kelly's body a jolt and her mind an eerie feeling of déjà vu, comparing it to Orleans Street's sudden merge with Pulaski Highway. The slowed pace extended Kelly's glance at a green sign that read Scotland Neck City Limits.

Kelly was twenty minutes early for her appointment with Tina. "Chadrick, let's burn the extra time by passing the destination and driving the length of this tiny town."

"Yes Ma'am, twenty minutes is plenty of time to see both sides of its three-quarter-miles worth of real estate."

Kelly reasoned. *I can impress the Charleses by having some knowledge of their hometown while getting a feel for the environment that had nurtured Donald Leonard Charles.* Rivaling any classic novel or movie depiction, Main Street did not disappoint. It had a wide avenue, two lanes of traffic in both directions, and cars parallel parked on the curbside. "Chadrick, I've never seen diagonal parking in the middle of the street."

"With this one exception, I haven't either and I've driven all over these parts."

Although three signal lights and several stop signs legally managed the minimal traffic flow, civility was the actual governor of movement across intersections—people jumped to be first at cordially yielding the right-of-way. "Chadrick, I find this town's charm to be best depicted in its two-story, brick façades. The bright and colorful awnings seem like those fake ones on movie sets."

"Yes Ma'am."

Some of the retailers lining that side of Main Street included a five-and-dime, a convenience shop, a drugstore, a furniture center, and two national fast food chains. Kelly associated some of what she saw with what she had read in a guide book about historic Halifax County. It was presented to her by First Lady Marylou the day before as a gift of hospitality. She compared photos to real life, matching up the modest list of social venues—Smokey's Bar and Lounge, the firehouse's weekly bingo, an all-night diner, a video arcade, and a movie theater. Trudy's Cut-n-Curl and Sir Charles's Barbeque Pit ranked high on the county's list of most popular businesses—both owned by members of the music executive's newfound family. She deduced, *My business-savvy gene must have come from my birth father's lineage.*

Kelly felt validated upon learning that Scotland Neck was first settled in the 1700s by Scottish Highlanders. *That fact provides a possible explanation for my fair skin, freckles, and reddish-brown hair.* Another article featured Joseph-Lee *Manor* as a historic landmark and provided commentary on how the estate had acquired its name. After a U-turn, Kelly viewed Main Street's opposite side on the trip back down the three-quarter-mile stretch. Her eyes connected with Willow-Matt's Funeral Home, a florist, a savings-and-loan, a Laundromat, and the offices of an attorney-at-law bail bondsman who also prepared taxes. As a final touch and convenient placement, a gas station was positioned on that end of town.

☙

Because of the incline and the distance of the house to the road, Joseph-Lee Manor's all-inclusive splendor wasn't completely visible until reaching the top, leveled portion of the driveway.

Oh my goodness, Kelly gasped. *The enormous columns and side entrance make this place look like a "Gone with the Wind" plantation. It's complete with whitewashed wood siding, black shutters, and dormers. How could it be anything else but a historic landmark?*

Kelly stood on the edge of the blacktop driveway and journeyed with her eyes before taking her first step toward Joseph-Lee Manor. She admired the geometric layout of the terracotta pavers, noting that their reddish color was a contrast to the natural greenery of the landscape. She heard her amplified heartbeat as she followed the pathway to the porch and climbed the four stairs. In less than a two-week span, she had gathered a lifetime's worth of information, landing her at the entryway to her birth father's family home. *This is it; I'm here, and ready or not, it's time to go inside.*

Before Kelly could ring the bell, one of the double doors opened. "Hello, Miss King, and welcome to Joseph-Lee Manor. Please come in."

"Is it possible to lower the volume of the formality by calling me Kelly?" she asked with a broad smile as she extended her hand.

"I'll work on it, but it will take time for me to get to that point of comfort," Tina explained. "Our first two brief encounters—on the church grounds and in the backseat of the town car—favored the side of strictly business and my naming game seems to be stuck on Miss King."

"That's fair enough." Kelly's head moved right, up, and left as she stood inside the two-story foyer. "This house is amazing. They don't build them this large and extravagant in Baltimore, where I grew up."

Tina didn't know how to respond so she moved forward. "Just as you hoped, we're alone. My Aunties Gina and Trudy, Uncle Ed, and Larry are at church. My Aunty Zooni is at her own house and Carlton is at Trudy's Place, our family's hair salon."

"Since I was early, I viewed the town from end to end and passed a beauty parlor along the way. Is that the one you're talking about?"

"If you passed a salon, it definitely was Trudy's Cut-n-Curl because there's only one hair dresser in town." Tina paused, tilted her head upward, and spoke with entitlement and pride as a Charles-Watkins-Smith clan member. "My Aunty Trudy opened it thirty-seven years ago in 1945 and it's been thriving ever since. In the last three years, it's been even more popular because of Carlton's talent and management style."

Hoping for a yes, Kelly asked, "I take it that Carlton will keep minding the store while you're pursuing your music career?"

Tina was emphatic. "He absolutely will not! We just brought on two graduates from Roanoke Rapids Beauty School, plus my cousin Hattie Mae, and Tony is the new manager. Other than when I'm with my father, Carlton goes where I go. We're a team. When he was fifteen and

I was ten, we made a pact. He said that Scotland Neck was our state of suspended animation. When we leave this place tonight, Carlton and I leave together—period, plain, and simple."

Struggling not to show her disappointment, Kelly contemplated, *This Carlton issue is a bump in the road—a slight problem that I'll find a way to gloss over.* "I think your loyalty is commendable."

"Not mine as much as Carlton's. He's twenty-two years old, has been off probation for almost two years, and could have left any time after that. He waited for me, and that's commendable."

Kelly followed Tina a few feet into the living room. *Did she just say probation? Great! That's another item on my find-a-way-to-spin list.*

Tina said, "I have a quirky habit of naming things that are important to me. This one is huge. Please meet Willie Chambers, my baby grand Steinway."

"So you play?"

"Yes, I do, and very well, according to my grades at ECU and Professor Milton, my piano teacher."

"Isn't ECU a university?"

"It is. I've been going there for two years as part of an early admissions program."

"Your background continues to get more impressive by the minute. You're quite articulate and have a sexy, sellable accent that I don't recognize."

"Nobody does. I guess it's a mixture of my moving about. Until I was ten years old, I lived in Europe in a military township in Germany. My adopted father and I still spend time there when we can. His name is John Chapman, but I call him Pappy John. He retired as an Army General and recently moved to Washington, DC. He's staying with a friend until his apartment is ready at the end of this month. I'll be taking care of the decorating because he is clueless about things like that."

Although having prior knowledge about the adoption, thanks to First Lady Marylou, Kelly maintained her deception and asked, "Adopted?"

"Yes, my birth father and mother were killed in a car accident when I was a baby. But I'd prefer not to discuss the details."

"Enough said. I'm very sorry about that." She turned back to Willie Chambers. "May I hear you play?"

Unaware of house rules, Kelly sat on the end of the burgundy chaise, placed there for aesthetics instead of for sitting—except for Aunty Zooni, the author of the stipulation. With no witnesses, Tina ignored the offense, sat at Willie Chambers, and gave a four-minute sampling of "Mozart's Piano Concerto No 22." It was her most difficult piece, presented as her final exam in Advanced Piano Classics. Kelly did not expect this demonstration of talent in a classical playground—fingers rising and falling gently on the keys and an effortless delivery of rhythm and expression. Tina ended her instrumental appetizer with a series of runs, playing notes in rapid succession up and down the keyboard. Kelly rated Tina's abilities as *HGT*, for highly gifted and talented and began to clap. "My! My! That was quite impressive. This weekend has been full of surprises and coincidences. I came here to attend Katrina's wedding and she happened to be marrying the son of your piano teacher. Meeting you is an unexpected pleasure." Caught up in her twisted reality, Kelly admitted, *At least that's partly true.*

"Your coincidence is my blessing. Professor Milton was going to introduce me to a friend in the music business once I got settled in New York City. Before that could happen, you showed up in Scotland Neck as a mystery connection that neither he nor I knew existed. Whether known or unknown, I met you because of the Professor. I'm really glad our teacher-student relationship ended with me doing something to make him happy, which was singing in his son's wedding."

Kelly was under the impression that, if things went well, Walden Records would have to work around Tina's scholastic pursuits. Now, she was in need of clarification. "End it? Isn't he a professor at the college that you are attending?"

"Yes, he is, but I'm taking a break from college. I'm stepping out on faith and following my dreams all the way to New York City. Our bags are packed, our flight leaves at eight o'clock tonight, and our apartment is ready to go. The part we didn't have figured out was how to make a demo and get it to the right people. With you offering that opportunity, all my plans are lining up in perfect order much more quickly than I expected. God is the only way to explain miracles like these and I'm really grateful."

Kelly wondered, *Oh, Tina, I wish I could predict your reaction to knowing how deeply entangled I am inside your miracle. Is this the moment I whisper the truth into your unsuspecting ears?* Feeling no heavenly signal of God trying to tell her something, Kelly let the moment pass, opting for self-preservation. She remembered her promise to deliver Arnie a demo by Wednesday and decided not to make a move that could potentially jeopardize that outcome. She reasoned, *After all, it's what Tina wants, so I'm looking out for her best interest.*

Instead of confessing, Kelly listened to Tina describe her well-chartered course to invade the island of Manhattan. She quickly deducted that Miss Charles's profile was not the typical rags-to-riches story. It was clear that pursuing a career in show business had been set in motion far before their chance encounter and would continue with or without the assistance of Walden Records. She deducted that she had been preempted by a unique support system that included emotional guardians in Pappy John and Aunty Gina and the financial advisement of an attorney, an accountant, and a banker. Although mentioning her trust fund, Tina gave no details regarding its stipulations or the peculiar involvement of her grandparents—the faceless Chamberses.

The reality check for Kelly was that a relationship with her younger sibling was not for sale. It was incapable of being purchased with possessions and pompous posturing. Though she had never used it for personal reasons, like taking vacations, Kelly would not be ordering up the private company jet because Tina and Carlton's first-class tickets to LaGuardia Airport had been secured for some time. Also, there'd be no inviting her little sister to stay at her Upper East Side condo because Tina had her own Upper East Side condo. Unable to manipulate the itinerary or circumstances, Kelly abandoned her futile efforts to accumulate easy brownie points. Instead, she shifted her focus to the personal pursuit of digging around the roots of the family tree while holding loosely to branches of professionalism.

22

A PRAYER GONE WRONG

TINA escorted her guest to the Great Room where she had prepped the coffee table with a pitcher of lemonade and another filled with sweet tea—plenty of ice in both. There was an assortment of cookies and banana sandwiches that were cut into little squares. In Kelly's Baltimorean mother tongue, a Great Room and Family Room were synonymous. This one had a gaming table in one corner and a recliner in another. A long sofa, a rocking chair, and an antique table-top grandfather clock were also part of the furnishings. Kelly's wide-angled scan of the room revealed porcelain whatnots, a collection of unique ashtrays, and a few vases holding fresh flowers. Prominent wall space held portraits of slain heroes—Jesus, King, Jr., Malcolm, and both Kennedys. Every console, table, and shelf not holding books or picture albums showcased dozens of family photos presented in small-to medium-sized uniquely designed frames.

Venturing within the interior, Tina and Kelly stood about four feet away from the room's focal point, a massive fireplace. It had a brass frame and screen and was surrounded by an oak cabinet man-telpiece—detailed with handcrafted carvings and finished with dark-cherry-colored shellac. Without externally reacting or appearing distracted, Kelly's eyes connected with the photograph that was her primary point of interest. *The man in that photo must be Donald Leonard Charles because many of my features are so similar to his. It's quite eerie and disconcerting.*

Tina boasted. "I call this fireplace's casing my *Mantel of Honor* because it holds photographs of very special members of my family." She paused momentarily and then continued. "To the far left is my Great-Grandpa Joe. His son and the person this house is named after is to the far right—my Grandpa Joseph Lee. Next to him is his wife Big Momma. They are my Momma Nin's parents."

The new big sister continued to look at the pictures. *They belong to me too—my Great-Grandpa Joe, my Grandpa Joseph Lee, my Big Momma, and yes, your Momma Nin is my Aunt Nadine.* Kelly had pieced together a fairly comprehensive family tree, thanks to the assistance of First Lady Marylou, other newfound relatives, and now Tina. Her insight increased as the heritage presentation continued. "My family is filled with lots of double-cousins like me and Carlton because brothers and sisters from three families married each other," explained Tina. "The relatives forming the love triangle are mainly a mix of Charleses, Watkinses, and Smiths."

Anxious to finish her oratory on family history, Tina inadvertently skipped Donald Leonard Charles and focused on the mantel's center photograph. Her concisely presented profile of Momma Nin covered much. "My Momma Nin attended Howard University, had a successful career in the army's nursing corps, and was one of the first black female colonels. She received her surgical training at Walter Reed Army General Hospital and served as charge nurse at several mobile surgical hospitals in Korea where she met her beloved husband and my Pappy John." Winding down her family overview, Tina hailed a doting mother that had succumbed to a heart condition, resulting in a premature death. She grabbed two items from a bookshelf that were enclosed in separate clear acetate pouches and shared them with Kelly King. The first was a family tree of sorts and the other was a yellowed-with-age clipping from an army magazine. The article contained a photo of Pappy John and Momma Nin posing together in formal ASUs—Army

Service Uniforms. While not reacting outwardly, Kelly was surprised to discover that Pappy John was a white man.

She read the caption aloud.

> *A brave and true military team, making things happen for America on European soil—General John Archibald Chapman and Colonel Nadine Bethany Charles, September 7, 1960.*

"Your Momma Nin keeping her maiden name was quite a bold move and modern approach for a time of rigid traditions," noted Kelly.

"Miss King, my parents married in 1951. Because of the ugliness of racism, much in their lives was kept separate. When returning home to the States for business or pleasure, their motto was secrets for safety and survival, especially the married name Chapman." Tina stated these words emphatically.

"I feel quite dim-witted for not reaching that conclusion on my own and grateful that you omitted the word *dummy* from the end of your last statement."

"I could never think of you in a negative light because I believe that you're brilliant and successfully infiltrated a career position with few opportunities for women."

"How perceptive you are Miss Tina, so let's continue now that I've climbed out of the jaws of ignorance to say that you're blessed to know so much about your family's heritage."

"My Momma Nin left me journals—more than two hundred letters about her life, about me, and our family. She painted wonderful pictures for me through her words. So far, I've received two volumes. They are a part of my inheritance, you see."

"Do you have a sample of one of the letters?" Kelly asked, hesitantly.

Without reservation, Tina said, "I have more than a hundred of them so far, but nobody sees my letters—not Carlton, not Pappy John, not Aunty Gina—nobody."

"Forgive me for intruding on something so personal. Changing the subject, once again, I do have another nosey question. How are your Aunty Gina and Momma Nin related?"

Tina was happy to answer the question, but wanted to establish some ground rules. "Although they were raised as sisters, my Momma Nin is the niece of my Aunty Gina. They're only two years apart and my Aunty Gina is the youngest although my Momma Nin is her niece." Tina paused to make sure appropriate emphasis was placed on her next statement. "If our relationship continues beyond making the demo, I'd like many of the things I'm telling you about my personal life kept private."

Kelly responded. "Not if, but when we get to that point, we'll sit down and address those concerns."

"I really appreciate your understanding and apologize if I sound a little punchy."

Because Tina was being so appreciative and apologetic, Kelly felt it was a good time to slip in the question she'd been dying to ask—hoping to bring into play a dialogue about Donald Leonard Charles. She pointed to the frame on the mantel, yet to be discussed, a photo of a young male soldier. Trying her best to appear matter-of-fact, Kelly asked, "So, who is the handsome young man earning a spot on this Mantel of Honor?"

"That's my birth father, Donald Leonard Charles—my Momma Nin's baby brother." Tina saying his name made it official—jarringly real to the big sister. Inwardly she acknowledged, *Donald Leonard Charles is my birth father. Tina and I share a strange commonality. We each have loving living fathers and a mutually shared dead one.* Once again, Kelly took a mental drive over a recurring speed bump. *What should I do with this secret sister discovery? Nothing right now,* she told herself.

As Tina returned the news clipping and family tree to the shelf, Kelly watched with curious apprehension—not knowing what to expect. Growing impatient, she waited. *Sister or not, Tina is the most secretive, distrustful, and eccentric young person I've ever met. Is she going to make me stand in front of this damn mantel for the entire visit?* As if sensing what her special guest was thinking and with a photo album clutched to her chest, Tina escorted Kelly King to the sofa. After inviting her to sit down, she presented her with what she considered to be a national treasure—not for its content, but because of its creator.

"My Momma Nin truly loved her baby brother and made this photo album to highlight his journey. You can look at it if you like. The layout and handwritten captions are unique and show my mother's creativity."

Arnie had trained Kelly well, so she called upon her skills as a bold-faced liar. "I'm very intrigued by art found in a person's unique handwriting. I would love to look at the photos—I mean examine the album's inscriptions." Kelly reasoned, *Maybe she's not that bad after all.* Tina was conveying warmth as best she knew how, as it was being felt physically on the bare arms of both women. The intensity of the July sun shined brightly through the three panels of windows—curtains held wide open by elegant gold tie-backs. Caressing the book delicately as if it was the Holy Grail, Kelly took possession of the album. She felt a bit guilty about her self-gratifying slyness but was impressed by the success of her deception.

The Great Room's two sofas had five loose decorative pillows scattered about. Kelly took the one from behind her back, placed it on her lap, and used it as a lectern to hold the irreplaceable artifact. She leaned forward, studying each photograph of the man responsible for bringing her into the world. Her thoughts were jovial and giddy as each image revealed something new. *That's my nose, my chin, my ears, my freckles. That's my smirk and the way I stand.*

Kelly used her eyes as a camera and her brilliant mind as a depository, imprinting each image of her father into her memory bank. She didn't want to alarm Tina by extending her gaze longer than what was customary—as she perused the photo album of a supposed stranger. Much too quickly for Kelly, she handed the precious album back to Tina, noting the exact placement of the priceless relic on the shelf. She pondered while looking at the pitchers of lemonade and sweet tea. *I could refuse these cold beverages and ask for a cup of coffee. Once Tina is out of the room, I could slip Donald Charles's album into this Louie briefcase. No one would miss it right away.* Such street-worthy thoughts demonstrated Kelly's desperation to connect with her birth father's lineage.

Intrusively, the even-keeled atmosphere was disrupted with commotion and voices coming from different directions. Aunty Gina, Larry, Aunty Trudy, and Uncle Ed entered Joseph-Lee Manor's kitchen from the back screened porch. Carlton came through the front door, rushed down the hall, and reached the Great Room before the church attendees could make it out of the kitchen. He was elated that his return to Joseph-Lee Manor had been timed perfectly. Having removed his shoes, he used his socks as skates and slid across the hardwood floor to his cousins' position. The two women stood up to greet him. "Hello, Kelly. I hope you enjoyed your alone-time with Tina. Obeying orders, I stayed away just like you asked."

"And, I thank you for indulging my request."

"Since Trudy's Place was closed today, I drilled Tony one last time before turning over control to him. Come Tuesday morning, he'll be in charge. In addition to Sunday, the salon is also closed on Mondays." Carlton was leaving Trudy's Cut-n-Curl and his precious red Mustang in the reliable hands of his steady. Although afraid to express it, he had strong feelings for Tony—much deeper than he knew how to handle. He made a confession. "Checking on Trudy's Place and the Mustang will give me an excuse to stay in constant contact with Tony. I'm really going to miss him like crazy."

The mature residents of the house grew closer to the Great Room. "Ready or not, here they come," said Carlton, "the older members of the family you wanted to meet—Aunty Gina, Aunty Trudy, Uncle Ed, and Larry." Sensing apprehension in Tina and Kelly, he spoke to his elders first. "Y'all are still supposed to be in church. It's just eleven thirty."

Aunty Trudy said, "Assistant Pastor Yates preached and ten minutes is all he can do, plus two more for his ending whoop."

Aunty Gina added. "And that worked out fine because I'm not comfortable with strangers in the house when I'm not here."

I guess I'm the stranger, Kelly surmised.

Attempting to prevent an avalanche of negativity, Tina jumped in. "Aunty Gina and Aunty Trudy, this is Miss Kelly King." Introductions of Uncle Ed and Larry weren't necessary because the two men were huddled in the corner on the far side of the Mantle of Honor.

Gina extended no handshake, just words, clarifying Tina's introduction. "Hello, I'm Mrs. Eugenia Fae Watkins-Charles and this is my sister Mrs. Gertrude Watkins-Charles."

Despite the cold reaction from her great-aunts, Kelly pressed forward with a cordial response. "Mrs. Watkins-Charles and Mrs. Watkins-Charles, it's very nice to meet you both."

Tina whined. *This is not the day for my two Good Fairy Aunties to act unfriendly.* Knowing their seating preference, Carlton brought two of the nice padded, high-backed wooden chairs from the formal dining room. Thinking of them as thrones, he positioned them to face the sofa where he, Kelly, and Tina were getting ready to sit, in that order. The coffee table served as a neutral buffer zone between the two generations.

After everyone was seated, Aunty Trudy broke through the ice. "Praise report, praise report. Guess who joined the church today? Larry opened up his heart, walked down the center aisle, and gave Jesus his hand. Once he's baptized and receives the right hand of fellowship, he'll be a welcomed member of the church."

Thankful for a pleasant topic, Tina shouted across the room. "That's great news—congratulations, Larry."

Aunty Trudy added. "And maybe that's one step closer to him and Gina stopping their sinful fornication, letting their flesh be used by the Devil."

Tina cringed. *No, no, no, Aunty Trudy. Don't go any further.* Carlton was determined to keep the train on the tracks. He took requests and distributed cold beverages to everyone. Tina took a long sip of her drink and Kelly followed. From there, the sky darkened. Zooni stormed into the room, instructed Uncle Ed to bring her a dining room chair, and sat down beside her sisters once it was properly positioned.

"Carlton Andrew Charles, I had to muddy my tires and risk denting my Cadillac to make my way around your little hot rod," scolded Aunty Zooni. "Next time, I'm gonna ram right into your bumper."

"That will keep your precious Caddy dent free," mumbled Carlton.

"What did you say?"

Gina jumped in to prevent a verbal assault. "Miss King, this is our older sister Arizona Watkins."

Prepped from before, Kelly was ready. "It's very nice to meet you, Mrs. Watkins-Charles."

"My name is Arizona Watkins. Ain't ever been hooked up with the Charleses and never will." Far from the truth, she had been engaged to a Charles, Carlton's grandfather, Andrew Charles, Sr. He was a handsome and kind man who had broken off his engagement to her and married Rebecca Smith instead. Being shunned by Carlton's grandfather was the reason for Aunty Zooni's displaced anger toward her great-nephew.

"I apologize. I guess I got things mixed up a little."

"A lot more than a little—and please, don't make that mistake again."

"Yes, Ma'am."

Trudy said, "It's kind of funny that me and Gina have the same last names. We married brothers. My husband Ed is over there in the corner—a Godly man and loving husband. Gina's Henry had wandering eyes—run off chasing skirts some time ago."

Zooni barked. "She doesn't need to know all that. And look at this coffee table. Trudy, I can't believe you put out those nasty banana sandwiches for a guest."

Kelly reasoned, *At least, my mean Aunty Zooni thinks of me as a guest.* Attempting to gain some positive points, she put one of the bite-sized banana sandwiches in her mouth, took four quick chews, and swallowed. Internally, she screamed, *I hate mushy foods.* "This little treat is quite tasty," complimented Kelly.

Trudy offered instructions. "All it takes is soft white bread, sugar-downed mayonnaise, and just-ripe bananas."

Zooni laughed, "Do you really think she's gonna run home and try your disgusting recipe?"

Aunty Gina spoke pretentiously. "I would've skipped church altogether and made more suitable refreshments, perhaps brunch food, if I wasn't ordered out of my own house."

Tina was having a difficult time gauging her guardian's loyalty. *Aunty Gina, you hardly ever make a full breakfast these days. You're supposed to be siding with me—not teaming up with Aunty Zooni.*

Volleying the negativity like a beach ball, Zooni asked, "Why is a big black man leaning on a big black car parked in the back of our house? His front tires are pressed down on the tomatoes in our garden."

Carlton said, "*Our* house and *our* garden? You don't live here. And why do you always gotta bring up color?"

"Because I only got two topics for you—tar baby or sissy, pick one."

"That was so uncalled for. I'm so glad that all I got is a few more hours to put up with your meanness."

As things started simmering, Uncle Ed walked over to the end of the coffee table and bent to shake Kelly's hand. "It was nice to meet you, Ma'am, but I need to excuse myself. I gotta spray pesticide in the fields."

Instead of shaking hands, Larry extended his well wishes from afar. "Ma'am, you take care." He walked over to Gina and she stood up. Larry gave her a hug, slid his hand down, squeezed her butt, and whispered in his deep voice that everyone could hear. "I can't wait to see you later—Ed, wait up!" The two men successfully escaped the Great Room.

Of course, Gina giggled. "Bye, Larry, see you later."

Tina placed her hands on each side of her forehead, slid her fingers down the long strands of her hair, and sighed. *My prayer has gone wrong. God, I asked for these things not to happen. This is a disaster.* She looked at Carlton with eyes begging to be rescued.

He reached around Kelly and grabbed Tina's arm, pulling her up and over to his side. "Kelly, just like you told me, I called your assistant Angela, who was very helpful. She explained how things are going to flow tomorrow. Tina and me-I mean—Tina and I will see you then. Right now, we have some last-minute errands to run before leaving for the airport."

Kelly stood and spoke with desperation in her voice. "You're leaving right now?"

"Absolutely," smirked Carlton. "This will give you time alone with our great-aunties. As I recall, that is your preference."

Kelly excused herself and walked a distance away to speak with Tina and Carlton in private. Hastily, she had learned a valuable lesson. *No more excluding Carlton. His retaliation is quick and really stings. Pouring salt into my wound, he's taking Tina and leaving me to suffer this interrogation alone. He definitely has the balls for entertainment management.*

At the outer edge of the Great Room, facing away from the Iron Ladies, Kelly held hands with Tina and Carlton and smiled. "I'm looking forward to the demo session. A limousine will pick you up—the two of you—from your apartment at seven in the morning. Our work at Walden Records starts promptly at eight. You should prepare to be there for ten to twelve hours. Make sure you're well rested because there's dozens of things we have to get done. My expectations are extremely high." Tina and Carlton went one way—leaving Joseph-Lee Manor. Kelly went the other—back into her great-aunties' fiery furnace.

Once outside Tina asked, "Where are we going? We can't leave Miss King alone with the three of them. My prayer has gone completely wrong. They'll torture her."

"If we stayed a few minutes longer, I would've exploded and you would've flooded the Great Room with tears. There was no point in the two of us helping things go from bad to worse." Although he did

not mention it to Tina, he was still slightly pissed at the music executive. "Kelly King will be fine," assured Carlton. "She's a grown-ass, big-
time business woman, right? If she conquered the world, she should be
able to handle the female version of *The Three Musketeers.*"

After picking up his steady from Trudy's Place, Tina, Carlton, and
Tony waited out the storm from the shelter of a booth in the diner.
They ate a little, talked a lot, dropped quarters into the miniature juke-
box on their table, and listened to their favorite tunes.

23

GREAT AUNTIES' GRILLING

DISCUSSING logistics about the next morning's demo session bought Kelly precious minutes to brace for what was certain to be incoming fire. She returned to the interior of the Great Room and stood on the sofa side of the coffee table barrier, waiting for instructions from her great-aunts. *Would they be more cordial if they knew I was their great-niece?* she wondered. *I'm really not sure—probably not.* As it did earlier during Kelly's one-on-one with Tina, the sunrays continued to stream through the three window panes. This time, instead of warming skin, it cast a spotlight on each older woman, adding an effect of superiority. As the inquisition commenced, the great-aunty committee of three spoke as a chorus. "Have a seat."

Zooni gave an additional command. "And scooch over—dead-center the sofa—so that we can get a good look at you."

Kelly appealed to her ego and sensibilities. *I don't have to subject myself to a great-aunties' grilling. Remember, Tina's going to New York with or without me. I should run for the door before my newly found feelings get hurt. Thanks a lot, Donald Leonard Charles. Oh damn, what do I do—what do I do?* In a few seconds, which seemed like minutes, Kelly reached a decision, sat down, and positioned her body in the center of the sofa as directed.

"It's a pleasure to be invited into your lovely home. It's absolutely breathtaking on the inside and out," said Kelly, with overemphasized delight. "There's an article about it in the county's historic manual, but the photo does no justice in capturing the magnificence of this fabulous estate."

Trudy said, "Oh, you talk just like Tina—proper and citified."

Zooni leaned back in her high formal dining room chair and folded her arms. "First Lady Marylou's been handing out that damn guide book again. How many copies did they print? Apparently, she's got them all."

Kelly looked for courage by scarfing down two more banana sandwich bites. "I can't seem to stop eating the little treats."

"See, with each bite, they taste better and better," bragged Trudy.

Zooni intended to be confrontational. "Must we talk just for the sake of talking? Miss King, I read three articles on you—New York City by way of Baltimore and back to New York City. They call you a no-nonsense drill sergeant. Why did you come to Scotland Neck and why are you still down here?"

"I came to attend my cousin's wedding. My schedule was freed up because of a long overdue vacation," Kelly replied with a hint of defense in her tone.

"And a wedding in North Carolina was at the top of your list of places to go? How often do you get to this part of the world?" asked Aunty Zooni.

"Just like Tina and Carlton's closeness, Katrina is my best friend and cousin. I had to support her and this is my first time down here." Kelly reasoned, *The atmospheric conditions in this room fluctuate from scorching heat to a freezing cooler. Being influenced by these three jewels, no wonder Tina is secretive and distrustful.* "I liked what I heard at the wedding and wanted to hear more. The second performance was quite impressive, so I invited her to come to New York to cut a demo for Walden Records. As you already know, Tina was headed there anyway. It seems that things are working out miraculously. At least, that is how your great-niece described the circumstances to me."

Trudy retrieved her glasses from her pocketbook to take a good look at the guest. "Now, you're talking my language! Miracles are God made. You kinda favor our family. Who are your kinfolk?"

"I beg to differ," Zooni rebutted. "Lies, lies, and more lies. She don't favor the Watkins clan—not one bit, but who are your relatives down here?"

I should take this opportunity to tell them the truth—to introduce myself as the long-lost sister to Tina, cousin to Carlton, and great-niece to the three of them. They'll probably throw me out with a good tongue lashing and an old-fashioned kick in the hind-parts—as my Nanna-Weezy would say. Kelly refreshed her lemonade as she pondered. "My family lives in Tarboro and my father and Katrina's father are brothers. You probably know them—the Browns." Kelly praised herself, *Great job at quick thinking. Katrina's father really is a Brown, but he doesn't have a brother. They'll never know. I just played my Harriet Tubman card, jumped in the river to fool the dogs. That should throw them off my scent.*

Gina finally broke her silence. "This town is very small, Miss King, so news travels fast—especially when it's about a meddling music executive. Word has it that you and First Lady Marylou were very chummy during the wedding. What you didn't know was that her primary purpose in life is to spread the good news of everybody's business," Gina said with a boldness that caught Kelly by surprise.

Trudy quickly added. "About that reception, people who were there came up to us at church, saying that you were asking questions about us. Why's you so interested in our family?"

Gina chimed back in for another round. "Then, at that Trevi's after party, Tina's little band of cousins—Rufus, Duberry, Clevon, and Cornelius—were quite bothered. Hungover or not, they are Mount Pleasant Hill's musicians for Sunday church services. This morning, they talked about overhearing you asking about Tina."

Zooni finished the grilling. "So, Miss King, if you want to know something about my great-niece or this family, you come directly to one of us in the future—if there is a future. You don't snoop around. My sisters and I don't take kindly to that sort of thing."

"Yes, Ma'am, I understand and that's why I'm here right now—to let you know my intentions. When I engage with a hopeful, it is customary for me to meet his or her family. I learn a great deal from that exchange."

Gina needed clarification and asked, "So, in your world that's how you see her. My Tina is your company's latest hopeful?"

Business savvy to the core, Kelly gained strength from her professional IQ and streetwise instincts, allowing her ego and anger from rejection to guide her thoughts and pronouncements. *I've dealt with people much bigger and badder—real cut-throats. I refuse to continue to be steam rolled by these three older ladies without putting up a good fight.*

"Yes, Ma'am, that is correct. At this point, that's what she is to Walden Records—a hopeful, who, in most cases, amounts to nothing." Kelly's personal opinion overrode her anger. "On the other hand, I see a promising future in Bettina Charles."

"Now that I believe," said Aunty Gina. "To be honest, my gut tells me that there's something deceitful about you. But, where my Tina's talent is concerned, you see what I see and know what I know—she's something special. I can tell she means more to you than odds and predictions. Anyway, I thank you for your support of Tina."

Kelly said, "The pleasure is all mine."

Quickly, Gina's strictly business attitude returned. "I have one final thing to say about this matter. If this game we just finished has a rematch, we will play it fairly. I have responsibility in Tina's affairs until she turns twenty-five years old. You come to me first, before you go to her. You ask me—don't tell me something that's already been decided. I hope that's clear?"

"I understand completely," Kelly said, as politely as she knew how, while trying to end the inquest. She envied the depth of love that the great-aunties had for Tina. *I'd pay dearly to have some of that.* Then a realization hit her. *Based on some of my moves since coming to North Carolina, I've literally already started writing checks.* Kelly decided to compliment the trio. "From the bottom of my heart, I want each of you to know that Tina is blessed to have three guardian angels that care for her so deeply."

Zooni expressed intention. "That's right, three great-aunties who care for her so deeply that they have no problem flying to New York City and whipping up on some ass if they need to."

Trudy strengthened her sister's threat with scripture. "You say so, Zooni! For the Lord said, 'He will deliver you into my hands, and I'll strike you down and cut off your head.'—First Samuel seventeen forty-six.—Praise the Lord for His Word."

Kelly's mental sigh was deep. *That's not the comeback I was looking for. I can't gain an inch with these three.* "Mrs. Watkins-Charles, Mrs. Watkins-Charles, and Miss Watkins, I thank you for your hospitality, but I must be going in order to be on time to catch my plane." Kelly shook each of her three great-aunties' hands, turned quickly, and rushed to the town car.

Upon deplaning, two of the Upper East Side's newest residents gravitated toward a man holding a sign that read Bettina and Carlton. As a welcome surprise, a limousine was sent by Kelly King. Tina and Carlton's upscale apartment was located on 86th Street near the Guggenheim Museum and Park and Fifth Avenues. Upon their arrival, two bellmen rushed to the limousine and grabbed luggage. Although the natural lighting had been extinguished by nightfall, the street lights provided adequate illumination for Tina to see Windsor East, the building that was her new home. Upon walking up three wide red-carpeted steps, the doorman said, "Welcome to Windsor East." Tina entered the lobby, looked up, and spun in a complete circle, absorbing it all—three crystal chandeliers, other decorative lighting fixtures, massive floral paintings, sculptures held on white stone pedestals, and parquet floors. *Our new home is more elegant than Carlton described and far greater than I had imagined.*

Carlton recognized and responded to Tina's look of being well-pleased as she nodded in the affirmative. "See, I told you, it was nicer than Teddy Pendergrass and Prince put together."

"Yes, you did."

By the time Tina had finished her 360-degree twirl; an overly animated person bounced over and introduced himself. "Good evening, Miss Charles, I am Curtis Frazier, office manager and chief concierge. I remained on post to greet you personally." In actuality, his presence was insisted upon by Kelly King. Curtis Frazier extended his arm and gave a very weak handshake. Tina smiled politely. *Pappy John says that a silent sign of strength in character is demonstrated through the power of a person's grip. Momma Nin said that certain behaviors are like a for sale sign—advertising the price of a person who can be bought for two cents.* Tina's first impression concluded that the frail handshake plus the exaggerated tone labeled Curtis Frazier as a two-cent purchase—unable to be trusted.

The Chief Concierge continued. "Just to give you some of the highlights, there is a resident-only bar, a fitness center, and a roof deck for grilling and relaxing. Although this is one of our older properties, Windsor East is one of our most preferred because of its location, architecture, and overall amenities. There's a waiting list because the average room size is much larger than most of our newer properties. In addition, the concierge service that we provide includes making reservations for dinner as well as procuring the best tickets to sporting events, the theatre, and concerts."

Carlton colorfully expressed his approval. "Tina, this ain't nothing but the truth on a day when everybody else is trying to lie to Gabriel to get into the pearly gates."

Curtis Frazier went further into his stamped-out overview. "Please follow me to our main security desk. As is the case with maintenance and the door and bellman services, security operates twenty-four seven." Curtis handed Tina a trifold brochure. "This is a listing of contact numbers for the services offered here at Windsor East as well as important tidbits. Now, I'd like to introduce you to Bernie Bazemore, one of our evening security guards. He has been an important part of the Windsor Group for more than twenty years. We felt it only befitting to place him here at our most popular property."

Bernie stood, leaned over the counter, and shook Tina's hand while lowering his head. "It's a pleasure to meet you, Miss Charles, and you can call me Bernie."

Firm grip, I like that. "It's nice to meet you also. I'm probably going to bother you a lot, so please call me Tina."

"There are house rules that require a *Miss* handle be attached to the front of your name."

"And I have been taught the same thing, Mister Bernie." Tina's brain computed warmth and kindness exuding from the face and voice of this fifty-seven-year-old man. Ahead of a process that generally took weeks, Tina was experiencing the pleasure of warm feelings. Bernie's presence lowered her overly cautious and distrusting flag to half-mast. Nonetheless, she was grateful to be in the elevator, headed to the twenty-fourth floor, to apartment 2407, and away from Curtis Frazier.

Once inside their apartment, Tina sat Brief de Vaughan down gently against a wall and restarted her twirling. She noticed floor-to-ceiling windows that stretched along the entire side of the jointly shared living and dining area. The window treatments were a spectacular accent as was the custom hardwood flooring that covered the entire square footage of the spacious accommodations. Finally alone with her best friend forever, Tina started squealing joyfully while jumping up and down. "Oh my God, Carlton, do you believe it? We are here in New York City in our own place and it is wonderful."

The living room furniture was classy modern that was finished in a neutral color. There was a plush, chocolate brown sectional surrounding an entertainment group with a centralized large television. The remaining seating was a set—all beige with polyester/rayon blended cushions, leather arms, and decorative wood feet with scalloped molding. The pieces included a love seat, a recliner for Carlton, and a chair with an ottoman that was set off in a corner by a window for Tina. There were also a two-tiered coffee table and a familiar glass curio that held Tina's doll collection. She could not bear to leave her precious dollies back in the sitting room of her first-floor suite in Scotland Neck.

Positioned in one of the corners was a six-foot tall artificial Ficus tree—looking nearly natural with silk leaves—held in a brown, plastic planter with matted moss. There was a rented piano in another corner, nowhere near the quality of Willie Chambers. The walls throughout the apartment were accented with color from lithographs of twentieth century black artists, including the masterful work of Varnette Honeywood. As she stood in her New York City apartment, absorbing its surroundings, Tina was extremely proud of her cousin/best friend. "I know it took a lot for you to set aside your glitzy self-expression. Everything screams classy-modern, the motif I whined to you about for weeks."

"Mister Montgomery knows he's thorough and fierce is as fierce does."

Through phone banter while Tina was in Colorado, both cousins agreed that the apartment's most amazing feature was it being retrofitted with two master suites. Using the momentum of her excitement, she ran into Carlton's bedroom. Her feet stopped themselves on the inside of his door. Surely, she had entered the room through a time machine, dropping her off in the early seventies. Like Joseph-Lee Manor's Great Room, Carlton had plenty of whatnots scattered about, but most of his were phallic to some degree. The entire space was multicolored, filled with lava lamps and black lights, which allowed his zodiac sign posters to glow in the dark. Some artwork was vintage black power, dominated with beautiful faces sporting huge afro-bushes. Of course, his largest posters featured the entertainers Teddy and Prince. Tina wondered, *What does my bedroom look like? There's nowhere to go from here, except to the deepest pit of tacky.*

Tina ran out of Carlton's room and into her own, which was located at the other end of the apartment. Upon entering, her mouth opened, her eyes popped out, and she started to sob. She was instantly elevated to a place of delight. There had been much deliberation and so many hours spent viewing catalogues, as well as actual visits to the furniture capital of the world in High Point, North Carolina. Tina's cottage-white furniture fit in her master bedroom perfectly. There was plenty of open space between her queen-sized bed, its foot bench, nightstands, mirrored dresser, and her vanity table and chair. Combined, they had a light and airy feel. There were satin nickel-colored knobs as well as two-tier molding insets on the front of each piece of furniture. The whiteness of her furnishings was counterbalanced by rich crimson bedding, curtains, rugs, and other accessories. Her private bath matched her overall décor as did Carlton's in his unique master suite.

The final room Tina inspected was the designer kitchen. To both cousins' surprise, a thoughtful gesture had been set before them. "Look at this," Tina gasped. Their eat-in kitchen table had been dressed, holding a welcoming spread—French Champagne and imported caviar on ice, hickory smoked summer sausage, cheese, and crackers. There was a card reading: "Welcome to Windsor East"—signed Kelly King. After filling their plates, Tina and Carlton sat on their private balcony overlooking a spectacular view of the urban landscape. They gorged themselves, eating and sipping Champagne to an above-moderate degree. It dawned on them that they hadn't eaten since midday at the diner in Scotland Neck. While enjoying the gourmet snacks, Tina expressed repetitious appreciation. "You and Tony did such an incredible job on decorating the apartment and I know you worked really hard. I thank you, I thank you, and I thank you so much."

Carlton screamed. "You are welcome and that's the last time I'm saying those words about this apartment. If you say thank you one more again, I'm gonna take all this Tina classic-modern furniture back and get the stuff that I really wanted to buy." His Tee-Tee received the message and ended her rounds of many thanks.

After placing Brief de Vaughan in the special safe designed for him in her bedroom's walk-in closet, Tina completely shut down. Although later than desired at half past midnight, a shower, a call to Aunty Gina, another to Pappy John, and prayers were quickly followed by sleep.

3:26 a.m. — Tina was shivering uncontrollably, sitting on the floor in the corner of her walk-in closet in her bedroom at Joseph-Lee

Manor. Her arms were wrapped around her knees as she rocked back and forth. There was excruciating pain originating from her vaginal area and the reason for it had yet to register in her spirit. Tina cried out loudly in her mind. *Aunty Gina, I need you so badly right now. I hear you calling my name, but my voice box won't work. I'm unable to move from this position, so please find me quickly.*

Tina opened her eyes to find herself wrapped in an ultra-soft, down feather-filled comforter. She could hear faint street traffic sounds and see skyline lights from her windows' open curtains. With reasoning restored, she understood that she was in her new bedroom at Windsor East, apartment 2407. She used that information and her voice as calming agents. "Bettina Bethany Charles, you are in your New York City apartment, cuddled comfortably in bed, and are extremely safe. There is 24/7 security that's just a push away, using this emergency button on the nightstand." Sleep arrived during the midway point of the eighth utterance of her reassuring mantra.

24

THE DEMO

Monday, July 12, 1982

"**AIN'T** this a bitch," said Carlton. That was his response to the place of disembarkation. The limousine dropped Tina and him off in an underground parking garage. Having spent seven consecutive years in an environment of fresh air, grass, trees, and flowery fields, they were claustrophobic by predisposition. They had no idea what the Walden Records' building looked like, but this totally obliterated their expectation. The shared pipe dream was that of people pausing to watch them exit the limousine, them stepping onto the sidewalk, and passing under a marquee that named the record company. In the vision, other hopefuls were there, but they were the lucky ones to be granted access.

In actuality, their experience was quite humbling. Instead of fanfare, Tina and Carlton were told to walk in the direction of the word *ELEVATOR*. It was painted in large red letters on a cement wall adjacent to glass doors that were their entry point. The actual witnesses to their grand entrance were three armed security guards—focused on procedural processing only. Tina mumbled. "Welcome to showbiz."

The next stop was a counter where two additional guards were seated. They were asked to sign the registry—input date, print name, indicate person visiting, and insert the arrival time. The next step was a problem for Tina because the ID that verified her identity was back at Windsor East inside of Brief de Vaughan in her closet safe.

Carlton scolded her. "I can't believe you don't have your ID card."

Tina snapped back. "It's your job to remind me of things like that, so from now on, you keep the stupid card." She had yet to transition from her backpack to a woman's handbag. She gave Carlton no leniency even though he was weighed down with her garment bag and a small suitcase of accessories. She had been instructed to bring two performance outfits and The Lovely was prepared with head-to-toe accents.

Carlton stepped in front of Tina and smiled. "Mister Security Man, unfortunately my acquaintance has left her purse and is unable to produce said identification. Can you please contact a Miss Angela whose last name escapes me? She, however, is the assistant to Miss Kelly King and can verify Miss Charles's identity."

Behind the security area, a manager holding a clipboard entered from a secondary room. "Bettina and Carlton Charles follow me right this way. Sorry for the mix-up, but you entered through the wrong glass doors."

Carlton smirked with an attitude of entitlement and victory. "Now that's more like it. In the future, please make our presence known to your staff."

"Consider it done, sir." The manager pointed to the set of doors they should have used, took photos, and created security badges with a chain to hang around their necks. Tina was cognizant of the fact that the ID lanyard now adorning her neck rested on top of *Love Golden*. Upon the security manager turning a key and pushing a button, they were on their way to the fourteenth floor. It was The Label's main receiving area. Although owning the entire building, Arnie Peters made a hefty sum leasing the first thirteen floors of his empire's headquarters. Some of his corporate tycoon acquaintances classified the twenty-four-floor structure as a low-to-lateral-rise as opposed to a full-fledged skyscraper. For Arnie, flying below the radar was a business strategy. He often boasted. "I have no problem running behind the big dogs, catching their fleas, and collecting the benefits that are attached."

When the elevator opened, Kelly and her Assistant Angela were standing there in front of a Walden Records' logo, blown up to gigantic proportions, covering floor-to-ceiling wall space. The iconic emblem was a recognizable fixture, appearing point-central on each of The Label's vinyl records. With an icy air, Kelly scolded. "You're late! Not acceptable."

Carlton defended. "Your watchdogs would not let us enter."

"Angela, make sure that issue is corrected."

"Yes, Ma'am."

Although five years separated Assistant Angela's age from Kelly's, Miss Executive Vice President insisted that her support team address her formally. It was her way of forcing respect for the corporate executive position that belonged to a person who happened to be Black and a woman. The one exception was Carlton. She was going to pick her battles with him carefully, and calling her *Kelly* was not worthy of an altercation.

Although anxious to get started, Kelly allowed her guests to walk around the reception area while she reviewed a checklist with Angela. The space was a brightly lit, airy showroom with marble flooring and a large receiving desk that accommodated three receptionists. The waiting area's design was a modern decor with comfortable leather seating—eight armchairs and a sofa. One wall was dedicated to six thirty-two-inch monitors continuously streaming music videos and concert excerpts. Kelly took them through glass doors to a gallery that displayed awards, sheet music, concert programs, and ticket stubs. There were framed poster-sized photos capturing milestone events throughout The Label's history. Also showcased was a priceless collection of memorabilia that included costumes, jewelry, handwritten song lyrics, newspaper clippings, a drum set, and several guitars autographed by the artists.

"Now, it's time to get busy, so follow me." Kelly worked her four-inch pumps hard, walking at a pace that required a slight jog from everyone else, except Carlton. He took extra-long strides with the length of his legs. As they rushed down a long hallway, Assistant Angela introduced herself, hands occupied with pad and pen. Tina and Carlton received the message that all activities had gone live and the mood was serious business. Taking an indirect route to the preparation department, Kelly guided them down a hallway entitled Corridor of Distinction. platinum awards were displayed on the walls that were replicas of million-dollar-plus selling albums. The engraved plates listed the artist or band, the album's name, number of copies sold, date, and name of the record company. With so many, the awards were a mere six inches apart. Although gold records were deemed such by ARC with a minimum of five hundred thousand copies sold, one million and up was Arnie's threshold for what merited celebration in this hallway. Those gold placards missing his mark were displayed in the memorabilia gallery that Tina and Carlton had just whizzed through. The opposite wall was covered with familiar faces of Walden Records' recording artists. Tina made a mental note to herself, *I plan to make it on both sides of these walls as fast as my hard work can get me there.*

After passing the wall adornments, they followed Kelly out an exit door, up four flights of stairs to the sixteenth floor, which was called *Center for Music and Choreographic Preparation.* Absent bells and whistles, this floor was lined with rooms reserved as rehearsal spaces. What Tina found interesting was the configuration. There were two doors close together—the first was panel-molded, textured, had a brass identifying number, and a narrow vertical window on the upper-left half, above the doorknob. The other door was solid oak with no frills. There was about twenty feet of wall space before reaching the next pair of doors with the same setup. Kelly stopped at Rehearsal Room 1604, the largest practice space, and knocked five times using a specific rhythm—*knock-knock—knock-knock-knock.* A strong, lively male voice said, "Enter, enter, if you're looking for a mild-mannered

Muse named Ellis." While Carlton and Assistant Angela remained in the hallway, Kelly stood behind Tina, grabbed her by the shoulders, and gave her a gentle nudge.

Receiving the cue, Tina moved forward into Room 1604. The featureless, brightly lit space contained a grand piano, a padded bench stretching across one wall, and an office chair positioned at a small desk, holding a phone, a container filled with sharpened pencils, and four-stacked bins filled with different colored paper. A second wall was dedicated to a one-way mirror—showing a normal reflection on the rehearsal side and a transparent window in the adjoining darkened observation booth. This explained the strange configuration of doors that Tina observed in the hallway. *There's one room for working and another for watching. I'm sure that judging of a hopeful's ability to keep up takes place in the observation room.* Tina was absolutely correct. All rehearsal rooms and studios were similarly configured, enabling Arnie, Kelly, and other executives to engage in covert monitoring. In addition, support staff, such as personal assistants, could be stationed nearby while not being disruptive.

Ellis stood up and caressed Tina's wrists with both of his hands as he pulled her toward him. His body frame was tall and thin and he took pride in describing himself. "I'm an eccentric, dreadlock-sporting, horoscope-quoting hippie forever." His locks were tamed and pulled back into a ponytail. Based on the fact that they were eighteen inches past his shoulders, they had been growing for quite some time.

Kelly said, "Ellis Ross, meet Bettina Charles."

"It's a pleasurable treat to meet you, little lady. There's been much said in a short time—many doubts, but I'm here to make them all believers. A brother from Washington State has a unique point of view—less tainted by the sinkholes of racism."

Tina asked, "You're from Washington State?"

"Born and bred in Seattle, little lady."

To Tina, that was a sign of a person ingrained with progressive thinking.

Momma Nih Lullaby Letter Excerpt

Seattle is where Pappy John and I were allowed to marry for the second time with the help of the Friends Encircled Organization.' After being married by the chaplain at the American Embassy in Korea in 1951, our nuptials were deemed null and void/not legal upon reentering the lower forty-eight—the supposed land of the free—for some. Beyond the true battlefield and upon finding a state that acknowledged interracial matrimony, we retied the knot on American soil—in Washington State in 1953. ■

Ellis Ross was a record producer extraordinaire and musical genius in motion. His talents included composing, arranging, and conducting. His instruments of choice were the piano, trumpet, and trombone, although he played several others proficiently. His long, thin, and lightning-fast fingers were ideal for use in his profession. Until reaching the rounded hook on the end, his nose was slender, and he had a pointy chin that matched his face nicely. His mustache was a bit thicker than what Tina considered to be ideal, but not unruly. His thin red bottom lip was a focal point because of its contrast to his milk-chocolate complexion.

Tina grabbed Kelly's hand, squeezed it tightly, and bunny-hopped in place two times. "Are you serious? I get to work with Ellis Ross—for my demo—really?" *Calm down, you have magic to do,* she reminded herself. She quickly regained her composure, staring at the slender face of someone she admired. He had deeply inset, coal-black eyes, which explained why the press described his gaze as *hypnotically piercing and sinister.* On the contrary, his eyes revealed to Tina a man with a healthy reverence and intense passion for music.

Because of his natural intellect and the musical genius atop his creativity, Ellis used unconventional measuring sticks. Positive and negative vibrations guided his decision-making process regarding his involvement in musical collaborations. Based on his enthusiastic behavior, Kelly was pleased that Tina hit a grounder to left field in Ellis's ballpark. Knowing his preference for one-on-one interactions, she left the two kindred-spirited musicians alone to become immersed in the ethereal realm of creativity. Carlton followed Assistant Angela, who followed Kelly away from Rehearsal Room 1604 to the executive offices. There, a multitude of tasks were waiting to be tackled.

Sharing the piano bench, Ellis ran through scales and other drills to get a feel for Tina's range and vocal IQ. He was quite impressed. About an hour into the session, he presented a sampling of three songs and had Tina sing segments of each to determine which was best suited for the demo. Periodically, the managing creative director and Carlton would enter Rehearsal Room 1604's observation booth to assure that all was going well with Tina and Ellis. Kelly instructed Carlton to knock on the door, introduce himself as a personal assistant, and ask if they needed anything. After administering *knock-knock—knock-knock-knock*, Carlton posed the question. As if meeting him for the first time, Tina's clinical answer was yes she required an additional something. Upon receiving further instructions, Mister Montgomery dashed away and retrieved a portfolio of sheet music from Tina's garment bag. Other than ad-libbing a colorful and comical word here and there, Carlton executed his duty as instructed, and Kelly was parent-of-a-child proud of his first music industry accomplishment.

It dawned on the older cousin executive that she had gained knowledge about family solidarity from her great-aunties' grilling session. She caught herself using a tiny bit of nurturing when dealing with both Tina and Carlton. As step one for Tina, she was with Ellis, the mastermind musician. Carlton's initial stride was shadowing Assistant Angela to learn the tricks of the trade and Walden Records' way of doing things. When opening her eyes beyond her judgmental tendencies, Kelly saw Carlton's many gifts and decided to let him dibble and dabble in various disciplines until he recognized more of his abilities and chose a path for himself.

⁓♌

After doing all that Ellis asked her to do and now in possession of her precious material, Tina unveiled her own pencil-created sheet music. "I'd like to start with this one," she insisted. "It's called 'Tell Me How to Love You.'" She played a beautiful melody, adding extra chords not on the musical score in order to show her piano prowess. Confirming what Kelly had told him, Ellis was impressed by Tina's musical reach as well as her self-assurance. *Look at the poetic license she's taking! I presented her with three studio songs and she's acting as if that exercise never happened. I know I must have planted a seed to create this musical whiz kid in an alternate universe.* Rejuvenated by Tina's total package, his new life's goal was to help her move his vision forward into the next generation.

As they worked through "Tell Me," Ellis assisted Tina with developing a bridge in the song's place of greatest impact as well as applying his genius in musical arranging overall. They used the colorful paper from the four bins to write instrumental parts of harmony and counterpoints. Both sides of the paper had twelve, preprinted staves. Ellis explained to Tina that each color represented a different instrumental family. Blue was for brass, white for strings, lime for percussions, and yellow for woodwinds. Ellis directed Tina as they wrote concepts for the guitar, drum, horn, and keyboard parts of the song. Then, entering 1604 from a smaller adjacent rehearsal space, the studio band joined them for Tina's first authentic creative jam session.

Assistant Angela and Carlton were busy coordinating on-the-fly demands from the creative team, including the ordering of food. Carlton was in love with his new job and all of its varied responsibilities. He had no intention of abandoning his talent as a stylist, but enjoyed the versatility of this position. Instead of being idle when there was no styling to do, he remained busy with coordination duties. He particularly enjoyed the fact that Assistant Angela and he were at the top of the support staff food chain, managing all logistical service activities.

After working with the genius maestro for twelve straight hours, Tina felt the burn of stretched muscles. In one setting, she had received tutelage that enabled her to, already, lift heavier weights as an artist. In this first connection, a great deal of the time was spent becoming acquainted musically—immersed in exchanges about technical and creative theory. It reminded Tina of the years spent under the wings of Professor Milton, who would always be the provider of her musical foundation. Tina hoped, however, that the time spent with Ellis Ross was the beginning of an anointed and appointed musical merger. She was open to his guidance, ready to be taught how to crawl, walk, and ultimately fly as a vocalist. She reminded herself. *Remember that the first hurdle is to get Arnie Peters on board.* By 10:00 p. m., they not only had one song, but they also had the framework for several others.

When the sample demo was finished, Ellis had a good report for Kelly. "I'm really digging this whole scene. Tina's a musical whiz kid, sharing my loose and free philosophy about the creative process, you know, not forcing things. My vibe and her fresh natural instincts made musical love tonight that was out of sight."

It had been a long day, but all were present in the rehearsal room to hear the final product—Tina, Ellis, the Studio Band, Carlton, Assistant Angela, and Kelly. Upon hearing the refined version of "Tell Me How to Love You," all expressed their unique display of pleasure. The studio band gave each other high fives. Assistant Angela patted her thighs and stomped her feet. Kelly displayed an expression of relief followed by a smile of joy and claps of approval. "Bravo!" she yelled. "I'm quite pleased."

Carlton stood up, raised his arms high in the air, and performed a swinging-hips victory dance. Tina burst into tears, having waited her entire life to hear herself on a recording with a professional sound.

Because Kelly had refused to interrupt the creative process over the course of that day, there was no time for anything else. Believing the recording spoke for itself, she made an executive decision to deliver the product to Arnie in its current form—no embellishments through audio mixing, no photos, and no video. In fact, Tina hadn't even seen what the actual recording studio looked like. All demo-creation tasks were executed in the rehearsal rooms.

By 1:15 a. m., the demo and the long day were a wrap. Kelly complimented Tina and Carlton on jobs well done and sent them to Windsor East. She ordered them to take the next day off—which had already begun—to relax, and return to The Label at nine o'clock on Wednesday morning. Within an hour, the demo recording was on its way to Los Angeles, being flown there on one of Walden Records' company jets. It would be on the founder's desk no later than 10 a. m.

25

CONFERENCE CALL CANCELLED

Tuesday, July 13, 1982

UNPACKING was the late morning activity for both Tina and Carlton, followed by lunch, a bus tour of New York City, and a walk up and down Times Square. They also thoroughly cased the perimeter of half a dozen Broadway theatres. Their goal was to gather as much information about their surroundings as possible in the least amount of time. Although exceptionally pleased with her stellar performance on the demo, Tina knew there were no guarantees and wanted to begin the search for an alternative route to her destination. Carlton was getting antsy and arrogant. "Why are we peeking into theatres when we already got our ticket to the big time?"

"There is no guarantee what's going to happen with that demo. I prefer to be proactive out here not just sit and wait to be summoned by Mister Peters."

"You're right because I heard that Arnie Peters is a high strung asshole and an impatient slave driver."

"There are lots of record companies scattered about that aren't stamped with a Walden Records' emblem. Without a Miss Kelly King type person to get us in the door, it will be challenging, but not impossible. We both learned a great deal about the music business in our one-day at The Label."

The executive suites of Walden Records were located on the twenty-second floor. Kelly and Arnie's plush business accommodations and support staff cubicles took up half of the floor's square footage. The two dynamos' specific office suites opposed each other, separated by a state-of-the-art conference room. It was used for legalese, contract negotiations, brokering of major deals with corporate sponsors, press interviews, and schmoozing with radio station owners and television executives. Earlier in the wee hours, Kelly ordered a quiet day of cooling down for her Artists Operations' Team. It involved catching up on administrative activities, having a catered staff lunch, and a half-day dismissal. During the two week vacation, heavy pressure had been applied to her team as they attempted to fill Arnie's Pop-Diva prescription. They had taken a daily verbal lashing as he rejected each of their recommendations.

No rest for the unofficial second in command because her schedule was booked. She had a half-dozen priority return calls and a lengthy teleconference. Several times during the day, she paused, tapped her nails on her desk, and stared at her *bat phone.* The direct line was so named because it was capable of reaching Arnie from multiple locations. She dare not call him, but prayed that he would contact her. After all of his yelling out demands, he was silent once the demo had been produced under her close scrutiny. *How can he be so cruel? Especially, with me enclosing a handwritten note in the package sprinkled with perfume. I told him that we worked until one in the morning and that the entire team busted their asses to get the demo done. On top of that, we completed the task a day earlier than I promised.*

2:30 p. m. Eastern Time/11:30 a. m. Pacific Time—After listening to the demo four times, Arnie made a phone call, gave explicit instructions to his executive assistant, and left his Los Angeles office. Assistant Angela informed Kelly that Shantelle had called with Arnie-orders. Serving as a go-between, Angela said, "Arnie wants a meeting scheduled for eight thirty tomorrow morning, Eastern Time. His list of attendees includes the department heads and team leads from artist operations, publicity, sales, and the art department. He also wants to see anyone else who worked on the demo not in those departments, including Ellis Ross. He said to have the studio band onsite and to also have Miss Charles on the premises—isolated and not to inform her about any of this."

"Will you get him on the phone?"

Assistant Angela's reply delivered disappointing news. "Shantelle informed me that Mister Peters is unavailable to speak to anyone until tomorrow morning's meeting."

How dare he refer to me as anyone? Kelly breathed deeply before posing her next question. "Does she know if he reviewed the tape?"

"Yes, Ma'am. She said that he listened to it several times, gave her instructions to pass on to you, and then left his office for the day."

"Well, Angela, I guess there's nothing else to do on our end other than make calls to inform the invitees. After that, you can leave for the day. Although I don't say it much, I appreciate your hard work."

Kelly had no idea what Arnie was up to. *What does this mean? I can't believe he's not communicating with me directly. Is he punishing me for not delivering the photos and video? If he doesn't like Tina, I'm certain he's going to take it out on my team—firing people to make a point and to express his frustration. That's exactly why I keep Mister lover-man boss at a distance. He is so unpredictable.*

Kelly redirected her focus on work. She had plenty to keep her busy. She made her way through one of three piles of urgent correspondence—identified as such by their red folders. At 5:30 p. m., she called it quits and headed for the private lounge in her apartment building. From her frequently occupied booth in a corner of the dimly lit bar, she listened to jazz while nibbling on appetizers that lined her stomach like a sponge, providing absorption for her heavy cocktail consumption. By 8:00 p. m., she had her fill and retired to her penthouse. There were no messages to return, so she pleased herself with the aid of a sex filled movie. It was one of those days where her power-broker activities didn't leave her completely satisfied.

While Carlton was barhopping until midnight with André Jenkins, The Label's lead choreographer, Tina spent the evening at the piano. She applied techniques learned from Ellis Ross to improve the composition of the songs she had written, strengthening independent and harmonious musical lines. She also worked on creating bridges and developing more sophisticated intros and outros. As promised, Carlton made it home before midnight—11:50 p. m.

Wednesday, July 14, 1982

8:00 a. m. Eastern Time/5:00 a. m. Pacific Time—Partaking in a breakfast buffet, all requested parties were assembled in conference room 2101 a half hour early. The catered meal was laid out on credenzas at both ends of the room. The timing was appropriate for the East Coast team, but Kelly was not a fan of beckoning the West Coast team members to a teleconference stand-up meeting so early in the morning. Gradually, in her camp in New York City, twelve of the company's top brass staked claim to seats at the conference table. The other six team leads sat in chairs around the walls. As part of the proceedings' preparation, staffers grounded themselves internally, bracing for high-voltage shocks soon to come. They would originate from the Los Angeles office, courtesy of Arnie Peters, and be blasted through the conference loudspeakers in New York City.

A smaller version of the breakfast buffet was delivered to Rehearsal Room 1604, where Tina and Carlton were sequestered, waiting for further instructions with a guard positioned outside the room. The eggs, fried potatoes, sausage, toast, fruit, and coffee rested on a rolling two-shelf cart. Having dined sufficiently, Tina sat at the piano, practicing new rhythms that she hoped to share with Ellis Ross.

Carlton sat on the bench on the other side of the room, putting together an outfit and accessories. "I'm assuming they're supposed to take photos and shoot video using the music from the demo you recorded last night. I don't want your dress to get wrinkled in this bag. They need to hurry up and tell us something. I'm trying to act professional, but if we're being kicked to the curb, I will be forced to express some colorful words as they escort us out the door. And what's up with Mister Security Guard standing out there in the hallway? Do they think we're gonna steal something? I already looked around and didn't see one thing that was worth sending to Tony."

Tina offered consolation. "It's definitely nerve-racking, but we're still here and that means something good, I hope."

⌁

Once Kelly was seated at the far end of the conference table, Assistant Angela dialed the Los Angeles office's communications line. After three rings, she disconnected the call, looking up at an indelible image. In real time, Arnie Peters entered 2101, gracing the room with his personal appearance. He put his booming voice to work immediately. "The fact that all of you are present proves that you do know how to follow explicit instructions." Resulting from his strong push, Arnie's chair rolled behind him as he stood in its place at the head of the conference table. With everyone seated, it added elevation to his five-foot-ten stature—a two-inch embellished height with the assistance of the special heels attached to his Bruno Magli shoes.

Arnie had the most beautiful eyes—dark brown, centrally set, and crystal clear—surrounded by a brilliant white background. He was a handsome man with a baby face. He wore a shabby beard, attempting to convey a visual more in line with his actual age of forty-five.

Arnie's skin tone was cocoa brown with natural highlights, giving his face a glow. His nose was moderately broad and more so in the area near his cheekbones. His nostrils flared when the temperature of his rage soared above ninety degrees—displayed much too often. His forehead was fairly pronounced and his hair receded slightly on each side of his temple, leaving a protruding patch of hair dead center above his brow.

Arnie injected humor with intent to be sarcastic as well as piss on his territory. "I'm pleased that no one had the balls or boobs to occupy the helm position at this side of the table in my absence. Apparently, my executive vice president has conditioned you well." Kelly stared Arnie down from the head position at the southern end of the table—displaying a stoic expression accompanied by silence.

Arnie continued. "I assembled leadership from the departments represented in this room for several reasons that will be unveiled slowly as we move forward. Right now, I want you to join me in congratulating the Artists Operations Division on a job well done. I offer specific kudos to Miss Kelly King for her outstanding leadership. The demo I received yesterday was executed brilliantly. And Ellis, your role as musical director is duly noted, appreciated, and surprising. You, a maestro genius, stepped in to assist in making a demo for a nobody." Applause broke out throughout the room and dissipated as Arnie's gesture of pressing down both his hands suggested a retreat to silence. "With that said, the game starts over and the work before us will be much harder, but the reward will be great."

After looking at Kelly, the record company owner scanned the room before continuing to deliver his message prefaced with words of reproof. Although directed to all, they were specifically pointed—meant to neutralize the praise that he had just delivered as well as reprimand and annoy his executive vice president. "Since I received no visuals, either still photography or video, to accompany the demo recording, I'm here to collect them in person. Other than Ellis and the studio band, who will be part of the performance, the rest of you will serve as the test audience." Low-level murmuring permeated the room. "Auditorium 2001 has been setup like a mini concert hall with one hundred chairs that shortly will have a butt seated in each one of them."

The hall on the twentieth floor was a multipurpose space that not only could be transformed to a performance theater, but also could be partitioned into eight brainstorming war rooms. Arnie's remarks kept flowing. "In addition to company leadership in this room, the remaining spectators will be made up from the best and brightest members of your teams—your choice." Arnie's next demand was specifically directed. "Kelly, have Miss Charles in 2001, on stage, in thirty minutes. Hopefully she can entertain us with a live performance of her little homemade 'Tell Me' song." Seeing how pissed she was, he made an adjustment. "Let's make that an hour from now." Although playing the big bad wolf to everyone else, Kelly King had passion powers able to tame and reduce Mister Peters to a willing, obedience trained puppy on many occasions. *I better not piss her off too bad and punish myself in the process. She's beautiful when she's pouting though.*

Angered by Arnie's temporary takeover of her turf, Kelly looked in the opposite direction when passing by her direct report. She couldn't remember a professional moment when her heart had sunk so low. She was a few blinks away from shedding tears in front of her staff and her lover-man boss. Assistant Angela acted as a human buffer, assuring her that no one got close enough to observe Miss King's emotional Achilles' heel moment. Kelly's angry thoughts were all valid and pointed. *All yesterday Mister Peters toyed with me by maintaining radio silence. Today, he shows up unannounced, undermining me in front of the leadership team—offering empty kudos as part of his tormenting tactics.*

Ellis Ross had left the boardroom early and was already in Rehearsal Room 1604, prepping Tina by the time Kelly administered her *knock-knock—knock-knock-knock* password. He opened the door and purposely pushed her backward into the hallway. He closed the door behind him in order to have a private moment with the music executive. "Please hear me good. At fifty-nine years old, I now reside beyond the point of playing childish games and ain't crazy about watching you and your boss exchange love taps, bruising each other's feelings. However, I gotta give Arnie his props. He reached back into an old bag of tricks—pulling out proof-is-in-the-pudding, sink-or-swim tactics—a trial by fire. He's a cold bastard, but his move is one that I would have made myself. Am I worried? Hell yeah, but he'll never know and neither will Tina. Since we're putting all our money on her, we've gotta go back into 1604 showing on the outside what we believe in our hearts—that she was molded to work in this industry." Knowing that she had insider allies in both Assistant Angela and Ellis, the executive vice president snapped back quickly, regaining an offensive posture—ready to theoretically kick Arnie hard in his jewel box.

By the time Ellis reentered the room followed by Kelly, Tina was dressed in her red mini, with large gold hoops dangling from her ears and pumps adorning her feet. Carlton was well into his application of makeup. He said, "Kelly, if the speed around here is always on fast-forward, then I'm gonna need an assistant. Y'all are tripping, asking for miracles in wardrobe, makeup, and hair faster than Liz Taylor can find a new husband. The Lovely has risen to the task, but y'all need to recognize." As Carlton finished grooming duties, Kelly and Ellis fed Tina as much information as possible, pertaining to what she was getting ready to experience.

With Assistant Angela monitoring the numeric elevator side panel, she, Carlton, Kelly, Ellis, and Tina were taking the ride to Auditorium 2001. All but Tina stared up at the encircled numbers as each lit to indicate the floor—as if possessing the power to influence the movement. After the elevator stopped on floors seventeen and eighteen, Tina broke the silence with an observation. "Unlike the elaborate lobby on fourteen, the other floor's elevator foyers have a modest sized logo with lettering that indicates the division name. I think the bronze, raised lettering is seriously cool."

Only Carlton responded. "Uh-huh Tee-Tee, that's really special."

"I also like how each floor is named by the type of work being done. With so much happening here, it's easy to get confused."

Kelly expressed concern. She turned to Carlton who was standing to her left and posed a low-volume question. "Does Tina understand what's about to happen?"

"No worries. When Bettina Charles talks about random stuff, it means that she is good to go. As for me on the other hand, I'm as nervous as a mouse cornered by a cat that hasn't eaten in days."

Assuming the leadership role in the execution of the trial by fire, Ellis escorted Tina into Auditorium 2001. Kelly entered the room and sat on the throne next to Arnie, dead-center, first row, about six feet from the stage. They were surrounded on all sides by the remaining observers—nine rows of ten seats each. Arnie's arms were folded and his expression was uninviting. In a rare, whispery voice, he spoke to Kelly. "Stay angry if it makes you feel better, but this whole scene is because of me trusting your instincts. After hearing the demo, I began making moves based on your word of how the total package was put together—looks and stage presence. In addition to that, I'm sitting in the center of a room filled with my leadership, showing off a talent that I haven't even laid my eyes on."

Delight rose up from Kelly's belly and created a slight grin on her face. *Finally, Arnie expresses relevant words of endorsement.* Now, she was not only nervous but also petrified.

Suddenly, a six-foot figure came walking over with a chair in his hands and stopped to the right of Arnie. It was Carlton. Without yelling, he spoke loud enough so that his targeted audience could hear him clearly. He expressed his wishes while placing his hand to the right of Arnie's head. "From this point down, I need all of y'all to scoot your chairs about twelve inches to the right."

Believing this to be an Arnie pop quiz, all of the staffers on that side of the front row moved their chairs down as instructed. When the appropriate-sized gap was created, Carlton slid his chair between Arnie and the director of the marketing division.

Seated to Arnie's immediate left, Kelly closed her eyes briefly and shook her head. *I was so caught up preparing Tina for this trial by fire that I completely forgot about Carlton—my colorful, loose-cannon cousin.*

Arnie looked at Kelly and asked, "Who is this maniac? He must be crazy, forcing his way to gain a seat next to me?"

As Kelly tried to catch her breath, Carlton spoke for himself. "Hello, Mister Peters. It's an honor to meet you. My name is Carlton-The Lovely-Charles-Montgomery, but you can call me Carlton-The Lovely-Charles-Montgomery. Psych, I'm just playing—trying to lighten the atmosphere." Carlton held out his hand until Arnie unfolded his arms. "Let's just start out on a first name basis, shall we? So, Arnie, you can call me Carlton. I'm Tina's acting mana—I mean personal assistant."

After a five-second shake, Arnie withdrew his hand from the grip of the stranger and turned to talk with Kelly. Whispering, he asked, "Who—how—what in the hell is this all about?"

Kelly whispered her answer. "Tina has an entourage of one and the two of them are inseparable. Carlton is Tina's cousin, her stylist, and her personal assistant. It's sort of a two-for-one package deal."

"Kelly, you have got to be kidding."

She looked him square in the eyes. "No, Arnie, I'm quite serious. Carlton is Tina's personal assistant and please, can we leave it at that?"

Having just made up with her, he decided to let it be Kelly's call—for now. Instead of acting ugly, he chuckled. "I can't wait to meet Little Miss Sunshine—a nobody with a personal assistant. This is hilarious. I need to get back to the East Coast more often."

26

TRIAL BY FIRE

9:30 a. m. Eastern Time and Still—Wednesday, July 14, 1982

AUDITORIUM 2001's observation booth was located directly behind the removable stage. Ellis had Tina stand at the entryway inside the darkened, narrow surveillance room until after his introduction. From there, her trial by fire was a short distance away—a four-step climb onto center stage. Before leaving her side, he squeezed her hand with a grip, conveying support and confidence in her abilities. Ellis spoke jovially to the test audience. "Hey, everybody, it's been a while since I've seen some of you Cats. You're still alive and kicking, so that's a good thing. I'm here to introduce Bettina Charles and she's about to serenade you with something fresh and funky. As you find yourselves grooving in your seats, let go and enjoy the ride. If you like what she's serving, let her know with your applause." Ellis joined the band at floor-level, stage-right and took his place at the keyboards. Before sitting, with a jerk of his head and a movement of his left hand, he gave the studio musicians a signal to start playing the introduction to "Tell Me How to Love You."

After the music started, Tina slowly revealed herself, gliding up the stairs into position. She moved to the beat of the song, willingly surrendering to the scrutiny of the onlookers. With eyes closed, she sank inside the melody—body swaying seductively. Like a narcotic injection hitting her bloodstream, she felt an intoxicating rush—a surge of pleasurable sensations. There was a warming on the inside of her body and tingling of the nerve endings on her skin. She licked her lips and moaned sensually, caressing the microphone with both hands. She opened her eyes and presented a wide smile, drawing the test audience into the provocative world where her suggestive lyrics resided. Recognizing The Label's owner immediately from print and television, Tina moved her head from side to side to reach everyone, but gave the head honcho special care throughout her performance.

Arnie was definitely pleased with Tina's physical package, giving her high marks on his mental scorecard for possessing all three of his H's—hue, hair, and height. There were no noticeable blemishes on her face and her neck, shoulders, chest, and arms had a velvety smoothness. *Passage of time is required to mature Tina's adorable, teenage face to that of a beautiful woman. That's definitely her inevitable destination. Until then, makeup and wardrobe will be used to artificially achieve the objective. Her hourglass frame is also in the developmental stage, but I give her high marks for its pear shape and potential. Even with a size deficit, she gets a passing grade for boobs because of their perkiness. She also scores high for my favorite feature which is her backside bump. It meets my criteria of roundness and accentuation.*

From uttering the first poetic phrase to singing the final word, Tina remained stationary, mouth close to the microphone, fingers and hands stroking it so as to invoke stimulating thought. Kelly enjoyed every second of watching her steady-handed boss break down under the alluring spell of a teenager. He was mesmerized, unable to control the movement of his leg and patting of his foot, reacting to the catchy rhythm of the song's hook. Internally, Kelly was no longer an impartial music executive, but the singular party responsible for delivering, quite possibly, Walden Records' recording artist of the decade. As well as adding points to her professional prowess, she was bursting with internal pride, knowing that Bettina Charles was her little sister. Similar to the gestures presented at Club Trevi's, Tina ended "Tell Me" by inserting and withdrawing her finger from her mouth seductively. She used the moistened finger to point to an unsuspecting man in the test audience, motioning him to come to her. This time, instead of being random, the intentional object of her sexually suggestive taunting was none other than Arnie Peters. He readjusted his male member. *I think she just got me off from the microphone and I enjoyed it tremendously. Stand down, Peters, stand down. It's your turn to make a move.*

The room was flooded with applause, whistles, bravos, and ultimately a standing ovation, led by the Artists Operations' Division and Carlton. In addition to remaining stoic, Arnie held tight to Kelly's arm to assure that she and he stay seated. "Arnie, let me go," demanded his executive vice president. "I want to give her a standing ovation as well."

"No. As top leadership, it's important for us to behave impartially." Kelly remained seated as instructed, but applauded with energetic enthusiasm and a smile.

The test audience's reaction conveyed a unanimous consensus that the sought-after Pop-Diva had been found. Arnie stood up, turned to his staff, and, once again, pressed his hands downward to silence his team. Per his request, he was given a cordless microphone to use as a bullhorn so he could engage in an awkward and unbalanced cross-examination of Tina. He took his seat, assuming the role of a playground bully with 100 well-compensated cronies backing him up.

After bowing, smiling, and bowing again, Tina turned to leave the stage. Arnie spoke in the microphone with authority. "Young lady, you have not been dismissed."

Tina took two steps backward, turned around, and faced Arnie and the test audience. He said, "The vocals, gestures, and emotion were well-executed—far above board. However, your feet remained stationary throughout the performance. That's absolutely acceptable here and there, but today's audiences expect dancing to be part of their entertainment experience. Besides your suggestive swaying, how well can you dance?"

"I'm a good dancer," responded Tina.

"Please speak into the microphone so we all can hear you."

Carlton said, "Miss Charles can dance her ass off, been doing it forever. Is this line of questioning necessary?"

Without looking in his direction, Arnie said, "Not talking to you."

Carlton snapped back. "Well, I'm talking to you."

Kelly shook her head in the negative as a nonverbal signal for Carlton to calm down. "Everything's all right. This is an executive-level conversation, so let us, the senior staff, handle this situation, Carlton."

Although receiving Kelly's message, Carlton's defensive sword had already been drawn. "Don't start nothing, won't be nothing. That's all I'm saying. Now, my lips are sealed."

Tina put her mouth close to the microphone. "My dancing is quite refined, you see."

Arnie turned his head and spoke directly in Kelly's ear. "What the hell does *quite refined* mean? And what kind of accent is that? Didn't you discover her in North Carolina?"

"I did find her there, but she's an army brat and was raised all over. Arnie, must we grill her in front of all these spectators? Let's go up to 2201 and finish this discussion in the conference room with just the team leads."

Arnie made sure Carlton could hear what he was saying. "If I'm going to roll our biggest dice on this girl, throwing in everything including the kitchen sink, I need to be damn sure she can handle the pressure. In addition to that, as a company, we need to know what grooming is needed in what areas. So far, she's shown very little in the dance department, so I want to see what she's got, right now. To answer your first question, hell yeah, I'm putting her on the spot. That's what a trial by fire is all about."

Kelly pleaded with him. "But I just took her through a similar drill at a club in North Carolina."

"Good! Then, she has been well prepared for round two." Arnie spoke into the microphone. "We would like to have a demonstration of your refined dancing."

Tina asked, "What style of dance shall I perform?"

With the exception of Kelly, Ellis, and Carlton, the test audience joined their boss in laughter. "What shall you perform? Young lady, you have my permission to improvise. You can dance any way you like." Arnie was convinced. *This kid probably doesn't have a rhythmic bone in her gorgeous body. We're gonna have to spend extra time and money teaching her choreography that looks as if it comes naturally.*

"In that case, I would like to dance to something slow and melodic like 'Endless Love.'"

Arnie screamed. "Somebody, make it happen quickly."

The audio mixer said, "Give us ten minutes and we'll be ready to cue the music."

While waiting, Kelly took Tina to the back of the stage. "How comfortable are you with doing this dance presentation? If you feel that it's too much, say so, and I'll pull the plug on this exasperating trial by fire."

"As always, I'm wearing my leotard bottoms and this flared mini dress is perfect for dancing. Since I don't have my toe shoes, I'll perform my routine barefooted."

Kelly clarified. "What I'm asking is whether you're emotionally okay with all that's happening."

"I've got magic to do, so I'm fine."

Kelly spoke enough Tina-ese to translate her little sister's idiom into: *Bettina Charles is ready to go.*

"Good. I like self-assured answers. If you can do something, grab hold of it. You have to be confident to make it in this business. I see that you're preparing, so I'll leave you alone to your process." While returning to her seat, Kelly prayed, *God please translate Tina's "magic to do" into being able to perform to Arnie's satisfaction.*

While Kelly and Carlton squirmed nervously, Arnie discussed other business matters with the department heads seated near him. Tina stood in the darkness of the observation booth and stretched to warm up the muscles in her body. It had been quite some time since she had performed a complete dance presentation. When the music was cued, Tina was ready. In the beginning of her routine, with her legs turned out, she performed a slow, deep-knee bending full plié. Her back was straight and properly aligned with her lower body. Her revelés were clean with heels lifted off the floor as she balanced on her toes. Her body control was exceptional during the execution of each passé, with a foot sliding above her knee and back down her standing leg. From that position, she transitioned to exacting pirouettes of controlled spins and turns on one leg. With a quick succession of a big step followed by two little steps, she performed several triple-runs in a circle. At climatic moments in the song, several grand jetés of long horizontal jumps to airborne splits carried her from one end of the stage to the other. Those were followed by five fouettés of quick whipping turns around her body from one direction to another.

Throughout Tina's routine, Auditorium 2001 became a concert hall with the test audience engaging in a chorus of "oohs" and "aahs" in similar fashion to the choir at Katrina's wedding. In habitual Kelly fashion, she mentally logged the spectator feedback as another previously lived moment. Tina ended her presentation with an arabesque—a difficult move made harder after dancing an entire routine barefooted. With her body leaning forward at a more-than-ninety-degree angle, she stood on one leg with the other extended into a standing split. From beginning to end, excellence in precision, strength, and balance was elegantly demonstrated through the poetry of her human form. The onlookers' approval was apparent and their rumbling was a subtle urging for their boss to announce the obvious conclusion.

Arnie asked, "Little Lady, your dancing was superb and totally unexpected. How positive are you about me signing you to a contract?"

"I'm one hundred percent sure that you'll sign me."

"Oh really? And, why is that?"

"You were the topic of a research paper I did in school. Articles referred to you as tough, a top business man, and superintelligent."

Arnie said, "I think that's an accurate description."

"If you are truly all those things, you'll sign me because it would be foolish if you did not."

Not expecting that response, Arnie chuckled and the test audience braced for an avalanche. "So, you think you're somebody who can handle this cutthroat business?"

"I was born somebody and I don't need show business to tell me what I already know. I want to be an entertainer because it's my passion. It's what I'm most comfortable doing—what I think I was born to do."

"And your response is most of the battle won, knowing what you want and owning it." Tina was getting a little tired of standing there on display. Arnie asked, "What kind of name is Bettina? It's probably one of those combining two into one—made-up names. Maybe we should tweak it a little."

Tina spoke loudly into the microphone. "Excuse me, but what kind of name is Arnie? Is it short for Arnold like the character on re-runs of a show called *Green Acres* that I watch with my great-aunties?"

Kelly was nervous, recognizing that Tina had slipped into her annoyed personality. It was manifested by her saying exactly what she was thinking. She prayed, *Please don't let this conversation go south by Arnie hitting back with a hard-nosed attitude.*

Carlton said, "Mister Oink-Oink, I mean Mister Peters, knowing Miss Charles as well as I do, I think it's time to get her off that stage."

Aware of Arnie's intolerance for backtalk, all grew silent. Many of their eyes bulged and ears perked up, awaiting an Arnie explosion. Surprisingly, he was jovial. "You know what, Miss Charles? I think you're a pistol, a real tough little fireball."

"And I think you're a grizzly bear—big, loud, and ferocious, but still furry and cuddly. Mister Peters, I appreciate this incredible opportunity and don't mean to appear ungrateful. With all respect, Bettina Charles was, is, and will always be my name. I want to be called who I am—Bettina Charles."

Not wanting to upset his new Pop-Diva, Arnie softened his approach while remaining strong to his team. "Bettina Charles is definitely original—it's catchy. I like it, so let's go with it."

Arnie motioned for Kelly to follow him onto the stage in order to address Tina and the audience from a vantage point of authority.

"Let's give Miss Bettina Charles another round of applause for her incredible display of talent in a pressure-cooker situation." After allowing ten seconds of applause, he continued. "From this moment on, regardless of the boiling point applied today during my trial by fire, Bettina Charles has top echelon status at Walden Records and will be catered to with the respect that comes along with the designation. I thank you for your cooperation and you are dismissed."

Within earshot of Kelly, Arnie shook Tina's hand and pointed at her. "I'm expecting big things from you. Prepare to work harder than you ever have before. You're going to need to draw from the toughness that you've shown today."

"Yes, sir, I'm ready to go." Assistant Angela escorted Tina to human resources where she signed a temporary agreement, enabling her to start immediately. The terms were simple. Tina agreed to perform music production duties for Walden Records as a paid consultant until her long-term contract was signed or at the end of a five-day period of performance (whichever came first). During that brief stint, there would be no claim of ownership to property, no liability, and no obligation assumed by either party—Walden Records or Bettina Charles.

Arnie motioned for Ellis to come and join him and Kelly. "After a well-earned, long lunch break, I would like you and Miss Charles to spend the balance of the day in rehearsal. All is at your disposal, including the production team of songwriters and musicians. They are to brainstorm with you and Tina and come up with a theme and structure in which to build the first album project. Start with the demo song and go from there."

Arnie and Kelly went into the dark observation booth behind the stage for an on-the-fly meeting. He said, "Ellis has agreed to serve as music producer on this first single, but I need him for the duration. Figure out a way to get him to commit, in writing, to an extended period of performance."

"That should be an easier conversation than the usual ones, when dealing with the full blown eccentric Ellis. He has become quite fond of Tina already."

During one of their earlier phone conversations, Kelly had explained to Arnie that Tina was backed by advisors that included a lawyer, an accountant, and a bank investment specialist. Even more important was the inclusion of her guardians—General John Chapman and Eugenia Fae Watkins-Charles. "Although you forewarned me, I'm baffled that our little nobody has her own negotiation team."

"I wish you would stop referring to Tina as a nobody."

"Until she proves herself, that's all she is to me. And step one in changing that perception is to get her team together, so a final contract can be put in place by COB tomorrow."

"That's an extremely tall order."

"And that's why you're handling it personally. Once the deal is done, I want 'Tell Me' recorded and an accompanying video completed ASAP."

"What about Carlton?"

"What about him? I already gave you the nod on him being Tina's personal assistant."

"And I appreciate that very much. He, however, wants his own personal assistant."

In disbelief, Arnie needed clarification. "Did you say that the just approved personal assistant is making a request for a personal assistant?"

"Yes, that is correct. I would like to assign the task to my assistant Angela, whose goal is to increase her support of me on the creative side of the business. Unofficially, I've given her small tasks and she's performed them well. I'll assign some of her strictly in-house administrative duties to someone else. Regardless of me allowing the rope to slack, she understands that my needs, as executive vice president, are still her priority."

"So, now you're telling me that the personal assistant named Carlton will have a part-time personal assistant named Angela who will need a personal assistant to assume many of her administrative duties?"

Kelly had to suppress her urge to laugh before she provided the president of Walden Records with an answer. "It sounds a bit bizarre when said all together, but, yes, that's pretty much what I'd like to happen."

"Somebody needs to contact Bellevue because my executive vice president is mentally ill and her disease is spreading over to me." Approving the uncanny request, Arnie said, "I've got bigger fish to fry, so this is your crazy call. Put Carlton on the payroll assigned to the creative team and give him his job-splitting assistant and so forth and so on."

Kelly forgot herself and gave Arnie a quick, suggestive kiss that parted his lips, penetrated his teeth, and sensuously swiped his tongue. "You believe in Bettina Charles as much as I do."

Arnie fought to maintain a stern look on his face while his stomach quivered and his male member pulsated. "Bettina Charles is your baby, so grow her up to this business quickly. I'm serving notice that I will be hovering." He left the dark observation booth chuckling to himself. *Did little Miss Bettina call me Arnold the pig and a grizzly bear? I need to vaccinate myself against our Pop-Diva's quick wit and charm. And my clock of tolerance is ticking on that Carlton character—Tina's uncouth and tacky extra baggage.*

27

THE CONTRACT

LEADERSHIP from contracts and the legal department joined Arnie and Kelly in his office for a working lunch. The main dish being served was the terms of Tina's contract—the line of attack for capitalizing on Walden Records' position of strength. As Arnie presented a handful of permissible, but unethical ways of maximizing The Label's advantage, Kelly had a conflicting position. In strategizing to close this particular deal, she had not sharpened her claws in preparation to tear holes in the pockets of the artist. At the same time, she was not on the gangway, preparing to board *Good Ship Tina*. As a middle ground, she presented a tempered alternative to their usual cutthroat business model. "With a brand-new artist, our profit potential is extremely high by design. Maybe we should enter these proceedings extending an olive branch—offering a few incentives—perhaps a signing bonus."

"And why the hell should we do that?" asked Arnie. "Where are your killer instincts?"

"I'm using them right now as a Serengeti Lioness—staking claim to a premium position in the high grass—lying low for those perfect opportunities to pounce. My strategy makes it possible for our company to feed each and every time we experience hunger—not just for food, but for bragging rights and prestige."

Trying not to be outdone, the director of contracts interrupted. "What you're recommending is contrary to the aggressive formula we're getting ready to propose."

"Absolutely! Miss Charles is coming to the negotiation table armed with an advisory team of her own. I suggest that we conquer with kindness—give a little to gain much more. If Tina is as successful as we think, we want to position ourselves for a lasting relationship— steadily filling our coffers."

Arnie banged his fist on his private office's round conference table as he addressed his closest advisors. "That's exactly why Miss King is Walden Records' executive vice president. Her foresight is incredible— a winner of wars not skirmishes. With that said, we're gonna sit here and develop a solution along the lines of what Kelly suggested."

While Arnie and his co-captain continued prepping for negotiations, Tina and Ellis sat on a bench in Bryant Park eating hotdogs, washing them down with grape and orange sodas respectively. After getting their fill, they walked a short distance to the branch of the New York City Public Library located nearest to The Label—Fifth Avenue and Forty-Second Street. There, they spent the afternoon researching the greats in Black music, ranging from gospel to blues. The library had an incredible reference department dedicated to Black entertainment. Their focus was on a timeline that stretched from the Harlem Renaissance period to the amazing era of Motown-Sound's heyday. It was Ellis's intention to ignite a fire in Tina prior to them recording a single note. He wanted her to embrace a legacy of greatness—paved with the dedication and sacrifice of musical legends that excelled in spite of tremendous adversity.

For several hours, Ellis and Tina read commentary and viewed photo and film footage of the greats, including Bessie Smith, Billie Holiday, Ella Fitzgerald, and Sarah Vaughan. In Ellis's opinion, the current throne was deservedly occupied by Aretha Franklin and

Tina's idol, Diana Ross. His concern was for the future and he had yet to find a suitable candidate to carry the Diva-torch into the next generation.

Ellis attempted to motivate Tina while providing insight about the industry. "Tina, I'm sold out on your talent, us making magic together, and you reigning as musical royalty. Mind you, the focus is far beyond the music these days. It's about building an image through wild dance routines, crazy costumes, and edgy videos—all with sexual undertones. You have to be able to handle those extras that are a part of the changing tide."

Before leaving the library, Tina understood the mission and accepted the challenge. "Ellis, I will do my best to maintain the high standards set in the past while stamping the present with my own unique musical signature. Although not thrilled about the last requirements, I'll do my best to adhere to the sex crazed, break dancing, and free expression sign of the times."

For the rest of the day, Walden Records buzzed with Pop-Diva business. Tina and Ellis juggled between working one-on-one and in concert with the artistic production team—developing concepts and perfecting musical arrangements. Kelly and Arnie had shifted their focus to addressing separate components of senior management responsibilities from the executive suites on the twenty-second floor. Carlton coordinated complicated logistics, causing his value to The Label to reap immediate dividends.

As Assistant Angela watched in amazement, Carlton convinced Tina's entire executive team—her attorney, accountant, and banker—to be present for contract negotiations in New York City at Walden Records the following morning. Petitioning the guardians to attend was not difficult, but required additional explanation. Aunty Gina and Pappy John were stunned by what their baby chicks had managed to pull off in less than a hundred hours from leaving the safety of

Joseph-Lee Manor. They were going to co-sign a contract for Bettina with Walden Records.

In addition to finalizing transportation, Carlton and Angela carried out layered duties. They hurried from place to place, supporting the intense and varied activities unfolding simultaneously in all the rehearsal spaces on the sixteenth floor. By quitting time at 11:00 p. m., the collective efforts of the music production team not only netted an album concept, but also the selection of five of its ten songs. Two were close to being completely arranged and several others were in various phases of development. From Tina, to Ellis, to Carlton and Assistant Angela, to the studio band, and the sound engineers, they all left Walden Records that evening having accomplished much and with a good understanding of their next steps.

Thursday, July 15, 1982

Many moving parts had come together in an attempt to get Tina quickly signed to a contract. One of Walden Records' private jets had been dispatched to transport Aunty Gina from North Carolina to New York City. Aunty Zooni delayed the process by accosting her youngest sibling. "Did you say a private jet is coming to pick you up from a private air strip in Rocky Mount with no one we know there to witness the incident?"

"That's what I said and I need you to drive me their right away."

"Oh, I'm gonna do a lot more than drive you. That plane won't be taking off, heading nowhere, without Arizona Zooni Watkins on board."

"I can't believe I'm saying this, but I could use the company and your brand of boldness would definitely cut down on my nervousness. Well, let's get moving. We gotta stop by your place, so you can pack a few things for the trip."

"We don't need to stop because I keeps me an overnight bag stocked and tucked away in the trunk of my Cadi at all times. I never know when a nice-looking man is gonna sneak up and steal my attention for a whole night or so. Gina, you ain't the only one with needs to be fulfilled or with the opportunities to do something about it. Zooni takes care of her business."

"Well, I already told Trudy, Ed, and Larry that they had to stay behind and hold down the Fort, so let's go. This is so exciting. Our little Tina is gonna be a singer with a contract and everything."

Because of the sister-to-half-sister interaction, the trip from Rocky Mount to New York City by way of Washington, DC was unique. The purpose of the stopover in the nation's capital was to pick up Pappy John and the members of Tina's estate executor team. Upon arriving at Walden Records' New York City headquarters, all meeting attendees gathered in the Narthex of Conference Room 2201 to meet and greet where coffee, tea, and pastries were being served. After escorting Tina to the official gathering, Ellis was introduced to her advisory team and family. Immediately, he was drawn to a certain someone. "Much obliged to meet you all, but may I have the name again of the one looking spry and not a sign of being shy?"

To test astuteness, both hands were extended to Ellis. "I'm called Zooni, but my name is Arizona Watkins."

"I don't see a ring, and must assume that you're happily single, but hopefully available to mingle," said Ellis Ross.

"How observant you are as well as hitting the nail on the head."

Tina was delighted to see one great aunty and quite concerned by the presence of the other one. The music industry hopeful used vocal inflection and facial expressions to register and alert Aunty Gina about her uneasiness and displeasure of having Aunty Zooni as part of the delegation. "Carlton told me that you were coming alone."

"Zooni tagged along to keep me company, to see your new place, but she won't be staying for the contract meeting. We already discussed it."

God, I thank you for small favors that are huge—like Aunty Zooni not being at the most important meeting of my life.

"Miss Arizona, since I won't be attending the meeting as well," added Ellis, "I'd love to show you around the building while the business is being conducted."

"That will be fine because I'm not fond of formal meetings." Ellis extended his elbow, Zooni hooked her arm through his, and they disappeared.

Carlton whispered to Tina. "Between Aunties Gina and Zooni, I don't know who is the most flirtatious and old-timey freakazoid."

Informally, most of Team Tina was well-acquainted and there to happily extend beyond their duties as managers of her trust fund. Although like family, Vaughan and Brown had assisted with Tina's affairs since she was five months old. Vaughan monitored the holdings of her trust and Momma Nin's volumes of letters. Brown managed her finances and his family's business was the leasing agent of her Upper East Side apartment. Straus had advised Tina personally since first beginning to explain the terms of Momma Nin's Last Will and Testament to her when she was twelve years old. Pappy John and Aunty Gina were her guardians with seven more years to supervise the trust fund and a lifetime to continue joyfully showering the starlet with love.

As her first order of business, Tina met with her team in a small office down the hall from the main conference room. She had done her own research on how some well-established artists had been taken advantage of by their record labels, resulting in the loss of rights to property, privileges, and profits. All were important but her property was paramount. With assurance, she expressed her absolute must-haves. "Nobody owns or will ever own my name, my songs, and my journaling. Do what you need to do—what you have to do—to make sure I keep ownership of those things. For me, they're way more important than money."

Upon entering Conference Room 2201, participants were positioned to pre-determined placement by Assistant Angela and a very professional acting Carlton. The careful compliance to configuration control resulted in the two factions seated opposite each other at the large and intimidating conference table. Team Arnie included Kelly, two attorneys—the legal department's senior and deputy directors—a transcriber, and an administrative assistant, who was there to monitor the audio recording of the proceedings. Formally, Team Tina included Fitzgerald National Bank's executive vice president Preston Vaughan and his executive assistant Shelly Patterson. Miss Charles's accountant was Douglas Brown, the managing partner at Anderson Pratt. Isaac Straus was senior partner at Straus, Goldberg & Feld and was Tina's attorney.

Straus, who led Team Tina, had brokered lucrative book deals that were similar in scope, but he had no experience playing the music industry's version of chess. To compensate, Attorney Horace Winslow was retained to assist with deal brokering on behalf of Bettina Charles. He was partner of a New York City-based heavy-hitting entertainment law firm and had opposed Walden Records in the past. Specifically, he had filed separate lawsuits on behalf of a handful of The Label's former recording artists. Although stepping in at each plaintiff's life support stage, Horace Winslow consistently found contract loopholes that forced settlements—restoring remnant royalties from Walden Records' rich repository.

At the beginning of contract negotiations, Arnie gave introductory remarks to be entered into the official record. "I appreciate you all coming with zero notice, but the music industry's bells never stop ringing. The good news is that Walden Records is excited about signing Bettina Charles. With that said, I must emphasize the fact that she is an unproven talent whose biggest advantage is having a contract with my record company. That sponsorship places heavy financial risk on the coffers of my Label and exposes us to embarrassing scrutiny if Miss Charles fails at this attempt to become a successful entertainer. Although sounding convincing, Arnie's latter statements were over-inflated and misleading conjecture."

With his posturing concluded, the point man on patrol yielded the podium to the top brass in his legal department. The rules were simple. Each side quickly initialed beside the line items that were standard and mutually agreeable. Haggling was required for those that were not. It was accepted that Bettina Charles hereinafter in the contract would be referred to as the "Artist." It was understood that Walden Records had the exclusive right but not the obligation to record, manufacture, and distribute the Artist's recordings by any means, including but not limited to albums, singles, cassettes, and video products. The Artist's appearances on television, in videos, in movies, in print media and on other performers' recordings had to be approved by The Label and outwardly documented as: "Courtesy of Walden Records."

Over the course of the three-year contract, Bettina Charles would produce two albums and perform as part of other seasoned entertainers' concert tours. The Artist was responsible for reimbursing Walden Records for 75 percent of the cost incurred in the production of her first two studio albums. The expenditures included recording time, manufacturing, packaging, marketing, and distribution. Because of Arnie's vision of creating large-scale music video products, Team Tina won the battle and Walden Records agreed to absorb expenses relating to the development of the two albums' mini-musical-movies.

Also to her advantage, Tina declined an advance, resulting in higher compensation on the royalty side. She did accept the generous offer of a non-reimbursable one hundred fifty thousand dollar signing bonus. In addition, The Label agreed to provide all work-related transportation, including private jets, buses, and other ground transportation, at zero cost to the Artist for business use only. Tina was able to retain possession of the brand name *Bettina Charles* and was granted complete ownership of all her created, copyrighted work and associated masters—all referred to as her intellectual property. Because of her fear, which bordered on paranoia, a safety copy of each of her masters would be produced and delivered to Bettina Charles in care of Fitzgerald National Bank. For the life of the contract, Walden Records was granted exclusive licensing of all her intellectual property for the purpose of promotion and distribution.

Relatively speaking, as compared to most deals with its artists, The Label had agreed to unprecedented concessions. This was balanced by Arnie loading Tina's contract with strict guidelines and penalties. With the exception of Bettina Charles's intellectual property, Walden Records had exclusive ownership of all other copyrighted, recorded material and associated masters. The Label had the right of refusal to record any of Miss Charles's copyrighted material and placed an aggressive opt-out clause on the overall deal. Bettina Charles could be dropped from the contract if her popularity failed to materialize or drastically dipped once established. Moreover, termination could occur if the Artist's second album sales did not meet or exceed the threshold of her first album's revenue. By contract end over two albums, Bettina Charles was required to produce three platinum singles (i.e., three songs selling a minimum of one million units each). If three platinum single records failed to be produced, Bettina Charles would owe Walden Records a penalty fee of five hundred thousand dollars and be subjected to the aforementioned release from contract.

Other than stickler points, much of the contract was a 360 multiple rights deal. In this arrangement, The Label would collect income from revenue streams that were traditionally off-limits. Specifically, Walden Records would receive a percentage of earnings from endorsement deals, tours, and merchandise. Tina was willing to bear such a heavy burden because it was the compromise to end the dispute over holding onto her name and intellectual property. Thanks to Kelly's mediation, Arnie did not appear totally unreasonable, leaving the door cracked for subsequent deals with his budding Pop Artist in the future.

Because of her age at signing, this initial contract would terminate automatically on Bettina Charles's twenty-first birthday—fifteen days short of a three-year deal. At the end of legal discussions, both sides of the table were lightheaded. For Tina, there was heavy short-term risk, but potential long-term gain. For Walden Records, unless the Bettina

Charles project was a complete failure, Arnie's record company was well insulated with the possibility of being in the possession of a cash cow.

Privately during a fifteen-minute break in the negotiations, prior to Tina, Pappy John, and Aunty Gina signing to finalize the deal, Horace Winslow expressed concerns. He stated that the execution of the contract would place an enormous psychological and physical strain on the Artist. In a personal plea, he warned. "As a family, I need each of you to understand that failure to meet the terms and obligations of this contract will most likely result in bankruptcy for Bettina Charles and potentially ruin her short career."

Aunty Gina asked, "What if the obligations are met?"

Pappy John added. "Or surpassed?"

"If that occurs, your little Bettina Charles will be a very wealthy young woman with instant clout as a shrewd player in the music industry."

After a glance at each other and no hesitation, Pappy John asked, "Where do we sign? Tina wants this and we're supporting her one hundred percent."

Over a working lunch, the legal teams on both sides remained in the conference room, fine-tuning the details. For Bettina Charles, however, by 2:00 p. m., the deal was done. She was Walden Records' latest recording artist, signed to an almost three-year contract beginning Thursday, July 15, 1982, through Sunday, June 30, 1985. Excluding legal, those involved in the contract negotiations joined Mister Peters in The Label's Executive Dining Room for a lavish celebratory, late lunch. Of course, Ellis Ross and Arizona Watkins were asked to join the festivities. André Jenkins was added to the invitee list as well. Kelly King assumed that it had been done by Arnie Peters and he assumed that she had extended the offer. Actually, Carlton had taken liberty and amended the final guest list to include the lead choreographer.

When all were assembled, twelve people were seated at the oversized table-in-the-round. The atmosphere was mellowed by the studio band serenading with a combination of mellow R&B ballads and smooth and easy jazz. A server was assigned to each guest as the five-course offerings were presented. In addition to family and members of Team Tina, many present were foundation blocks in the formation of an evolving music industry inner circle team to undergird the young artist.

Bettina Charles was sandwiched between her new ally and music mentor Ellis Ross and Arnie Peters, The Label's prime minister of power. Kelly King was, among many other things, Tina's day-to-day manager and André Jenkins would be her chief choreographer. Carlton was, above all else, still Tee-Tee's very best friend.

The mixture of personalities at the roundtable made for interesting conversation. Sitting next to Aunty Gina, Kelly made an attempt to improve their relationship. "Aunty Gina, I want to—."

"I beg your pardon, but what did you call me?"

"I meant to say Mrs. Watkins-Charles."

"That's better."

"I just want you to know that I will look after Tina as if she were my sister."

"As long as you do right by her in this music business thing, that's enough for me. The *being a sister part* is not necessary."

Douglas Brown said, "Eugenia—if it's not too forward to call you that—in the times that I've spoken with you face-to-face through all of these years, you continue to look more beautiful."

"Thank you. And please, call me Gina."

Shelly Patterson said, "Mister Chapman, saying this might get me fired, but there's a glow about your face that is intriguing."

Pappy John answered. "And in you, I see a beautiful sunset."

Carlton said, "André, I really appreciated you taking me out and introducing me to so many people the other night. I had a great time."

"No problem, but it was hard for me to share you, something so delicious, with everyone else."

Immediately following his flirtatious comments to Carlton, Mister Jenkins turned his attention to the bank vice president seated to his left. "Mister Vaughan, I can recognize a fresh tan from a mile away. Have you recently sunbathed anywhere special?"

"I was just in the Bahamas a week ago."

"I certainly hope you were able to let the sun shine on other parts of your body," teased André. "It's a shame to waste good sunlight."

"Actually, all of my body received an adequate amount of heat."

Ellis's crooning had nullified Storm Zooni as she spoke to him coyly. "Mister Ross, your hospitality has been a pleasure. The way you explain things is very funny and fills me with energy."

"In that case, I'm here to ignite and delight whenever you need a charge."

"Your kind offer is very tempting."

Ellis moved close to Aunty Zooni's ear. "I'm not tied to nobody and I like what I see. I bet it's nice and tight, hasn't been used in a while, huh, Arizona Watkins?"

Aunty Zooni's answer was open-ended. "There's only one way to find out."

Arnie turned to Kelly and expressed his pleasure about how the day's events had unfolded. "Throwing this luncheon was an absolutely great idea. It's unfair for you to be so intelligent and beautiful at the same time."

Kelly responded. "Hearing that from you makes me blush all over."

"Then, my most important work of the day is done."

Prompted by Arnie at the end of the dessert course, everyone raised their glasses for a toast to Tina. "It has been a pleasure celebrating this wonderful merger. I look forward to meeting again when Bettina Charles sets the mark and breaks records in this high-stakes music industry."

Tina and Carlton spent the remainder of the day with Pappy John and Aunty Gina shopping and walking the neighborhood that surrounded Windsor East. In his protective mode, the father warned his daughter about potential dangers. "When you leave the apartment by foot, always let a security guard, a bellman, or the doorman know where you're going and when to expect you back. Whenever possible, I want you to have someone with you."

"I know, I know," Tina said impatiently. "You tell me the same thing every time we talk."

An entrance to Central Park was four blocks from Windsor East. Pappy John had Tina show him her routine upon entering the park. She pointed out the place where she liked to sit and *maintain*. "Tina, don't sit on that bench," her father warned. "It's too close to those bushes. Make sure you have an exit in mind at all times."

I wish Pappy John's rules applied to nightmares. That seems to be the place I'm most vulnerable and continuously in danger and terrified. I wish my own mind would stop tormenting me so. Where can I go to get help for that?

Convinced that the top ten rules of safety were understood, the evening was spent in reflection and celebration at Windsor East's apartment 2407. Tina and Carlton showed off their new living quarters to Pappy John and Aunty Gina, ate carry-out Italian food, drank wine, and sent up salutes to Momma Nin. To the cousins/best friends' relief, attending to other matters with Ellis Ross, Aunty Zooni was a no show at the open house affair.

In the back of the limousine, Kelly's strong tower disposition was bulking under the weight of helplessness. Her best-made personal plans were failing to reap the desired results. It had been a long and exhausting day that would be filed in her memory as unforgettable. She was happy and sad in equitable amounts. Tina, Carlton, Aunty Gina, and Pappy John were celebrating together and she had not been invited. Since things on the business side had turned out so well, she questioned her judgment in having not revealed her secret sister identity. *If I had told the truth during the great-aunties' grilling in Scotland Neck,* she speculated, *maybe I'd be celebrating with my newfound family in Windsor East—maybe.*

Upon unlocking the door to her penthouse, Kelly's nose was assaulted with a wonderful fragrance emitting from within. Twelve vases filled with various colored roses were scattered about the entire two-story square footage. As with past occurrences of this unexpected floral pleasure, there was no point in looking for a salutation and closing on a cleverly crafted card. The thought behind the gesture was appreciated and made Kelly blush just the same. She didn't need a note to inform her that the sender was Arnie Peters.

The next morning, at the sensible hour of 9:00 a. m., good-byes were exchanged, guardians were heading home, and the cousins were on their way to Walden Records for Tina's first official day as a recording artist. Aunty Zooni arrived at the airport just in time to enjoy the flight heading south on the luxurious private jet.

28

3.7.2.85

---

66 **T**RANSPORT is approaching for three seven two eighty-five," said the entrance booth attendant who broadcasted the information through a two-way radio. Pertinent vehicles, dressing rooms, rehearsal spaces, and studios were tagged. In addition, security detail, personal assistants, and other relevant staff were badged—all with Tina's artist product identification number. The two assigned security guards, Assistant Angela, and the director of human resources were there waiting in Walden Records' underground parking garage.

As Carlton and Tina exited the limousine, he said, "Now, this is more like it.—They know that Bettina Charles is all that, a bag of chips, and a soda, but bolder." In the elevator while bypassing the first thirteen floors, Assistant Angela pinned Carlton's badge in the correct position—left side lapel. It was black, one by three inches in diameter, and embossed in white lettering with the product ID: 3.7.2.85.

Held for specific reasons or having been previously visited, floors fourteen, sixteen, eighteen, nineteen, and twenty-one were skipped. Stops were made on other floors to emphasize divisional functions. Maintenance, the security office, and first aid were located on the fifteenth floor. When stepping off the elevator on floor seventeen, the separation of the Performance Preparation Division's two corridors was overstated with a half-wall divider, and security servicing both areas. There were signs with arrows identifying each—artists to the right and dancers, choreographers, and other supporting cast to the left. Both corridors' floor plans were very similar, with three sections on each side—wardrobe, hair and makeup, and locker rooms. In addition, certain staff and artists were assigned a more permanent space.

Although a department head, Kelly instructed a particular team lead to meet with Tina and then join the session in progress in 2101. The director said, "My name is Zina Shelby and I run this division. When a video is being produced, things get pretty crazy—lots of people to manage. Many of them are temporary workers, here for a day or two. The main reason for the separate corridors is to protect our artists. We've had real issues with fanatical types." After showing the common areas for the different aspects of grooming, Tina was assigned private quarters—accessed using a cipher lock—already labeled: 3.7.2.85. She was given a code and provided with instructions for using it. Of course, she gave the combination to Carlton and they both practiced, successfully opening each door several times.

Tina expressed concern. "Carlton has always done my hair and makeup. How is that going to happen here?"

"We have union workers. Carlton's new job will be to train your team and manage them. He can assist, but he must allow the team to be involved."

Tina remained silent, but thought, *I won't make a problem until there is one, but Carlton has to be in the mix at all times. I depend on him for everything, especially for my sanity.* Product 3.7.2.85 became a human rag doll when the lead stylist and an assistant from the wardrobe department came over and began taking her measurements. While Zina Shelby continued talking as if everything was normal, the wardrobe lead maneuvered Tina's body parts and took measurements while the assistant recorded them. They included her overall height, inseam, arm length and width as well as measurements of her waist, bust, hips, thighs, and calves. From a standing position and in turn, each shoe was taken off and replaced with a foot-measuring device. When that was done, Tina balanced herself by holding onto Carlton's shoulder as she returned each pedal extremity to its pump.

Zina Shelby said, "We don't make costumes, but we are responsible for maintenance and organization of them for the artists, background singers, dancers, and so on. When on tour, a stylist team is an important part of the travel crew—in charge of costume upkeep and booth dressing during the live show. The size of the styling team depends on the magnitude of the production."

After measurements, swatches of fabric were held up against Tina's face and skin while photographs were taken—random shots, no posing. Tina did her best to focus on the information being presented to her as part of the orientation, as opposed to focusing on the physical activity. She did not want to appear so unfamiliar with the process. The next stop was Marketing Operations on the twenty-first floor. There, she whizzed through Sales and Promotions. Fascinated by the work products and equipment, she paused for a closer examination of the creative activity taking place in the Art and Printing Departments. From there, she walked around a corporate apartment on the twenty-third floor, a corporate suite on the twenty-fourth, and was allowed to peek inside 2400, Mister Peters's penthouse.

Intentionally, Arnie and Kelly were absent, allowing their highly skilled staff to execute the orientation. For an hour after the tour, the human resources director gave Tina an overview of company procedures and its obligations to her as an artist. The final task was delivering their prioritized project to the twentieth floor's Product Development Department. There, she was handed over to Idella Stephens—the delegate for decorum. She wore a light-bulb-shaped, curly wig—full on the top and gradually tapering to three inches below her ears. Her black, thick-rimmed glasses hung on a white beaded chain and adorned her face along with a pair of pearl earrings. They were a half inch in diameter and had a matching necklace. Idella Stephens wore a Sunday-go-to-meeting black dress trimmed in a white cord whose hemline rested four inches below the knee. Her panty hose were skin-toned and thick like tights and her shoes were patent leather with a strap and a wide heel. It was said that the stoic soul did not own a pair of pants.

Authoritatively, Idella Stephens shooed everyone away.

Tina asked, "Can Carlton stay with me?" Then, remembering her new title as recording artist, she demanded. "Carlton Charles Montgomery is staying with me."

"Who is Carlton?"

"He's my personal assistant and cousin."

With a sanctimonious aura, Idella Stephens said, "If the answer is yes to any of my questions, he is welcome to stay and do my job, if you like. Is Carlton appearing on stage with you?"

"No, Ma'am."

"Will Carlton be performing in your videos?"

"No, Ma'am."

"Will Carlton be responding to your interview questions?"

"No, Ma'am."

"Then, Carlton, you have ten seconds to let the door hit you where the good Lord split you."

Carlton whispered. "Ooh, Tina-girl, you know I love you, but I gotta go. Miss Shirley Chisholm's look-alike is too grand for me."

Once Carlton was out of the room, an introductory conversation commenced. "I am Miss Idella Stephens, your product development coordinator." Stephens was a sixty-five-year-old ambassador of etiquette and protocol—cool, collected, and dignified—the inventor of personal growth and improvement instruction.

Tina curtsied. "It's a pleasure to meet you."

Having worked for several of Arnie's mentors and with some of the best artists of all time, The Label's owner coaxed Idella Stephens out of retirement with ego-boosting and carte blanche privileges. Most record labels no longer engaged in artist development activities and Arnie did so sparingly. To remove the mentality of a personal attachment and the assumption of a long-term investment, he changed the department's name from Artist to Product Development. It was Kelly who convinced him that product promotion was crucial in Bettina Charles's case. "To reap premium benefits, the development process should be geared to career building as well as image shaping," argued Kelly.

Miss Idella Stephens began her first official session. It was an identity reinforcement exercise. "Lesson one is about name recognition. With a few exceptions, the Walden Records' staff will refer to you as Miss Charles. If you're called by any other name, you do not respond period."

"Why?" asked Tina. "All of them are older than me. Some are very much so."

"You're Bettina Charles and they aren't. It's that basic. My next question is very easy as well. Are you a top entertainer?"

"Not yet."

"That is the wrong answer. You are a celebrity. The game is all about image, prestige, and an understanding of who you are. In order to be a Pop-Diva as they call it today, you have to breathe it, eat it, and receive it to believe it."

Tina replied proudly. "I know who I am as a person."

"And very quickly, you will learn who you are as a personality—as three seven two eighty-five."

"Why am I being referred to as a number?"

"Contrary to what the public perceives, an artist is a product to the record company, plain and simple. Awareness of that fact is a gift that you will use to your advantage."

"How is understanding that I am a product helpful?"

"Young lady, what does a product do? And that is a rhetorical question. It makes money. The record company makes money when its product does well. If you work every minute of the day far beyond exhaustion, you will be successful. Making money and moving The Label forward and crossing over to the masses is Arnie Peters's current pursuit of prestige. Therefore, I encourage you to accept your three seven two eighty-five status, know your self-worth, insist on the best, pick your battles carefully, and reject things like drugs that will be used to control you. Without them being aware of it, get to know your enemies. That list will be long. On the flip side, your fingers will suffice to count those you can trust and depend on in this vinyl disc making business." Miss Idella Stephens moved on to another lesson. "What is your best angle when taking photographs?"

"I don't know. I haven't taken any professional photographs as of yet."

"I don't know is an unacceptable response."

Tina was amazed as she witnessed Miss Idella Stephens grab a professional camera and start taking pictures while directing her to pose in certain ways. "Angle your body to the right, pull in your gut, poke out your hips, and smile. I want you to do the same thing to the other side. As the next move, put both hands on your hips, look directly at me, and smile playfully. Now, look dead center the camera again, but this time don't smile. Drop your head, lift your eyes, and stare at the lens in this camera seductively."

Tina complained while doing what she was told. "Some of these body positions are quite uncomfortable. They don't feel right."

"Who cares about how you feel? Your feelings are irrelevant to the presentation of your package. You grin and bear it."

Tina was really missing Carlton because of her language comprehension deficit. "Miss Stephens, I'm not familiar with the term *grin and bear it.*"

Idella Stephens had not been prepped on Tina's backstory and assumed Miss Charles was being sarcastic. "I want you to repeat after me. It doesn't matter how I feel, but how I think and act are crucial."

Tina repeated. "It doesn't matter how I feel, but how I think and act are crucial."

"Say it again, Miss Charles."

"It doesn't matter how I feel, but how I think and act are crucial."

"That's what *grin and bear it* means."

Miss Idella Stephens had Tina perform a slew of drills—walking, sitting, standing, smiling, laughing, and crossing and uncrossing her legs while keeping her back straight. Over lunch, in addition to monitoring her every word and eating posture, Idella Stephens drilled her client using interview questions. She had no issue with Tina's habit of adding the words *you see* to most of her answers. It was a quirky, confident affirmation and far better than saying *you know*. Overall, the teacher was quite pleased with 3.7.2.85's package and presentation.

"Miss Charles, your parents did an exceptional job in developing your core, absolutely superb home training. You have class, grace, poise, an outstanding deportment, and an excellent command of the King's English. All of the above makes my job much easier and your ability to grasp the information more plausible. My tweaks are for the purpose of polishing what is already in place. Since you are far ahead of the game, our sessions will focus on developing more pronounced and exaggerated gestures and a clever attitude, bordering on arrogance. What we create will be the cornerstone of the Bettina Charles public image. And by the way, I am here for you, Miss Tina—not for the one whose name is printed on my check. Finally, what we discuss is private—not to be shared even with Carlton. He is trustworthy, but also a troubled soul."

Under the table, Tina used her thumb to hold down her pinky, leaving three fingers erect. One was for Carlton, one for Ellis Ross, and the third was for Miss Idella Stephens. So far, they were the only people in this record-making business that she trusted.

Coinciding with Tina's orientation and training, Kelly and Arnie had returned to Conference Room 2101, conducting a lengthy brainstorming session. The company's top brass and team leads had reconvened and Kelly was comfortably seated in her usual position at the head of the southern end of the table. After being dismissed by Idella Stephens, Carlton and Assistant Angela joined the conference room meeting to receive marching orders just like everyone else.

Arnie said, "Two days ago, I stated that the reason for bringing you together would slowly be unveiled. Today, I'm back to tell you that the reason should be crystal clear." Arnie sat down at the helm of the table and stood back up before the clock's second hand could make a full revolution. "A hundred of our best and brightest staff came together, sampled the product, loved her, and have been charged with spreading the word throughout our international company. I want our marketing team on the phones rounding up sponsors—encouraging them to board the Bettina Charles train on day one or we will leave without them. That is not to be delivered as a threat, but as a promise. I want the names and numbers of those former friends who passed on our deal."

Those seated at the table or around the walls put pen to pad, capturing the points relevant to their specific departments. Arnie continued. "Three seven two eighty-five is the prototype that I've been talking about for more than a year. Now that we've signed our female Pop-singing heartthrob, we're going to develop an action plan that charts a course leading us to a destination called *Platinum Debut Album* for Miss Three Seven Two Eighty-Five."

As only Kelly King could get away with, she stood and completed her boss's statement. "We're going to do this right, build a house of cards out of brick that won't crumble under the pressure-cooker environment of the music industry. We've got the expertise and Miss Charles has the rest—talent, youth, beauty, natural charm, and intelligence."

Arnie focused on his number one priority, making money. "With this amazing merger, I'm expecting our efforts to pay off in a big way."

With a steady stream of success and money, Arnie's overzealous excitement about Walden Records' potential icon was personal. Being the R&B hit-making King no longer made him the talk of the town. Things had fizzled out and Arnie was bored pure and simple. Having a Pop-Diva under contract was his ticket to professional relevancy. With so many vehicles—recordings, radio, television, music videos, and print media—an artist could be blasted to superstardom in a flash. The status came with Paparazzi trailing, admittance to the hottest clubs, red carpet events, galas, private parties, and access to the best tables at the top restaurants at any time. Bettina Charles was being prepped to position Walden Records at the top of that VIP list, reaping those benefits of royalty.

After lunch, Tina and Miss Idella Stephens parted company with an understanding that, until further notice, they would connect on a daily basis either in person or by phone. In addition, Idella Stephens would be monitoring and critiquing rehearsals, performances, and interviews.

Walden Records' Headquarters

Midtown West Thirty-Seventh Street

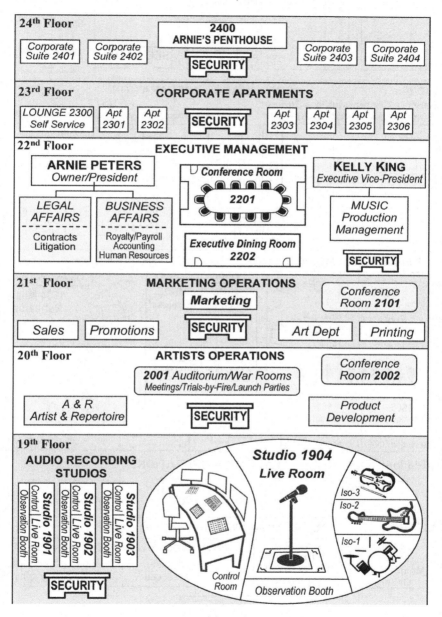

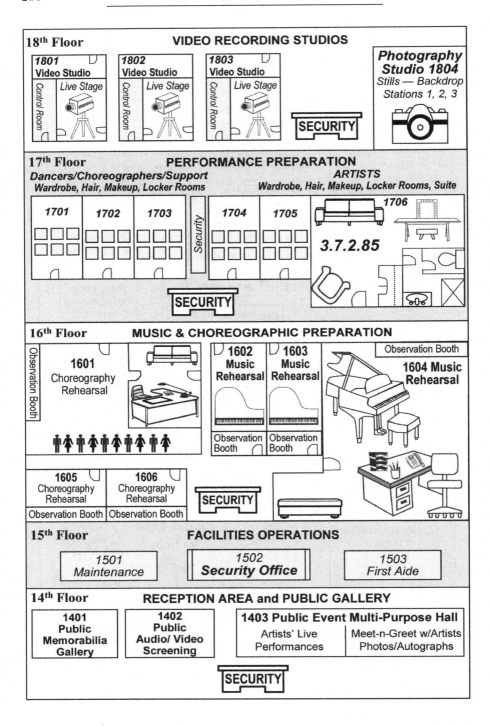

29

LIVE ROOM RECORDING

Friday, July 16, 1982

ELLIS Elite Productions was a hit-creating business whittled down from twenty-five people to one—the eccentric maestro himself. Negative attitudes, lackadaisical work ethics, and inability to consistently implement his vision were reasons he had become a lone-soldier operation. He subcontracted recording support when doing an individual project or worked with those provided by the customer. As an independent record producer, he had a steady flow of flexible agreements with several music labels. His unwavering condition was the right of refusal, enabling him to reject participation in a project without explanation. In his mind, he had a proven system for selecting musicians, assistant audio engineers, and performers. He explained his process to Tina. "I choose my artists, musicians, and production teams based on a notion caused by the motion in the ocean and then give complete devotion to the process of creating something beautiful."

Although expressed differently, Tina found Ellis's appreciation of the art form of music similar to that of her longtime teacher. She had no problem comprehending Ross's poetically stated explanations and was honored to sit at his feet. Tina sent up silent praise. *Although I slammed the door on working with Professor Milton by leaving school early, Ellis Ross was sent through a window to serve as my music industry father. For that, I am truly grateful.*

The sentiment was mutual. In Tina, Ellis Ross found a daughter to nurture. It had been years since he felt so excited about working with an artist and had never felt such a kindred connection. Opposite his obstinate deportment, he entered into a three-year retainer agreement with Walden Records. It made The Label his most favorite client relative to his dealings with one artist, Bettina Charles. Contrary to The Label's credo, Ross was granted creative authority and autonomy. As Arnie predicted, Ellis requested that Kelly King serve as his executive producer, the scenario he desired. In that arrangement, the record company's commander in chief was positive that he would be fed accurate updates and have the ability to implement his agenda through his executive vice president.

Walden Records' staying the course as an independent record company was a strong selling point for Ellis. He appreciated that The Label kept most of its production processes in-house. With that, he had his choice of four state-of-the-art recording studios from which to work his magic. In addition, the staff writers were seasoned veterans that he sporadically had the opportunity to work with over the past twelve years. The reason for the infrequency of a musical alliance was the fact that the six-member team was signed to exclusive songwriting agreements with Walden Records. Their collective achievement was making hits whose masters belonged to The Label. As a singular directive, their current task was to use their assembly line process to crank out tasty tunes for Bettina Charles.

Ellis was a creature of habit. He chose Audio Recording Studio 1904 as the production home for him and Tina because it had served him well in the past. The studio's design was circular like an arena. He and his protégé stood at its center on a six-by-nine-foot Persian area rug—covering a small portion of the room's well-polished, butterscotch-colored hardwood flooring. There was one room in front of them and three small rooms behind them. Each was separated by transparent glass.

After a full morning, Tina welcomed the opportunity to tackle a challenge directly related to music, although she was still unfamiliar with the setup. Her enthusiasm caused her to grab Ellis's arm and tug on it hard. A touchy-feely reaction was the travel companion always escorting Tina's excitement.

"Little Lady, I'm pleased to introduce you to the *Live Room*. It was designed as the ultimate environment for acoustical control. This is where your vocals will be recorded." Looking at the space about six feet in front of them, he continued. "My control room is on the other side of that glass. It's my baby, the place where I perform little miracles." After walking over and looking inside the room, he began to point things out. "All those gadgets are my electronic toys—my multi-track recorders, audio monitors, equalizers, and most importantly, my electronic audio desk."

Continuing to walk around Studio 1904, Tina attempted to absorb much quickly. Because her eyes and head were out of sync, it manifested itself as flightiness to some of the production team being introduced as they walked about. She said, "I can't believe that I'm really here—not only in a recording studio, but one owned by Walden Records."

Tina followed Ellis to the back of the studio and described each small area in turn. "These three spaces are isolation booths. That drum kit and those electric guitars are secluded because of their loudness."

Tina walked to the final isolation booth to the far right where a harp, flute, and three violins were set up. "Those instruments aren't loud at all. Why are they separated?"

Ellis loved Tina's astuteness and willingness to ask questions. "I also use the iso-booths to segregate instruments whose impact I want to manipulate—to achieve a certain exactness and precision in the

quality of the sound. You're going to be blown away by the string arrangements I've added to 'Lost in Love.'" Tina was excited to learn
that her wedding song would be one of her first recordings after "Tell
Me."

Both the isolation booths and the Live Room were soundproofed—retrofitted with double-layered walls and reinforced with
the highest quality absorption material. Ellis took Tina's hand, guided her back to the carpet in the center of the room, and had her sit
on a stool in front of a microphone. "I want you to consider this Live
Room your dugout, your home court—the place where you will be
fruitful and multiply—giving birth to outstanding harmonic compo-
sitions. And unless you have questions, this studio introduction is
over. It's time for us to get down to the business of making beautiful
music."

Tina's soul was trapped inside a place of jubilation and she had no
questions. *Bettina Charles, you finally made it home.*

As the meeting in Conference Room 2201 was drawing to a close,
Kelly slipped out as department heads brown-nosed Arnie. After placing an important phone call, she had Angela, Carlton, and Zina Shelby
report to her office. Once there, Kelly sent them on an assignment to
the Garment District. Its epicenter was a few blocks away from Walden
Records headquarters. She gave them explicit instructions. "I just spoke
to Artella and informed him that an artist's measurements, swatches,
and photos will be hand-delivered to him shortly. With them, he will
create sketches of his recommendations for costumes and then you
three plus André Jenkins, Tina, and I will sit down and make some
determinations."

Excited, because there was an attraction, but wanting to throw off
the scent, Carlton asked, "Why André?"

"He's the lead choreographer and we're preparing for video productions and performances," answered Kelly. "Tina's costumes have to be dance-worthy as well as visually pleasing."

Carlton thought, *I had no idea all this extra stuff behind the scenes was involved in music-making. As long as I get paid on time and have chances to look at luscious André, I'm on top of the world.*

Kelly continued. "I stressed to Artella that his design team approach this project as if preparing for the Fashion Parade, creating a unique look. In the meantime, he's going to let you comb through his ready line and select six to ten body-hugging garments. I'm thinking sexy mini dresses—different colors, similar styles, and noticeable variation near the top of each costume." Kelly did a nose to nose with Carlton. "Since you've been serving as Tina's stylist for some time, I need you to take the lead on this and make smart decisions. The costumes will be used for shooting the 'Tell Me' video and you, Carlton, are the only one that knows the song."

Assistant Angela asked, "What is our target date for shooting?"

"It's up to Arnie, but I'm guessing it will be tomorrow at the earliest. I want you to prepare for that with everything in place tonight—ahead of schedule!" The music executive clapped her hands. "Let's go, people. This train has taken off and is moving quickly." After sending the trio away, Kelly thought strategically. *I wouldn't put it pass Arnie to make an issue out of creating Tina's first video. If he does, I've outlined a concept and have moved forward with costumes. That should position me a few steps ahead of his impatient game—I hope.*

As Assistant Angela, Zina, and Carlton rushed along, The Lovely asked, "Is Kelly talking about Artella, as in America's hottest new designer—Antwan Artella?"

Angela said, "Exactly! He creates costumes for our biggest artists. Arnie subsidized his gallery's start-up home base about four blocks from here. Enough talking—we gotta fly."

"I wasn't built with wings, so you mean fly as in walk-jog real fast?"

Because of Carlton's lagging, Assistant Angela and Zina were eight feet ahead. Angela looked back and yelled. "Stop talking and catch up with us!"

"Y'all are tripping. The soles of my feet aren't accustomed to lifting more than six inches off the ground—at least not when I'm in a standing position." Nonetheless, Carlton dug within himself and caught up with the two veteran team members. They ran from Thirty-Seventh Street, down Seventh Avenue, and turned up West Thirty-Fifth to Artella's, located on Ninth Avenue.

Ellis gave instructions while adjusting the studio vocal microphone to the height of his musical daughter's mouth. He handed her high-quality headphones and exited her musical home to enter his own. Tina adjusted the heavily padded headphones to her liking—completely covering her right ear to block out all external noise. The other headphone was muted by its placement against her hair and behind her left ear. Once situated in his playground, transparent soundproofed glass separated them physically—he in his control booth and she in Studio 1904's Live Room. Creatively, their eye-to-eye connection enabled a continuous spiritual bond, developing an instinctive, nonverbal system of communications. When needed, Ellis instructed Tina through hand movements in the fashion of a choir director or orchestra conductor. While laying her vocals over the track, Tina could clearly distinguish between the fullness of the instruments and the resonant tones of her voice. This enabled her to meld almost effortlessly with the music.

Kelly did not want to interrupt the creative process that was well on its way in Studio 1904. To perform her executive producer-management roles, she monitored the proceedings, peering through the observation booth's one-way glass. The need-to-know people were quite aware of the observation booths attached to each rehearsal room on the sixteenth floor. However, only Arnie, Kelly, and the heads of security and maintenance had access to the ones on floors eighteen and nineteen. Most of the staff had been told that the rooms attached to the studios were electrical closets that they should avoid at all times. The room was illuminated by low-level emergency lighting, and Kelly sat in the darkness, drinking coffee and, periodically, smoking a cigarette. Privately, she prayed. "God please allow everything to go well with the recording of Tina's first single. I am so emotionally invested in its success, both for me and for my little sister."

With headgear in place, Tina sank into the silence of the room. Initially, she was so aware of her breathing and heartbeat that she wondered if their sound would be picked up through the recording devices. She asked Ellis to give her five minutes before beginning the recording session. With it, she executed her process of *maintaining*—breathing in and out while counting down from ten. Then, she consciously logged this experience as occurring twenty-four days short of the seventh anniversary of Momma Nin's death. To commemorate, she placed two fingers on her lips, kissed them, and held them high in the air, saluting her Shero. After that, she uttered two basic sentences before beginning to record her first official single. "Ellis, let's go. I've got magic to do."

E-Ross, as he was known throughout the music industry, pushed the applicable button on his console and the playback started. A clear, professional sound emitted from Tina's headphones, sending a satisfying jolt to the receptors in the auditory cortex of her brain. A deferred dream of a high-quality acoustical experience had been realized. Isolated in 1904's Live Room, seated on a stool in front of a vocal-specialty microphone, knighted with a headset crown, Tina began to sing. There were three television monitors positioned above the control board, streaming the live feed of the video being captured.

Round one of the recording session was for Tina to create the background segments of "Tell Me." Having tweaked the song to have a more refined chorus, Ellis directed her to sing it over and over, in different octaves, key changes, and alternating parts—alto, first and second soprano, and even some deep, rich dips into the lowest depths of her register.

After about thirty minutes, Arnie joined Kelly in the observation booth. He took the lit cigarette from her hand and finished smoking it while handing her a fresh, hot cup of coffee. He stood beside her as they watched their budding Pop-Diva in the *Live Room*. Tina had no idea that she was being monitored. Arnie asked, "How are things going?"

"They're going very well."

"By the way, did you receive my flowers the other evening?"

"Yes and thank you. They were lovely."

"I know you don't like me making overboard compliments about you in front of the team. Now that we're alone, in this booth, in the dark, I want to say *way to go*. You've done a fantastic job with this project so far."

"Just so far?"

"Hell, yeah, so far. We've got a long, long road ahead of us."

Kelly began to snicker and then it turned into a giggle.

"What's so funny, Miss King?"

"Forgive me. Your *long, long road ahead* comment took my mind to a naughty place, but I'm back." Kelly chuckled again and returned her facial expression to its prior serious countenance. "Since we're showing appreciation, I want to thank you for not boiling over the top on Tina's first few days of dealing with you—the Wizard of Walden Records. I'm sure an explosion is coming, but I'm glad it didn't happen the other day in front of a hundred people." Arnie started laughing.

Kelly asked "So, what did I say that was so funny?"

"It's exhilarating to know that you're monitoring the coming of my boiling points and explosions," Arnie admitted.

"Well, somebody has to be brave enough to try and keep you in check."

"Every now and then, I get lucky enough for you to take the time to examine me that closely."

"Yes, I guess you caught me on one of my softer-side days."

"Well, I really like those days and wish they would happen more often."

After moving close enough to touch shoulders, Arnie held Kelly's hand for at least sixty seconds before she reclaimed it. He interpreted her not sliding away from him as a very good sign. He squeezed a handful of plumpness and changed positions to stand behind her. Kelly asked, "Arnie, what are you up to?" The executive vice president knew she was in danger of succumbing to desires. *Arnie's hands are palming-a-basketball sized. I can't help but give him high marks for his special skills in fondling and stimulation.*

"In a few seconds, it will be quite obvious," he answered. Secured in his backdoor position, Arnie wrapped Kelly in his arms, caressing her body—conveying a readiness to help carry her emotional baggage. With no resistance, he pressed forward. His lips and tongue connected with her neck, driven by an alluring combination of a flowery scent and a sweet nectar taste, which emitted from her skin.

Kelly referred to Arnie as a scruffy guy because of his soft, unkempt short-haired beard that she found attractive. Its unruliness complemented his pointed personality. As her neck received his advances, she tilted her head, giving him additional access. Thinking, *Oh, the feel of his lips on my neck is so enticing.* Chill bumps from the tickling sensation began to form on her skin as the interior muscles in her garden began to throb, petitioning for a higher level of attention.

Kelly warned. "You know this is highly inappropriate, so I must administer self-defense." Her retaliation caused Arnie's eyes to pop wide open and then close as the pace of his breathing slowed down. Kelly had freed her right arm from his caress, reached back, and caught hold of his scepter and precious stones. Increased bulging was the result of her skillful massage. She had been there before and was a stickler for getting to the point of a matter. Outwardly, Arnie wanted to suppress his hunger, but his judgment was clouded. *This woman's touch consumes me.*

Kelly cautioned. "This behavior is contrary to the vow of chastity between us."

"I know," he answered. "We have an agreement."

Kelly batted back. "And if you honor it, I'll never speak to you again."

While embracing Kelly from behind, Arnie administered his hands' artistic skill set—rubbing her breasts as his pelvic region worked on its own accord, making known a stiff stance of cooperation. He added ear nibbling to his mouth's mission. He unfastened button one and then button two on her jacket, pulling her blouse out of her skirt. With hands now positioned inside her blouse, he lifted both breasts out of their tucked-away position inside her bra. Applying simultaneous titillation, his hands fondled her cups and his fingertips entertained the tips of her nipples, causing their firmness to increase.

In round two, the work in the Live Room was growing in intensity. There was a learning curve for Tina to overcome. Continuously, she fought to keep her true emotions in check. The vehement stimulation of the experience was exasperating. The newness of this wonderful journey was overwhelming, creating a heightened level of consciousness. Tina sang the melody and verses in a linear format—exactly as they appeared on the sheet music. The accompaniment that she was singing to had been modified. In addition to the instrumental components, background vocals of some of what she sang in round one had been added to the musical track being piped through that right headphone into her ear. Tina sang over it, laying down the vocals of the various verses, and the newly arranged bridge and chorus.

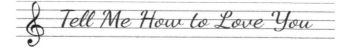

Tina sang:

> *Tell me when to come and what I need to do*
> *Tell me anything except that we are through*
> *Tell me what to say and what I need to know*
> *Tell me when to turn and tell me where to go—*
> *Please—tell me—tell me how to love you.*
>
> *When you tell me this time*
> *Tell me how to make you mine—*
> *When you tell me this time*
> *Tell me that we're doing fine—*
> *When you tell me this time*
> *Tell me that we'll walk life's line—Together*
> *Please—tell me—tell me how to love you.*

Back in the observation booth, Kelly's field of sweet-smelling flowers was intermingling with the rugged, masculine, earthy scent of Arnie's pheromones. Kelly's right hand committed a penalty of encroachment, having reached a hand-to-foreskin connection inside of Arnie's pants. Meanwhile, King Peters refused to be outdone. He took his left hand and slid it down Kelly's torso, reaching its target and exploring her southern region. While not being intrusive, his fingers delicately tilled the top layer of the garden—causing its internal moistness to seep to the surface. Kelly was wild for Arnie's three-finger tricks—welcoming their power over her.

Through the speakers, the "Tell Me" song filled the atmosphere and combined with the darkness, causing the observation booth's temperature to rise. Each party's evasive maneuvers failed, allowing their bodies to surrender to passion's dance, hips moving to the rhythm of his till and her massage respectively. Kelly turned and faced her prey, making her job less taxing as she not only unbuckled his belt, but unzipped his pants. She pushed Arnie hard and his back hit the wall in the twelve-by-ten-inch booth. "This is harassment and I'm going to have to report you to human resources," he warned.

She said, "Good. We'll go together and make dual reports."

Arnie slid Kelly's thong down to her knees. "This is so unprofessional," he said about his own emphatic move.

Kelly jiggled her body, causing her thong to fall to the floor. Then, she stepped her way out of it. "Your idle threats do nothing but drive me forward."

Demonstrating his kingliness, Arnie kneeled and kissed his queenly prize all over her southern region. His lips were succulent and their abilities drove Kelly mad. The bottom one's plumpness had the capacity of engulfing its objective with high esteem. He serviced her profusely with all the adoration he possessed—respecting her as an accomplished powerhouse, loving her secretly as a woman. From that conviction, he used the strength and domination of his tongue to deliver bull's-eye blows to her weakest point of submission. Arnie remained at his post until she executed a forceful change in shift. After pulling on his shoulders and motioning him to stand, Kelly dropped to her knees and took hold of a mouthful of fore-play. He received what he could, but his longing to enter the garden was the most dominant of all his desires.

As round three, Tina ad-libbed the melody and harmony segments to both the verses and the chorus. "Instead of singing the lyrics straight," Ellis instructed. "I want you to create sexy sound effects of moans, groans, oohs, and aahs. Also, while matching the song's rhythm, make up words from what you're feeling about the messages found in the lyrics and the beat. I want you to give me a natural groove." E-Ross was thrilled by the fact that Tina was so coachable, listening carefully and executing as directed.

In the booth, there was no submissive soul present—no cordial relinquishing of power. Arnie was hanging onto the ledge of sensibility and was concerned about Kelly's comfort. "The blanket," he mumbled. After kicking off both shoes, he freed his legs from the confinement of the pants wrapped around his ankles. While pulling his precious cargo along, Arnie made his way to the second shelf in the metal cabinet and retrieved a soft and fluffy padded quilt. He had placed it there as a result of previous bouts of their alpha-male-female impassioned, impromptu behavior. They were victims of failing to comply with the rules they coauthored for the good of company deportment.

With both villains refusing to disengage the suction of their kiss, the off-balanced choreography carried them from the steel storage cabinet to the spot on the industrial carpeting where the quilt was thrown out. After being assisted to a lying position, Kelly sent a subtle invitation to her deliverer with moans and sensual body movements. Opposite her unflappable professional demeanor, she needed this counterbalancing pause to quench her secret desire to be taken, manhandled, and possessed. At this juncture, Arnie was the solitary soul meeting her lofty requirements. With a more direct plea, she beckoned him, and then begged him to invade.

In turn, his desire to enter the garden was on equitable footing with his need for water, food, and oxygen. Kelly's mouth watered in anticipation of the stiff rod's intrusion. With the aid of the low-level lighting, Arnie admired Kelly's beauty as he descended upon her, taking his time to savor the moment. He placed her hand on his rock-solid pistol, creating a shower inside her pleasure palace. Its width and length were equally impressive, causing her hand to voluntarily stroke it up and down. At that pivotal point, she was on fire and he was enraged. After a few gentle tries, he abandoned his politeness and forced his way deep inside her inner court. It had been a while since she had a visitor, so pain was experienced as the breakthrough unfolded. This heightened her satisfaction, and Kelly enjoyed the momentary discomfort. It was pleasurable, like biting down on something tart and chasing it with something sweet. The controlled, rhythmic movement of Arnie's instrument was masterful, allowing Kelly to easily follow the motion. The concerted effort caused both participants to wallow in the enjoyment of overwhelming delight.

Even in the pursuit of pleasure, they engaged in a sexual power struggle. In a wild rowing session, Kelly basked in the satisfaction of being mounted—enjoying the intense grinding. Then, a shift in position occurred, causing Arnie to acquiesce. Kelly sat up, head back, hands touching his abdomen for balance. Using her backward-bending lower extremities, power and rhythm guided the up-and-down movement of her ride. During the engagement, there were many false-positive quivers, reaping elevated levels of gratification. They were followed by tremors where passion's sweat oozed from their pores and blended together. Having flipped positions again, their wild kisses assisted in lowering the volume of their cries, released unavoidably as a part of their indescribable satisfaction.

After a lengthy seductive encounter, they had reached the exhausting point of collapsing from an overdose of exultation. Yielding to satisfaction was euphoric, magical, and overpowering. As the hose spread fertilizer all over the garden, they held onto each other tightly, needing that support to bear the intensity of the overwhelming level of pleasure. Arnie so badly wanted to reveal his hidden desire to permanently occupy the land, to be granted the power to continuously plow—perhaps, raising crops in the process. As he quivered, moaned, and praised her so beautifully, Kelly returned his accolades while treasuring their sharing in this brief moment of mutual relinquished control.

Although feeling the added weight of Arnie's limp body on top of hers, she refused to budge from that position. Her arms held him close—seeing him through the completion of his release. *These few and far between encounters with my lover-man boss are incredible.* Indeed, they represented Kelly's outward expression of intimacy—the only affection she would allow at this point in her relational maturation. Similar to her cousin Carlton, she had a phobia about serious commitment and was afraid to trust another person that deeply—especially one as deceptive and devious as Mister Peters.

Disengaging their love-link, they lay there, staring at the ceiling.

Arnie asked, "Will you stay at my place tonight?"

"You know I'm not prepared to do that. Agreeing to spend the night denotes something more substantial and open to public scrutiny."

"The hell with what the public thinks."

"We discussed this before and my answer is the same. All my attention is focused on The Label and that's where I want it to be right now. Please try and understand."

"I can't say I do, but I respect your wishes just the same." Arnie was disappointed, but was accustomed to her rejection. Whatever time they spent together had to be enough—for now. He knew that they were a powerful force, even if she refused to openly acknowledge it.

In their opposing office suites, the two powerhouses showered in an attempt to wash away their naughtiness. Carrying on with their duties, it appeared to everyone else as if nothing out of the ordinary had happened.

30

ALL NIGHT VIDEO

DECOMMISSIONED by the power of Kelly's kryptonite, the long hot shower did nothing to wash her presence out of Arnie's mind. Unable to break the spell she had cast on him, he had been left in this emotional debilitating state—feeling like a bruised man, far too many times. Once again, he licked his wounds with mental consoling. *With all I've accomplished, my ego can withstand being dropped down a peg in my personal life. Besides, no one that matters knows about me and Kelly anyway.*

After laying vocals over the final track, the Live Room work was done and Tina joined Ellis in the control booth. Just like in the rehearsal room, they shared a bench seat at the console. Ellis's expertise as a mixing engineer was at the top of his multifaceted skill set. He was known as a musical mad scientist with amazing instincts. Respecting Tina's desire to be a student of the art form, he gave her an overview of his process. "As we go forward, you'll see my desk light up like a Christmas tree." The instructor pointed as his student looked on. "These gain knobs, this auxiliary section, and the like are boring controls and mumbo jumbo tools for a connoisseur like me and my technicians to worry about. The happenings I want you to focus on are the levers located on the bottom of this console—the assign buttons—very self-explanatory. I've doled out functions of sound expressions to each switch."

While pointing them out, he guided Tina's hand in order for her to move the different levers up and down. "The full instrumental track is assigned to lever one, your straight melody is on two, the harmony is three, and your vocal swell is four. From there, it gets unruly with designations for ad-lib, bridges, horns, drums, breakdowns, and so on."

Tina was awestruck. "This equipment is the best!"

Ellis added his special twists to the multi-track recording synchronization process by manipulating song segments of Tina's three-part harmony—her singing above and below the melody. His understanding of her style of expression enhanced and expedited their production work in the studio. There was no lengthy discourse about musical point of view. In fact, Tina and Ellis often reached similar conclusions on the placement of musical accents, adding body and emphasis to the song's background. As part of her naming game, Tina called her special vocal sound effects *Nice-Spice*—to be used as one of her musical signatures in many of her recordings going forward.

Multiple times, Ellis copied the musical string of Tina singing the straight chorus verbatim—according to the sheet music. Then, in looping it all together, he produced an intricate background of what sounded like the contribution of many voices. In actuality, it was all vocals sung by Bettina Charles, executing many roles in her choir of one. Listening to the play-back, Tina was overcome with emotion. Like being knocked off balance, the awareness of fulfilling her dream of making a record kept hitting her in waves.

Creating flavorful and appropriately placed emphasis, Ellis's use of the console's reverberation unit added echo effects that entered and slowly exited the song. "Oh yeah, the send and receive of this reverb is right on, adding an extra lift of wonderful *oomph*. Man, this groove is hot."

While Ellis treated Tina, Carlton, and Assistant Angela to a celebratory dinner, the audio-recorded work of art was passed to the reliable hands of Daniel Weeks. He was The Label's mastering engineer and leader of the studio production team, charged with preparing the final recording product for reproduction and distribution. Of course, Arnie had to give his approval before anything left the building.

9:00 p. m.—The production team assembled in close quarters in Studio 1904's control room. In addition to Tina and Carlton, the inner circle included Kelly, Arnie, Ellis, Assistant Angela, Idella, Zina, and André. Along with Daniel Weeks, they sat and listened to the "Tell Me" track. During the song's second play, Ellis said, "I always give a nickname to each of my musical babies. I named this track *Impromptu Sex.*"

Kelly and Arnie's eyes connected from opposite sides of the mixing console. Separate and confidentially, they accepted ownership of the befitting categorization. Arnie contemplated, *I've got to find a permanent remedy to break that woman's spell.*

Kelly thought, *Arnie's poison potion is irresistible. I should be ashamed of myself, but I'm not. I was long overdue for a recharge.*

The unanimous opinion of those hearing the final version was that the "Tell Me How to Love You" song was a knock out-of-the-park that garnered four runs batted in. Although sold on the single after hearing it the first time, Arnie held his approval until after the fourth play of the track. During each review, his internal anger meter continued to rise. The looks in everyone's faces were a bit too relaxed for him. He wondered, *The members of this so-called inner circle must think I've gone soft or stupid. Between Ellis, Idella, and that Carlton character, I've given them a little too much freedom and power. Shit, even Assistant Angela is acting a bit too special. Now, it's time for me to retake the steering duties of this wheelhouse.*

Kelly offered praise. "The execution of this first track is an exceptional demonstration of teamwork." She looked at her watch and said, "Great job everyone and since it's after ten on a Friday night, enjoy your last free weekend until further notice from here on out. We'll get started early on Monday—say a breakfast planning meeting at seven thirty. Everyone's internal clock needs to be set on long days until further notice." Respecting the presence of their founder, Kelly looked to him for confirmation. "Arnie, what do you think?"

"I agree that things are going to get a hell of a lot harder, but instead of Monday, it begins tonight with filming the 'Tell Me' video. Before dinner, I took the liberty of having Shantelle set things in motion." Arnie placed a call from the control room's phone and was told that everything was in place. "Good, the only people missing from their respective positions are surrounding me here in this booth and that better change in the next sixty seconds." The room cleared with the intensity of a stampeding herd of buffalo. As a professional, Kelly understood that it was Arnie's call and her job to guide Tina through a strenuous process that would occur over the time-span of a solitary, long night.

High activity, focused on a common purpose, was the atmosphere in the applicable departments. Having received Arnie's forewarning at the end of Tina's trial by fire, staffers were not surprised to be called into work during off-hours. It was neither the first nor the last time for such urgency. After causing the storm, Arnie retreated to several phones in his office suite, manning them in telethon mode—talking on one receiver with a caller—left holding on another. Kelly King was everywhere coordinating everything—her ultimate place of comfort. She had Carlton work with Zina to assure there was noticeable variation in hair and makeup in correspondence with each wardrobe change. Assigned an errand, Assistant Angela darted down a flight of stairs to 1801 and delivered a sketch-a-script to Keith Murray, the video technical director. The document contained notes that had been scribbled on a lyrics sheet of the "Tell Me" song.

Keith Murray asked, "What the hell is this?"

"It's Miss King's concept for the video," answered Assistant Angela. "She wants you to work the details out with Ellis Ross and have her scenes timed to the musical track ASAP." With the message delivered, the personal assistant to the personal assistant moved to her duty post at Carlton's side.

Ellis took it from there, getting Murray to open the window shade of his narrow-mindedness in order to examine Kelly's concept in its purest light. Its simplicity was ingenious—to promote Tina's image by emphasizing her beauty and sexy sassiness through numerous costume changes, seductive body poses, and playful dance moves. Those shots would be combined with film footage from Tina's audio recording of the "Tell Me" track. The video's magic would be made by Murray adding special effects and mixing all of the elements filmed into fast-paced cuts to compensate for the lack of props, little set design, and a cast of one. "Now, we're cooking with gas," said Ellis. The two cagey veterans were working cooperatively, directing the crew on how Kelly's concept would take form.

On floor sixteen, Tina had just completed her thirty-minute rehearsal session with André Jenkins. It was more than enough time to absorb his input. His basic choreographed routine would be added to her freestyle moves—to be used during the video filming. With dancing action plan in place, Tina followed her handlers up the stairs to floor seventeen. After showering, she received an expert shampoo, blow-dry, and curl, courtesy of Carlton. For the duo, it represented a familiar activity in a series of current events. Although reluctant to do so, he had inched forward in transitioning the styling duties to a shared responsibility. As part of the process, Carlton used show-and-tell as his method of training the three-member cosmetology crew assigned to 3.7.2.85. Armed with beauty supplies, he methodically instructed the onlookers. "Separate and comb through a small section of hair. Glide the curling iron down the strands from top to bottom to straighten.

Next, use wrist action only to angle and twirl the curling iron three times and release. Voilà! A perfect curly twist is created."

Tina was grateful and pleased to have Carlton leading her team, laughing at the reactions of those unfamiliar with his straightforward mannerisms. "And if anyone accidentally burns Miss Charles, retaliation will be swift—a punch in the face delivered by yours truly," he warned. "Now, let's move right along to makeup. Administer concealer and foundation using circular motions that give a mini face lift with each application. Please note that makeup removal is just as important as putting it on. Prior to having your face nose to nose with Miss Charles, assure that your breath is minty fresh." He touched his mouth and blew a kiss.

Saturday, July 17, 1982

1:30 a. m.—Upon the completion of heavy-duty grooming and Carlton's training session, final styling preparation activities relocated to Video Studio 1801. That is where the groomers retreated to a small concave in the far back, right corner of the Live Stage. When Kelly entered the changing area, Tina's head-to-toe makeover was complete—dressed in costume one: a red, skin-clinging mini dress and three-inch matching heels. There was one problem the creative director noticed immediately—*Love Golden* had to go away.

Kelly said, "Tina, the necklace has to come off."

"I've seen photos where other artists were allowed to keep their jewelry on. This necklace is a part of who I am."

"I'm sorry, Tina, but it has to go. It doesn't fit with the overall concept." Tina slid the golden wedding band up and down its chain, turned, and held her hair up while Kelly removed the cherished heirloom.

"Don't worry—it will be safe with me. I promise." The senior executive placed the necklace in the small pocket on her suit jacket. With the jewelry issue resolved, Tina grabbed hold of Miss King's extended hand and walked as she was being guided onto the set. Once there, the big sister asked, "Although you look amazingly beautiful at this early hour in the morning, how do you feel?"

Tina answered. "I feel good, but a bit dizzy, trying to figure out who to listen to and where to focus."

"Unfortunately, it gets worse from here. Instructions will be delivered from many different directions—shouted over the intercom, from Murray in the production control room, from the floor manager's verbal and nonverbal signals out here on the live stage, and from me. In general, prepare for Arnie to micromanage off and on from this point forward. Fortunately, he's missing in action at the moment. Regardless of everything else, concentrate on singing along with the track that will be blasted through the speakers."

Kelly guided Tina through an obstacle course of floor cabling and cords to each of the three two-hundred-and-fifty-thousand-dollar cameras, which were five feet tall and bulky, but easy to move. She spoke into her headset's microphone. "Murray, go live on camera one." Then, Kelly turned to Tina. "See the red light?"

"Yes, I see it."

"That means the camera is rolling—that you're being filmed on camera one, two, three, or all of them. We'll cue you by saying, *Camera two in three, two, and one.* After you hear one, your job is to sing to the light of the camera that we call out as if it were an audience. Move naturally and in rhythm with the music. Other than dancing, the majority of the filming process is similar to a television news shoot—much easier than the full productions that are to come. There also will be four additional cameras." Kelly pointed her finger toward the ceiling and both women looked up. "Two cameras are unmanned and positioned above us to capture overhead shots. The two remaining will be mobile, maneuvered by camera operators who'll be tracking your motion. We'll instruct you when to sing directly to the moving cameras as we go along. Do you have any questions?"

I have about a million of them, starting with the definition of a television news shoot. "No, I don't have any questions at the moment." As Kelly bounced away to tend to her next line item, the floor manager positioned 3.7.2.85 in the center of a green screen, gave her instructions for the first scene, and backed away. The rookie artist prayed, *God, please help me.* Then, she encouraged herself. *Bettina Charles, you can do this. Block out everything else and perform to the red light, your audience. It's your favorite thing.* After that, Tina was in a zone and Tosha Ray was fiery.

The music was cued, the red light flashed first on camera two, and the filming began. With a setup that was similar to the audio recording, the video control center was located in a glass-enclosed cockpit. Technical director Keith Murray piloted from the visual control board and Ellis Ross provided musical direction from an adjacent audio console. A camera control unit, video switcher, lighting board, and character generator were some of the equipment being operated by technicians seated around and behind Murray and Ross.

The video monitor wall was above the director's head and held nine television units used for previewing graphics, special effects, input of each studio camera, and extra footage. The units were arranged in two rows of four—some color, some grayscale, and the largest screen was in the center. It was the reference monitor, displaying the combined studio footage. From his microphone, Murray called out commands to those seated around him as well as those wearing headgear and positioned in the live studio—the camera crew, the floor manager, and Kelly King. A headset was available should Arnie Peters show up and make a request for one.

6:00 a. m.—Four and a half hours into the production process, Tina had sung the entire song directly into the camera in each costume— red, black, yellow, blue, and green. With every wardrobe change, much took place behind the partition in the changing area. As Carlton monitored and yelled most of his instructions using an operatic voice, Zina Shelby and two of her wardrobe assistants' intimate access to Tina involved hands-to-skin engagement. They helped her in and out of clothing down to bras and undergarments—leaving no room for modesty. Hair, makeup, and costume adjustments were executed simultaneously. At times, six pairs of hands reached over, under, and around each other to implement their particular duty in the beautification assault being administered to 3.7.2.85. The film sequences were repeated with every costume change. Tina danced freestyle mixed with her choreographed routine. She twirled, dipped, swayed, turned to her right, and walked to the song's rhythm—the length of the green screen—about ten feet. Then, she reversed her body position, repeating the movement in the opposite direction. The shot selections and Tina's timing were a magical merger consisting of close-ups, establishing shots, full-body shots, follow shots, and freeze-frames.

By the time Arnie entered the control room, the final scenes in the last costume were being shot. Tina was dressed in her older sister's favorite color: fuchsia. Kelly had relocated to a seat at the top of the control room out of the way. Her concept was being carried out beautifully—no longer a need for interference. Noticing Arnie's presence and accompanied by Angela, Carlton tipped into the control booth and stood out of sight in the back entryway of the dimly lit room. Heeding Assistant Angela's advice, he remained silent—for the moment. Arnie sat down next to Kelly and they both stared at the central, live-action monitor—viewing from an audience's perspective. Arnie asked, "Are you sure she hasn't done this before?"

"I'm positive that she hasn't."

"When the camera light flashes, she's right there, singing to it. With each cut to camera two or three, she nails it, bull's-eye. Her stares into the lens carry a perfect amount of emotion that equates to a connection to the intended audience—the fans watching on their TV screens. The pouty mouth, subtle hesitation, and playful flirtation are dead-on."

Kelly reminded her direct report about her prediction. "Do you remember what I promised to deliver during last week's phone call from the hotel in North Carolina?"

"I do. And boy, did you come through. Look at her go. The way she pushes back her hair, her hand gestures, and her body motions are natural looking and inviting. It's as though she's making love to the camera and that is the appropriate allusion!"

"Whenever you enter a booth, the subject of making love is a consistent thought."

"That's because production equates to money, my supreme definition of satisfaction, next to you." Although tempted, Kelly did not respond to her lover-man boss's comment.

Creeping forward from the darkened entryway, Carlton tapped Arnie on the shoulder. "Excuse me Mister Peters, but I need to inform you that—."

Surprised, Arnie jumped to his feet. On his home turf, it was an unwritten rule that no one entered his personal space uninvited and touching him was out of the question. "Where the hell did you come from and why are you anywhere near me?"

"I'm here to do my job. Miss Charles is extremely exhausted, so the shooting of this video needs to end real soon—like in the next few minutes."

Fatigued and anxious about Tina's success, Kelly had, once again, forgotten about keeping an eye on Carlton. While glancing at his wristwatch, Arnie addressed his response to his executive vice president. "Is he talking about product 3.7.2.85 that's been under contract for all of thirty-six hours?"

"I certainly am—unless there's another video being shot in this building at this particular time."

"Apparently, you haven't been properly schooled, but I call the shots around here."

"Not where Tina's health is concerned."

"You and your concern can go straight to—."

Kelly interjected herself as the ending of Arnie's statement to Carlton. "Why don't we all calm down and have a fresh cup of coffee." Using her body as a neutral zone, Kelly slid between the two strong personalities. "Angela, pour us all coffee, please."

Saved by perfect timing, Keith Murray said, "And that, my friend Mister Ross is a wrap!" Ellis turned from his mixing console, looked up in Kelly's direction, and gave a thumbs-up sign that denoted the video's completion.

7:30 a. m.—Kelly's, first response was silent gratitude. *Lord, I thank you for intervening just in the nick of time.* "This conversation is a moot point because we're all done here." Kelly grabbed Carlton's arm and pulled him along as she yelled instructions over the intercom. "Cast and crew, meet me in the center of Studio 1801's live stage." Once assembled Kelly said, "Tina, you were fabulous and kudos to the entire team for a job well done. It's Saturday morning so enjoy your weekend. I'll see you back here on Monday—early—at eight o'clock sharp."

Arnie interjected. "People, this is what I expect from you—a quality single and a video delivered quickly and under budget."

Unaware of the minor bickering, Tina was relieved that her heavy coat of armor wasn't needed because the forecast for a Mister Peters' blizzard did not come to fruition. *Now, I get it,* she concluded. *Arnie's not mean after all. He just wants your best and I'll work hard to give him that all the time.*

During video editing, Arnie's behavior was surprising. "Murray, we're exhausted arguing about what frames to keep in or cut out. All the takes are usable so you and Johnson work it out. After grabbing a few hours of sleep, I have other matters to attend to. Have a final video and stills for me to review on Monday." Jerry Johnson was The Label's director of photography and the stills Arnie requested were his responsibility. Because of time constraints, he was forced to conduct a fragmented photo shoot, borrowing Tina after wardrobe changes in between filming segments.

Later that Evening, Saturday, July 17, 1982

5:10 p. m.—After giving security at Windsor East telephone approval, Tina opened 2407's front door and let in her unexpected guest. The Pop-Diva-in-training was disheveled—hair pointed in various directions, eyes opened halfway, dressed in a white tank top and striped-cotton pajama pants. "Come in, Miss King." Kelly followed her into the kitchen. Along the way, Tina scratched her head while yarning. "I guess I filmed something wrong on the video? I'll wake up Carlton. Give us about an hour to get ourselves together to go back to The Label?"

Now, standing in the kitchen, Kelly clarified the reason for her unplanned visit. "Oh no, Tina, I just left the studio and everything's fine. Matter of fact, you were incredible. I'm here because I wanted to return your necklace. I promised that I'd keep it safe and didn't want you worrying about it for what's left of the weekend." Kelly placed the bag she was holding on the counter. "Here, let me help you put it on." Tina turned and held up her hair and Kelly hooked *Love Golden* into place.

"Thank you, Miss King. Between you and me, my necklace is called *Love Golden.* It was a gift from my Momma Nin and is extremely important to me. It's irreplaceable."

"Well, from now on, I'll be the keeper of *Love Golden* when you have to take it off—if you like."

"I'd like that very much. Although I love him dearly, Carlton gets too distracted to place my necklace in his care. Besides, I overburden him with enough as it is."

"Consider it done." Kelly pointed at the rather large bag. "I know you like Chinese food, so I picked some up, figuring that you and Carlton probably slept most of the day and had not eaten. It's more than enough to last for several meals."

Tina emptied the bag's contents, opened each container, and placed them onto the kitchen table. "Let's see. We have shrimp-fried rice, peppered steak, shrimp toast, egg rolls, General Tso's chicken, and—."

Carlton popped into the kitchen, grabbed the final container from Tina's hands, and opened it. "Crispy beef is the bomb. My nose smelled this Chinese food and woke the rest of me right up. Kelly, welcome to our glad-pad by the way."

Tina added. "Yes, Miss King. Thank you for being so thoughtful. These are all of our favorites and we'd love it if you would join us."

"Yes, Kelly thanks for the grub and Tina would love the company. No offense, but my bed, my TV, and now this food will be on a private date for the rest of the evening." Carlton made two piled-high plates and disappeared to his room.

"That would be awesome, because I'm starving, too," said Kelly. "By the way, what I saw of your apartment looks fabulous."

"Thank you. I'll give you the full tour when we're done eating. Forewarning, Carlton's room is a little out there and he loves to show it off."

"I wouldn't expect anything less from Mister Montgomery as he calls himself." Although exhausted in her thirtieth hour without sleep, Kelly was in heaven as she made a move closer to befriending her little sister.

31

VERBAL AGREEMENT

Tuesday, August 3, 1982

STAYING on schedule to finish the debut album required a minimum of twelve-hour workdays for Tina and crew and sixteen-hour workdays for Kelly. In Arnie's absence, she had driven activities forward with minimal fallout. "Tell Me" and "Lost in Love" were put to bed first, prior to Arnie's self-dismissal. Four singles had been added to the completion list by the end of the sixteenth consecutive day of audio recording. That left four songs to be produced out of the ten needed for the album. Each finished track was sent to Arnie, who had returned to the West Coast office. With no fanfare, Shantelle communicated the big boss's four-out-of-four endorsement. From there, each approved single, in turn, was passed onto Jenkins and Murray for choreography and video preparation.

During that same time span, Kelly instituted a one-on-one breakfast meeting with Tina in Executive Dining Room 2202. The straightforward ground rules banished the attendance of the Bettina Charles's image, product 3.7.2.85, and encouraged free expression from the newly-signed artist—a real person. Two weeks after the daily summit's introduction, a more casual method of communications between the secret sisters was evolving slowly. Kelly gave instructions, offered advice, and answered each of Tina's questions even if a bold-faced lie was required to do so.

At the breakfast meeting, Kelly explained to Tina that her attention had to be divided. "As hard as you've been working, I have to stretch you even further based on The Label's target album release date. Time has to be squeezed into the schedule for you to work on the videos we plan to release in conjunction with certain singles. Starting today for example, you will begin working on choreography for the 'Lost in Love' video that will be filmed here in the studio." Tina sipped her hot tea with extra honey and lemon and listened carefully. "After working with Ellis on music production this morning as usual, I need you to report to André Jenkins on floor sixteen following a break for lunch."

"No problem. I am determined to become a great artist, and I know I have to work hard to get there. Besides, I love every minute of the creative part of what I'm doing, especially when nobody's yelling."

Kelly reached across the breakfast table and grabbed Tina's hands. "The one thing I can guarantee is that the yelling comes with the territory. The sooner you learn to deal with it, the better off you'll be. And when you need to fight back, do so. I warn you, though, to choose those battles carefully."

"Yes, Ma'am. You sound just like Miss Idella and that's scary."

"I'll try not to make that mistake again. One Idella Stephens is helpful and more than enough." The sisters shared a good laugh.

Choreography Rehearsal Room 1601 was the largest of the three dance practice spaces and had a private office with two doors—one leading to the hallway and the other into the studio. As lead choreographer, André Jenkins was able to perform administrative duties while being a short distance away from the dance floor. It was a real convenience for whenever he was hit with a burst of inspiration.

Video recording equipment was onboard, enabling his fresh ideas to be captured immediately. In addition to the office entryways, there was one more door that led from the hallway directly into Rehearsal Room 1601. That was the way Tina had entered the wide-open studio.

While waiting patiently for André to appear from his office, Tina prepared her body for dancing by stretching and gliding around the now brightly lit room. Her last visit to this studio was brief—a thirty-minute rehearsal for the "Tell Me" video with low-level lighting only in the front portion of the room.

She had no idea that a staff writer was exiting the private office undetected as André and he had just concluded their chemical and physical interaction. Tina's interest was piqued by life-sized cutouts of ten of Walden Records' mega stars lining the back wall of the large rehearsal space.

Upon joining her near the cardboard likenesses, André said, "I see you're admiring our little shrine."

Tina answered. "Absolutely. Seeing the faces of music royalty is very inspiring."

"That's exactly what they are designed to do, among other things," said André. "Push new artists like you to aim for that level of greatness and recognition."

"What do you mean among other things?"

"Miss Charles, this is a tough business. If the artist drops in popularity for an extended period, Arnie has the cutouts cut up into pieces and removed—always when people are present to witness the figurative falling from grace process. Mister Peters prides himself in sending subtle messages by making examples out of his human products."

Refusing to focus on negative thoughts, Tina changed the subject and turned to face André. "I'm a big fan of your choreography and am excited to be working with you for an extended period of time. By the way, there's something white above your lip on the right side."

André wiped his face. "Thanks. I was just finishing up my lunch with something sweet and delicious—a chocolate éclair with yummy white cream on the inside." André chuckled. "Oh dear, I guess some of it squirted out."

As Tina and André talked, dancers entered the studio. Once all bodies were in position, the choreographic instruction commenced. Although intricate, Tina had no problem keeping pace with the eleven professional ballet dancers. Of the six males, one of them served as her love interest. When the final routine was presented before Kelly, Carlton, Angela, Ellis, Keith Murray, and Idella Stephens, all agreed that André s choreography was brilliant. Its artistry of grace in motion matched the "Lost in Love" track and scripted concept perfectly. As the dancers and Keith Murray exited Choreography Rehearsal Room 1601, Arnie entered the studio, followed by Tina's high-powered consultant from the entertainment law firm. They split the ballet dancers down the middle and interrupted the lighthearted conversation of the inner circle team. They were seated on or standing near the bleachers in the front-left area of the room.

Kelly walked halfway across the dance floor and hugged Arnie, hoping the gesture would influence his frame of mind. "I thought you were still in Los Angeles. I wish you'd give me a little notice before popping up out of nowhere."

"My Company, my choice to show up when I damn well please." All but Tina and Carlton were clued in as to which Arnie they were dealing with. It was assumed that the insecure persona was there for a muscle flexing release by reinforcing rigidity to the rank and file. That was his smoke screen. After hearing and sharing Tina's music out West with industry experts, his possession of America's next megastar was the consensus. Arnie's goal was to assure that three seven two eighty-five was in his complete control. With Bettina Charles doing his bidding, his reign as record industry emperor was assured.

"For all of you who don't know, this is Horace Winslow. External to The Label, he's one of Miss Charles's legal advisors." Arnie showed up to show out. "I want Tina, Ellis, and Kelly to meet Mister Winslow and me in Conference Room 2201 in fifteen minutes."

Kelly struggled to maintain professional deportment. "For God's sakes, the child is dressed in a leotard and tights. We'll meet you there in an hour after she's showered and changed."

⁓

Upon entering 2201, Tina's heart was pounding and her hands were trembling. She asked herself, *What did I do to lose my contract already?* Finding strength and safety in numbers, she entered the room followed by Kelly, Carlton, Ellis, Idella, Angela, Zina, and André Jenkins.

Arnie said, "What the hell is this? You're trying to run a train on me?"

Tina responded on behalf of her entourage. "We've all been working hard and all of us are going to be impacted by whatever this is." Tina looked at Horace Winslow and asked, "Is it all right for members of my inner circle team to be here?"

Winslow answered. "It's permissible if this is what you desire."

"In that case everyone stays."

"Well then, all of you sit the hell down." Everyone but Tina took a seat at the conference table.

Arnie said, "That especially applies to you, Miss Charles. Sit down!"

"No thanks—I prefer to stand."

Arnie was going to win this round. "Well, I have nothing to say until you do." Tina sat down. Then, he instructed The Label's transcriber to read the excerpt from the contract.

The transcriber read:

Walden Records, with or without provocation, has the right of refusal to deny the recording of any of Bettina Charles's copyrighted material and associated masters—all referred to as her intellectual property.

Tina's frown demonstrated her confusion. "You were pleased with the singles we recorded and approved each and every one of them—so far."

"That's true, but you have not met the terms of our verbal agreement. In several conversations, you and I agreed that you would record one of The Label's songs for every two coming from your little Bettina Charles catalog. I've received six out of the ten needed for the album and not one originated from my songwriters—my company's coffers—the same thing."

"It wasn't intentional. I was trying to finish the album by doing what I could do best and quickly, like you asked me to."

"Many have tried to play me, but none have succeeded. I gave you rope, left you alone, and waited to see what you'd do. Perhaps, we should start over and produce an album with all internal-company songs. Or, maybe, I'll pull the stopper from the drain, shelve the project until further notice, or squash the deal altogether."

Seated next to her, Tina turned and addressed her question directly to Horace Winslow. "I'm under contract. Can he do that?"

"Miss Charles, I'd like to take this conversation offline. Please follow me."

The bratty Tina emerged. "No. Just answer my question. Can he do that?"

"To maintain your branding, we relinquished a great deal."

"So what does that mean?"

"Mister Arnie Peters on behalf of Walden Records is within his right to refuse to record your music and/or cancel your contract altogether."

Ellis interjected. "Arnie, there's no need for threats and a heavy hand. The Little Lady has integrity and incredible drive. You'll both win if you give her some creative space."

Kelly said, "Arnie, we stand to make major money and you own the rights to hundreds of songs. Tina's few won't make or break us. Can't we just forget about this senseless verbal agreement?"

Tina's word meant everything to her and she was devastated that Arnie accused her of being conniving. "I've tried, but so far the click in my head that makes magic has not happened with the material your songwriters have presented to me." *I never cheat, but how do I prove it to him?* Tina posed her bright idea to Winslow. "What if I guarantee four platinum singles or repay The Label its one-hundred-fifty-thousand-dollar signing bonus—as soon as I can?"

Quickly, the bonus had been eaten away. In addition to her and Carlton's living expenses, Tina had repaid Pappy John, made repairs to Joseph-Lee Manor, and purchased gifts for her great-aunties, her great-uncle, Larry, Tony, Rufus, Duberry, Clevon, Cornelius, Cousin Alonia, and a new friend—she had met since moving to New York.

Winslow said, "Tina, negotiations don't work that way. As Mister Peters is well aware, your contract is not up for renegotiation. The deal is done and the ink is dry."

Arnie assured. "I'm quite aware of the rules. Changing the terms of the contract is not my idea, but your client's asinine offer."

"Can't I make a new verbal agreement to prove my loyalty?" asked Tina.

Impatiently, Winslow answered his client. "Nothing would be legally binding, but I can't stop you from playing silly honor system games with Mister Peters."

Unlike Douglas Brown, Preston Vaughan, and Isaac Straus, Horace Winslow was a hired consultant with no personal allegiance to Tina. "In that case, Mister Winslow, can you please leave?"

"Yes, I can, if there's nothing else I can help you with legally."

"No, there is not, so that is all."

Horace Winslow shook several hands and left the room.

Once the conference door closed behind Winslow, Tina continued her plea. "Arnie, I'm not trying to deceive you, but being creatively handicapped won't work for me. In my brief time with Ellis, I've learned that my major means of expression is through the music I create. If you let me keep that control, we can make a verbal agreement about anything else."

Ellis said, "He needs you just as much as you need him to feed his hunger to top the Pop charts."

Idella Stephens said, "Tina, don't make a deal with the devil."

Kelly said, "If your music fails, then we fail too. There's no need for additional agreements of any kind."

Carlton stood to his feet, grabbed Tina's hand, pulled her up, and guided her to a corner of the room. "Tee-Tee, we didn't get this far, this fast for no reason. Make the damn verbal agreement, so we can finish what we came here to do—create music and hear your songs on the radio. Other than Mister Napoleon Asshole, everybody else is cool—Kelly, Ellis, Zina, André, and even hoity-toity, Idella Stephens."

Carlton's advice made the most sense to Tina. *If things don't work out, Carlton and I are the only ones that could end up back in Scotland Neck.* Tina returned to her seat. "Mister Peters, I want to do whatever it takes to continue moving forward."

Arnie imploded with internal joy, certain that Tina and Carlton's support beams were collapsing under the pressure of his empty threats. He had no intention of delaying or dismantling their momentum. Kelly attempted to reason with her lover-man boss. "I can't believe you're being so obstinate when everything's been going so well."

Arnie was careful to temper his tone to the woman who held his heart while holding firm to his position of strength. "Kelly, I appreciate your hard work, but I'm handling this one my way." He paused and scanned the faces of his disloyal team. "Matter of fact, I want everyone but Tina to vacate this conference room right now." André, Zina, and Angela retreated quickly followed by Idella Stephens's slow saunter out of 2201. Using his inside voice, Arnie spoke to Kelly directly although everyone still present could hear. "By the way, if I keep Tina on, I'm thinking about replacing you as manager and creative director. Miss Turn-Coat King, you can go now." Along with Kelly, Carlton and Ellis had not budged from their seats. Arnie's volume increased. "I said I wanted everybody out."

Tina's emotions were hot and heavy and her feeling of being cornered had kicked-in. "Carlton goes when I go and I want Ellis Ross to stay as well." Kelly's heart sank as she pressed her hands on the table to assist in standing as a precursor to her exit. "And Miss King is not only staying in this room, but she is my executive producer, creative director, and any other decision-making person—as long as I'm here at Walden Records—even if it's just for five minutes more." Kelly sucked in her tears and readjusted her derrière in her conference room high back chair.

Arnie stopped himself from overplaying his hand. *Dial it back Peters before Tina bails on you. That's not a part of your plan.* "Fine, they can stay, but nothing changes. What is your new proposal, Miss Charles?"

"All I can do is to reaffirm the verbal agreement I already made. I'm not saying each and every song, but I am a writer who has a lot to say. Let me keep my musical voice and you and Walden Records can have everything else. Publicly, I'll go where you want me to go, do what you want me to do, and say what you want me to say. In private, however, I will express my opinion to you and The Label as usual. I can't change all my colors, even for you, Mister Peters. Well, those are my terms. You guys handle my image and I continue working with Ellis and the musicians—writing and recording my songs."

Arnie relented. "You are a tough little cookie, but I accept the terms of our strengthened and witnessed verbal agreement." As mysterious and abrupt as his appearance at the New York headquarters, his immediate departure was just as strange.

Wednesday, August 4, 1982

3:00 a. m. Eastern Time/12:00 a.m. Pacific Time—Tina knocked the phone on the floor while struggling to answer it in the darkness of her bedroom. After pulling its coiled cord and positioning the receiver to her ear, she said, "Hello."

"It's Arnie Peters and I have explicit instructions for you and only you to follow, Miss Three Seven Two Eighty-Five."

11:00 a.m. Eastern Time/8:00 a.m. Pacific Time—A sense of triumph filled his being as Arnie watched his 3.7.2.85 creation exit the private jet and walk gingerly down its steps. His amazing rush of adrenaline was proof positive that she had passed his test and assured his dominance over her. As Arnie leaned on his limousine's back door, Tina ambled over to him and stopped about twelve inches from his smirk-filled face. "Good morning Tina," he said much louder than was necessary for face-to-face conversation.

Her low volume response was the exact opposite. "Just as you requested, I'm here. What do you need me to do?"

Arnie spoke after blowing a big puff of smoke in Tina's face. "Welcome to Los Angeles. I gave an order and you followed it. Good girl. Now, I'm convinced that you're trustworthy and will honor our verbal agreement."

"Like I said all along, I try not to lie, as in keeping my word. So, what now? I'm three thousand miles away from New York City—missing a full day of production time." Tina abruptly stopped talking as she struggled to hold back her tears of frustration.

Arnie moved in close—lip-to-lip, he planted a wet kiss on Tina's cheek. Then he shouted, spraying spittle on her face. "Now, get your ass back on that jet, go back to New York, and finish my damn album!"

32

A VOW OF SILENCE

HUMILIATION and disgust characterized Tina's emotional state after being subjected to a bully-instigated trip to Los Angeles. On the three-thousand-mile return flight, she weighed her options regarding damage control. In general, Pappy John and Aunty Gina would wage war if made partially aware of her subjection to cruel treatment and excessive pressure from Arnie Peters. And specifically, her creative team's reaction to this unnecessary roundtrip test flight would also be unfavorable. Carlton would hurl pieces of his mind, Kelly King would argue, and Ellis and Idella would protest on principle. Tina concluded that any overt response would be counterproductive to finishing the album. As an alternative release, she placed a symbolic ice pack on her bruised ego—using a human sounding board that had no family or music industry affiliation.

At 7:15 p. m., more than sixteen hours after the beginning of Tina's day, the same person who witnessed her departure was there to welcome her back to Windsor East. Since moving into the building, Tina spent many of her free evenings with Bernie Bazemore—especially when Carlton was out being Carlton—therefore, unavailable. Serving as her connection to the outside world, she trusted him with her private thoughts and he shared stories of life beyond the confines of her contract.

Having received a call that Bettina Charles was on her way, Bernie was ready with a listening ear, rippled potato chips, and Tina's favorite dipping concoction—a ketchup and hot sauce mix. There was soda to wash it down, accompanied by a soothing serenade of Sarah Vaughan's music playing softly in the background. A cassette recorder, a nineteen-inch color television, a VCR, and a mini refrigerator were gifts from Tina. Bernie's security shift was from 7:00 p. m. to 7:00 a. m. and she wanted her fifty-year-old friend to be comfortable. In addition, his duty station was moved to a low-glass-enclosed cubicle where monitoring Bettina Charles was his primary assignment—courtesy of a Tina request to Miss Kelly King.

"Hello, Mister Bernie. Is Carlton here?"

"No, Miss Tina, the ledger indicates that he hasn't been in since yesterday."

"I guess he stayed overnight with one of his new music industry friends. Carlton's a social butterfly, you see."

"Yes, that has become quite clear."

"Well, at least I've got you." Tina entered the half-door and took a seat beside Bernie Bazemore. With snacks prepared, she gave a recap of her day set to jazz classics that included "My Funny Valentine," "Misty," and "Moon River." After her verbal testimony, all Tina's attention was occupied once the VCR started playing the movie *Lady Sings the Blues*. It had been recorded as it aired on one of the national network channels. Tina's taste in music and movies had been influenced by virtue of her being raised by a mature village. Therefore, in many ways, she and Bernie Bazemore were contemporaries.

Thursday, August 5, 1982

Hugging a back and side wall at the entrance to the kitchen, Kelly and Tina's morning breakfast summit took place as usual. The barely visible table offered the level of privacy required for each woman to speak candidly. To keep their meeting under an hour, their menu was preplanned a week at a time. Accordingly, French toast and omelets were served—Kelly's with cheese only—Tina's western-styled with salsa. "Why did Arnie have you travel all the way to Los Angeles and back in a single day?" asked Kelly.

Without looking up from her plate, Tina answered. "He did it for no real reason."

"That doesn't make sense," Kelly said with disbelief.

Tina continued eating. "Exactly."

"Why didn't you call me before getting on that plane and what did you discuss once reaching Los Angeles?" Kelly looked at the date indicator on her watch before expressing sentiments that were more personal. "This is our seventeenth breakfast meeting and nothing shared has left this table. I've granted most of your special requests and provided an explanation on the few instances when I could not. I thought we'd made strides in trusting each other."

"We have made strides and you've been really great overall. It's just that there's not much to tell." Tina took a sip of her hot tea and continued. "It was an Arnie test to see if I'd keep our verbal agreement. He ordered me to Los Angeles and I went, spent ten minutes with him there on the tarmac, reboarded the plane, and flew back here to New York. That's what happened."

"I can't believe he'd do something so childish and vindictive. He's going to hear an earful from me. Just wait until we finish eating this breakfast."

"Miss King, what I need from you is a vow of silence. Please don't say anything to Arnie about the verbal agreement test. I'm certain that a bad reaction from you is part of his exam and I intend to pass. As far as yesterday is concerned for everyone else, I was out sick. That's what I need us to agree to."

Kelly tapped her nails on the table for five seconds before reaching a decision. "I'm furious by what he did, but if you insist, I'll keep quiet. Basically, there's been a lot of deal brokering lately. Two days ago, you solidified a verbal agreement with Arnie and now negotiated a vow of silence with me."

"You're absolutely right. I'm asking you to help me survive in this new and crazy music business. It's one where I'm being hit with grenades and am throwing stones to defend myself."

"Oh wow, Tina, that statement gives me a glimpse of things from your point-of-view. The music industry makes you jaded, insensitive, and forgetful about the imbalance of power that is heavily weighted in favor of the record companies. I can't do much about systemics, but I can offer an olive branch to at least make you feel better. In addition to my vow of silence, I apologize. I'm truly sorry you had to go through the nonsensical Arnie ordeal."

"It's okay, really it is. I heal pretty quickly."

"Since I can't say anything, I'd love to make up for it by taking you out—doing something special from me to you."

"Even though you did nothing wrong, doing something special would be awesome."

"In that case, your something special happens tonight. Your workday will end at two o'clock sharp. If Ellis doesn't release you promptly, security will come and escort you out of this building. I want you to exhale, get dressed up, and meet me in the lobby of Windsor East at four thirty."

Tina's eyes sparkled and her wide smile was engaged. "I'm really excited. Thank you so much." After giving Miss King a tight hug, she rushed off to begin her abbreviated workday with Ellis Ross. Taking a moment to cherish the affection, Kelly went to her office to make plans for the evening.

1:00 p. m. Eastern Time/10:00 a. m. Pacific Time—Kelly made a call to Arnie's bat phone. He answered with adrenalin pumping, prepared for a heated altercation. "Hello, Kelly. I know that it's you. I've been sitting here waiting for your call."

She spoke using a forced calm voice. "That's so very sweet! It's just been a few days and you miss me already. Maybe you shouldn't have rushed in and out of town so quickly."

Expecting colorful metaphors, Arnie was confused and decided to play along. "So, what's going on?" he asked.

"I know we're under pressure to finish the album and videos, but I need a favor or two or three."

Arnie reasoned, *Oh, she's coming through a sarcastic side door so let me steady myself.* "What is it, Miss King?"

"I wanted to make this an early day for both Tina and me. Even though she told me she was fine, she looked tired or sad or maybe both. I thought it would be nice to take her to dinner. I want to reiterate Walden Records' commitment by spreading a little cordial care and concern—coming from you and me as senior management."

"I think that's a great idea."

Kelly hesitated to convey apprehension in her delivery. "My second request is that Tina and the entire creative team be given a four day hiatus this Saturday through Tuesday. I know that it's short notice, but I completely forgot that Tina has some kind of family thing in DC. I figured it would be a good opportunity to give the whole team a break before I push them hard the rest of the way to the 'Tell Me' album's completion." She paused for a snide remark from Arnie, but he said nothing. "Oh, there's one more thing. Carlton's birthday is on August eleventh, and I wanted to have an office party with hors d'oeuvres, a special cake, and a humorous birthday card. I plan to forge your name in big writing. I know Tina would appreciate the gesture."

"Kelly, Kelly, you're excellent at this morale-boosting thing and you sign my name better than I do. Well, your entire plan really makes Walden Records look good and I like it. You've got a green light from me on all your requests. If you like, you can give me a call during funny man's party and I'll give an insincere birthday greeting. Are you sure you weren't a mother in a previous life?"

"That's very funny. You know you're full of it, don't you?" Kelly scolded. "Well, I need to close out a few things before I leave for dinner with Tina. Unless you have a concern, I have nothing else to request or report."

Arnie said, "Oh yes, there's one big thing on my end. I'm in the process of finalizing the budget to fund the remaining five videos—my mini-movie-musicals. In the meantime, get the album finished, including sample cover designs for me to review. Shantelle will get the video budget to you when I'm done—within a few days. I'm a bit surprised, but your phone call was painless. On that good note, I'm hanging up."

"I feel the same way and won't call and bug you again unless I'm desperate. Take care." Kelly hung up the phone and exhaled. *I made it through the call without breaking my vow of silence. He's such a prick, but he's my prick, and I love every inch of that man. However, Tina was right; he was waiting with bait. Although not biting, I had to make the call and say something. Mister Peters is many things, but stupid is not one of them.*

Arnie was pleased with Tina for scoring 100 percent on his six-thousand-mile endurance test and for maintaining confidentiality. Details of his dastardly deeds were withheld from Carlton as well as Kelly—so he thought. *Now, I'm certain that Tina will honor the terms of our verbal agreement. With all that I'm doing for her, I have to be the one calling the shots.*

Instead of feeling like the big man on campus, Arnie's heinous treatment of Tina at the airport gnawed at his conscience like a mosquito swarm. *My profession and position requires me to be a brute from time to time, but I went too far. The yelling and blowing smoke in her face was cruel even for me. Saying yes to Kelly's laundry list of requests that benefit Tina was the closest I could get to apologizing—understood that way or not.*

4:20 p. m.—Tina stepped off the elevator into her apartment's lobby looking beautiful from head to toe. She was wearing a red, sleeveless cocktail dress—with a sequined fitted bodice that had a drastic flare ending slightly above the knee. Before leaving, she placed a sealed letter on Bernie Bazemore's security desk, letting him know what was taking place.

It read:

> Miss Kelly King is taking me out tonight for a New York City adventure. I'm all dressed up and have no idea where we're going. I'm way excited and will give you details later. Just like you told me, when I think I can't take another step, God will jump in with a blessing. He's sending Miss King as an angel who is treating me like a little sister. I'm grateful because I really need this right now. —Tina

Touted for its superlative Venetian fare, Kelly chose the award-winning Italian restaurant Belle Sapori for the special dinner. From the breakfast summits, she had learned much, including Tina's favorite cuisines and the fact that she had no food allergies. Looking around the restaurant, Tina was energized by the elegant but lively atmosphere. There were many large parties with representation from babies to grandparents and all ages in between. The tablecloths were white linen adorned with fine china, assorted crystal glassware, and forks appropriate for each course. A large crowd had gathered at and around the bar, positioned off to the left in a separate alcove. Visible from the main dining room, the bar patrons were a lively group, enjoying themselves in a standing-room-only celebration.

Upon being seated, sparkling water was poured and extra lime was presented on a small plate. Sinatra music was playing at a moderate volume, being piped through recessed ceiling speakers. After glancing at the menu, Tina said, "Since this is one of your favorite restaurants, I would love it if you ordered for us both."

"Thank you for the vote of confidence." Kelly motioned to the waiter who had only ventured a few feet from their table.

He said, "I understand that you will be attending the theater at eight o'clock this evening. All has been set in motion for you to leisurely enjoy the meal and get to the theater on time."

Tina interrupted. "We're going to the theater?"

"Absolutely! We couldn't have a first outing without including your favorite pastime." Addressing the waiter directly, Kelly said, "We'll be sharing two of your family-sized portions. Let's start with the Gamberi Al Forno. Your baked shrimp drizzled in the spicy tomato sauce is divine."

"Indeed, you are correct," answered the waiter.

"After that, we'll have the Pollo Al Limone. Tina, it is outstanding— sautéed boneless chicken breast with lemon and cerignola olives."

The waiter added. "That is accompanied by caper berries and sautéed Mesa Greens. Also, would you like a beverage in addition to the sparkling water?"

"We would like a wine of your choosing."

The waiter said, "I recommend the pinot grigio mastered in Veneto, Italy. The aromatic notes of green apple and blossoms add a delicate bite to accompany your excellent main course selections."

"If that is all right with you, Tina, we'll take a bottle? Feel free to change whatever you like."

Tina smiled. "It all sounds yummy, and thank you."

Kelly patted the back of Tina's hand. "Tonight, it's just me and you—no record company—no album—zero stress. With that being said, I'm ordering you to lower your guard and have a good time."

Tina explained. "Unlike when I'm singing, which feels so natural, one-on-one encounters are awkward for me. But you are making it wonderful. I had no idea that you were so down-to-earth."

"Let's just keep that a secret between me and you." Kelly shaped her hands to look like claws and scrunched her face. "Be very aware that the Lioness will be ever-present when lurking inside the walls of Walden Records."

Miss King's jovial demeanor had healing power, causing Tina to laugh and lower her defenses. Halfway into the second course and the bottle of wine, Kelly had mustered the courage and was ready to make an admission. After stuttering, she abandoned her prepared script and went there. "Although I know you'll be shocked, I have to make a confession."

"Ooh, this sounds serious, so go ahead. I'm listening."

"Arnie and I have an intimate connection."

Putting the next forkful of food in her mouth, Tina's reaction was benign. "You two have worked together for years. It makes sense that you're friends. Even the Great Grizzly Bear deserves companionship."

"That's true, but comradeship is not what I'm trying to convey. By intimate, I mean—sexually intimate."

Tina dropped her fork and put her hands over her mouth. "Really, you two are a couple? Oh my God! I would have never guessed that in a million lifetimes!"

"Although this is slightly slutty to say, we aren't actually a couple. I won't allow this thing between us to go as far as an official relationship. Arnie's too mean, crazy, and impulsive for that. I'd be in jail for premeditated murder."

Tina hissed. "And, I'd be your cellmate for helping you bury his body." After giggles from both women, Tina asked, "What attracts you to a man like Arnie?"

"He's extremely intelligent and powerful, and his rough edges are alluring. The more I try to despise him, the more he turns me on. He's my sex toy with special skills. When he arrives at my figurative doorstep, he rings the right bell each and every time."

Tina laughed and laughed and laughed. "Oh, come on. It can't be that funny. This is my romantic life you're mocking."

"I'm sorry Kelly, but it's not just funny, it's hilarious to me—you and Arnie? Wow. But, I promise, my lips are sealed and no one will hear it from me—not even Carlton."

The executive vice president's face took on a serious expression. Tina followed it with her own look of serious concern. "I'm sorry, Kelly, I didn't mean to hurt your feelings."

"No, you didn't hurt my feelings. You called me Kelly several times with no Miss attached. It's the first time you've done that and it touched my heart unexpectedly. I'd really like us to be friends. We're both savvy enough to separate our professional and personal interactions."

"Kelly-Kelly-Kelly. Saying it now feels right to me and I would like us to be friends as well. I appreciate everything you're doing, especially the way you look out for me—like a big sister. Saying thank you is not enough." Under the table, Tina folded her thumb diagonal the palm of her hand, leaving four fingers erect. One was for Carlton, one was for Ellis Ross, one for Miss Idella Stephens, and the fourth was for Kelly King. An additional person had been added to the list of people she trusted completely in the music business.

"Please don't thank me for doing what is an absolute pleasure." *I want to tell her the truth so badly, but not tonight. Stacking it on top of Arnie's obedience test would be too much of an emotional shock for her right now. I'll figure out a way to tell her real soon. I have to.*

The waiter returned to collect their dishes. "Are you interested in dessert?" he asked.

Kelly rubbed her hands together. "That would be a yes, indeed. We each will have our own. We'll take the Panna Cotta please."

After devouring their desserts with time to spare, the secret sisters left the restaurant well-satisfied. The theater was a short, one-block walk and Tina could see the marquee. Her breathing became audible and she wanted to ask but was afraid of an inaccurate assumption. Kelly quickly put Tina out of her misery. "Yes, that is what we're going to see."

"Are you serious? That's what we're going to see tonight?" Kelly loved how Tina made her feel like such a Shero.

Kelly stopped halfway down the block and lit a cigarette. "Get all of your jumping-up-and-down and heavy breathing out before we move another inch closer to the venue. People know me in there. We've got time, so you jump and pant while I enjoy this after-dinner cigarette. Eating, sex, and talking on the phone are the top three reasons why I can't seem to quit smoking." Once the cigarette was sucked down to the butt and Tina had cleared the jumping from her system, they elegantly glided into the theatre. Looks of envy were pointed their way as they followed the usher to their seats—third row, extreme center. Each woman's hand carefully cradled a playbill whose cover revealed three long, Black female legs draped in gowns and the smash hit's title *Dreamgirls.*

Knowing musicals were Tina's favorite source of entertainment, Kelly had paid two thousand dollars to get the rightful owners to surrender their premium tickets. She could have paid less, but didn't have the time to haggle. Having already seen the play three times, Kelly spent the entire show watching her younger sibling off and on, enjoying each raise of her feet off the floor, her chuckling at humorous dialogue, and the brilliance of the light in her face that never dimmed. It was as though an extra spotlight shined specifically on Tina. Seeing her innocent glee was refreshing and fulfilling. As a stirring song ended one of the musicals most dramatic scenes, Tina and the main character executed a similar gesture. The leading lady stretched her hand out toward the audience while Tina squeezed Kelly's hand tightly. At that pivotal moment, the executive vice president was overcome by an epiphany, realizing that she loved Tina in a way that she had yet to fully understand. The adoration was similar to her love for Katrina, but stronger. Tina was a stopper that plugged a hole in her heart, one that Kelly had long accepted as an unfillable void. She had been given a gift of a maternal instinct and a baby sister in whom such affection could be showered.

33

NO-FLY ZONE PROTEST

LOVER-MAN boss approved, Kelly granted four consecutive days off for Tina and crew, warning that intense pressure would be applied once they returned to The Label. "Use your days wisely," she warned. "They are the last of their kind until the album and videos are put to bed."

Friday, August 6, 1982

At that morning's breakfast summit after thanking the managing directstress for a wonderful evening, Tina did something that was inconceivable with any artist up to that point. She declined Kelly's offer to receive city-to-city transportation in a Walden Records' jet.

"That's a first. You'd rather fly commercial?"

"Oh no! Absolutely not! I'm not a fan of long lines, delays, and security. Unfortunately for me, your generous offer came at a bad time. I have five more days left on my no-fly zone protest."

Kelly was eager to hear the explanation. "Your what?"

"It's me and my dad's response to what happened last year—August 5, 1981, to be exact."

"More details, please. My mind is still drawing a blank."

"I'm talking about last year's big strike when President Reagan fired all those air traffic controllers. It was eleven thousand of them who missed his forty-eight-hour deadline to return to work."

"Oh that. I remember it vaguely, but what does that have to do with you and your father?"

"Without taking sides, Pappy John and my outrage was about constitutional rights."

Assuming the posture of an active listener, Kelly leaned forward and smiled. *Crazy thinking like that is a good reason why adoption should have a cut-off age.* "What an interesting dinner table topic for a father and his daughter."

Kelly's mockery flew right past her little sibling's ability to comprehend. "Pappy John said, 'It's a sad day when an American's right to redress grievances is punished so severely. Those union workers were not only fired, but banned for life—no chance of being rehired.'" Tina tried to mimic Pappy John's serious-looking facial expression. "My dad said, 'Tina, never forget that boycotts and protests were the greatest weapon against injustice during the civil rights movement.'" Tina made a gesture, signaling that she was now speaking on behalf of herself. "Kelly, it's all about the freedom to peaceably assemble and petition, you see."

"Your father is quite the activist, especially for an older white man, and I say that as a compliment."

"I guess. Well, to show our indignation, Pappy John and I made a pinky swear that we wouldn't use air transportation for the first eleven days of each August—one day for every thousand government workers that were fired."

"Bravo to you both. This, however, brings up a crucial *no-no.* As a performer with Walden Records, you're not allowed to take a public stance on any issue unless directed and scripted by us. It's in your contract. Your father and daughter boycott is cute as long as it remains a silent activity. Are we clear?"

Tina wasn't crazy about the demanding attitude of Kelly King—the Boss. She reminded herself to separate professional matters from personal ones. "Yes, I understand." *My goodness, I wonder if the contract states how many times I'm allowed to breathe in sixty seconds.*

Not wanting to end her special time with Tina sounding like a dictator, Kelly changed the subject. "Regardless of how you get there, I know you're excited about your special trip to Washington."

Tina was grateful for a conversation shift, wanting to share a personal matter with Kelly. "When you visited me at Joseph-Lee Manor, I mentioned my dad's move back to the States."

"Yes, I remember."

"Well, he's been living out of cardboard boxes since his arrival—having to stay with a friend for more than a month. Now, that he's finally moved into his apartment, I'm going to spend part of my time off getting him properly settled. I ordered all kinds of things by catalogue that he hasn't even touched. My dad is good at maintenance, but awful at organizing. Since my mom's death, keeping him structured has been a job that I gladly perform. Pappy John means everything to me."

"You're really blessed, just like me, to have a special closeness with your father." Tina's eyes began to swell.

"You're so right, and I've leaned on him so much in the past seven years since Momma Nin's death. I've pretended to be strong, but inside it's been really hard."

"I can't begin to imagine what you've gone through, but I applaud your courage."

"And I'm gonna need every bit of it. The more important reason I'm going to Washington is to pay a special tribute to my mom—just me and my dad. The only people that know about it are my Aunty Gina, Carlton, and now, you—and I'd like to keep it that way."

"Absolutely, and I appreciate you trusting me enough to share."

"The major event takes place on Tuesday, August 10. It will be the seventh anniversary of my mom's passing and openly discussing it makes me feel quite emotional."

"I want you to know that I'm there in a blink if you need me."

"You've already done something amazing that has helped me tremendously. By giving everyone the four days off, the focus is not on me—no explaining to do. No Arnie screaming about how I'm costing him money."

"Oh yes, I've heard that Arnie proclamation way too many times."

"I appreciate these meetings and the extra care you've been giving me, especially your sisterly advice. Because I'm away from Aunty Gina, your womanly support is very important to my life right now. I'd be quite lost without it."

∽౧

6:00 p. m.—Later that evening while on the train, Tina made good use of her time, reviewing video scripts and fine-tuning her lyrics. It took increased volume and a harmless nudge for the cabin steward's statement to register. "Ma'am, we've arrived in Washington, DC."

Pappy John was there at Union Station, waiting with a smile, a single rose, and a warm fatherly embrace. Tina reminded herself to solely focus on helping Pappy John get settled and try not to dwell on Momma Nin's tribute that was three days away. To do that, she leaned on a Bible verse her Aunty Trudy insisted that she memorize.

"Therefore do not be anxious about tomorrow, for tomorrow will be anxious for itself. Sufficient for the day is its own trouble."
— Matthew 6:34

9:00 p. m.—Tina had arrived at Pappy John's and was assessing the enormous tasks. His humble abode was a three bedroom apartment that was a part of the Watergate—a five building mixed-use complex located near the Kennedy Center in a Northwest Washington, DC neighborhood called Foggy Bottom. It was one in the same—a recognizable address to the masses. In 1972, one of the offices in the multi-purposed facility was the place where unprecedented breaking and entering took place. The end result was wiretapping of the Democratic National Committee's headquarters. The unparalleled political scandal earned the Watergate make mention in an infamous chapter of American History. Throughout her life, Tina had accompanied her adopted parents to the historic building to visit friends who lived there. Now, Tina was elated that the familiar address was Pappy John's new home. She could rest easier because he was surrounded by friends who loved him and would care for him in her absence.

Over the next two days, Tina and Pappy John unpacked boxes and unraveled bubble pop plastic that had been wrapped around new furniture and appliances. Underwear, socks, T-shirts, and pajamas were rolled and aligned in dresser drawers. Jackets, pants, and shirts were organized by color and segregated to one side or the other of the walk-in closet—according to designation as business or casual. All bedrooms were dressed and extra bedding and towels were placed in the two linen closets. With a grocery store on the lower level of the building, it was easy to fully stock Pappy John's cabinets and refrigerator with enough food and cleaning products to last him for months.

The walls were adorned with artwork and the shelving was filled with framed photographs. With photography as a hobby, most of them were taken by Pappy John and were very dear to his heart. An entire wall was dedicated to photographs of Tina from preschool to her twelfth grade graduation. The only items that had been set up in advance were the entertainment center and the component set that came bundled as a unit. Tina was not wired to perform busy tasks with her hands without music. Therefore, while working, they were supported by sultry vocals of the greats—singing tunes like "They Can't Take that Away from Me," "Georgia on my Mind," "Little Girl Blue," "Spirit in the Dark," and "Today, I Sing the Blues." Pappy John was definitely a major contributor who had helped nurture Tina's old soul.

Come Monday afternoon, the home setup project was done and the two engines that could were already geared up for continued stimulation. They wanted to make the most of their short time together and switched their attention to one of their favorite leisure activities. Taking in two movies back-to-back, they transported their minds to a fanciful world of make-believe through the wonders of Hollywood entertainment. As paraphernalia-possessing Trekkers, they rooted for the *Enterprise* while watching *Star Trek II: The Wrath of Khan*. At its conclusion, they jogged three blocks down F Street to the second theatre, making it to their seats as the last preview was showing. The movie was *An Officer and a Gentleman* and the themes were apropos for Pappy John's love for the military and Tina's youthful thoughts of romantic notions.

Tuesday, August 10, 1982

Patriotic reverence was an automatic mental response when Tina and Pappy John's feet made contact with the hallowed ground of Arlington National Cemetery. Upon taking in the overwhelming site of more than three hundred and fifty thousand white grave markers, Tina concluded that the nickname *A Garden of Stone* was befitting and self-explanatory. The burial headstones were aligned symmetrically in such an honorable and dignified fashion. She encouraged her spirit. *This is indeed the most suitable place for my American Shero to take her rest.* Although tears rarely accompanied her thoughts of Momma Nin these days, they did on this occasion. It was a very personal and private commemoration, marking the seventh year of the passing of Colonel Nadine Bethany Charles-Chapman. With heavy hearts, Tina and Pappy John looked down at the tombstone. Her remains rested in cemetery Section 21, an area set aside for those who had served as nurses. Tina reflected on the honor bestowed on Momma Nin during the interment. Her mental journey transported her back to 1975.

"Pumpkin, this is your last chance to say goodbye, so try and pay close attention during the ceremony." Taking her father's counsel to heart, Tina had no problem remaining alert while at Arlington Cemetery. Her eleven-year-old eyes became a camera in spite of her grieving. Staying near Pappy John, Aunty Gina, and Carlton, they followed closely behind her mother's flag-draped casket. It was held on a caisson and was being pulled by six black horses. The Old Guard wheel team was the escort—three on each side of the coffin.

Tina's little body jumped with surprise during the three-volley rifle salute. Grateful that calm was restored, she listened intently to the solemn serenade of Taps being played on a bugle. While seated under a dark canopy, Tina sat in the second chair between Pappy John and Aunty Gina watching Momma Nin's flag being meticulously folded. Then, she inhaled a comforting smell of mint that emitted from the breath of the honor guard that kneeled before her as he placed Old Glory in her outstretched arms.

Tina listened closely as he spoke directly to her. "Ma'am, on behalf of the president of the United States and the people of a grateful nation, may I present this flag—a token of appreciation for the honorable and faithful service your loved one rendered this nation."

NADINE BETHANY
CHARLES-CHAPMAN
COL
US ARMY NURSE CORPS
WORLD WAR II
KOREA
JAN 6, 1921
AUG 10, 1975

Refocusing on the current tribute seven years later, an eighteen-year-old Tina kneeled and placed flowers in a sanctioned cone furnished by Arlington Cemetery. It resembled a bridal bouquet and had a variety of pink blooms that excluded carnations—Momma Nin and Tina's least-favored flower. After remaining at the resting place paying silent reverence for about an hour, Pappy John performed a very difficult task. He wrapped his arms around his daughter and escorted her away from the gravesite. It required him supporting the weight of her limp body to the awaiting limousine. To Tina, walking away and leaving Momma Nin behind was like waterboarding torture all over again.

From Arlington Cemetery, Pappy John and Tina were driven across the Fourteenth Street Bridge, arriving at their next destination fifteen minutes later. Feeling a very slight hot breeze on a typical humid August summer day in the nation's capital, The father and daughter stood on the east side of the Washington Monument, about ten feet from its base. They were looking down the Mall at the US Capitol Building—one of Momma Nin's favorite vantage points. From that position, they each released seven pink balloons into the atmosphere—one at a time. They both were silent, watching their rise upward alongside the 555-foot height of the obelisk honoring America's first president.

Later that evening, after a lovely dinner, Pappy John took Tina to Union Station where they said their goodbyes. Then, a well-earned nap quickly ate away almost four hours of travel time. Bettina Charles had arrived in New York City and a switch in her mind immediately returned her focus to the business of completing her first album. Carlton had accompanied the driver and met Tina outside of Penn Station. "Welcome back—Little Miss Freedom Rider. I'm glad your No-Fly Zone Protest is just about over."

Wednesday, August 11, 1982

9:00 a. m.—The morning's breakfast summit had come so quickly that Tina felt her trip to Washington, DC had been a dream. Laying business aside, Kelly offered the only weapon in her arsenal that seemed fitting—a listening ear. She lent it as Tina gave an overview of the tribute to her American Shero and shared a few special qualities about her Momma Nin.

Once Tina was ready, Kelly steered the conversation to something she knew would be uplifting. "The Label's throwing Carlton a surprise birthday luncheon today."

"Although extremely shocked, the thoughtfulness pleases me a great deal. I'm certain that it was organized by you and not Arnie Peters. May I help set things up?" asked Tina. "I'd like to add a few touches that only I know about the honoree—my personal assistant, cousin, and friend."

12:30 p. m.—Carlton was extremely moved by the birthday surprise, especially the end of the celebration when Tina presented her personal assistant with an eighteen-karat yellow gold rope chain—twenty-eight inches long.

After two hours of fun, Kelly made a brief speech to end the festivities. "Once again, Carlton, the Walden Records family wishes you a very happy birthday. Now, fun and games are over and it's time to get down to the serious business of completing this album."

34

MINI-MUSICAL-MOVIE MAKING

DOLLARS determined, Shantelle sent Arnie's unprecedented seven-figure budget to Kelly King. His goal was to make a mark in the changing tide of a 1980s America. A growing middle class and an overall higher standard of living assisted in creating a materialistic generation with a free-to-be-me attitude. This was accompanied by liberal spending habits. Arnie was keenly aware that the change was driven by technology. Home video cassette recorder usage and cable television access were increasing exponentially—moving quickly toward both becoming American household mainstays. This phenomenon enabled quick and easy access to news, the latest trends, and music videos. As a result, an embracing of differences and the merging of cultural appreciation were redefining popular music. Recognizing that his sellable product was almost ready, Arnie increased his marketing efforts, knocking on specific doors of particular media moguls.

❧

Upon it reaching her desk, Kelly perused Arnie's budget and was stunned by his allocation of funds. The substantial financial investment was a clear indication of his commitment to the "Tell Me" album project. The funds added several more logs on the fire that fueled Kelly's determination to deliver her lover-man boss's bar-raiser mini-musical-movies. Starting with a distinguished group of industry experts, the adage of receiving high quality for top dollar was not an exaggeration. Keith Murray's video production staff was supplemented with two award-winning movie directors. André Jenkins was supported by three groundbreaking choreographers. Jerry Johnson remained at the cinematography helm as director of photography. In addition to leading the lighting and camera crews, all facets of production relied upon his visual astuteness.

Including Kelly, Ellis, and Tina, there was a ten-member leadership team that collaborated in lengthy war-room sessions. In them, video concepts were turned into storyboards that expanded into sophisticated scripts, calling for elaborate and hi-tech implementation. The cast was comprised of dancers, actors, extras, and of course Bettina Charles. The technical gear included cameras, lighting, and audio equipment as well as several fog machines. All were operated by a crew of highly-skilled personnel. Tina was impressed by the intricate sets and the realistic props.

The multiple hat wearing Kelly focused on financial considerations by working closely with the business affairs department to tightly manage expenses. She renegotiated quotes from outside vendors, often obtaining an additional 10 percent savings at a minimum. She had a reputation for substantially coming under budget. One of her cost-saving measures involved start-to-finish scene completion—even if all-night shooting was required. This enabled sets to be broken down or converted for use in another scene and extra bodies dismissed as opposed to lingering, eliminating the need for their downtime to be charged as an overhead expense.

Exhaustion was far too limited a word to define the effort expended to fulfill Kelly's edict of a continuous push toward project completion. The remaining five big-budget productions were geared to creating an image as well as promoting the music. This was accomplished through makeup, hair, costumes, fake body piercings, and dance routines—overemphasizing edginess, sex-appeal, and boldness. The eighties punk-rock craze received special attention exhibited in the costumes worn in two of the videos. The wardrobe included spiked hair in a variety of bright colors, fingerless gloves, holey fishnet stockings, wide belts wrapped around miniskirts, and long striped socks whose tops extended above the knee.

The choreography was dominated by break dancing, an American craze that spilled over from the seventies—known then as pop-locking. Those dance routines were the most physically challenging and included twists, handstands, kicks, flips, jumps, and full body spins on the ground—usually ending in an arm-folded pose. On-location filming took place in and around Manhattan, including a cement wall and playground backdrops in Harlem and a college campus across the Hudson River in nearby Hoboken, New Jersey.

One video concept mimicked the craze of a dance-off between rival street gangs with music blasted from a boom box. Tina was dressed in acid-washed jeans, a hooded sweatshirt, head and wristbands, and a pair of red classic Converse. After spying on the activity from a distance, her character carried an oversized piece of cardboard and imposed on a congregating crew. She spent a few moments as an observer, standing on the sidelines looking cute. Shocking members of both gangs as well as a crowd of spectators, she tossed out her makeshift dance floor and joined the competition—out-dancing all the male-only participants.

In Rehearsal Room 1601, hours of repetition had been required to make the complicated choreography appear seamless. Tina's bruised body was documented as coincidental consequences that were a casualty of the creative process. Product three seven two eighty-five's costumes were extremely seductive—skin-hugging gowns, several styles of sexy mini dresses, tutu-mimicking skirts, corsets, satin camisoles, and bodysuits with padded shoulders. Of course, the movement was sexually suggestive.

As part of the video production process, several all-day choreographic rehearsals were required. During those long sessions, Tina, André, and the cast of dancers were immersed in perfecting video dance sequences. Kelly capitalized on one of them, sneaking a short distance south to visit her parents on Baltimore's Orleans Street. Another conference with her mother was needed. This time, it was Kelly who delivered the confessions. She sat down with Kay-Dee in the kitchen. "Mom, I'm scared and I really need some advice."

"I'm right here as always. What's wrong?"

"When we spoke on the phone on the night of Katrina's wedding, I failed to mention several huge things that happened. Basically, I lied to you. I not only found out about Donald Leonard Charles's Aunty Gina, but we had a long talk. I visited the house called Joseph-Lee Manor and met the rest of the family that included her two sisters. One was very religious and the other was mean as hell. During those several hours, I never mentioned that I was their great-niece."

Kay-Dee said, "Even though that was a huge story to leave out, it was your decision not to tell me or them. You said that you were taking things slow, so what you did wasn't that bad."

"I'm not done confessing. There was one more discovery that was even bigger than that."

"I can't imagine anything bigger than what you've already told me."

"It has been a heavy load to carry, so I'll spit it out quickly. I discovered that I have a little sister that's twelve years younger than me. Her name is Bettina Charles and she's the young woman I've been telling you about—the one that I discovered in North Carolina."

"You mean the girl that you said was super talented and on her way to becoming a big-time singer?"

"Yes mom, she's the one."

"That's great news, isn't it? You've always wanted a little sister. What did you say to each other when y'all first found out?"

"We said nothing because she doesn't know. I can't figure out a good time to barge in and tell her. She's so happy about her career and we've gotten really close—like sisters, strangely enough. Now, I've made a mess of things, covering up the secret under a whole bunch of lies."

"You know I been there and it's not easy to tell the truth because the timing never seems right. All you can do is pick one of those wrong times, dive in with the truth, and beg for her forgiveness. Don't be like me, giving life to a lie for years. The longer you wait, the worse the penalty for both of you."

"Thanks, Mom. Your advice means a lot. I pray that I don't lose her, but I'm going to tell her the truth as soon as we're alone when I get back to New York."

"It's the right thing to do and I'll definitely be praying for the both of you. As soon as this hard part is over, I can't wait to meet her."

"Once I leave, please tell daddy for me. It hurts too much to have to repeat the whole twisted story again."

⌒つ

Wednesday, September 8, 1982

Five weeks after the verbal agreement and working through the Labor Day Weekend, the "Tell Me" album and its six associated videos were finished. Although they were not a requirement under the verbal agreement and they took more time to adapt to her musical style, two of the four final tracks came from the Walden Records catalogue. No matter the difficulty, Tina felt it was the right thing to do. She was keenly aware that her recording artist opportunity was made possible courtesy of Arnie Peters. To show her sincere appreciation, Tina recorded the songs and vowed never to bad-mouth him in public regardless of his evil bullying and malicious behavior. Arnie was internally touched and shocked that Tina recorded two of his songs but showed no outward appreciation.

⌒つ

In wait mode with a stay-put restriction, Tina and Carlton spent the day resting and watching movies at Windsor East. At six-thirty that evening, they received a call from Walden Records that Arnie was back in town. They were told to dress in party-going attire and report to Auditorium 2001 immediately. Tina said, "What now? Carlton, I don't think I'm up for another trial by fire. That's what happened the last time I was told to report to that room."

"I know, Tee-Tee. They need to cut this perfectionist bullcrap out. We should've finished these damn videos a week ago, at least. They done got on my last good nerve. I'm gonna try not to go there, but my mouth is prepared to cuss about six people out—Ellis, Keith, Jerry, André, Kelly, and Arnie. Now enough is enough. Shit!"

"I agree. And this time, we'll cuss them out together."

Having willed their tired bodies out of transport, Tina and Carlton didn't speak to anyone. They held hands, stepped off the elevator, and walked slowly toward Auditorium 2001. The two doors were held open for them by security guards. Inside, it was difficult to see, because the lights were low, but the audio was piercing. Arnie's voice rang loudly through the microphone. "On behalf of the Walden Records' family, I say congratulations! Bettina Charles, your first album project is a wrap." The lights came up and a crowd was clapping, whistling, and yelling well wishes.

Including one invitee each, there were more than two hundred people in attendance. The room was set up for a party with a dance floor in the middle, tables surrounding it, and chairs against walls throughout the space. There were four elaborate food stations, three bars, several disco balls revolving, and a DJ blasting club music. Confetti was being thrown and champagne was splashed at Tina and Carlton. In turn, she was hugged by the inner circle team—Keith Murray, Jerry Johnson, Zina Shelby, André Jenkins, Idella Stephens, Assistant Angela, Ellis Ross, Kelly King, and Arnie Peters.

The party went on for hours. The DJ was amazing, the food was fabulous, and the alcohol was popular. Everyone was in varying degrees of intoxication. Tina was flat-out drunk. Having danced continuously for two months, she chose a sit and slurp celebration. Kelly kept her company with two exceptions—a few whirls to her favorite tunes and an hour-long retreat to the observation booth—both with Arnie Peters.

At one point, things really got crazy. Carlton ran over to Tina and Kelly. "Hey, y'all, check out how Idella Stephens is boogieing down on the dance floor. She said that she was hot, pulled off her wig, and told me to hold it. I'm not walking around with this thing. Y'all keep it." Carlton tossed the wig on the table between the two sisters and pranced away. That kept Tina and Kelly laughing for the rest of the celebration, which ended on cue.

At two o'clock in the morning, Arnie took the microphone. He yelled. "It's been a blast. On behalf of the entire Walden Records family, we congratulate our young superstar—Miss Bettina Charles. Now, the party is over, so everybody go the hell home right now." Auditorium 2001 cleared out quickly. As the catering crew cleaned up, Arnie walked Kelly to the elevator. He kissed her gently on the lips. "I'm escorting you all the way down to the garage to your transport."

"Thank you very much, but that won't be necessary."

"Necessary or not, I'm doing it anyway."

"If you insist, but I wanted to go up—not down." Upon exiting the elevator, Arnie picked Kelly up and carried her into Penthouse 2400. Inside, wild kissing and tearing off of clothing commenced. It led to lovemaking—not ending until sleep caught up to the height of their satisfaction.

35

THE MELVIN GRINAGE SHOW

Thursday, September 9, 1982

LOOKING at the clock radio, Arnie noted that it was 10 a. m. and coaxed himself to an alert state of mind. His last recollection was around five fifteen in the morning. Apparently, he had dozed off while watching a solar eclipse or something equivalent that was rare and worth the wait. He logged it as his greatest dream realized—even higher than his accomplishments in the music industry. It was a fact. Kelly King was lying next to him sleeping peacefully, straddling him with an arm and a leg. His mental instructions were specific. *Peters, rise. Relieve yourself. Bring her coffee, smokes, and order some food. Oh yeah—Have a glass of water and two aspirin ready, in case she has a hangover.* Arnie was trying to demonstrate that, when it came to Kelly King, he blazed trails in showing care and concern. He thought further. *I love this woman madly and am not about to mess this up.* Then, he eased out of bed to obey the orders he had given to himself.

While eating brunch on the bedroom's balcony, Kelly acted on a sudden urge to share. "Arnie, I need to tell you something very important, very private, and not work-related. Well, it is—kinda-sorta. If you leak this in anyway, I'm done with you and your record company—for good—and I mean it—this time."

"Miss Kelly King, I promise that I will not betray your trust."

She tapped her nails on the table and bit her bottom lip. "With a pile of lies, I've kept our Pop-Diva in the dark about a shocking secret. Around two months ago, I found out that she's my sister."

Arnie chuckled.

"What I confessed is far from funny."

"When you stop telling jokes, I'll stop laughing at them."

"Well, stop it then because it's not a joke. She is my little sister."

"She's your what?"

Tears formed in Kelly's eyes and her cadence sped up. "I said that Bettina Charles is my sister. We have the same father. He's been dead for a long time, but that doesn't matter. Tina is my baby sister. She's twelve years younger. So now that you know, be your asshole self and say something—any—something!"

Arnie allowed the words to compute coupled with receiving confirmation through Kelly's sensitive emotions and speed of speaking. He jumped to his feet, hitting his knee on the table during his rise. "Holy shit!" he yelled. "You're serious. I knew something extra was attached to your commitment to her. I knew it! But, I had no idea you two were sisters—as in sibling sisters, holy shit!"

"Arnie, you said that already!"

"I'm sorry, but that's what keeps coming out. This is so damn unbelievable. And, if this is true, you have to tell Tina—like immediately. A huge investment has been sunk into that girl."

"What do you mean if it's true? Do you think I'd make something like this up for the hell of it? Are you kidding?"

"I didn't mean it that way. I'm trying to process this as well, you know. Let me rephrase. Since it's the truth, you have to tell Tina—like yesterday. At some point, the press will find out and we've got to figure a way to spin it without hurting our Pop-Diva."

"Are you kidding? This is going to destroy her."

"Not if it comes from you first with all the passion that you have. I've seen you with her and now, it all makes sense. I know that what you have for her is love and her best interest in mind."

"Oh Arnie, you're so right. I've tried to demonstrate how I feel about her and that's got to amount to something. I'll work on telling Tina and you work on keeping it contained—away from the press and eventually shared with the public by us. Will you work on doing that for me?"

"Absolutely—of course, I will. Like everything else that's been thrown our way, we can and we will fix this. Now, don't get mad, but between me and you—damn, this is a doozy—holy shit!"

12:00 noon—As Arnie returned from walking Kelly to the elevator, his housekeeper handed him the phone. After ending the call, he dialed Shantelle, gave her a list of instructions, and scrambled to begin his own preparation.

2:00 p. m.—The Live Room in Studio 1904 was buzzing with activity. The studio band was in place, Ellis was directing from the grand piano, and Tina was at the microphone. Arnie was in and out of the control room, pacing back and forth, watching the monitors and listening to the sound being projected. His point of view was that of a television spectator, critiquing and coaching in concert with Ellis. Although the cornerstone song of a smash hit musical, Tina was vaguely familiar with the tune and memorized the words as the crash course progressed. Twice, she stammered over the same phrase, stopped, noted that she made a mistake, and asked to start over.

Idella stepped in and added a third subject matter expert to the coaching staff's roster. "Young lady, it's unacceptable to lose composure—in rehearsal, in an interview, or in a performance."

Watching from a distance, Carlton whispered to Angela. "Yeah, Tina, don't lose control like Idella and her wig did last night—Miss Stephens, please."

"But I stumbled over a word."

"Yes, and there was only one problem with what you did."

"W-w-what was the problem?"

"You acknowledged it as an error. From this point on, if you trip, hiccup, sneeze, or say the wrong words, sing your way out of it with a smile on your face. Remember that you're a magician up there on stage and there's no such thing as a mistake. People will see and believe what you want them to if you're convincing enough."

Tina took Idella Stephens's directions to heart. She vowed to never again react to a slipup. "Yes, Ma'am, now I understand."

After tweaking the song's subtle nuances more than a dozen times, the two mavericks were satisfied. Ellis said, "Yes, yes, yes, that's where we need to be in terms of musical arrangement. Arnie, what do you think?"

"I'm good. Structurally, I think we're there."

Ellis said, "Now, we need to perfect a seamless performance for Tina. Band, I need you to wait on her, prepare for slight tempo shifts based on her phrasing. Tina, don't worry about the musicians. In fact, don't even listen to them. Hear the music in your spirit. Take your time and give your voice permission to submerge deep inside of the lyrics. You have to remember that Melvin Grinage's band and key musicians from our studio will merge to back you up. His conductor will not surrender his post, so I will be a part of the studio audience and can offer no help during the live performance. If you have questions, you need to ask them now."

Tina paused to deliberate. *Between Arnie, Ellis, and Idella, my education is much harder than with Professor Milton.* Then, she encouraged herself, *You got this. Listen, learn, let go, and let God.* "No, I don't have any questions at the moment." That statement had become Tina's go-to response whenever she was uncertain and holding back on a handful of never to be asked questions.

∽◯

3:00 p. m.—After leaving Arnie's place, Kelly went straight to several stores because she was out of just about everything, including eggs, milk, fresh vegetables, toothpaste, and feminine products. Upon reaching her building, the concierge greeted her with an urgent message. "Miss King, they need you at The Label right away in Studio 1904. We'll take care of your packages and will put your groceries away."

Thirty minutes later, Kelly entered 1904's Live Room as Arnie and Ellis were tag-teaming instructions. Her quick scan computed a band, a camera rolling, intense lighting on Tina, and an engaged inner circle team.

Ellis instructed. "The song title sums it up: 'Made It Home.' You have to serenade the audience by carrying them along the journey to this far-off, unfamiliar, and unfriendly land, which has you trapped. Get them to root for you in your search to make it home."

Kelly broke up the continuity. "Arnie, what the hell is this about? The album is done. We had a party last night and-and other things happened after that. Have all of you gone mad? Why is this child singing a cover song from a 1970s musical? What does that anthem and a Pop-Diva have in common?"

"We chose this old award-winning song because it's a catchy tune with familiar lyrics, to everyone except Tina, that is."

Ellis added. "That's right—and it's the perfect ballad to showcase her range, vocal dynamics, and control."

"The bottom line is that Ellis and I believe that this song will go over well with the diverse television audience that Tina will be serenading tonight on *The Melvin Grinage Show*." Arnie looked at his watch. "We have three hours left to prepare and could really use your input."

Arnie's focus and absence of cussing and sarcasm were truth-telling indicators. Kelly said, "Oh my God, you did it and so quickly. You found a way to introduce Bettina Charles to the world—oh my God!"

Arnie replied. "Kelly, you said that already. As you know, Melvin Grinage and I go way back. Each time you sent one of Tina's completed tracks to Los Angeles, Melvin critiqued it alongside me and he loved them all. He went further to say that, when a slot came available, he wanted to feature Bettina Charles on his show. I didn't mention it because promises take a long time to be realized in this business, usually."

Kelly added. "Melvin Grinage switches the taping location from Los Angeles, to Vegas, to New York City in a blink of an eye. I guess it was Manhattan's turn in his rotation—how fortunate for us."

"Exactly. In commemorating Sullivan's anniversary, he's doing a two-week stint here at the Piedmont. Today, he called me because his guest singer cancelled and he wanted to give the slot to 'the girl with the enchanting voice.'"

As she jumped up and down, Tina said, "And that's me. Isn't it wonderful? I'm going to be on live television tonight."

"It's absolutely fantastic. The garment I have in mind is perfect for the broad audience that watches Melvin's show. It's a sophisticated and sassy costume that Artella designed especially for our Pop-Diva and delivered to me a few days ago. I always keep a 'go-to' outfit for my top artists for special occasions. I didn't know that Tina's would be needed so soon."

Arnie replied. "That's great news and perfect timing. Zina's team has been working on choosing a costume and you have the answer. Hurry down to Performance Preparation and have Tina ready for dress rehearsal within the hour."

～⊙

Sixty-five minutes later, Bettina Charles was back in 1904 standing at the microphone. Stunning was the word that Arnie used to describe his Pop-Diva. She was dressed in Kelly's magical color—a fuchsia gown made of two very different body-clinging fabrics—stretchy polyester at the top and shimmering satin at the bottom. Because the garment transitioned from one cloth to the other at Tina's hips, the point of emphasis was that area, highlighting her slim waistline, curves, and backside bump. The puffy short sleeves were off the shoulders, anchored in place by their elastic edging. With the ring slid to the back next to the clasp hidden under her hair, *Love Golden* was allowed to remain in place. Its chain rested delicately against Tina's skin. Her earrings were diamond studded, mounted in eighteen-karat white gold, which caused the jewels' brilliance to illuminate all the more.

Kelly said, "Zina and I agree that this look is ideal for television— elegant with a modern twist—sexy, but tastefully so. And Tina's sparkle of innocence still shines through."

Not wanting to over-prepare, Arnie's dress rehearsal ended after a single run-through. Prior to departure, Tina changed into all black, The Label's standard travel attire. It was worn by the artist and the accompanying entourage that included security. This enabled a hover into a protective engulfment if required. For this engagement, Tina's version of The Label's standard, all-black travel attire was an oversized tee shirt, black leggings, a baseball cap, and high-top Converse sneakers. In case of an overly aggressive air conditioning unit, a zipped-down, hooded sweat jacket was held by the lead of performance preparation, Zina Shelby herself. With the difference of skin-tight sweat pants, Carlton's black garb was the same as his cousin's.

Tina wondered, *Why is this all-black clothing thing necessary, when no one knows who I am? I guess this is another one of those grin-and-bear-it situations.*

10:40 p. m. Eastern Time—Arnie was seated in the guest chair next to the desk of the host. When the camera went live, Melvin Grinage said, "We're back from our station break and joining us is Arnie

Peters—the brilliant founder of Walden Records. He's here tonight to introduce someone special. And she must be incredible because this man has never personally presented any of his artists."

"You're exactly right and you know me better than most."

"Yes, I'm honored that you're here, but surprised."

"Melvin, I had to do this myself because I'm so impressed with the scope of this young lady's talent. She's definitely Pop-Diva material with the raw talent to be a superstar."

"Audience, I have to tell you that my good friend here gave me the privilege of listening to each single as Miss Charles's first album took form. With every track, I was blown away. She truly has a golden voice—incredible chops—but also, she's gorgeous and sophisticated."

Arnie said, "You know, Melvin, that I'm one of the pickiest, meanest son of a guns out there. But, that voice broke through my hard shell."

Melvin Grinage said, "Folks, wait until you hear her. She's just eighteen years old. Ladies and gentleman, here she is—Walden Records' newest recording artist—Miss Bettina Charles."

While the studio viewers clapped, the band began to play as Tina approached the microphone. So humbled by the audience's warm reception, she pressed her hands in a praying position and bowed her head to convey gracious appreciation. When the song's lengthy introduction ended, the first few phrases sung by Tina were barely audible—quiet as a mouse. That enabled the listeners to zero in on the beauty of the canvas—hoping that this newcomer had not lost her nerve on live, national television. By the twelfth lyrical utterance, an indication of Tina's vocal prowess presented itself. The build of the song enabled that thing—that thing that makes greatness great—to rise from Bettina's belly. It entered the melody through her vocal cords and took over.

The audience hung on to every syllable, note, and turn of a phrase. Tina's gestures included several movements where her arms stretched out wide—as far as they could extend. A smile of hospitality was part of the presentation. Instead of being received disingenuously, Tina came across as an innocent girl, petitioning all observers to assist her in the quest to make it home.

On the latter part of the song, Tina smiled her way through because it felt so good, so right. She knew it was her turn—her coming out—her shining moment. She exhibited such poise and grace that those within her inner circle struggled to contain their emotions. Arnie viewed the performance from his seat on the set next to Melvin Grinage. Carlton, Kelly, Ellis, and Idella sat second-row center as part of the studio audience. Zina and her stylists displayed glee while waiting in the wings. Her entire close-knit team held onto each syllable, inflection, and gesture. Then, at the appointed time, Tina elevated to an anointed place, floating above herself. Idella wondered. *We know, but do we really recognize the significance of this vessel that has been placed in our charge.* The overall performance was a success. Tina truly owned the stage and the live audience. The song "Made It Home" was so well received that Arnie decided to include it on the debut album.

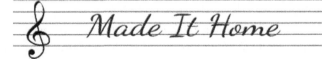

In this cold world—I'm on my own
Lots of people—yet all alone
Each harmful deed—causes an action
Danger lurking—a chain reaction

Days are empty—the nights are long
There is no light—all has gone wrong
Each way I turn—there is rejection
No helpful words—and no affection

To each its own—there's no respect
Not what you give—it's what you get
From evil acts—lives gone too soon
Joy can't squeeze in—there is no room

In all put out—nothing was gained
A broken spirit—is what remained
The wicked flaws—caused me to see
The worst in them—rubbed off on me

Loud voices came—lent me their ear
Pushed back the ones—that I held dear
Support removed—out of my sight
Many gone wrong—can't make one right

From where I was—I looked to you
Your opened door—saw it, walked through
So here I am—now it's my turn
To share with all—that which I've learned

Now, I can feel—the gentle breeze
Flowery fields—and lots of trees
Smiling faces—are all about
My faith in you—guided me out

The oceans waves—the skies so blue
The grass so green—the birds fly too
And from now on—great things I see
I'll do my best—now that I'm free

No longer lost—nor on my own
It's crystal clear—I made it home
I'm sitting high, atop a throne
The battle's won, I made it home
Guided me back—no more to roam
A fresh new start—I made it home
New faith I claim, I'm not the same
No more to fear, I'm finally here
I made it home, I —made—it—h-o-m-e

36

FAMILY TRADITIONS

IMMEDIATELY following *The Melvin Grinage Show*, Arnie boarded his jet and returned to Los Angeles. The next morning, he met with the programming director at *National Video Television* whose screening team was impressed with the Walden Records product. Arnie's sales pitch was concise. "The power of this Bettina Charles video is in its simplicity. Because she is a brand-new talent, our focus was all about image building—introducing our Pop-Diva's amazing voice while emphasizing her beauty and sex appeal. The five videos that follow this one are all grand productions, true mini-musical-movies."

As promised, NVT ran the "Tell Me" video that same night with a trial by fire of airing it at 9:45 p. m. The results were impressive. The phone rang demanding more plays, resulting in a run every four hours. When the requests kept coming, "Tell Me" was placed in the programming rotation, running once every hour. Shortly thereafter, Arnie received a call from NVT requesting immediate delivery of the next video.

The business-savvy Mister Peters had offered *NVT* a four-week exclusive run of the first three videos. After that the game was on and *Mission Black Television* joined the party. Although in its infancy stage and not airing daily, *MBT* was the only Black cable station and a significant portion of its limited programming was dedicated to streaming music videos. In addition, the three big television networks began featuring Tina's mini-musical-movies on shows like *Soul Video Nation, Rocking Gold,* and *Video Groove.* To capitalize on Tina's television debut and *NVT* video plays, Arnie released the "Tell Me" album as soon as the distributors were ready—five days later.

From there, Tina and entourage hit the road, engaging in a slew of personal appearances on local radio, on affiliates of network television, at record stores, in night clubs, and special events. The engagements varied, involving interview, photo, and autograph sessions. Appearing to be spontaneous and based on audience enthusiasm and media coverage, Arnie would give the nod for Tina to perform the tracks he wanted to market. Cities toured included Philadelphia, Baltimore, Washington, DC, Miami, Los Angeles, and middle-American hot spots in between. As the singles climbed the charts, the crowds quadrupled in size, often taking Tina hours to smile for photographs and sign album covers and posters. In less than three months, she had circled the continental United States and gone from personalizing each autograph to scribbling a facsimile of her name.

Saturday, January 1, 1983

While making and marketing her debut album, Tina had missed summer's yielding to autumn's beautiful colors, receiving a mere three-day break for Thanksgiving and five days during the Christmas holiday. Because she performed on New Year's Eve in *Times Square,* the three great-aunties brought the first meal in January and their holiday traditions from Joseph-Lee Manor in Scotland Neck to Windsor East in New York City. For Aunty Zooni, it was a short trip. Abruptly retiring, she had spent the holiday season at Ellis Ross's brownstone in Brooklyn. Hattie Mae had taken a bold and potentially dangerous step, causing her to miss the family gathering all together.

A disgusted Aunty Trudy explained. "That sin filled heathen wore my daughter down, he wore her down. I tell you."

Aunty Gina added. "Hattie Mae accepted Vernon's umpteenth I'm sorry and went back to him in DC."

"Sisters, don't fret too hard," snarled Zooni. "Once she's black and blue and tired of him beating her silly, she'll be calling and we'll go rescue her again."

Desiring to show her appreciation, Tina extended an invitation to the King and Queen of Walden Records. The building's chief concierge Curtis Frazier escorted them up the elevator and told them to knock on the door of apartment 2407—as he had been instructed to do by Miss Bettina Charles.

It didn't ease Kelly's mind or settle her stomach that she had visited the apartment before. As she walked down the hallway, it seemed to be closing in on her like a tunnel, requiring her to take a series of deep breaths. *You can do this Kelly. You can handle the iron ladies. Really, you can.* "Arnie, knock on the door," she demanded.

"These are your secret relatives, not mine. I don't see why you insisted that I tag along—and especially so damn early." Arnie grunted as he knocked. "It's just eleven o'clock in the morning and we were up working most of the night." Including Tina, The Label had been monitoring several of their hottest artists' performances on various televised New Year's Eve celebrations across the country as well as in Europe.

Aunties Gina and Trudy peeked through the crack in the chained door. "Who is it?" they asked while looking at who was knocking.

Both Arnie and Kelly were speaking like ventriloquist—throwing their voices at one another with a Cheshire cat grin—broad ear to ear toothy smiles, with teeth clenched tightly. "Their staring right at us through the crack in the door," said Arnie.

"Just shut up, keep smiling, and play along," demanded Kelly. She answered her two great-aunties. "It's Kelly King and Arnie Peters."

Aunty Gina directed. "Miss King, please take three steps back and let Mister Peters enter first."

After Kelly moved backwards, the door sprang wide-open and con-fetti was tossed above his head as Arnie's foot crossed the apartment's threshold. "Happy New Year," yelled Tina, Carlton, Tony, Aunties Gina, Trudy, and Zooni, Uncle Ed, Larry, and Ellis Ross. Coffee, tea, Champagne, mimosas, and Bellini cocktails had been flowing with hors d'oeuvres for over an hour. Tina hugged Kelly, introduced some, and presented others while Tony grabbed coats.

"Get your butts in here, so we can eat," yelled Ellis. "I have officially been indoctrinated into the family's folklore and mysticism. You see, in order for Miss Tina's humble abode to be appropriately blessed and protected, three-men that didn't sleep here last night had to be among the first seven people to cross the threshold after sunrise on New Year's Day. Then, they have to stay and eat a meal. Ain't that something?"

"You're shitting me right?" asked Arnie.

"No he's not kidding and please, mind your mouth. I'm Trudy by the way—Tina's second oldest great-aunty and an anointed and ap-pointed soldier in the Army for the Lord."

"Well, congratulations and it's nice to meet you, Ma'am."

"Tony and Larry slept here in sin last night," Aunty Trudy con-tinued. "So, they don't count. Me and my Ed was the first ones to en-ter the apartment this morning and my sister Zooni and Mister Ellis came right behind. Now, you, Mister Peters are the completion. We get blessed along with the dwelling—for performing the act of cross-ing the threshold in purity of thought and deed."

"I've been described in many ways, but having purity in any form most definitely was not on the list," said Arnie.

"As I was saying, good spirits have officially been ushered in—one for the Father, one for the Son, and one for the Holy Ghost. Praise the Lord."

Arnie's mind reeled. *What in the hell is the name of the planet where these folks came from? Kelly-Kelly, you're going to owe me big time if I make it through the day.*

"You met me at the contract luncheon," said Zooni. "The tradition also says that the more men partaking in the first meal the bigger the blessing. With the five men represented here, this apartment should be safe and secure for the entire year."

"Zooni dear, you stand corrected," said Ellis. "There are six men present. Does that increase our favor?"

"To play it safe, I counted Carlton and Tony as a half-a-man each."

Tina interjected. "That's because they're younger than forty. Isn't that right Aunty Zooni?"

"You interpret your way and I call it, like I see it."

Carlton shook his head and waved his finger to match the cadence of each snappy word. "I know you don't want me to get to calling what I see."

Aunty Zooni ran with that statement. "Like how I see the spook who sat by the door. You better go guard somebody's entryway while you still have teeth."

Arnie laughed. "Zooni, I like you more by the second and the insult."

Tina pulled Carlton's fingers down as she redirected the conversation. "You see, Arnie, our New Year's Day traditions have been in the Charles-Watkins-Smith family for as long as anyone can remember."

Kelly interrupted with a complement as she pinched Arnie's leg hard and twisted it. "Your powerful presence is why Tina wanted you to be a part of this holiday celebration."

"Ouch!"

Carlton made quote signs with his fingers. "You better convert that 'ouch' into manly man powers. They will come in handy when it's time to chow down on that hog head minced barbeque, those black-eyed peas, and collard greens. Each man has to eat a double portion and then the protection is secured."

"Don't forget about the candied yams, the macaroni and cheese, potato salad, and slaw," added Aunty Trudy. "Although Cousin Alonia couldn't be here, he cooked up enough food to refill Simon Peter's boat after off-loading the fish that he got from Jesus."

Arnie was perplexed. "What did she just say?"

Aunty Gina provided more detail. "You see, young man, the hog head barbeque is for good luck, the black-eyed peas are for good health, and the greens are for financial blessings."

Arnie turned to Ellis. "These are the most unusual and hilarious old wives' tales that I've ever heard. I need to put this whole scene on tape and release it as a comedy album."

Carlton was offended. "All jokes aside because this stuff is serious. And you're the one who needs to be taped—not for records but for film—Mister Bonaparte."

Arnie sneered on the inside. *He's lucky Tina's protection has my hands tied—for right now.* "Mister Gutter-ball, I resent that disparaging comparison, and I've heard you say it more than once."

Over their almost six-month acquaintance, Arnie had developed a low-tolerance for Carlton—believing that he had too much mouth, was cocky, disrespectful, and unpredictable.

"Carlton, be quiet before you piss him off," demanded Tina. "Except for Pappy John, my main village is here and I'm in a very happy place."

Kelly spent most of the day, warming and serving food, washing dishes, and saying, "Yes, Ma'am and no, Ma'am." Her heart was performing somersaults the entire time because it was one of the most fulfilling days of her life. She was part of a close-knit family—one with a peculiar brand of unconditional love for each other. She counted herself as a member even though no one, but Arnie, knew that she belonged to the village. As it pertained to Mister Peters, the master of plotting revenge, he talked himself out of raining down terror on Carlton. Instead, he decided to err on the side of caution and let the irritating horse-fly continue to buzz around—for now.

4:00 p. m.—Aunty Gina and Tina were camped out on the left side of the plush, chocolate brown sectional. They loved football and had been watching games most of the day. After an extended *Times Square* performance in the cold the previous evening, Tina was napping on and off with her head resting in Aunty Gina's lap.

Arnie made an observation. *These great-aunties treat Tina like a baby. That explains why she acts like a spoiled ass brat.*

As part of family tradition on this first day of the year commemoration, kinfolks at odds or who had little in common had to engage in, at least, one activity together—a truce of sorts. In addition, every Charles-Watkins-Smith gathering included a 300 piece jigsaw puzzle that each attendee had to assist in putting together. A completed project was achieved seventy percent of the time. With that, it was Larry and Aunty Trudy's turn at working the puzzle that was a third of the way finished.

Larry pumped his fist. "Hey check this out. The puzzle part I just put together spells happy holidays."

Aunty Trudy said, "That's the Lord blessing your hard work on learning how to read. You know the Bible says, 'Study to show thyself approved unto God, a workman that needeth not to be ashamed.'— Second Timothy two-fifteen."

Aunty Zooni spoke loudly, adding her special brand of encouragement. "And Zooni saith, keep trying Larry. Soon, you'll test high enough to enter the sixth grade."

With insults still flying, Carlton, Tony, Uncle Ed, and Aunty Zooni were playing spades. "Dammit Ed, if you're gonna be my partner, you gotta grow some balls. Count them kings as books when you're holding the damn aces to that suit and it's early in the round. Matter-of-fact, just move. Kelly, make me a fresh vodka and orange juice and you and your freckles get over here and be my partner."

"Yes, Ma'am," Kelly said with an elated attitude. Although terrified to make a wrong move in the card game, she was floating on a cloud just the same—by virtue of being counted as a member of the herd.

Trudy warned. "Zooni, enough with the foul language. If my ears are burning, the Lord most certainly is not pleased and aiming a lightning rod in this direction."

Ellis and Arnie spent time alone on the balcony, braving the chilled air. "That Zooni is a seasoned lioness, one that gets her jollies off by bullying the rest of the pride," said Arnie. "Somehow, she's put a spell on you—a man known to have the attention span of a two year old when it comes to women."

Ellis cackled with his tongue making peek-a-boo appearances in and out of his mouth. "Don't knock it until you rock it and don't quit it until you get it! Besides, as I get older, I need stimulating conversation in addition to my romps. Being like-minded is important to me now."

Arnie sneaked a quick look through a gap in the vertical blinds. "That Zooni of yours is very striking—possessing that Lena Horne classic beauty. And look at all of the women in this family from the top down to Tina." Arnie licked his lips and continued. "They all got it—elegance, confidence, spunk, and-and hell—I'm just gonna say it. They all got that small waistline and perfectly-sized junk in the trunk."

Ellis shook his head in agreement. "Maybe, it's a Carolina thang because your Kelly has it too. Her momma's from that same neck of the woods, you know."

Arnie held his tongue, but his mind screamed. *Ellis, how perceptive you are. I wish I could tell you that Kelly is a blood member of this clan of beautiful booties as well.* "What do you mean—my Kelly? We were driven over here together, but we're not together-together."

"Yeah, right, Arnie. This is Ellis Ross you're talking to—a discerning Cat that knows both of you closer than I'd like to."

9:00 p. m.—The day had winded down and finally surrendered to the night. Food, drink, parades, football, card games, a 300 piece puzzle, conversation, insults, and laughter had contributed to a memorable christening of the New Year.

37

NEWCOMER OF THE YEAR

SEVENTEEN months had passed since the release of Tina's first album that made it in the history books as one of the highest selling. The neophyte recording artist had worked very hard without a significant break for her to pause, reflect, and recuperate. Her efforts, however, reaped a multitude of award winning accolades. In addition to being nominated for more than thirty awards from music academies around the world, Bettina Charles had been crowned "Newcomer of the Year" in five countries. Emphatic in her determination to, at a minimum, personally accept those five crowns, her travels around the world were a tedious journey. Tina gave a rare ultimatum to Mister Peters. "If the fans and the academies named me 'their best newcomer,' the least I can do is show up to accept the awards. As it relates to all of the other nominations, I guess I have to figure out a fair way to pick and choose." With his eyes on selling more albums, Arnie made the process easier by making all of the other selections. With that, Bettina Charles made personal appearances at the ceremonies with the highest television ratings in which she was also a featured performer. Weathering the logistical storms, Arnie and Kelly were in the auditoriums to "modestly" nod and give personal support to each of their budding Pop-Diva's shining moments.

Sunday, February 26, 1984

Unable to be matched, Tina's acceptance speech at the grandfather of award shows stood alone as the most memorable. As the nominations in her category were read, her mind reeled to the past—to Tee-Tee moments—those of the little girl looking in the mirror, speaking into her hairbrush, and pretending to win the award. *Oh my God, it's no longer a dream. I'm nineteen and a half years old and I'm here—at the Shrine, sitting in this audience. I'm so grateful and I truly don't care who wins.* Tina was speaking so loudly in her own head that she didn't hear her name being called. When feeling Kelly's nudge on her left side and Carlton's harder leg bump on her right, she concentrated on the moment at hand. While turning her head from left to right, looking for the winner, she smiled and clapped fervently.

Carlton screamed. "Tee-Tee, it's you crazy girl! You won, so get up there and get your award." Tina looked up to see herself on the large monitor. She jumped to her feet, hugged Carlton, Kelly, and then Arnie as she squeezed by him and two other people to clear the row. Once in the aisle, she took off and ran full speed to the stage, skipping several stairs to reach the platform. Upon arriving at the podium, the "Newcomer of the Year" took hold of her golden gramophone and altered her grip to a tighter one. She had not anticipated the award being heavy as she set it down carefully on the lectern. After clearing her throat, she began to deliver her first public speech since her brief salutatorian address at her high school graduation.

Gramophone Award Acceptance Speech One

This is my first time being up here and I'm really excited and also very nervous. Absolutely first, I thank God for blessing me with my peculiar brand of talent. I thank Carlton who was my first manager and is my best friend and personal assistant. He's the one who willed my career into existence. I thank my entire family for keeping me grounded. The ones that smother me the most are my dad, Pappy John, my Aunties Gina, Trudy, and Zooni, my Uncle Ed, Tony, and Larry.

To my fans, you bought the albums, so this award belongs to you. Okay, I see the warning light, so I need to hurry along before the music starts playing. I've been watching this show my entire life, so I know how it goes.

Laughter spread throughout the auditorium and a loud voice yelled out from the balcony. "Take your time because we love you, Bettina Charles!"

Tina chuckled:

And I love you too, but let me keep going. H'm blessed to have been taught by two genius musical fathers—Professor Milton and Ellis Ross. I want to thank my creative team led by André Jenkins, Jerry Johnson, Keith Murray, and Daniel Weeks. I send my love and thanks to the rest of my inner circle and appreciate all you do to care for me daily—Assistant Angela, Idella Stephens, Zina Shelby, and Bernie Bazemore.

Because of their importance, I saved these two for now. I want to give a special thank you to the royalty of Walden Records—Arnie Peters and Kelly King. You are the earthly reason the public even knows my name. Thanks for your brilliance and for taking a little time out of your busy schedules to believe in me. Lastly, I thank my heart of hearts—my mother, Momma Nin. Although she left her earthly dwelling, she is flying with the angels. Once again, I thank you all very much.

The theme music played and Tina left the stage with the heavy gramophone award held high over her head. Before the night was over, she gave an incredible performance and collected two more gramophones. Those two speeches were very brief.

Gramophone Award Acceptance Speech Two

I thank you all. But especially, I thank my awesome fans. You guys really rock!

Gramophone Award Acceptance Speech Three

This is absolutely incredible. Again, I thank you.

Being a gracious winner and performing at award shows was not an excuse to slouch on Arnie's other duties as assigned. Tina continued to be moved from one strategic point to another. A crucial part of fulfilling her Walden Records' obligations included fielding questions from the press. In so doing, Arnie was collecting future favors, limiting the on-the-fly interviews to a few handpicked reporters at a time.

Reporter One: *Miss Charles, when seeing yourself on billboards, posters, or in print, what is your reaction?*

Tina: *I feel awkward when I see myself on a magazine cover or when I see my face on a tee shirt that someone is wearing. It's me, but it's not me. It's very difficult to explain. You see, singing and performing is what I do. It's not who I am. I try to keep that in my mind at all times.*

Reporter Two: *How do you feel about your fans?*

Tina: *I'm humbled, grateful, and a bit overwhelmed by the responsibility that goes along with this "superstardom" thing. I appreciate the awards and my fans' vote of confidence. I try to work overtime for them every day.*

Of the numerous prestigious recognitions, one award was supreme over all the others. Tina fulfilled the pinky-swear promise that topped all of her other pinky-swear promises to that point—thanks to Ellis Ross. As a lecturer, he had connections with several institutions of higher learning. In the 1985 spring semester, upon approval of her home university registrar's office, Tina enrolled in a course entitled: Vocational Technology. It was an optimal solution for a person going to school while working full-time. Class attendance was by means of correspondence with the exception of oral exams. The course requirements were a series of interim submittals and the final deliverable of a twenty-five page thesis. The subject matter was real-life experiences related to a candidate's field of study.

For Tina, the exacting task involved extensive research and writing, tacked on to her already over-extended schedule. Before, in-between, and after rehearsals and performances, Tina worked on her school assignments. On her days off, she could be found at the nearest library buried in a book, reviewing reels of microfiche, or exploring other reference materials. Although camouflaged in thick-brimmed glasses and a baseball cap, the disguise was unnecessary, as most of the library patrons were on quests for knowledge far more important than chasing down an entertainer. In that same vain, the Ivy League institution hosting her class was accustomed to high-profile students. Accepting no excuses, some of Tina's submissions were rejected—sending her away to make modifications on three separate occasions.

Misreading Tina's focus on her studies as snobbish behavior, other entertainers labeled her as unapproachable.

The National Intrigue
SLEAZE-LINE—*Bettina Charles the Snob*

A few weeks ago in the green room at the Gramophone Awards, Bettina Charles kept her head buried in a book as an excuse to avoid being cordial.

Overheard by many, her much older handlers addressed her as Miss Charles. A nameless member of her inner circle said, "You either suck up or be fired for disrespecting Walden Records' little princess."

Also wanting to remain anonymous, several well-established entertainers labeled her as a snobbish prima donna. One said, "What nerve—a fresh-faced kid insisting on being called Miss Charles. How dare she ignore and disregard a room full of proven entertainers, most with a minimum of ten years' experience in the music business."

One night, opting to walk and be on her own, Tina left the library that was near Windsor East and went to her neighborhood supermarket to pick up ingredients—ground beef, lettuce, tomatoes, black olives, shredded sharp cheddar cheese, sour cream, and hard tortillas. She had a taste for homemade tacos and the motivation to make them. With no pressure from knowledge-seekers in the library, she had abandoned the glasses and baseball cap disguise and forgotten to restore it before entering the grocery store. While waiting at the checkout counter after gathering all of her items, she heard rumbling from four teen-aged girls in the adjacent line. Assuming they were giggling about boys and general high school drama, she ignored them—being in deep contemplation about her thesis. While watching her items move toward the cashier on the conveyer belt, she looked up and saw her image plastered on the front of *Scene Teen Magazine*. Advising herself, she said, *Pretend it's not you.* Two of the girls switched lines and were separated from her by one waiting customer.

While she returned her checkbook and non-driver's ID to her backpack, the clerk said, "Have a nice day, Miss Charles. Oh my God—I just waited on Bettina Charles." The teenaged girls started screaming. Tina smiled, grabbed her bag of ingredients, and darted out of the store. She ran up the street and around the corner into the alley entrance of Windsor East.

An hour and a half later, she sat in Bernie Bazemore's cubicle sharing the taco meal. "Miss Tina, you have to face the fact that you're a big-time star now. The days of roaming around on your own are over."

"It's not that easy to change because I feel the same. I'm still me."

"Well, you really need to wise up quickly. I don't want you to get hurt roaming around by yourself. Mister Peters would go crazy if he found out."

"Yes, he'd probably fine me for breaching a clause in my contract. Wow! As a little girl, I remember performing in the mirror, pretending to be a famous singer. Deep inside, a part of me always knew I'd make that dream come true. But, running and ducking in alleys to get away from people wasn't in any of my dreams."

Friday, May 4, 1984

As a result of remaining persistent, the fourth submission and her oral presentation were a charm. Tina had successfully defended her thesis paper and earned thirty credit hours in the process. That was seven more than she needed to complete her requirements. More than a year before the prescribed deadline, Tina graduated. Finally given a Pop-Diva perk, she was allowed to be escorted across the stage when her name was called. The university president shook Tina's hand but presented the degree to Pappy John. Paying for extra copies, she hung one each at Joseph-Lee Manor, Les Vésinet, and Windsor East. Pappy John displayed the original degree on the wall in the Foyer of his Watergate apartment. He planned to look at it and smile each time he entered and exited. Tina kissed the final copy and tucked it away inside Brief de Vaughan. She spoke aloud softly. "Momma Nin, this one is for you."

38

RESERVED ON RETAINER

CAMPED out at Walden Records for three weeks of planning and rehearsals, Tina, Kelly, Ellis, and lead choreographer André Jenkins produced a quality rookie live show. Leaning heavily on performance fundamentals, the short program was dominated by flat-footed belting out of the lyrics. In addition, her dancing was effective, her stage presence was excellent, and her rapport with the audience was superb. The critics agreed that Bettina Charles not only had an amazing voice but also had the potential to become a great live entertainer. During her first four months of touring, her steady schedule rotated between serving as the opening act for a past-his-prime performer with a loyal following and revving up the crowd in preparation for the hilarity of a top comedian.

Saturday, September 15, 1984

As fallout of fulfilling an Arnie favor, touring for Tina became eventful, requiring an extemporaneous performance plan. It was deemed such because a great deal of improvisation was required.

Due to a sudden illness early on performance day of a top headliner, the budding artist was asked to be on standby and rushed from New York City to Las Vegas. Her instructions were to wait in the wings in the event that the artist was unable to complete the show in its entirety. Luckily, the venue's orchestra was the headliner's musical accompaniment that would be playing for Miss Charles if required. Therefore, preparation was all about the music and involved a two hour rehearsal with Tina singing and Ellis teaching parts to unfamiliar, but extremely skilled musicians. They quickly absorbed the sheet music's technical essence and nuisances while following Conductor Ellis's direction to reach the desired interpretation. All the while, Tina's musical father privately prayed that the headliner would pull through and their assistance would not be necessary. That evening and thirty minutes into the show, however, a brief apology was given as the headliner was being carried off of the stage. Bettina Charles stepped in and performed for an hour and a half with rave reviews.

When the news leaked out mysteriously to the press by an anonymous Walden Records' staffer (Arnie), Tina responded to inquiries by downplaying her heroic intervention.

Interviewer: We've been told that you have a special knack for dealing with the unanticipated, able to step in and pitch-hit for an established artist at a moment's notice. You were able to clear the difficult hurdle of meeting the high expectations of a disappointed audience that did not pay to be entertained by you. How do you really feel about being put in such a precarious and vulnerable position?

Tina: I don't view such situations in a negative light, so, for me, there was no problem. Miss Idella Stephens, my product—excuse me—my artist development coordinator taught me to embrace unforeseen circumstances as skill sharpening drills. They are unexpected opportunities instead of a setup for failure.

Walden Records immediately capitalized on the mainliner's career ending mishap and Tina's good fortune. A unique marketing concept was dreamt up in Arnie-land, supported by his Serengeti Lioness, and implemented by product three seven two eighty-five. For an exorbitant fee, Miss Charles could be placed on retainer and if available would open, close, or replace an artist with minimal notice. Although surprising to The Label's marketing leads, the phone rang off the hook with takers of the unusual arrangement. Added to her credentials, Bettina Charles was an emergency responder who was excellent at putting out fires.

By the sixth month of performing as a relief pitcher, Tina had perfected her delivery of situational services to an exacting degree. Managers of headliners, venue executive directors, and tour promoters had signed up to pay a retainer fee whose sticker price had doubled. As Tina traveled about, the diverse audiences were an excellent means of promoting her second album project and test-driving their corresponding dance routines. Originally produced as video choreography, each routine had to be modified to suit the parameters and limitations of performing live on stage.

Tina was grateful that this particular, last minute engagement landed her in Washington, DC where she'd be performing the next evening at the historic Constitution Center whose doors first opened in 1835. She and Carlton arrived in the city at 8:00 p. m. in order to spend a few hours with her father. Instead of staying in the hotel with the rest of their small crew, they'd be spending a few nights at Pappy John's Watergate apartment. It was Carlton's first visit and he thought that the decorations were fabulous. "Pappy John, I know you have two left hands when it comes to decorating, so way to go Tee-Tee. You laid this place out just the way I taught you."

Saturday, March 23, 1985

7:30 a. m.—Prior to leaving the Watergate and being driven to National Airport in Tina's transport, Pappy John awakened the two twenty-something partners in crime and gave them marching orders. They would be staying in his apartment for a few nights without his supervision. "Make sure the water and all the lights are off, the windows are closed, the kitchen appliances, and the iron, Carlton, are unplugged." Mister Montgomery was an ironing fanatic who felt that the slightest wrinkle in his clothing was a personal indictment against him. A long hug was Tina's last act of saying goodbye to her father. His baby sister and her Aunty Ava was having major surgery later that day. Pappy John planned to be with her in Boulder, Colorado throughout the recovery process—for six weeks at a minimum. He wasn't the only family member, however, with open-ended plans to leave Tina. In two days, Carlton would be taking extended leave from his cousin and The Label to tend to loose ends in Scotland Neck—left dangling for a significant period of time.

After getting a sufficient amount of sleep for the over-exuberant young adults, Tina and Carlton took transport to the venue. In approaching these retainer engagements, regardless of performing in the concert rotation—first or last—Tina was always revved up and prepared to give her all. Because it was not her show, she had to plan for the unexpected. There would be different set designs and lighting at a minimum and varied musicians and backup singers on the extreme end of the spectrum of the unpredictable. Because of the short notice, her four dancers were already booked in Las Vegas and unavailable to serve as window dressing during her performance. With the absence of stunts and acrobatics, Tina's live presentation would include three costume changes, extensive dancing on her part, and a heavy reliance on her vocals and personality.

11:00 a. m. — When Tina and Carlton entered Constitution Center, the venue was bustling with activity. It was being prepped to host events in both its auditoriums. The larger concert hall was where "The Newcomer of the Year" would be showcasing her talent. The smaller production site, seating eight hundred, was a theatre in the round—hosting a special opera performance the next evening. It was the entertainment portion of the Center's annual fundraising gala. As the cousins cleared the entryway into the interior of the historic hall, they both were encountering a mouth opening and jaw dropping experience. They walked across the wide lobby that was set apart by gold and black flowered patterns embedded in the beautiful red carpeting.

Scattered about the hall, Tina and Carlton were surprised to find stone and marble sculptures of archaic nude legends and mythical creatures. Their attention was drawn to the wide-range of lighting fixtures that included a variety of crystal chandeliers, pendant lamps, and classic incandescent bulbs held in unique polished brass canisters. The intricate details on the ornamental railing and decorative doors seemed to be originally designed for the discriminating taste of royalty. Upon entering the concert hall itself, Tina paused to pay homage to a demonstration of magnificence displayed in its truest form. The theatre had a proscenium design that was indicative of the ancient Greek and Roman structural style, enabling amazing acoustics. There was a series of archways in the ceiling and a huge curtain encased in a rectangular frame that separated the stage from the auditorium. This structural styling enabled a frontal view of the stage only. There was no back or side perspective offered to the spectators.

To concentrate on the job at hand, Tina did as Aunty Zooni commanded on a regular basis—she pulled herself together. While standing on the stage, she directed her attention to where her audience would be seated. Slowly panning the room, she paused at varying intervals to examine the organization of chairs carefully. She looked down at the pit, moved her head from right to left, probing the main level-orchestra. Then, she tilted her head up and focused on the box seats that took precedence in the first row of the upper level. They started at the front—stage right—and wrapped all the way around the entire semi-circled seating area. The intermediate mezzanine tier was next. Finally, Tina scanned the balcony. Just like three years earlier at Club Trevi's, she stood on her tiptoes and stretched her neck to see the last row and the far-off seats in the rafters. With no respect of person, her intention was to touch everyone through the projection of her voice, the reach of her eyes, the gestures of her body, and the consideration of the audience as a whole in her heart.

In order to create such synergy, Tina engaged in a venue test-drive. After she viewed the auditorium from the stage, she and Carlton moved around the concert hall, took a seat in random sections, and spent ten to fifteen minutes viewing the stage from that particular audience member's vantage point. Upon taking in the sought after information, she moved to a different location in the auditorium and repeated her point-of-view assessment. Tina felt very fortunate to be afforded this rare opportunity to perform at Constitution Center. It was the result of The Label granting priority booking to one of the early takers of the retainer services of Bettina Charles. Later that evening, she would be closing for August Osborne in this larger concert hall as a surprise guest performer. Her client and head-liner was surfacing from a three-day, no sleep, drug binge. His managerial camp was well aware of his limitations in stamina and decided to have him open up the show, attempt to perform for forty-five minutes, and relinquish the featured time slot to the girl with the golden chops. After all, August Osborne was known as a trailblazer who was on a mission to promote the next generation of talent. In his camp's opinion, Bettina Charles was a leader of the pack. That was the planned excuse he'd present before disappearing to his hotel room and an awaiting saline drip to combat his severe dehydration.

As they sat in the empty audience and observed the stage, Carlton posed a thought provoking question to Tina. "Can you imagine the day when it's our turn? You'll be the headliner and we'll be sitting in an auditorium like this one—watching your set being put together?"

"Based on Arnie's timeframe, that might take forever. He wants me to have about a dozen of my own hits and tons of this—opening for other artists' experience. Until then, you keep dreaming and I'll keep jotting down my ideas."

"No worries, based on the attention that you're getting now, it's gonna happen much sooner that you think. You've already got six hits and in a short time since its release, this new album has taken off."

"I certainly hope so because I feel like I'm ready to tour on my own."

As Tina's attention was drawn back to the stage, she was impressed, watching the precision of the construction crew as they worked in cooperation to assemble the set. Carlton sat next to her, skimming through a brochure about the venue. It was his job to clue 3.7.2.85 in on pertinent facts about the concert hall and the city in which they were touring. During the performance, Tina would use the information to interject comments pertaining to that home turf. In this case at Constitution Center, she would say something that resonated with the audience of 5,000 people strong.

Kelly King encouraged Tina's implementation of the practice for different reasons. "Throwing a few facts around about the venue and locale impresses theatre management. They're the ones who work with the promoters regarding booking. We need them in our corner when the time comes to negotiate percentages for your solo tour."

Carlton's eyes got big and his mouth flew open. "You have got to be kidding me. This is too childish for words."

"What is?"

"It's not what, but who." He moved over close, shoulder to shoulder with Tina and shared the brochure. "Look who's on the trustee board of this concert hall—Victoria Chambers. Your grandma-ma is listed as a governing trustee on page 15, and on the next page, she's listed as a member of the leadership circle."

Tina disputed. "It could be another Victoria Chambers, you see."

"Don't you remember the latest check when the Chamberses did something so unlike themselves? Instead of their attorney's office, they put a home address on the envelope. It was to a house in McLean, Virginia and that's a DC suburb. I was born here and ran the streets for fifteen years. Trust that I know all the nukes and crannies where rich folks live."

"The fact that they live in this area doesn't prove it's the same Victoria Chambers."

Carlton kept flipping through the pages, not stopping until he reached the back inside cover. "Hate to bust your bubble, but now I'm sure it's them. It's written right here in black and white—a color for each side of your family. Victoria and William Chambers are listed as legends in the ovation circle. 'Each year, they contribute fifty thousand dollars to Constitution Center in honor of their deceased daughter Christina.' There's no question they're talking about your birth mother and look at this. The Chamberses have been donating the money every year for the past twenty-plus years. That's the same amount of time you've been on this earth and your mother's been dead."

Tina's heart started to beat rapidly and her stomach began to flutter. "Alright, it's them, woopty doo," Tina said minus enthusiasm. "That's all they get from me because I don't care. They're experts at spreading money around—being big-time philanthropists." Tina used her finger to glide through every word of the two paragraph write-up. "This story is all about their accomplishments and doesn't mention anything about having a Black grandchild. They're such big hypocrites."

Attempting to make her feel better, Carlton joked. "I hate to be the one to break the news, but technically, you're high yellow and I'm Black. Ask Aunty Zooni."

Tina giggled and rolled her eyes. "Thanks Carlton. That laugh eased the queasy feeling in my stomach. You're just plain stupid, but I love you just the same, you see."

Tina turned her head away from her cousin and returned her attention back to the transformation unfolding on the stage. Internally, however, she hoped that Carlton would find more details to report. He closed the first booklet, opened another, and continued his probe. The second document was a marketing leaflet. It dedicated a page with photos and a summation to each event taking place in that current season.

"Here come the Chamberses again on the fourth page of this pamphlet. They sponsor the 'Rising Stars Opera Training Program' and the year-end grand opera performance." That figures their preference in music would be hoity-toity.

"Wait a minute now," defended Tina. "I love opera too. My favorite operas are La Traviata and La Bohème. Tina was no stranger to the refined arts, having received long needled injections of the classics—symphonies and Shakespearean theatre in addition to opera. Since being aware of herself, mandatory cultural enrichment was at the top of Momma Nin's list of entertainment for her adopted daughter. Tina was so confused about the possibility of encountering her grandparents that she continued to ramble. "I also love Tosca. The last opera Pappy John and I went to see was Turandot. When Luciano Pavarotti sang his famous aria, Nessun Dorma, I almost fainted. He was incredible. At the end of the show, I got a close look at him and everything."

"Alright already, I get the point. You love opera. You love opera. You—l-o-v-e opera! I'm positive you inherited that gene of spazzing out about boring ass entertainment from the Chamberses. They say that the fruit drops close to the tree and knocks you over the head."

Tina rolled her eyes and bumped her cousin's shoulder. "That's not even close to how that saying goes."

"Whatever." Carlton continued to scan through the brochure. "Damn, Tina, your grandma-ma is on the platinum gala committee too! Oh no, stop the show, something's about to blow! Wait here. I'll be back."

"Where are you going?"

"No worries. You just stay right there. Until I get back, I'm 'Kunta Kinte' and you're 'Kizzy' which means *Stay Put.* And that means you keep your butt planted in that seat until I get back."

In Carlton's absence, Tina tried to distract herself by focusing on individuals on the stage while humming the tune of "Finally Made It Home." Her mind, however, was stayed on the Chamberses and her cousin/personal assistant. *I know I'm thinking crazy, but, I really want to know more about them and I can't believe I'm feeling this way.* Tina's heart palpitations and stomach quivers returned as she vocalized questions that no one was around to answer. "Carlton, where are you? What could possibly be taking so long?"

Twenty minutes later, Carlton reappeared and ran over to Tina. The fact that he was winded was obvious as he began to speak. "You ain't gonna believe this if I joined the military and came back a hero."

"Believe what Carlton, believe what?" Hearing direct commentary about her grandparents was causing Tina to experience a variety of emotions all at once. Her impatience was the most outstanding.

"First of all, let me give myself, The Lovely, props for being so damn smooth. I sashayed up to Miss Polly Shipley's office. By the way, she's the artistic director of this Constitution Center and her assistant was the person who escorted us in here earlier. With that said, you owe Miss Shipley a five thousand dollar donation. That was my excuse for going to see her."

"Your hands always seem to be directing my checkbook, so no problem. It's worth the money to get this information. So, go ahead and tell me what happened."

"I knew you were interested. First of all, I was right. Those are your grandparents and they do live in McLean, Virginia. And, I was going to suggest that we go there and sneak through the back of the house to take a peek at them. That, however, won't be necessary because they are hosting a gala—right here in this building—tomorrow night."

"Carlton, some things aren't funny. You shouldn't play with me about something like that. It's too much of a coincidence."

"Well, it's a God thing then because as crazy and unreal as it sounds, it's the truth. I swear." Carlton showed Tina the glossy one-page marketing slick. "See, they'll be here tomorrow night to smile, showboat, and be praised for their giving spirits."

Tina smirked. "That's probably easy for them. They should be experts at smiling and being phony."

Later that evening, Tina's surprise performance at Constitution Center was an overwhelming success that garnered her three standing ovations. She made a promise to the Washington, DC audience that she would return and the next time would not be a surprise. Loaded with extra energy, Tina met with *MBT's* two concert winners and their guests. They were young adults like her and didn't seem to mind that she was not August Osborne. After leaving the concert hall, Tina, Kelly, and Carlton were driven a short distance and had a late night meal, at arguably, DC's top Chinese Eatery. It was the first of many located on H Street Northwest as part of Chinatown's restaurant row and one of a few sit-down dining establishments in the entire city to stay open until three in the morning.

In addition to not mentioning anything about her grandparents to Kelly, Tina had not made a decision to deal or no deal with the Chamberses that next evening. With free-time to spend in Washington, Tina and Carlton had a full day to decide on the "if," "when," and "how" of project "Surprise-Surprise the Chamberses."

39

VALET PARKING VIOLATION

6:00 p. m.—Sunday, March 24, 1985

OUTISIDE of Constitution Center to the extreme right, Tina and Carlton were leaning against the far edge of the building. There, they could view the action occurring in the front while staying out of sight. With the questionable weather and wind of late-March, the two bandits were relieved that the temperature was holding steady around fifty degrees. Absent heavy coats, Tina and Carlton were chilly, but not freezing. For more than an hour, they watched the valet parking attendants, the arriving guests, and venue ushers. Those exiting the vehicles were dressed in formal attire—furs and gowns and expensive tuxedos. After walking the red carpet that had been placed on the sidewalk, the guests were greeted at the front entrance and directed to one of two half-walled coat check rooms. From there, they were offered champagne and hors d'oeurvres and joined a noisy, excited crowd at the gala reception. It was taking place on both sides of the large lobby. Many people went back and forth to the silent auction tables, attempting to outbid their fellow gala participants in order to possess the coveted items. They included exotic getaways, professional sporting event tickets and memorabilia, gourmet baskets, signed artwork, furs, and jewelry.

Upon arrival, each attendee's name was broadcasted through a two-way radio and crossed off a master list that was being managed at the box office. This was an invitation only event with no exceptions. With every luxury car or limousine's arrival, Tina endured a Ferris wheel experience. Her expectations rose high with anticipation then her spirit dipped low with disappointment. This occurred each time the valet manager announced a surname other than Chambers. Tina turned to Carlton and began to mentally prepare herself for the possibility that her faceless grandparents would remain that way—a mystery. "Maybe the Chamberses are already here," reasoned Tina. "We don't know what they look like."

"Nope, I was specifically told by Polly Shipley that they always drive themselves to this event, and their permanent parking space is right over there." Carlton pointed to a pull-in parking spot that was one of six premium spaces and was the only one still vacant but for two orange cones. The space was located a mere fifteen feet, to the right, and caddy corner from where he and she were staked out—both were dressed in their all black travel attire. Tina's was accented by a baseball cap and thick rimmed glasses that were similar in style to those belonging to Idella Stephens. Miss Shipley also told me that your grandfather recently purchased a new blue Rolls-Royce and he does that religiously every two years.

Tina adjusted her baseball cap. "That explains why they're not being dropped off in a limousine like the majority of these rich old fogies. They like to show off and the new luxury car is probably my grandfather's latest toy. That makes me feel so much better about taking their $25,000 graduation guilt money gift three years ago. That was my first and only physical connection—me touching a check that my grandparents had touched. It's so pathetic, but I kept the envelope and still touch it from time to time. I hate how they mess with my emotions."

"Tina, please don't get all mushy and sad on me—not right now. You were having fun sneaking around on this stakeout. Don't you agree?"

"Yes, but it won't continue to be fun if I don't get to see them and possibly have a chance to look into the eyes of the rich and the phony."

"They'll be here. I promise."

Tina began to rationalize. "You don't have the power to make such a promise. Maybe something came up and they're not coming. We should forget about this and go back to Pappy John's. I guess I'm getting frustrated and angry at myself for allowing the Chamberses to let me down again."

Carlton began to sense Tina's pain. "Tee-Tee, it was your idea to come, so if you've changed your mind, let's head back to Pappy John's or we can catch a movie. It's still early, you know." Continuing to look in the direction of the valet podium, Carlton's eyes grew wide and his stomach churned with excitement as he heard the name Chambers being broadcasted. While viewing a Rolls-Royce slowly heading towards him, Tina, and the reserved parking space, his prediction had produced results and his promise was fulfilled.

The ever optimistic Mister Montgomery tapped his little cousin on her back because her body was turned away from him as part of her pouting ritual. "Be frustrated no more because your grandparents have arrived."

Tina was so nervous and excited that she backed up about six feet on the side of the venue before getting the courage to move forward and return to her position at the building's front edge. By then, the Rolls-Royce had paused in front of them with a fifteen feet distance of separation just as Carlton had predicted. Once the two orange cones were removed, the car pulled in and the ignition was turned off.

"Look at that brand spanking new Rolls. They got it like that." Unbeknownst to Tina and Carlton, the Chamberses' chose to drive themselves to Constitution Center as a designed plan to lose the chauffeur for the evening here and there to be on their own. It made them feel vibrant and carefree in the presence of their fellow philanthropic friends.

"I just love watching the life of the rich and not so famous," whispered Carlton.

"What?"

"They're not famous like you and that might keep them up at night."

Somehow that registered with Tina. — The majority of the parts of the four-door, full-sized Rolls-Royce were built by hand. That included the body that was molded from a single piece of steel by a master craftsman and finished in royal blue. The stainless steel flying lady and grille were not only hand-crafted but also signed by the artist. The tires were wide whitewalls and the rectangular headlights had twin lamps.

Both the driver and passenger doors were opened by valet attendants simultaneously and the sixty-something grandparents were assisted out of the vehicle. Tina's heart was racing, unsure of how she would feel when she laid eyes on them. This scene had played out in her mind for most of her life—two and a half months short of her twenty-first birthday. In every dream sequence, however, she would awaken as the blotted-out faces of her grandparent's drew close to her. Now, she was a few minutes short of another of her secret and delayed dreams fulfilled.

"Tina, look at your grandma-ma. Other than suffering from size zero malnutrition, she's gorgeous for an older woman." As Tina struggled to breathe and was unable to speak, Carlton's chatter made up for her temporary disability. "Miss Victoria's gown is the bomb—royal blue to match the Rolls-Royce, beaded bodice, and chiffon full-length skirt. And your grandpa-pa ain't trying to be left behind. He's all distinguished-looking, like Pappy John, handsome, and wearing the hell out of that black custom made tuxedo. No wonder you're as pretty as a picture. Girl, you got good genes from both sides."

As they stepped on the sidewalk, Tina and Carlton moved about six feet forward, so that the granddaughter could get a good first look. Her grandparents returned the stare with their own smug glance. Contrary to etiquette, William Chambers continued to look at them while changing positions with his wife—placing her to the outside of him—closer to the street and away from Tina and Carlton. Her grandfather's demonstrative message in his subtle action angered Tina as she waited for the Chamberses to continue moving forward. During the delay, acute hurt and frustration had set up a campsite in the pit of her stomach.

"Carlton would their noses be turned up at us if they knew I was Bettina Charles the famous singer?"

"With those two, Tee-Tee, I can't say for sure."

"Maybe my skin color offends them so much that nothing I have done or ever will accomplish would matter. I'll never be good enough for them." Tina began to think irrationally. "Since they're so ashamed of me, I'll give them a reason to feel that way." The Pop-Diva waited for her grandparents to move ahead ten more feet past her and Carlton. With intent to be destructive, she headed for the Rolls-Royce and jumped in on the driver's side. By this point, the Chamberses' attention was completely focused on the synchronized movements of their grand entrance.

Carlton couldn't believe what he was seeing. "Oh glory to my Lordy." He rushed over to the passenger side and leaned on the Rolls-Royce with his butt pressed against the window. Facing forward, his eyes were stayed on the very busy valet attendants. With both hands behind his back, he used them to open the car door as he squatted to quickly duck inside. "Bettina Charles, I can't believe we're sitting in this car. You need to hurry up and get your warm and fuzzy feelings or—whatever it is that you got in this car to do."

The interior plush carpet matched the exterior paint job. The beige leather interior was made from the hide of specially fed bulls. They were raised in a climate too cold for mosquitos, causing there to be little to no blemishes in the raw hide. The wood grain trim shined, making it possible to see a reflection.

"Tina girl, we need to get out of this car before we get caught." Carlton was torn—filled with equal amounts of caution and curiosity. He scooted down in his seat while opening the glove box. "This car is outrageous, smells like new money, and has power everything—windows, locks, steering."

Noticing the key in the ignition, Tina turned it, and the car's engine began to purr.

Mister Montgomery closed his eyes for prayer that his crazy cousin could hear. "Dear God, I must be dreaming. So Lord, please wake me up and let me see and hear that Bettina Bethany Charles didn't just start the engine of two old white people's brand spanking new Rolls-Royce." Carlton opened his eyes and the scene had not changed. "Are you crazy? Turn the key and cut this car back off!"

Just before entering the middle doors of Constitution Center, Victoria Chambers realized and made her husband aware that she had forgotten her purse inside of the car. William and his wife backed out of the entryway and walked a short distance to the valet podium. Seeing red brake lights engaged on his car, William Chambers questioned the activity. "What is your worker doing? Our vehicle never moves from in front of this building. That person must be new. It's your responsibility to make that known. Anyway, stop them quickly because my wife left her purse in the car."

Upon counting his team and including those who were parking a vehicle and not present, the valet manager knew that something had gone very wrong. He spoke with the phone receiver against his face, held their by his shoulder. "We're on top of this and I'm contacting the police as we speak. Unfortunately, Mister Chambers, the person driving your car is not a member of our valet service squad."

As a valet attendant tapped on the Rolls-Royce's passenger door window, Tina shifted the car in reverse, backed out hurriedly, put the car in drive, and sped away. "Now, I know you've gone mad. You better stop this car right now!" demanded Carlton. "Once we jump out, you follow me. Run as fast as you can and don't look back. Let's move on three. One-two—." Tina pressed down on the gas and the car zoomed down the street. While speeding ahead two additional blocks, she had one hand on the steering wheel and the other moving around, patting on gadgetry. Inadvertently, she cut on the wiper blades, rolled the windows in the back of the car halfway down and then up again, and turned on the emergency blinkers. The car swerved and Carlton yelled. "What are you doing?"

"I'm trying to roll down this window and turn on the radio."

"Tina, you need to focus on driving. And, why in the hell do you want to listen to music while driving a stolen car? Shit, you done already turned us into 'Bonnie and Clyde.' Please don't cause a wreck too. I'm too young for plastic surgery. And there's no procedure in the world that can copy and repair the beauty of this face."

Carlton turned on the radio and pushed the button to roll down the driver side window. When it was halfway down, Tina stopped him. "Alright that's far enough, it's cold in here."

"Oh Miss Nutso, why ask me to roll down the window if you are cold?" Tina found her grandmother's small rectangular purse lying in the middle panel and threw it out onto the street.

"That's why and thank you. Now, roll the window back up."

Carlton recognized Tina's hurt was the part of her that had taken over and was acting out. To attempt to reach her sensibilities, he calmed his voice all the way down. "Listen Tee-Tee, I know you're hurting, but we have to take this car back right now. The driver gets the most time, so stop the car and let me take the wheel."

"There's no way I'm going to get you in trouble."

Briefly, Carlton's anger meter rose. "We're already in trouble! I'm the one with the juvie record, so stop the car and move over."

"Pappy John got it erased, remember?"

"Erased and sealed are two different things. My record is sealed not erased."

"It doesn't matter anyway because I said no and I mean it! I'll crash this stupid car if you try and stop me." Tina began to reflect on her prior grief moments. — "You know what Carlton?"

"What Tina."

"It would have been better if the Chamberses were dead all this time. Instead, they've been living here in the DC area—a place I've visited all my life. Without that graduation check sent directly to me, I might have never learned this important fact."

"That's true, but now you know. Just take a chill pill to give yourself a little time to process the information. Then, you can do something about it that won't land our asses in jail."

Tina rolled her eyes at her cousin. "I can't trust my own family to be truthful—not Aunty Gina, Pappy John, and maybe even Momma Nin. Not one lullaby letter mentions my grandparents address. Somebody should have told me where they lived."

"So, you could do what? Go over there and burn the place down. Please don't be angry with the part of the family that has always had your back."

"I must be an awful person for the Chamberses to hate me so much."

Reminding himself to think rationally, Carlton lowered his voice again. "I don't believe they hate you, and this might be the night that brings you guys together. As soon as we get this car back, maybe some of your answers are there waiting for you."

"We'll find out shortly, so tell me how to get back to the venue."

"Take the next two rights." He waited until Tina had done so. "Are you sure you don't want me to drive?"

Poking out her lips and taking on her spoiled brat demeanor, Carlton's little Tee-Tee drove up onto the curb, hit a parking meter, and swerved left back down to street level. She turned and looked at him. "I'm quite sure I don't want you to take over the driving and don't ask me again!"

"Okay, I get the message, so don't cause any more damage to this fancy ass car that doesn't belong to us." Carlton took a deep breath before giving Tina further instructions. "Tee-Tee, everything is going to be fine. After going through the next light up ahead—make the next two rights—and we'll be back in front of Constitution Center. — My next instructions are straight-up serious."

"I'm listening."

"Once we're in front of the building, you need to pull over, stop the car, raise both of your hands up high, and do whatever they tell you to do. It's been a minute, but I remember this drill like I know all of my names."

Tina did as her cousin instructed after executing an additional step. After stopping the vehicle, she withdrew the key from the ignition and placed it inside of her bra. Looking straight ahead, the very nervous and frustrated Carlton saw none of Tina's last moves.

After pulling them out of the car, the four male, DC Police officers frisked Carlton thoroughly and performed a light pat-down of Tina—careful not to touch her private parts. Then, both suspects were cuffed and taken to the venue's security booth on the side of the building. The Chamberses went there as well but used a different route to get there. Their concern was Victoria's purse and the whereabouts of the car keys. Once inside the enclosure, the security guard said, "Before the police take you away, we need you to tell us what you did with the keys to the vehicle."

Carlton insisted. "I have no idea. I guess they're still in the car."

Tina yelled. "I might know but I'm not telling."

Carlton's mental squealing was piercing. *Oh hell, Tina done took those dang blasted keys. We're in enough trouble already.*

The police Sergeant asked the next question. "Where is Mrs. Chambers's purse?"

Carlton answered. "We never saw a purse."

Tina was trying her best to hurt her grandparents. In the small booth, she was close enough to touch Victoria Chambers if it were not for the handcuffs. Tina admitted. "I saw the purse and threw it out the window. It's in the street about three blocks from here."

Carlton rolled his eyes. *Now, I know we're going to DC Jail for sure—right to Central Booking.*

One of the police officers removed Tina's thick rimmed glasses and baseball cap. Her hair fell down beyond her shoulders. Victoria Chambers shouted. "Christina, oh my God, it's my baby!"

In addition to being Constitution Center's creative director, Polly Shipley and Victoria Chambers were close. She did her best to perform her professional duties as it pertained to place of employment while consoling her longtime friend. "Victoria, I know you're upset because you're not thinking rationally. Your precious Christina has long passed on. That's Bettina Charles, the singer. She performed here last night and this situation doesn't make sense." Polly Shipley moved closer to Tina. "Why would you, young lady, be involved in something so thuggish and sinister? Are you under the influence of something?"

William Chambers said, "I don't want to make a big scene out here in the open. Polly, we need to deal with this matter in private. Let's take this to your office at once."

A freelance photographer hired by the venue had followed the disturbance. After hearing the name Bettina Charles and getting a glimpse at her face, the journalist slyly snapped photos of a side view of Tina being guided away in handcuffs. *This image will be in somebody's paper in the morning and on network television in the afternoon,* he assured.

On the way to the office, William Chambers had a low-level discussion with the highest ranking of the DC police officers. After the brief conversation, the Lieutenant left the group in order to make a private phone call to the chief of police. Once the door was shut and all were inside the office, Victoria Chambers sat in a side chair and was given a glass of champagne. Polly continued her reprimand of Tina. "Young lady, you need to explain yourself and do so right away. If it had not been for quick thinking, you could have ruined our affair. In addition to that, you have devastated the Chamberses."

"Polly, we're fine," responded William Chambers, "and we won't be pressing any charges. Please unhandcuff the both of them right now."

Polly Shipley said, "Now, neither one of you, my good friends, are making sense."

Victoria Chambers stood up and squeezed between her husband and Polly who was standing close to Tina. Once free from the handcuffs, Carlton rubbed his wrists and sighed in relief. "We're sorry for making a disturbance and will just mosey along out of your way. Can someone please direct us to a back entrance? Then, y'all can get back to your highfalutin affair. It's been real."

Polly Shipley held tight to Tina's left arm and had a venue guard keep her still by firmly holding the other. The creative director was adamant. "With what you've done this evening, we can't just let you run off to potentially create another disturbance. I insist that she's taken to the police station to at least be put through the process."

Using a very low volume, Victoria pleaded with her friend. "Polly please, that won't be necessary. I know this will shock you, but Miss Charles is not a criminal, she's our granddaughter."

"This is a private matter and we need all these people to clear out," William Chambers added, but much louder and with authority.

As everyone, but Polly left the room, Carlton was allowed to use the phone, called Kelly King at the hotel, and told her to come quickly. She had spent the day in Baltimore at her parent's home and returned to DC that same evening as opposed to spending the night and dealing with the Washington Metro Area's dreadful, morning rush-hour traffic. Early the next day, Kelly was scheduled to meet with Team Tina's advisors. Her mission was to make it very clear that Walden Records was extremely interested in resigning Bettina Charles.

As the Chamberses requested, Walden Records' executive vice president was escorted to an adjacent office to give the complicated family time to speak in private. There, she was briefed by the venues' creative director on William Chambers's sanctioned version of the events involving Bettina Charles and Carlton.

While that took place next door, the Chamberses attempted to have a civil conversation with their granddaughter as Carlton sat back on the sofa and listened silently, praying for a breakthrough. Tina stood up as her grandparents approached her. Victoria Chambers asked, "Bettina, do you need anything—anything at all? We'll take care of it immediately."

"Wow, after all this time, the first words you say involve offering more things. An apology would have been nice for ignoring me—my entire life. To answer your question, no, I don't need anything—not from you anyway—and I never will."

William Chambers said, "We were trying to do the right thing and didn't mean to hurt you."

"So, your version of not hurting me is staying away? It's obvious that we don't speak the same language in addition to me being the wrong color."

"That's not what I meant and your color is fine. You're absolutely beautiful." refuted William Chambers.

"Since when—today? I know you've been sent pictures of me through your lawyers my entire life. Here lately, it would be quite difficult not to see me on some type of media outlet."

"You're right and for some time now, we've been working on a dialogue strategy with a qualified therapist."

"Besides driving that expensive car, it seems everything you do requires the advice of some type of professional or another," Tina chuckled. "Well, this one you get for free. If you're concerned about my silence, don't worry. I don't want anyone to know that I'm connected to either one of you. By the way, please stop sending me those guilt gifts and checks. Money can't pay for everything. If it did, I would have bought me real grandparents a long time ago."

Carlton covered his mouth with the tips of his fingers. "Oh dear, if you can't say amen—say ooch and ouch."

Victoria Chambers started to cry and William Chambers raised his eyebrows. "I guess we deserved those harsh words and many more."

"If you're not going to send us to jail, may we please go now?"

"W-w-we're not trying to hold you. We just want to stress our desire to try and, at least, begin to communicate with you directly in the future."

"That won't be necessary, but I will be following in your footsteps as it relates to philanthropy. I'm working hard and am accumulating my own wealth. I have plans for the money you've placed in my trust fund. When I gain access to it at twenty-five, I'm donating every penny you sent me through the years to my favorite Black charities."

Tina turned away just long enough to retrieve the keys from her bra. In facing them, she positioned her body to be at a central point—equal distance away from both William and Victoria Chambers—about nine inches from their faces. She pressed the Rolls-Royce's car keys into her grandfather's open palm. When her skin touched his, it made this pathetic introduction all the more real. Tina needed to say her last words and retreat before the bath water overflowed. "I'm afraid it's much too late for a family reunion at this point in my life. Tina sat back down next to Carlton."

Alerted by venue security that the meeting was over, Kelly was escorted into Miss Shipley's office and looked at Tina and Carlton in frustration. They were seated on the sofa looking like two lost puppies. Polly said, "In spite of the Chamberses' refusal to press charges, I feel better releasing them to a responsible party. I have to show that some penalty was administered. Otherwise, it won't go over well with our board of directors."

Kelly was left in the dark about the Chamberses being Tina's grandparents as she shook their hands. "On behalf of Walden Records, please accept our sincere apology and appreciation for not pursuing this matter any further. If you're in need of concert tickets or anything else, don't hesitate to contact me." She handed William Chambers her card and he did the same. Upon directing her attention to her little sister and cousin, her pleasant demeanor disappeared. "Come on you two, let's go."

Tina looked back before exiting the office door. "I would say that it was very nice to meet you both, but I'd be lying."

In the end, Tina was ticketed for driving illegally, fined for doing so recklessly, and released to the care of an executive representing Walden Records—Kelly King. Despite the request not to do so, an additional check was written on Tina's behalf by her grandfather. William Chambers had observed the photographer snapping photos and purchased the camera and all the rolls of film for an undisclosed amount.

Once Tina, Carlton, and Kelly were seated in the back of the limousine, the budding Pop-Diva lost control. Tina banged her fists into her knees and started to sob uncontrollably. Then, periodically, a squeal was added to her weeping. "I hate them! I hate them! Oh Carlton, I hate them!"

Tina's cousin wrapped her in his arms and rubbed her back and hair. As a result of her face being buried in her best friend's chest, the sound of her excruciating howling was muffled. Carlton kissed the top of Tina's head and added rocking to his comforting embrace. "Tee-Tee, I know. I know. Just let it all out. Everything is going to be okay. I promise."

Tina's sobs got louder and the piercing release of pain was unbearable. It caused Kelly to abandon her plan to reprimand their behavior with cussing and idol threats. Kelly's body was frozen and her thoughts were skewed. With no solace to offer, she looked at the business card she had been given and asked a question. "Who in the hell are William and Victoria Chambers?"

Still rocking her gently, Carlton responded with tears pouring down his face. "Those two assholes are Tina's grandparents and that was her first time meeting them face-to-face or speaking to them at all—for that matter."

"Oh, I'm so sorry," mumbled Kelly.

Tina started kicking her feet again while continuing to hold on to Carlton tightly. "This hurts down to the core of my heart. They make me ill and I hate them with every ounce of the pain that's locked inside of me."

Because of the seriousness of the situation, Kelly accompanied Carlton and Tina to Pappy John's Watergate apartment instead of being dropped off at the hotel.

40

DAMAGE CONTROL

SLEEPING pills were required to calm Tina down once they were back at Pappy John's Watergate apartment. Kelly and Carlton remained by her side until she had fallen asleep. Returning to the living room and while drinking a glass filled with 90 percent vodka and ten percent orange juice, Kelly made the dreaded call to the bat phone. Taking very quick breaths, she regurgitated the details—not allowing Arnie to interrupt until she had given the complete, redacted incident report.

Arnie said, "Really, no shit. They posed as valet parking attendants, stole a Rolls-Royce, went for a joy ride, came back to the scene of the crime, and were arrested. I'm sure that Carlton talked Tina into this mess. What kind of weed were they smoking?"

"It's not that cut-and-dry," defended Kelly. "They were not under the influence of any substance and did not pose as valet parking attendants. The blame for this fiasco should not be placed on Carlton. By the way, Tina was the driver. The good news is that no charges were filed. It was all a big misunderstanding."

"It was a misunderstanding my ass. I know you're holding back on some nitty-gritty details."

"I am, but at the present time, they aren't important."

"Well, regardless of who did what, I love it. It's brilliant and gives our starlet a bad girl edge. You can't make up stuff like this and you know that we've tried. I just love free publicity!"

To show her control over the situation, Kelly stretched the truth. "Although Tina's very fragile right now, I really gave her an earful and am keeping a close eye on her. As it relates to Carlton, I've placed him on administrative leave with pay until further notice. He's been asked to stay away from headquarters and is returning to Scotland Neck in the morning."

"It's about time you did something to slow that character down. You're showing you've got balls, boobs, are in control. Hell, you know what I'm trying to say."

"Listen Arnie, it's crucial that you let me deal with this. I don't want you coming behind me. I need you to promise that you'll back off and not say anything to Tina about this matter."

"You've handled it well to this point, so if it's that important to you, I guess I can leave it alone."

"I guess isn't good enough. I need to hear you say the words: I promise."

"Dammit, I promise. I'll let it go, but just for this issue only. If she does something else, I will be right back in her face as usual."

"That's fair and thank you."

After a heavy duty discussion, six cigarettes, two of her specialty drinks, and periodic tapping of her nails, she had convinced her lover-man boss to stay in Los Angeles and continue attending to other matters.

With Tina's insistence and Kelly's reassurance, Carlton carried on with his plans to take a few months off to attend to Trudy's Cut-n-Curl business in Scotland Neck. The shop had failed inspection due to faulty wires, plumbing, and the evidence of critters. Carlton was highly concerned because, over the three-year period of being away from Scotland Neck, he and Tina had sent money to be used to make repairs and upgrades. In addition to that, Carlton had admitted to Tina how much he missed Tony. She refused to stand in the way of the two of them getting together and formally committing to each other. To convince Carlton to continue with his plans, Tina had to do a great deal of reassuring him. "The one thing I can promise is that my drama will be waiting for you when you get back. At least, one of us should escape this madness. Besides, getting Trudy's Place back in service is crucial to me as well. It's important to the entire family." Tina wrapped her right pinky around Carlton's, but had two fingers crossed behind her back. "I triple time promise that I will call you to come running if I need you."

Monday, March 25, 1985

7:00 a. m.—The next morning, everyone was on the move. Two Walden Records' jets flew out of DC. One carried Carlton to North Carolina where he was met by ground transport in Raleigh to be driven to Scotland Neck. Tony was waiting inside of the limousine to surprise him. Tina and Kelly were flown back to New York City. There was no way the Rising Starlet was going to stay in apartment 2407. The press was camped out at Windsor East, waiting to pounce on Bettina Charles.

The reason the press wasn't looking for Tina at Kelly King's residence was because the Serengeti Lioness came up with an ingenious plan. Bernie Bazemore pretended to be a snitch with a secret to sell. He went to Curtis Frazier. "This could lose me my job, but my family is in hard times right now, and I could really use a helping hand." For a nominal fee, the lead concierge of Windsor East put the security guard in touch with a buyer.

A sleaze-line reporter for *The Orbit* met secretly with Mister Bazemore and dropped two crisp one hundred dollar bills in his hand.

"If you know the whereabouts of a certain somebody, three more like these could mysteriously land in your possession."

Bernie replied. "If a total of thirteen more Benjamins found their way to Bernie Bazemore, then an old man's memory might suddenly return."

After pocketing a thousand dollars for himself and five-hundred for Curtis Frazier, Bernie told the sleaze-line reporter that Bettina Charles was hiding out at The Crystal Plaza Hotel. To substantiate the claim, he checked out one of the town cars and drove Miss Charles to the said location. With two security guards dressed in black suits and old gold ties, he made sure Tina was seen being led into the hotel through the kitchen by way of an alley entrance. As provided in his detail, Miss Charles was dressed in a gray sweat suit, wearing a pink scarf that was splattered with an apple green pattern. Then, out of view, two security guards still dressed in black suits, had switched to royal purple ties. Bernie made sure Tina was not seen as she exited the building through the laundry's loading dock located on a ramp on the far left side of the Plaza. She had changed into her Walden Records' black travel gear, wearing a cream scarf with a crimson red print. They drove Tina in heavy traffic across the Verrazano Bridge to Long Beach and back to Manhattan in a different vehicle, a Chevy conversion van. With its two-tone paint job, the driver pulled into the underground garage of Kelly King's Upper East Side apartment building a few hours later with Tina in tow.

After getting her secret sister settled in her penthouse, Kelly reported to The Label to work with the legal team on damage control. As Assistant Angela intercepted calls filtered through Legal, the executive vice president responded to questions from reporters who represented various media outlets, including newspapers, magazines, and radio. It was decided to respond to only one television inquiry "Today's Entertainment." It was the number one program in its seven-thirty timeslot and highly-regarded as a reputable source of show business news.

As planned, Kelly King spoke to the television program's producer who contacted her in search of a formal statement. "The purpose of this conversation is to inform you that Bettina Charles will be our lead off story for this evening's broadcast. Would you like to make a statement on behalf of Walden Records?"

The Executive Vice President agreed to give brief remarks on and off camera, using The Label's legal department's carefully crafted script. By the time she neared the statement's conclusion, her demeanor was emphatic. "Miss Charles nor the young man who accompanied her were charged with any crime. She, however, is devastated that her actions could be misconstrued in such a malicious manner."

At two thirty, the music mogul shifted gears, making her role as nurturing big sister her priority. She switched locations, had Angela forward calls to her home office, and told her to cut them off completely at five o'clock. Already speaking with Pappy John and Aunty Gina and in Carlton's absence, Tina refused to talk or see anyone except for Kelly.

6:00 p.m.—After eating a light dinner, the sisters sat close together at sofa-center in silence with Tina periodically grabbing Kelly's hand. The tight squeezes coincided with the teasing of the upcoming report entitled "Bettina Charles's Alleged Crime of Grand Theft Auto." The segment had been advertised during each commercial break for at least a few hours leading up to the show's live airing.

7:30 p.m.—With no more delay, the appointed time was at hand. In a black textured background, the show's logo appeared on the top of the television screen with a moderate sized square underneath. It displayed cuts to quick video excerpts of the top stories being featured as a different reporter for each promo teased the segment, using voice over that was phrased in the form of a question. While the catchy theme music played, a graphic of the show's logo danced around the screen. Flipping sideways, it appeared to be shot from a laser beam and heading straight toward the home television viewer. The next graphical technique was a 360-degree spin that ended with the logo positioned upright and all movement stopped to a freeze-frame. The next cut was a wide-angle shot of the studio, zooming in to an establishing shot of the two grinning co-hosts—seated at the anchor desk. Once the theme music stopped, the animated talking heads began broadcasting.

Today's Entertainment
Live Broadcast—*Bettina Charles the Alleged Car Thief*

Good evening everyone, I'm Ron Wiley, and I'm Maryann Hartley, and this is Today's Entertainment.

The next cut was to a medium close shot of the anchorwoman. A graphic box was positioned to the right of her talking head. It streamed a montage of still shots mixed with video excerpts of the Pop-Diva while the newscaster delivered the lead-in story.

Last night, America's musical sweetheart, Bettina Charles was detained by Washington, DC police for allegedly stealing a made-to-order 'Silver Spirit Rolls-Royce.' With witnesses present, the starlet casually slid behind the wheel and sped away. From there, she pro-ceeded to take the very expensive vehicle on a joy ride through the streets of the nation's capital. Sources say that the wealthy victims of the crime who owned the vehicle were attending a private gala at Constitution Center. Yes America, it was the same venue where Bettina Charles performed the night before. Their names have not been released to the public. Lucky for Miss Charles, the benevolent philanthropist insisted on not pressing charges even though their vehicle sustained considerable damage.

Reportedly, Miss Charles was cited for operating a vehicle with-out a valid driver's license. Shortly, thereafter, she was discharged to Walden Records' executive vice president, Miss Kelly King.

Releasing a brief statement earlier today on behalf of the record company, the music producer said, "Miss Charles is an amazing artist with an impeccable reputation. This entire matter was a misinterpre-tation of events, relating to the filming of a music video."

"So far, Today's Entertainment has been unable to substantiate that claim or receive a statement from the Pop-Diva herself."

⌒⟲

Kelly threw a cloth napkin at the television screen while quickly analyzing the report. "What a blatant attempt to destroy your good reputation. In presenting just the facts—as they claimed, omitting Carlton from the story all together was a huge fact to leave out."

"At least that's one thing that makes me feel good. Carlton doesn't deserve to be caught up in the middle of my mess. I'm the one who decided to get into that car and speed away."

Kelly added. "Another good thing is that the press hasn't been able to track you down."

Tina folded her hands and looked up at the ceiling. "Oh yes, for that I'm truly grateful. Way to go Bernie Bazemore. After paying that good for nothing Curtis Frazier, I told him to keep the thousand dollars."

Kelly squeezed Tina's hand. "Instead of dealing daily with the Press gunning for you at Windsor East, I want you to stay here with me at my penthouse indefinitely. What do you think?"

"With Carlton gone and the paparazzi camped out at my apartment, my choices are limited. I gratefully accept your invitation because, honestly, I don't feel strong enough to be on my own right now. — However, my departure date will be whenever Carlton returns."

41

BREAKING BREAD

BUNKING at Kelly's place was in its infancy stage and Tina was experiencing something new. Although twelve years older, Kelly was the youngest woman she'd allowed in her intimate space. The connection felt like a sisterly bond—Kelly was someone she admired, someone who was trustworthy to keep her girly-girl secrets. The two women had agreed not to mention the Chamberses or anything having to do with the alleged grand theft auto incident.

With schedule conflicts, this sit-down dinner was the first home-cooked meal shared together at Kelly's upscale accommodations. The top level of the two-story apartment had two guest rooms and a spacious master suite, all with private baths along with a fully equipped exercise space. The main floor's rooms included a spacious, step-down living room, a large office with a double-door supply closet, a cozy den, and a formal dining room off the eat-in gourmet kitchen. Kelly's private sky deck had a spectacular view of the cityscape. There was also a decorative baby grand that Tina assumed was a music industry prerequisite because piano playing was outside of the executive vice president's gift area.

While Kelly watched and interjected chitchat, Tina did most of the food preparation. Although aware of her little sister's southern influences, she was surprised at Tina's kitchen savviness, particularly her knife skills—quickly chopping and sautéing onions, green and red peppers, and fresh mushrooms. Snapping off and discarding the woody ends of the stems, she used a double-boiler to steam the asparagus. As instructed, Kelly nervously punctured the baking potatoes in preparation for them to be nuked in the microwave.

After seasoning the twelve-ounce rib-eye steaks and waiting for them to broil, Tina dressed the formal dining room table. When the meal was prepared, the sisters sat down in the formal setting that included lit candles. "Wow, not only do you know your way around the kitchen," said Kelly, "you dressed this table so elegantly. Working long hours and traveling so much, I seldom cook for myself. And in general, culinary art is not on my list of fun activities."

"It's been a while for me as well," Tina said modestly, "but I enjoy cooking. As dressing tables go, Momma Nin taught me a memory-reminder—BMW-W. The *B*read plate goes on the left, the *M*eal plate is in the middle, and the *W*ater and *W*ine glasses are on the right, in that order."

"That is very clever—BMW-W. I'm depositing that into my memory bank from now on."

"She also told me that flatware placement simply follows the order of usage, starting outside and moving in toward the plate. Since most people are right-handed, the knife and spoon are laid on the right side and the fork on the left. Momma Nin drilled it in my head, telling me that the blade of the knife always faces the plate."

"You never stop amazing me. I say it again. You're much different from my other artists—so extremely refined."

"I wanted this dinner to be special as a way of saying thank you for allowing me to stay here in your beautiful penthouse."

After a few bites of food in silence, Tina asked an intrusive question. "I know this is none of my business, but with Baltimore so close to New York City, do your parents ever visit? In the almost three years we've known each other, I don't recall you mentioning them being here in Manhattan."

"They've only been here once and that was awhile before your demo. In my mom's words, they prefer to keep a low profile—not interested in the glitz and glam that go along with what I do for a living."

"She sounds like my great-aunties who despise the *showbiz* thing. Because of the fans, Joseph-Lee Manor had to be enclosed with a wrought iron fence, electronic gate, and twenty-four-hour security. Even though they don't complain, I feel bad that their world keeps changing along with mine."

Kelly added. "I know how your Aunty Zooni is doing. Ellis Ross is occupying all of her time."

Tina giggled. "And, if I didn't like him enough, keeping Aunty Zooni happy is another reason why he's on my favorite person list."

"Since you brought up your great-aunties, how are the iron ladies doing?"

Tina chuckled. "They're still the same—precious, opinionated, and hilarious. They get together and watch me on award shows and on other TV appearances. Then they call me and want to talk about it at length. It drives me crazy, but it also keeps me grounded. Even with Ellis Ross in her life, my Aunty Zooni still has plenty to say. She gets on the phone and starts barking. 'Girl, I don't give a damn about everybody puffing you up. I'll climb through this phone and whoop your ass just the same as always. By the way, I'm glad that you won the award. You were way better than the rest of those gals.'" Tina and Kelly giggled.

"Your Aunty Zooni is truly a piece of work."

Tina nodded and smiled. "My Aunty Gina told me that Aunty Zooni is my biggest fan, carrying my picture around and listening to my music. However, in a million years, I won't let on that I know she's a fan. My fear of Storm Zooni won't allow it."

Enjoying the conversation, Tina remembered an observation that piqued her curiosity. Roaming around the penthouse, she had been intrigued by Kelly's den. It was circular with no windows. The furnishing was limited to a tan leather recliner and matching armchair that shared an end table with a lamp in the middle. Other than a narrow, floor-to-ceiling bookshelf, the plentiful wall space was for showcasing awards, certificates, degrees, and plaques made of wood, metal, and stone. Tina was drawn to five gold records that commemorated the artists Kelly managed whose albums reached the mark of a million units sold.

Tina said, "You know that I name everything—my dolls, my briefcase, and my piano, for example."

"Yes, I remember my visit to Joseph-Lee Manor and you introducing me to your Willie Chamber's piano."

Tina's mood saddened and Kelly connected the dots. "Oh Tina, now I understand. William Chambers is the source of your baby grand's name." Kelly realized her error. "Please forgive me for mentioning your grandfather."

"That's okay, really. It's hard not to bump into the Chamberses some of the time. I-I-I just don't understand how the two people who performed an over-the-top grandparent action by buying my amazing piano are the same people who refused to have physical contact with me all of my life. I have no regrets about the Rolls-Royce incident."

"At least, you finally got to meet them face to face."

"You know something Kelly, there aren't too many days that go by when I don't think about how much I needed them when Momma Nin first passed away. I was a helpless eleven year old who needed their physical presence. They sent money and gifts instead of hugs, kisses, and reassuring words that things were going to be okay. What angers me so much is that the color of my skin kept them away. They punished me for something I had no control over and would never be able to change."

"Tina baby, I'm so sorry for the pain and loneliness you had to endure. At least, they attempted to apologize at the Rolls-Royce incident."

"I appreciate your sympathy, but am unable to accept an apology from my grandparents right now. They abandoned me to deal with my grief and anguish alone. Even a guilt gift as magnificent as my Willie Chambers piano doesn't make up for their crime of almost twenty-one years of unavailability."

"Since this subject is so raw to your nerve endings, let's go back to your naming game conversation."

"That's a great idea. As I was saying, my Momma Nin told me that my birth parents took care in naming me. They chose Bethany for my middle name in honor of Momma Nin, my father's sister. I showed you her picture in the Great Room."

Kelly interjected. "Don't tell me. It's right on the tip of my tongue. Oh yes, her picture is resting in the center of what you called The Mantle of Honor."

"It means a lot that you remember the names I created and the special details about my personal life in general—information I don't share very often."

"You are very important to me—not just product 3.7.2.85. I know that it's hard to trust people in this business, especially me, because of my relationship with Arnie—forgive me for bringing him into the conversation. Please continue telling me about how you were named."

"My birth mother came up with Bettina to get close to her name, Christina. She felt that Bettina flowed better with Bethany. That's how I became Bettina Bethany Charles. I think it's the coolest thing and a special part of my birth parents that I will always have to remember them by." Tina paused to eat a yummy scoop of her baked potato, which was dressed in sour cream, butter, and fresh chives. "Well, that's my big birth parent story. I don't like talking about anything else having to do with them."

"I know how private you are, but I'd really like to know why you have no more to say about your birth parents."

"It's mainly because I only have two stories to tell. The first is how they came up with my name. The second is how they died as told to me by my Momma Nin because it happened when I was a baby. The death story is one that I absolutely will not talk about."

"I respect your wishes 100 percent."

"Well now it's my turn to ask you a nosey question. I looked at the degrees hanging on your wall in the den and saw that your full name is

Kelly Donnita King. I know it must be connected to a big naming story and I want all the details."

Kelly almost choked on her steak as the question took her by surprise. *Little Sister, you have no idea. My name comes with a tale that could blow your mind—or worse than that destroy our relationship.* Kelly slowly chewed the piece of rib eye in her mouth while thinking of a suitable reply. She swallowed and cleared her throat before answering. "My mom named me after my great-aunt: Kelly-Louise. My mother, Kay-Dee, lived with her and my Uncle Frank when first moving from North Carolina to New York City. Nanna-Weezy was my pet name for her and she was more like a grandmother to me than a great-aunt."

"Wow, we have that in common too. A great-aunty helped raise you just like my great-aunties helped raise me."

Kelly worked hard to pull back her tears. "Yes, she and my Uncle Frank passed away fifteen years ago.—The grief pain is still very fresh and I prefer not to talk about it."

"I most definitely understand how you feel and gladly change the subject back to my naming game question."

Kelly was praying for a subject change far removed from naming conventions, but Tina wouldn't let it go.

"I don't get it. If your aunt is Kelly-Louise, where did Donnita come from?"

I don't want to talk about this subject either, but it's better than the latter conversation. "Nothing that special—Donnita was the name of one of my mother's childhood friends. 'It had a ring to it,' was how my mom explained it. I don't use Donnita, unless it's on an official document like the degrees that you saw."

"Well, Bethany is real special to me. When I was growing up, Momma Nin called me Bethy in a soft, sweet voice whenever she was pleased with me or when she treated me like a baby."

"Bethy is cute. It fits you well."

"No one calls me Bethy, but you can if you like—only when we're alone."

Kelly placed her hand over her heart. "Wow, Tina—I mean Bethy— once again, you offer a part of yourself that money can't buy. That touches me deeply."

"Well, you calling me Bethy is the best way for me to express how honored and blessed I am to have Kelly King as my pretend big sister slash close friend."

Kelly held back her tears, which derived from conflicting emotions. She was elated, having connected with Tina so intimately. She was also furious with herself for further burying the truth underneath whopper-sized mendacity. *My lover-man boss and I have been so busy collecting retainer fees that we've allowed the secret sister issue to remain a dormant volcano. In these three years, I've told Tina so many lies that I can barely keep them straight in my mind.*

42

SWEET AND HONEST TESTIMONY

Friday, April 19, 1985

RING-RING-RING-RING. Click. The phone rang four times, disconnected, and fifteen minutes later, it started ringing again—ring-ring-ring-ring-ring. Click. The second attempt consisted of five rings with no response. Tina was comfortable ignoring the first and second set of rings. Although made to feel that this was her home away from home, on day one of Tina moving into Kelly's penthouse, it was made clear that her private phone was off-limits unless it was an emergency. Maintaining her deceit was the reason for the stipulation. Kelly didn't want her little sister to accidentally be given too much information from Kay-Dee, Ben King, Kathy, or Katrina. Other than Arnie, Angela, and Tina, those aforementioned family members were the only ones with the phone number to that private line. Tina vocalized her thoughts as a result of the third series of chimes. *Most people call once, maybe twice, but never three times on Kelly's personal phone.* The younger sister had no problem following orders and using the business telephone exclusively. It was connected to an answering machine, enabling the Pop-Diva to screen calls. In the case of Kelly's personal phone, there was no answering machine. Her philosophy was that, if it was important, the person would call back. That made no sense to Tina, but it was Kelly's phone and her right to create silly regulations. Again, Tina spoke aloud to herself. "Since the person keeps calling back, it must be important. It could be a family emergency. I will be forced to break the house rule if that phone rings once more."

On the third chime in the next series of rings, Tina answered. "Kelly King's residence, may I help you?"

Kay-Dee said, "Kelly, it's your mother. I've been trying to reach you all week."

"Ma'am, my name is Bettina and I'm staying with Kelly. She's not here at the moment, but I expect her soon."

"I thought the accent was different, but I wasn't expecting someone other than Kelly to answer the phone. You said your name was Bettina, as in Bettina Charles?"

"Yes, Ma'am, but you may call me Tina."

"Your voice is so precious and not what I imagined—not superstarish at all. It's a shame that we haven't met over these three years, but I hope to do that soon—maybe in a few months."

"That would really be nice."

"The reason I'm calling is that me and my husband are renewing our vows with a big ceremony—dress, cake, and everything. My sister Kathy is my maid-of-honor and best friend—just like you and Kelly."

"Yes, Ma'am, your daughter and I have become very good friends."

"God works in mysterious ways. He turned my secret into a vessel to bring you two sisters together." Tina was confused, curious, and needed clarification.

She interjected what she could. "Yes, Ma'am."

"God rest his soul. Donnie-Lee has two beautiful and successful daughters who found each other after all these years. That is a sho'nuff miracle."

The sister reference went right over Tina's head, but she wondered, *Why would Kelly discuss my birth father with her mother?*

Kay-Dee pressed on with her sweet and honest testimony. "It's funny how genes work. Looking at you on TV and in magazines, Kelly favors Donnie-Lee the most. She's got the freckles, the eyes, the nose, and everything. While growing up down there in North Carolina, wherever you went, you could always find a Charles, Watkins, or Smith. Your big family was scattered all over Halifax County."

"Yes, Ma'am. I do have a rather large family." As the unveiling of the truth continued, Tina began to receive the message, was baffled, and needed to hear more. "I get confused by all the small towns around Scotland Neck. Which one is your hometown?"

"I'm from Tarboro—about twenty minutes south, straight down Route 258. It's been a long time, but I'll never forget that drive. I was always excited when we were on the way to Mount Pleasant Hill Baptist Church, knowing Donnie-Lee would be there waiting for me. Kelly was born in New York City because people who made big mistakes were always sent somewhere up north."

Tina wanted to be certain. "I've heard my family members refer to my father as Donnie, but never as Donnie-Lee."

"It's cuz we was sweet on each other. Donnie-Lee was my pet name for him. When he'd sing a solo at church, your family would insist on him being introduced as Donald Leonard Charles—all prim and proper."

Tina put her hand over her mouth while descending to a squatting position. From there, she flopped and her tailbone took the brunt of the impact of her backside hitting hard against the floor. Tina's legs were sprawled out in front of her. The telephone's coiled cord stretched from the base of the phone that was still above her head on the corner of the desk. She forced herself to speak because she needed to know more. "Oh, yes, Ma'am, now I remember Kelly mentioning the town to me. So you said that you and my father were sweet on each other. I'm unsure what that means."

"Forgive me, child. I've never lost my Southern phrase turning. It means that we were going together. Honestly, it's kind of silly to say that your daddy and me was sweet on each other. By fooling around and ending up pregnant with Kelly, we went a long, long way past sweet. Well, that was a lifetime ago and a whole lot of water under the bridge. I've been with Ben King for thirty-two years now and he's been my rock. It's funny though. A woman never forgets the one that breaks through on that first time." Tina had no counter to that statement. "Sweetheart, are you still there?"

"Yes, Ma'am, I'm right here." By this point, Tina's tears poured out so profusely that mucus was running from her nose. She was devastated.

Kay-Dee directed the action. "I need you to write this down for both you and Kelly."

"One moment please—I need to get something to write with." Tina walked around and sat behind the desk, grabbed a wad of tissue, and blew her nose. It took several forceful pumps from her abdomen and a handful of tissue to clear her nostrils. With pad and pen already on the desk in front of her, she returned the phone's receiver to the side of her face. "Miss Kay-Dee, I'm back."

"Our church scheduled the vow renewal service for Saturday, August 8, at one in the afternoon." As Tina wrote, her hand trembled. "That's a long time from now—more than enough for you both to clear your schedules. Listen at me bossing you around just like I do Kelly. Get used to it because we're one big family now. Just in case Kelly doesn't call me back, make sure you tell her and get it put on her calendar and yours. Tina, will you promise to do that for me?"

"Yes, Ma'am, I'll make sure Kelly knows and that it gets placed on both our schedules."

Kay-Dee could hear the raspy difference in Tina's voice and noticed that the enthusiasm was gone from her inflection. She asked, "Are you all right? You sound different."

Tina refused to reveal to Kay-Dee that her sweet and honest testimony represented crucial puzzle pieces—unveiling a stockpile of inexcusable deception. "I have allergies that hit me when the weather starts to change at this time of the year."

"Well, feel better. Alright, Sweetie, I hope to see you at the celebration if not before. Good-bye now."

Tina hung up the phone, skipped as many steps as she could while running up to her designated bedroom. She opened Brief de

Vaughan, pulled out volume one, and started searching for certain letters. It had been a long time since she had read some of Momma Nin's earlier writings. Fiery anticipation caused her brain and hands to work against each other, delaying her searching process. After thirty minutes, Tina sat in the middle of the bed, frustrated, but determined. Finally, she reached a letter that mentioned Donald Leonard Charles, the church, and a girlfriend.

Volume I: Lullaby Letter 27

Dear Tina, at seventeen years old, your father experienced his first love, but we did not have a name. All he would tell Big Momma and Gina was that his girlfriend went to our family's church, Mount Pleasant Hill Baptist. Because her parents were very strict, they met secretly in and around the church.

Tina skimmed through the letter in search of particular details.

As hard as Gina tried, she never figured out the mystery girl's name. The wonderful thing was that the girlfriend pieced together the fragments of Donnie's life.

I'm sure I remember reading something about a town. Where is it? Tina continued to scan quickly and her persistence started to pay dividends. *Here we go. This part tells me more.*

One day, Donnie came home devastated, telling Gina that his girlfriend had abruptly moved away. Her parents sent her to live with a relative up north without giving him a chance to say good-bye. Although feeling very depressed, he eventually gave up on having a reconnection. — Momma Nin ∎

Tina's frustration drove her determination to find the sought-after detail. She encouraged her psyche. *I know there's more. Keep looking, Tina. Don't give up.* She scanned through a few more letters and zeroed in on the clues she sought. "Oh my God, this is it!" she screamed.

Volume 1: Letter 31 Excerpt

As Donnie assisted me with the waste reduction project, we talked five times more than we worked. We discussed the young lady who had broken his heart. He tried his best not to name her. He told me that she lived in Tarboro, a town about twenty miles from Scotland Neck. He said that he overheard his choir director and a deacon whispering about a young lady, a former choir member being sent to New York City. Almost slipping out a name he said, "I wonder if they were talking about my Kay?" ■

Between her conversation with Kay-Dee and Momma Nin's letters 27 and 31, the puzzle pieces were connected. There was no doubt that Kelly was her older sister. *How could someone be so conniving?* Tina asked herself. *I was stupid for trusting her. First it was the Chamberses and now it's Kelly King. God why is all of this madness happening to me?*

To be certain that Kelly noticed her promptly, the Pop-Diva reclined on the living room sofa that was located in plain view of the front door. Her head rested on an arm, a throw pillow was behind her back, and her feet were propped on the lower cushion. In an attempt to show disrespect, she didn't bother to remove her shoes. While waiting to confront the enemy, Tina stared at the ceiling with lights dimmed, television on with no sound, and soft music playing. Two bottles of Riesling were her companions. Positioned in an ice bucket on the coffee table, they were within reaching distance. The wine consumption lowered Tina's ability to show restraint and filter her verbosity once Kelly was standing over her head.

43

DÉJÀ VU EXPERIENCE

FULL of exuberance, Kelly said, "Hey, Tina, I come bearing cute outfits from the biggest show of the Fashion Parade. When these two dresses were modeled on the runway, I knew they were perfect for you." Hearing no response, she placed the garment bag down, turned the knob on the recessed lighting all the way up, and focused her attention on Tina. A scan of the evidence conveyed that something was very wrong. She saw a puffy face, tear tracks, an empty wine bottle, and another one half-way finished. Fearing someone was ill or had died, Kelly spoke in a soft voice. "Oh my goodness, what's wrong?"

Tina sat up, turned her body forward, and placed her feet on the floor. "You're what's wrong, Donnita—the name coming from one of your mother's childhood friends. What a deliberate liar you are." Kelly sat in the side chair closest to where Tina was sitting on the sofa. At that moment, there was nothing she could do but listen. "You told me that there was nothing special about your middle name. The fact that Donnita comes from your real father's first name is pretty darn special to me. It's been three years of lies upon lies. That's not normal behavior. How could you keep being deceptive all this time?"

Kelly realized that the scene being played out was a 360-degree déjà-vu experience. She had assumed her mother's position and Tina had become a 1985 New York City version of her 1982 Orleans Street self. Kelly tried to counter with a word, but Tina blocked it, determined to complete her full frontal assault. "From the moment you first said hello to me, you knew that we were sisters. Everything from that point on was a lie. Now, I know why you and Arnie are so close. Both of you are ruthless, only caring about bottom lines, money, breaking records, and controlling people's lives."

Kelly reached out and touched Tina's arm. Tina jerked it away. "Please! Don't touch me. Don't you ever touch me again! Other than greeting my fans, I don't like it when people I don't know put their hands on me. I'm unsure of who you are, but I do know what you are—and that's a selfish, lying bitch!"

Kelly begged. "Please! Let me try and explain."

Tina wasn't interested in hearing Kelly's excuses. "There's nothing to explain, but I do have a question and I need to hear the answer coming from your own lips. Is Donald Leonard Charles your father?"

"Yes, he is, but there's—."

"Thanks for finally being honest. That's all I need to know. Excuse me." Unsteady because of the wine, Tina staggered up the staircase to the bedroom that had been designated as hers. Kelly followed closely behind, but stopped at the doorway. Tina went into the walk-in closet, returned with a medium and two large-sized suit cases, and threw them on the bed. Planning to stay longer than she had admitted, there were at least two, five piece luggage sets worth of belongings to remove. For tonight, she'd take what she could.

Kelly knocked on the open door and asked, "May I please come in?"

"You own the place, so it's up to you, Miss King." Tina went back into the closet, grabbed a big armful of clothes, and stuffed a portion in each of the larger pieces of luggage. Using a duffel bag, she crammed it with some of the contents from the dresser drawers. Another trip to the closet was necessary to retrieve a carry-on tote. She took it into the bathroom and filled it with toiletries. By the time Tina was done, the room was a disheveled mess, as she had intended.

Kelly pleaded. "You are so right to be angry with me, but I don't want you to leave. The press is still hounding you. If you like, I'll go to Arnie's so you can stay here."

"Thanks, but no thanks." With unmitigated gall, Tina walked down the stairs to the living room, grabbed the garment bag holding the two dresses from the Fashion Parade, brought them back up to the bedroom, and stuffed them in one of her suitcases. Tina's intent was to be sarcastic and hurtful. "Yes, I'm taking the new dresses you bought for me at the fashion show. Lord knows, I've definitely earned them. This whole setup was all about the great Kelly King striking gold once again with her latest find, Bettina Charles."

While struggling to close one of the larger suitcases, Kelly put her arm inside, attempting to delay Tina's progress. Momentum had already impacted the motion, causing the suitcase to slam hard against Kelly's arm. In the manner of a grade school punishment, Tina ran to a corner and stared at the wall.

She spoke loudly. "I didn't mean to slam the case down on your arm, but you can't stop me from leaving. I need to get out of here right away."

Kelly kept her distance and massaged her arm as she spoke. "No need to apologize. I deserve a hurt arm and much more. I'm a coward and a selfish one at that, but for much different reasons than you think. It wasn't about credibility—well, it was about credibility. I'm proud that I had something to do with your success. I wanted it for you more than anything else I've ever done."

Tina said, "Finally, I hear a few facts coming from you."

"Please listen to those facts. Hear how it happened and maybe you'll understand. I went to North Carolina to my cousin's wedding to find answers about myself. I had just learned about my real father a few days before that. My mother had hidden the truth from me for the entire thirty-years of my life at that time. I stumbled upon my real identify, reading it on my birth certificate."

Kelly took Tina's silence as permission to continue. "That day at the wedding, practically everyone who was anyone in Edgecombe County was there. In addition to that, there was Halifax County representation that included members of your—my new—our family—mainly officers of Mount Pleasant Hill Baptist Church. It was the perfect setting for me to fish for answers to get to know the new me—this Kelly Donnita Charles person. Before learning anything about you, I sat in the third pew in that church, drawn to an amazing voice belonging to a beautiful girl. Your stage presence and confidence were so polished, and searching for new talent is part of what I do."

Tina watched the video in her mind as Kelly spoke. "The pastor's wife was sitting next to me. As you sang, I asked who you were. The information that came back blew my mind. First Lady Marylou leaned close to my ear and told me that your deceased father was Donald Leonard Charles—my father. In searching for information about him I found you as a byproduct of that discovery. At that moment, my life changed forever. I was no longer an only child."

Tina's voice had calmed slightly. "But you sat in that church like nothing was happening."

"You looked so happy up there singing in the pulpit. I couldn't just barge up, shock you with the truth, and steal your joy. I figured it had to be God, setting up such a perfect situation. I don't call on Him the way that I should, but I know a miracle when I see one. To create a beginning for us, I used my position as the big music executive, stumbling upon a new talent. That is what actually happened."

Tina turned her head, faced Kelly, and asked, "When were you going to tell me? The funny thing is that you did to me what your mother did to you. How could you hurt me like this when you know what this lie feels like? You stole my right to be shocked or angry or maybe even happy and I hate you for that."

Kelly walked closer to Tina, being sure not to touch her. "I forgave my mother, so Bethy, hopefully you can forgive me."

Tina wiped her tears. "First of all, don't ever call me Bethy again and, secondly, you don't deserve my forgiveness. By the way, before I forget, your mother called to tell you about her vow-renewing ceremony—August 8 at one o'clock. Finally, I want you to know that your lies have crushed me even more than meeting the Chamberses. How similar you are to them. The main difference is that they used money and you used kindness—pretending to be my friend. At least my grandparents have the excuse of age and racial ignorance. Besides losing my Momma Nin, this is the worst feeling ever. Now that I've listened to your explanation, will you please leave me alone? I really need to be by myself."

Before leaving, Kelly made a final appeal. "Regardless of how we got to this point, we're here. You and I are sisters. I want you to know that I love you so, so very much and I need you to be in my life. Please, think about giving us a chance. We need each other." Kelly left the room and closed the door behind her.

Tina made an SOS phone call to a person she knew could be trusted. "I need you to sign out one of the town cars and pick me up at Kelly King's place right away."

Tina moved her luggage to the front door of the penthouse, sat on one of the large suitcases, and waited. In less than thirty minutes, she opened the door after the third quick knock. Bernie Bazemore spoke to Kelly King as he loaded Tina's belongings onto the building's luggage cart. The demeanor of the usually upbeat corporate executive conveyed helplessness as she stood a short distance away with her arms folded and a lit cigarette in between her fingers.

While holding Brief de Vaughan, Tina said, "Miss King, my commitment to Walden Records and my professional responsibilities won't change. In terms of you and me, business is our only relationship. I'll send for the rest of my things later."

In the back seat of the town car, Tina's mind started to reel. *Oh God, please help me. Where am I going to go? Because of the press staked out at Windsor East, I can't go there. Carlton is where he should be in Scotland Neck with Tony. Pappy John is in Colorado with my sick Aunty Ava. Aunty Gina is with Larry and I can't deal with my other two great aunties right now.*

Bernie asked, "Where are we off to, Miss Tina?" He had to call her name three times. "Miss Tina—Miss Tina—Miss Tina."

Coming out of her fog, she answered. "Yes."

"Where do you want me to take you?"

The water from Tina's dam of tears broke. "Mister Bernie, I don't know."

"Then, leave it to me. Everything's gonna be okay." For many years, prior to Tina tripling his salary, Bernie worked at The Hawthorne Astoria part-time. The hotel was like Fort Knox, equipped with private garages, underground tunnels, separate elevators, and security to match. The facility was retrofitted and accustomed to hosting heads-of-state from around the world as well as others with a high-profile status. Bernie secured Tina one of their VIP suites.

Back at the penthouse, Kelly was on the phone with her mother. Upon figuring out that she had revealed the truth to Tina, Kay-Dee called, confessed, and begged for Kelly's forgiveness. "I'm so sorry that I failed you again."

"No, Mom, honestly, you did me a huge favor. Even though it hurts so badly, I'm relieved that it's over. Tina knows the truth and I'm finally free from covering up one lie with another. Although I lost the newly formed relationship with my sister, the minefield of deception has been destroyed."

"I don't believe you've lost Tina forever. I'm sure she'll come back to you in time. Look at us. You forgave me and we're closer than ever before."

"Unfortunately, Mom, I don't think my disaster is going to have a happy ending. Tina's been through so much in her young life. She opened up to me and I stabbed her in all of her old wounds—justifying my behavior in the name of helping her career. That's unforgiveable."

44

A COMPLICATED LOVE SONG

S EVERING play-to-real sister ties and moving out of the penthouse were Tina's immediate private responses to losing faith in Kelly. Her public retaliation was a rampage of mischief, doing her best impression of a "princess gone wrong." As related to the dating scene, taking it seriously was the last thing on her mind. Doing it publically, often, and without Walden Records' stamp of approval was ideal payback. Most importantly, dating restrictions were not mentioned in her contract. When tasting the town on her down time, Tina hired Bernie Bazemore to command her small and discreet personal security team. As the body guards maintained their distance in the front and each side of the Pop-Diva and her guest(s), Bernie took the rear position of the diamond-shaped formation.

Armed with trusted security, Tina began clinging to renegade athletes, washed-up actors, and general celebrity bad asses. August Osborne was her most favorite escort and chastised by The Label the most. Being twice her age, Arnie considered Osborne's ability to influence the young starlet his greatest threat. Carlton explained the parameters to each man eagerly volunteering for the unusual escort assignment. "From where I sit, dating Bettina Charles is a guaranteed, golden ticket to publicity and social relevance. Anything intimate is up to her, of course."

For those interested in seriously dating the Pop-Diva, Tina came prepared with a statement. "To be perfectly honest, the purpose of these dates is for the cameras to capture us hanging out. As real dating goes, I have a boyfriend who is not endorsed by Walden Records. However, if I'm ever on the market, you're at the top of my delectable man go-to list." A perfectly planted semi-seductive kiss would end the conversation as cameras clicked and bulbs flashed.

Playing publicist from North Carolina, Carlton would calm Pappy John, Aunty Gina, the Aunty-ettes, and other close family and friends. "Tina's spike in public bad girl behavior is a Tee-Tee coping mechanism. It's her way of dealing with her Chambers-anger as well as this stardom thing." To concerned members of the inner circle, he had a secondary response. "Tina is just giving Tosha Ray a little more room," he reasoned. "She's allowing her alter-ego to show up on and off the stage. Anyway by design, Pop-Diva's misbehave. That's what they do."

Keeping her word, Tina never directly bad-mouthed Kelly publicly, but the casual nature of their morning summits were a thing of the past. At the sit-downs, product three seven two eighty-five would receive instructions, while giving business-related feedback only. "Yes, Miss King, I understand. Yes, Miss King, I'll be there on time."

Kelly would try to breakthrough. "Is there anything that you'd like to say to me of a personal nature?"

"No, Miss King, I do not."

"Tina, I'm sorry that I hurt you. For the hundredth time, I apologize. How long are you going to continue torturing me like this?"

"I don't know, but three years would level the playing field. Listen, Miss King, I have an interview to try and not cry my way through. Can we end this conversation, so I can do my job?"

"Sure Tina, I didn't mean to upset you."

After ten minutes to brush her teeth and touch up make up, it was time for public relations.

Citizen's Magazine
An Emotional Bettina Charles Bares Her Soul

Interviewer: You've given me permission to ask two questions regarding recent accusations of your public displays of "bad girl behavior," so let's get that out of the way. Supposedly, you stole an expensive luxury car, took it on a joy ride, and caused extensive damage. Is this allegation true or false?

Tina: Because the incident was taken out of context, it was neither. I did not steal anything, the ride had nothing to do with joy, and the damage to the car was minimal. Basically, it was a harmless prank that was misreported—a-a-and part of a video shoot.

Interviewer: And let me add that no charges were filed.

Tina: Yes, you're absolutely correct.

Interviewer: This next incident was reported by several witnesses. While dining at an exclusive restaurant, you protested overdone lamb chops by complaining loudly and tossing one of them at the maître d. You were asked to leave and were ultimately escorted out of the fine dining establishment prior to completing the meal.

Tina: Everyone has a bad day, makes mistakes when their tired and punchy, and I'll leave it right there. By the way, that was your second rumor mill question, so I'd like to move on.

Interviewer: One of your fans wrote-in with a two-part question. Alicia wants you to describe a happy place or feeling that money can't buy and on the flip-side, what causes you great sadness and pain?

Tina: When I'm on stage, I'm home and feel like one of the popular girls in school. It's my happy place where I'm most lively. It's where I recognize that my talent is a God-given gift—a blessing that I need to cherish and share.

Interviewer: And the source of your greatest sadness and pain is—?

Tina was absolutely not going to mention the passing of her precious Momma Nin and was grateful for her close-second reply.

Tina: Let's see, the dreaded flip side. — Often when I'm off stage, during the silence, I'm left to confront the ugliness that accompanies this thing called fame and fortune.

Interviewer: Ugliness, you say—how so?

Tina: I'm referring to the backbiting, deceit, and greed that go along with this business. People pretend to be your friend and then they lie to your face and behind your back. Knowing who they are and having to deal with them on a daily basis is the tragedy.

Interviewer: Because you're so private, I'm sure my final question is a difficult one. In the past three years, a lot has been written about your life and most of the time you remain silent. What I and the world would like to know is how does Bettina Charles define herself? This is your chance to set the record straight.

Tina: You're right. It's a difficult question. I wasn't prepared for such thought provoking inquiry. It takes care and reflection.

Interviewer: Granting me this exclusive is rare and appreciated, so take all the time you need.

Tina paused for a little more than two minutes. She sipped water slowly during the first minute. To pull back her tears, she closed her eyes and engaged in the activity of *maintaining* during the second.

Tina: I-I guess—no—I'm certain that I communicate best through my music. So, that's the only way I know how to define myself. To me, my life is a complicated love song—with each verse revealing the joy and pain of my journey. You see, my fans' love and support keep me going. Their energy pumps blood to my heart and maintains the tempo of my soul.

And what can I say about the press, the paparazzi—people like you. Wow! Your twisted reports are the echo—broadcasting the embellished version of my life's lyrics. What I consider to be melodic musical arrangements of my every day, normal activities, you guys twist into drama that I barely recognize. It's as though you play the tracks of my life backwards.

The activity in my public life is my album's big picture—my musical score. It's guided—closely directed by my record company. The owner and executives call the shots. They're the strong personalities whose opinions not only drive the pace of the rhythm but also de-termine which song will be played and when. Truthfully, I'm at a low point. My record is scratched and pain and loneliness keep playing over-and-over.

Interviewer: You are definitely a songwriter, describing yourself so poetically. Your answer was really deep and clearly demonstrat-ed that there's incredible intelligence behind your drop-dead, gor-geous exterior. Yet, while applauding your honesty, you painted a dark and quite sad self-portrait.

Tina: Perhaps the flip-side of my complicated love song will be a fist-pumping, happy-glad anthem.

Interviewer: And quickly, fans like me will make it Walden Records' and your next platinum single that is if you re-sign with them.

Sunday, June 30, 1985

Bettina Charles, the birthday girl, was given an additional title "America's Rough-Edged Sweetheart." Regardless of her going on joy-rides in borrowed vehicles and throwing a few tantrums, the public was pleased with the girl who graced the cover of *Citizen's Magazine.* It was a special edition entitled: "The Top Twenty-Five No The Top Twenty-Three Personalities of the Year." Bettina Charles was on the leader board and the youngest person who made the issue, receiving unanimous votes in three categories. That was the reason there was not twenty-five honorees. Tina had been deemed the most beautiful, the most talented, and the most intriguing—for being very private and misunderstood. Tina was tickled by the article's claims. *Just like in my high school yearbook, they're deeming me the most this and the most that. Three years have passed, but, off stage, I feel like I'm still at my life's starting gate.*

Although angering Arnie to an irate degree, Tina declined his initial and three subsequent offers for Walden Records to host a publicized twenty-first birthday celebration. In its place, she opted for a Scotland Neck private gathering of those she considered to be her very close family—bloodline or not. In addition, Carlton had been gone for two and a half months and she missed him terribly. The attendees were Carlton, Aunties Gina, Trudy, and Zooni, Uncle Ed, Larry, Tony, Ellis, Rufus, Duberry, Clevon, Cornelius, Cousin Alonia, and yes, Pappy John. He made the trip down to North Carolina to Halifax County to Scotland Neck and to Joseph-Lee Manor.

The atmosphere was lively—loud music was playing, people spoke over each other, jokes were told, and the laughter was continuous. A buffet was provided courtesy of The Pit and wine and booze were flowing. After blowing out the twenty-one candles on her birthday cake, Tina opened her homemade gifts. They were part of another family tradition called heart to hand gift giving. Each participant had to conceive of a gift in their mind, send it through the love in their heart, and make it with their hands. The gift opening and explanation ceremony was unique as well as hilarious.

Some of Tina's gifts were practical like Aunty Trudy and Uncle Ed's burgundy and gold hand sewn Bible cover. Uncle Ed's contribution was ordering and ironing-on the football emblem of his great-niece's favorite team, the Washington Redskins. In addition to his food, Tina loved Cousin Alonia's sweet pickled watermelon rinds and he gave her two jars as his present. Although absent, Hattie Mae mailed her gift—a hat and scarf that she knitted. Ellis gave Tina a hardback bound book of their sheet music from the "Tell Me" album. It even included their penciled-in notations.

Aunty Gina's gift came with now and later specifications. Her crocheted pouch was flawless. It was a five by seven, red and white striped pouch with two equal sized compartments on the interior. An elastic loop that hooked around and a button served as its means of opening and closing. Aunty Gina instructed. "Look at the gift in the front of the pouch for now and save the envelope in the back for later when you're alone." As directed, Tina pulled out the gift stored in the front partition. Garnering immediate laughter, it was a strong piece of cardboard holding six condoms of different sizes and designs. Affixed with safety pins, they were aligned in two columns and three rows.

Aunty Gina bragged. "Larry's contribution to the gift making was neatly pinning all the condoms in place and they are a collection of my favorites. The one called 'The Tickler' with the ridges is really special."

"That's too much gross information," yelled Carlton.

Aunty Trudy placed her hands in a praying position. "Lord, teach my sister to bridal her tongue when her flesh overtakes her mind."

Aunty Zooni chimed in. "By the way Tina, with all the dates you've been on lately, you better make sure you keep those condoms with you at all times."

Ellis added. "Especially with the jive turkeys you've been hanging around—not a decent man in the bunch."

Pappy John's expression was serious as he turned to make eye contact with his daughter. "Above all else, think of safety first—always have an escape route in mind."

"Alright already! I get the safety message, so stop ganging up on me," Tina demanded.

Carlton insisted. "Now, can everyone take their noses out of the 'been grown' Bornday woman's bedroom. Let's move on to the next gift please."

Rufus, Duberry, Clevon, and Cornelius's joint gift was a quadruple hand fan—made by taping four of them together. All were borrowed from Mount Pleasant Hill Baptist Church. Stretching two feet wide, the bronze Jesus fan was attached to MLK, Jr. in brown and that was attached to the Willow-Matt's Funeral Home design. The fourth attached hand fan was a recent addition and commissioned by Tony. It advertised Trudy's Cut-n-Curl in celebration of its fortieth anniversary. In addition to a color photo of the newly renovated salon, the lower right corner of the hand fan displayed a restored, gorgeous black and white photo of a twenty-six year old Gertrude Watkins-Charles. It had been taken in 1945 at the salon's grand-opening ceremony. As the band of four cousins gave Tina their unique gift, Tony presented a box of fifty Trudy's Place hand fans to the business pioneer herself.

With a big hug, Aunty Trudy said, "I've always said that Tony was a kind person and a hard worker, fitting nicely into the family. He has God's favor, you know."

"On what planet did that conversation take place?" asked Carlton.

Aunty Trudy snapped back quickly. "It was somewhere near my pocketbook crashing down on your head, Carlton Andrew Charles."

"Aunty Trudy's firing back with threats while saying my whole birth name. I'm taking the hit and leaving that alone."

Aunty Zooni's gift was next and Tina opened the wrapping tentatively. Carlton went further and scooted his chair back a few feet away from his cousin/best friend. "Let me get out of the way just in case," he mumbled. Aunty Zooni's package contained a two-part gift that garnered immediate snickering. There was an old white gym sock filled with stones in the foot portion along with a small, pocket-sized can of "Mace."

"What's homemade about either one of your presents?" asked Pappy John.

Aunty Zooni was ready with answers. "It's always the white man that requires verification, but I've come prepared. I had to earn the money, write the check, and lick the stamp to order the Mace. Secondly, I dug in my yard for the stones and cleaned them off. Then, I had to wash Ellis's stinky sock and stitch up the hole before dropping in the stones."

"Oh yeah, Tina reach in the bottom of the sock." Ellis directed. "Zooni wrote instructions and that also counts as homemade."

Carlton said, "Look at how Ellis is taking up for his woman. Aunty Zooni must be rocking your world."

Accompanied with a high five, Ellis responded. "And, I'm a cat that loves to be rocked."

Tina read her Great Aunty's handwritten instructions aloud.

Aim for the eyes when spraying your intended target, followed by continuous blows to the face and head with the sock of stones. And put some strength behind it with your skinny self. You need to eat more vegetables and take a daily vitamin instead of all that gyrating all over the television.

Happy Birthday from Zooni,
Your favorite great-aunty

Aunty Zooni's gifts caused Tina's eyes to water and Aunty Gina to complain that her cheeks were hurting from so much intense laughter.

Finally, it was Carlton's turn. "Abiding by the rules that joint gifts were allowable, The Lovely, Tony, and Pappy John worked together. By me being back in Scotland Neck for over two months, the strain of our long distance relationship has been repaired."

"You're supposed to describe your gift not perform a half hour soap opera," said Aunty Zooni. "Please get to the damn point."

"The point is that we need some time to prepare for our presentation. Please, talk among yourselves, eat, drink, and be merry until we return." Carlton, Tony, and Pappy John left the Great Room and all but the music grew quiet for about ten seconds. No one had a clue about what was going to transpire.

Twenty minutes later, Carlton returned first and cued a particular song from a movie soundtrack album. Tony entered the room holding the latest "Instant" camera, followed by Pappy John, pimping to the beat of the song. Tina screamed, kicked her feet, and screamed some more. Aunty Zooni shook her head and burst into laughter. Everyone else expressed themselves jovially in one manner or another.

From head to toe, General John Chapman was dressed like a "Blues Brother." He was sporting a white, button-down oxford shirt and everything else was black. He wore regular suit pants with a two-button jacket, a two-inch thin necktie, a fedora pimp/gangster hat, super dark, detective sun glasses, and boots. Carlton even glued thick long sideburns on Pappy John's face and used a black ink pen to draw a crucifix on his left hand as well as write J-A-K-E on his fingers—one letter per digit. Then, Pappy John folded his arms and had Tony snap an "Instant" photo. However, General John Chapman wasn't finished. He did his best to "Shake a Tail Feather" as the song that was playing by Ray Charles suggested. After that, everybody got up and joined him in dancing. By a unanimous vote, Pappy John won first place for giving the best present and receiving the most laughs.

In addition to heart to hand gift giving, Tina stole private moments during the party to give one on one thanks in advance for a collective and thoughtful gift. For a few months after the celebration, her great-aunties would open and answer birthday greetings from Bettina Charles's fans. Those that they deemed most moving or required her personal attention were forwarded to their great-niece.

⤳

At the party's end while standing in the driveway, Tina said goodbye to her father. "Thank you for dealing with the crazy family to be here for my birthday."

"There's nothing I wouldn't endure for you, and I know you understand my hasty departure."

Tina grinned, "I absolutely, positively understand."

"Now hold out your hand to receive the last part of my bornday gift."

"What else could there possibly be?" Tina asked as she held out her hand.

Now, clear and fully developed, the chilled-out dad presented the "Instant" photograph that Tony had taken earlier to his daughter. "Pumpkin, here's the more relaxed picture you asked me to take three years ago at the Denver airport. Although late in arriving, it's less businesslike and definitely shows my softer side."

The exchange of I love you and a tight embrace preceded Pappy John's exit as he jumped in the back of a chauffeured town car for the ride back to DC.

⤳

The comic relief during Tina's heart to hand gift-giving activity was a welcomed interruption to her sadness. Although reaching a milestone Bornday and professionally, living inside her realized dream, Bettina Bethany Charles was miserable. It was 11:00 p. m. and she sat up in her Momma Nin inherited bed watching the final sixty minutes of her twenty-first birthday fade away. Tina saved the reading of certain birthday cards for this private moment. Skipping the stamped out corporate greetings written by the card companies, she only read the personalized inscriptions. A huge grin illuminated her face as she opened a card signed by her Walden Records' inner circle team.

Although most of the cards that remained were contentious, Tina had made a decision to read them in spite of the anticipated pain and anger they could cause. Determining that the temperature would not change, she dove into the cold water and began the challenging exercise.

Victoria Chambers: You probably think that we're monsters, but we are not. The world we were born into didn't allow for what we faced. In not knowing what to do, we did what came natural—threw money at what we considered to be an enormous problem. In 1964, we felt helpless. Not only did our only child run from us and join the military, she married a Black man and had a baby. We counted her behavior as punishment to us, her overly protective and snobbish parents. Writing this birthday greeting proved that expressing feelings is much more difficult than signing a check. And, as you requested, there will be no more of those.

William Chambers: It never dawned on us until we laid eyes on you the night you borrowed the Rolls-Royce that perhaps our daughter Christina was in love. The adoration she found happened to be with a Black man named Donald Leonard Charles whose cultural experiences were vastly different from ours. We were ill-equipped to deal with such a scenario. Even now in 1985, it's still unusual to encounter an interracial couple in our circle. Maybe that suggests that we should branch out and make new acquaintances outside our comfort zone—one that is apparently very shallow. This is my first expression of a feeling I, now, believe was there all along. We love you Miss Bettina Charles and would like to have a chance to at least talk by phone periodically if not start over.

> Happy Birthday, your grandparents,
> William and Victoria Chambers

Arnie Peters: Today, you're not only a woman, but one without a record deal. You are officially free from me and Walden Records if that is your desire. Obviously, I recommend that you stay on your current trek and complete our unfinished Pop-Diva business.

Although I've never mentioned it to anyone except Shantelle, a meeting to discuss and possibly sign you to a new contract has been on my schedule for three years. Back in nineteen eighty two by the end of your trial by fire, I knew you were something special. Never has my vision of an artist's success extended so far into the future. That is why your company identification number is three seven two eighty-five. Three represents Tuesday, the third day of the week on the Christian Calendar. That's right. Although it's not stamped on my forehead, I am a baptized believer. Anyway, the number seven denotes the month, the number two identifies the date, and eighty-five indicates the year of the pre-scheduled meeting.

It would be nice if you kept the appointment—Executive Conference Room 2201, 10:00 a. m, on Tuesday, July 2, 1985. Whether you accept or decline my invitation, it's been an amazing journey. By the way, this note was not prepared by Shantelle or by Kelly. I spent an hour in the drugstore searching for the perfect card and did my own two-finger typing of these words from me to you.

Happy Birthday, Arnie Peters,
Forever a Wise Ass Son of a Gun

Kelly King: I'm sure a greeting from me doesn't brighten your day, but I would be remiss in my duty not to wish you well on your twenty-first birthday. I really screwed things up between us and miss the closeness we had developed. I pray every day that, in time, you'll be able to forgive me. Although I don't deserve such a wonderful gift, you are my little sister and that is an amazing miracle to me.

There is so much that I would love to share and teach you, giving you the benefit of my life's experiences—the highs and the lows. Obviously, lying to you continuously is at the top of my list of mistakes. The punishment of losing your respect and trust is unbearable. I know that this is a very stressful time in your life. In addition to your managing the pain recently caused by me and your grandparents, you have to decide on a record company and sign a new deal. If I can help you in any way, please give me the chance to do so. All I want is for you to be happy. I truly believe that bringing us together to tear us apart can't be God's plan. Please know that I will never give up on you—on us rebuilding our relationship.

Happy Birthday,
Your sad sack sister, Kelly

Tina retrieved Aunty Gina's red and white striped crocheted pouch gift and took a moment to admire its craftsmanship. Slowly, she unlatched the elastic loop from around the button, and pulled out the envelope. Addressed simply "To Bethy," the sender was obvious.

Momma Nin: Happy twenty-first Bornday, Bethy. I'm so weak these days that I've stopped writing you letters. Pappy John loaded the volumes up and took them where they'd be safe until the appointed time for you to receive them. This birthday card may indeed be my last written words to you. Poor Gina had to make three trips to the five and dime for me. After looking at more than twenty-five birthday cards, I chose this one—blank on the inside to fill with my own thoughts and a breathtaking scene on the outside. The front of this card reminds me of Les Vésinet. There's a lake with lily pads, Easter green grass, wildflowers, and birds flying overhead. The girl that is depicted in the scene reminds me of the hope that I see in you. She's sitting on the grass—looking so content and appreciative. My twenty-first birthday wish for you, Bethy, is to make difficult days easier by tapping into God's gifts of earthly bits of peace and serenity. They can be found in the great outdoors—in the seas and in the landscapes. God designed them for mankind to admire, using the proficiency of one of His fingernails as a paintbrush.

Between eighteen and twenty-one years old, I'm sure you've bumped into some difficult life challenges—ones that leave your soul empty. When they occur, engage in my formula of maintaining and become that little girl on the cover of this birthday card. Take in big gulps of God's natural gifts. Use them to refill your inner-spirit with that wholesome beauty.

Now, as it is difficult for me to speak, the smiles we exchange and the looks in each other's eyes reveal more than a library worth of words. Love is the strongest, so don't ever forget the potency of your power because you are loved. It's the agape kind—selfless, sacrificial, and unconditional. Know that God's love will be with you when I no longer can.

Happy Bornday,
Momma Nin, August 7, 1975

Tina's heart fluttered upon recognizing that Momma Nin passed away three days after authoring that birthday card's greeting. With that, she pressed herself from her valley of sadness to a plateau of gratefulness. Her family, especially Pappy John, had gone all out to make her happy. His presence, however, did not change her circumstances. As tears accompanied her feelings of anxiety and uncertainty, she returned each birthday card to its envelope, placed them neatly inside of Brief de Vaughan, got down on her knees, and prayed.

Dear God, I thank you for allowing me to reach my twenty-first birthday and for my family and friends that helped me celebrate. Please, fix my heart and stubbornness, so I can forgive the hurtful acts of William and Victoria Chambers and Kelly King—someday.

When blowing out the candles on my birthday cake, my wish was one of desperation. At this turning point in my career, I need your guidance in figuring out the right fit and signing a new contract with whatever record company that happens to be. You know what's best over me and all my advisors put together, even on our best day of reasoning. Regardless of my decision, grant a special blessing for each member of the Walden Records' family, especially Arnie Peters. God, I really need your help to sort out the strange event that keeps haunting my dreams. I'm afraid and feel like I'm losing my mind. As requested, you've given me fans that express how much they love their Bettina Charles. As each day rolls by, I'm unsure if I like myself at all—a person I don't know very well. Please reveal to me the truth and send an angel to help me confront my demons. In Jesus name, I pray, Amen.

Tina climbed into bed, closed her eyes, and felt an amazing peace engulf her spirit. By the time she was fast asleep, Momma Nin's birthday blessing had come to pass in the form of a heavenly inspired dream. Her Bethy was transported to a beautiful field on the bank of a clear water lake. There was shrubbery, trees with beautiful cherry blossoms, and a florescent blanket created by fields of yellow, pink, and purple flowers. The watchable wildlife included deer and sheep grazing and geese walking about. Grandeur was also presented in the form of waterfalls and mountains in the distance that seemed to be caught up in the air—ultimately intermingling with the endless expanse of the sky. Tina stood up to chase a blue jay when a single fluffy cloud appeared and gave her a ride. Bettina Bethany Charles had been lifted above thoughts of record companies, music executives, dismissive grandparents, and a secret sister. There would be opportunities to deliberate and manage those concerns in the future.

3:26 a. m.—Unfortunately, Momma Nin's inspired dream didn't keep Tina asleep for the entire night. Chilled to her bones, a frightened Tina sat up in bed with tears running down her face. She turned the lamp switch to full brightness, reached in her top nightstand drawer, grabbed her journal and a pencil, and began to write what she recalled.

July 1, 1985—The visions are back and more in focus this time. Now, I'm certain that this recurring nightmare is much more. It's an awful, ugly memory.

Tina paused her writing to slide *Love Golden's* wedding band up and down its chain. When her heartbeat and breathing normalized, she continued journaling.

A man I know was in this room with me. Before awaking fully, I sensed a presence and smelled a vaguely familiar scent of cologne mixed with whisky. Because my nightgown had been pulled up to my shoulders, I was exposed from there to my toes. I felt icy cold, partly from temperature, but mostly from fear. The weight of his body pinned me down as he stared down at me with a crazed look in his eyes. The shadowy man-monster was holding my panties between his teeth until stuffing them in my mouth by squeezing my jaw tightly on both sides.

My voice retreated to the back of my throat and I struggled to keep breathing through my nose. Would I wake up with Momma Nin in heaven by the time this thing was over? The answer was no and I felt the will to fight return to my being. The heat of his breath hit the side of my face. I endured each horrific second with my eyes closed tightly, both fist clenched, feet in a ball, and my body board stiff. The feeling from there was horrendous pain—stabbing, excruciating pain.

Unable to tolerate more of the horrid recollection, Tina shook her head violently in an attempt to disrupt the agonizing memory. She ended her journaling, returned the writing tools to the night-stand drawer, and turned the lamp switch to its dim setting. As a steady stream of tears flowed, Bettina Bethany Charles lay on her side with the covers pulled over her head.

Trivia

1. What is Carlton's birth father's name?
2. What is the name of Tina's necklace given to her by Momma Nin?
3. What is the name of Club Trevi's Head Bartender?
4. What is the name of Club Trevi's Head DJ?
5. What does the GTS stand for in the radio call letters: WGTS?
6. At Joseph-Lee Manor, whose room was next to Carlton's?
7. What is the Name of Tina's High School?
8. What is the name of Pappy John's sister?
9. When is Tina's Birthday?
10. What was the title of the first play Tina saw in the 1970s?
11. Where was Ben King stationed in New York City?
12. What street did Kelly park her rent-a-car on when visiting her parents in Baltimore?
13. What is Assistant Angela's Last Name?
14. What is First Lady Marylou's Last Name?
15. What folder did Manuel literally file his illegal substances under?
16. What is the name of the city where Aunty Zooni lived?
17. What are the names of the five slain heroes hung in the Great Room at Joseph-Lee Manor?
18. What are the names of Tina's band of four cousins?
19. Who is Tina's entertainment idol?
20. How many people were seated at the roundtable at Tina's contract negotiation luncheon?
21. When is Carlton's Birthday?
22. What is the name of Tina and Carlton's New York City apartment building?
23. What is the section number where Momma Nin is resting at Arlington Cemetery?
24. What was the Charles-Watkins-Smith family birthday tradition called?
25. What were the four choices of hand fans that the band of four cousins used to make Tina's birthday present?

What's Next?

The story continues with a music deal decision, a sister-to-sister situation, movie making—maybe, hitting rock bottom—hopefully, and the antique lace of love—for certain. I encourage you to stay with me in Bettina Charles's world, journeying with her through valley and victory experiences.

The Pop-Diva's Dilemma:
Everybody has somebody. The fans have Bettina Charles and Bettina Charles has Tosha Ray. Tee-Tee has Carlton but Tina is alone. Will she remain that way is the question.

Made in the USA
Coppell, TX
22 November 2019